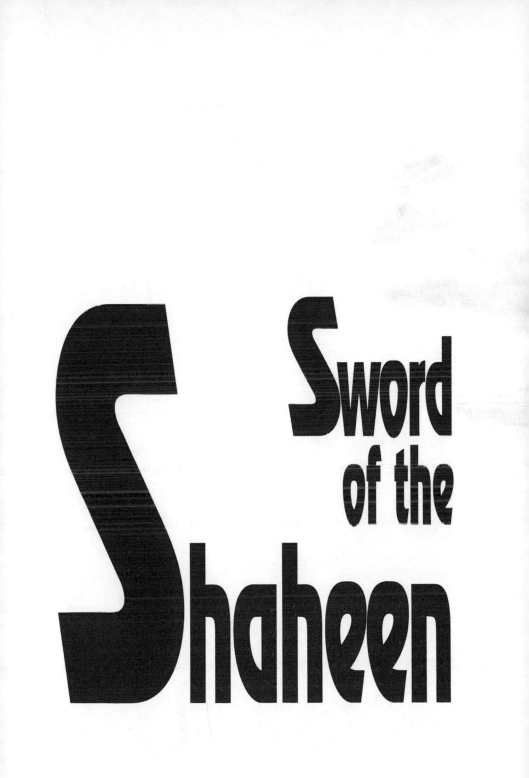

Also by M. E. Morris

Alpha Bug
The Icemen
C-130: Hercules

An M. E. Morris Novel

Sword
of the
Shaheen

PRESIDIO

For Kathleen, Kenneth, Susan, Mark, Dorothy,
Dennis, Michael, Christopher, Matthew,
and the son I never knew.

Copyright © 1990 by M. E. Morris

Published by Presidio Press
31 Pamaron Way, Novato, CA 94949

Library of Congress Cataloging-in-Publication Data

Morris, M. E., 1926–
    Sword of the Shaheen : a novel / M.E. Morris.
        p.   cm.
    ISBN 0-89141-328-6
    I. Title.
PS3563.087444S9   1990
813'.54—dc20   89-39292
                                                                              CIP

Printed in the United States of America

And when he opened the second seal, I heard the second living creature saying, "Come!" And there went forth another horse, a red one; and to him who was sitting on it, it was given to take peace from the earth, and that men should kill one another, and there was given him a great sword.

The Apocalypse of St. John the Apostle
Chapter 6, Verses 3–4

Prologue

The Soviet Bear swung around in a graceful arc to its new heading, its long, slim nose pointing down across the western Atlantic toward Cuba. The deep blue of the midsummer sky formed a perfect canvas for the swath of white that the silver Tupolev-95 was painting across it, the condensing exhaust from the aircraft's four massive turboprop engines streaming aft almost to the limit of the eye. Only to the south were the heavens interrupted. There, high, tufted cirrus cobwebbed the stratosphere as though some giant spider was releasing frantic spurts of its gossamer silk in a futile attempt to weave its web around the entire earth. Farther south, the cirrus lowered and became more dense as it disappeared across the horizon. Perhaps the spider was able at least to cocoon the Southern Hemisphere.

Ninety-three miles off the right wing tip of the vintage reconnaissance bomber lay the coastal waters of Chesapeake Bay, around which nested a major complex of American naval and air bases.

Comrade Pilot Sergei Isatovaka had no doubt that somewhere within that vast assemblage of military bases, two swift jet fighters were even at the moment taxiing hurriedly toward the end of their duty runway. Without pausing they would soon be screaming skyward toward the seven-mile altitude of the cruising Russian aircraft. The experienced Sergei alerted his crew.

"Be watchful, comrades. Let me know when our friends appear." Nonchalantly, he resumed sipping from a paper cup of *akroshka*. Normally eaten as a cold broth, the rich soup, with its strong base of fermented dark bread and heavy with firm chunks of vegetables and bits of meat, was routinely provided warm in large thermoses for rapid nourishment on the long flights down across the Atlantic. It tasted delicious and filled the void that had developed in Sergei's stomach over the past hour. His youthful Georgian navigator had thoughtfully passed around portions to all of the flight deck crew. Sergei sat relaxed, comfortable in the familiar routine. They were very close to the American Air Defense Identification Zone—the ADIZ, the Americans called it—an offshore imaginary line that roughly paralleled the East Coast of the United States and within which no seaward aircraft was allowed to enter without prior permission. He had no intention of penetrating the restricted airspace, but it was standard procedure to fly close enough to tickle the curiosity of the Americans and test their reaction times and tactics. It was a game they played on each trip down this way, and this was his twentieth within the past two years.

The first to alert the crew was his electronics countermeasures operator. "They're closing . . . about ninety kilometers out."

Hmmmmm . . . about eight minutes, figured Sergei. Would it be the stubby-winged Eagles out of the USAF's Langley airfield or the arrowlike Navy F-14s with their dual crew positions and variable-geometry wings?

"F-15s," decided Sergei aloud.

"Tomcats," challenged his copilot, and to show his confidence that they were being intercepted by Navy swept-wings he placed a ten-ruble note on the console between them.

Sergei grinned and laid a matching bill over the other.

"Twelve kilometers and closing fast," reported his radar operator.

Sergei eyed the twenty rubles and licked his lips teasingly.

Within seconds, two sunlit blurs whizzed out from beneath the Bear's belly and pulled sharply into a vertical formation roll before topping out on their backs several thousand meters above and ahead of the cruising Soviet aircraft. For a moment, the winged spots hung suspended, a dark duo on the bright blue canvas, then they laid descending twin arcs of their own willowy contrails as they swooped down to approach the Bear head-on.

Sergei picked up the twenty rubles. The interceptors might be too far away to identify visually, but they had to be F-15s. The big twin-tailed interceptors always played their boyish hey-look-at-me game of surprise. If they had been Tomcats, they would have closed quietly and would now be positioned just aft of and below his sun-up wing tip, tucked in tightly as though tethered to the bomber by an invisible cable.

The approaching Eagles split apart about five kilometers out, each taking a side of the Bear as they passed. Within moments they returned, sliding smoothly into position off Sergei's left wing tip for their ride, which would probably be about forty-five minutes long before they would be relieved by another air defense team from one of the Florida bases. Sergei would be able to wager another ten rubles. He glanced back and tried to visualize the flight leader's countenance behind the green visor and tightly fitted oxygen mask. Although he couldn't see any of the man's face, he knew there was a smile. The aviator had raised his gloved left hand and was holding his middle finger stiffly aloft. Sergei laughed and returned the obscene gesture, then placed his hot cup of soup next to the window before taking a delicious sip in full view of the American. The warm vapor of the soup clouded the inside of the glass. The Eagle pilot nodded, his shoulders shaking as it became his turn to be amused.

They were professionals, he and the Americans, although the fighter pilots were probably only half his age. But, like Sergei, they were skilled in their own flying specialty, which at the moment joined Americans and Russians in the common bond of airmen. The sheer joy of their shared experience overshadowed their political and military differences, and they flew side by side in a gentle aerial ballet, their simultaneous movements a response to the subtle choreography of the upper air winds. They were brothers in the sky. Oh, if the times were right or the cause was urgent, they would not hesitate to kill one another, but never without that unique respect they held for their own kind. They were aerial knights, the last practitioners of a mythical code of honor spawned by King Arthur.

The Bear bounced slightly and the Eagle pair inherently matched the bob as the three sky machines entered the unstable air over a developing south Atlantic storm. Low-level clouds appeared and before long the tops of some of the clusters were boiling through thirty thousand feet, an occasional one reaching up to almost touch the cruising international formation of Bear and Eagles.

After awhile, the bumps became more consistent and a bit more violent. Sergei preferred the American aircraft to be farther out and made a pushing motion with his hand to express his concern. The American flight leader nodded in understanding and slid his two-plane section out and back to a more relaxed position although still in a parade formation. Sergei gave him a thumbs-up in appreciation. Both he and the Eagle pilots understood the infallible law of physics that stated that two bodies cannot occupy the same physical space at the same time, and neither desired to prove it.

The next twenty minutes were quiet, if somewhat bouncy.

These were the times that Sergei enjoyed; he was relaxed, confident in the pursuit of his profession, and even enjoying the companionship and respect of the two potential adversaries who had joined him and his crew. They were probably about the age of his own son, and he could not help but wonder what would happen if they should meet at some future date. Vladimir Sergeiovich Isatovaka was a squadron leader in the Soviet Air Force and an accomplished Tupolev-26 bomber pilot. It was not beyond comprehension that Vladimir and the Eagle pilots would someday meet, for Sergei knew that his son's swing-wing strategic bomber was programmed to attack the U.S. East Coast in the event the horrible day ever came. Realistically, he knew that the Eagles had a slight edge and his son would most probably die while the face behind the mask and visor would likely live. But live for what purpose? The horror of it all caused Sergei to just sit quietly and study the structural details of the two Eagles.

Sergei's flight engineer broke the silence. "Oil pressure on number one dropping," he abruptly announced.

Sergei leaned onto his side window and stared out at the far left engine. The pair of four-bladed counterrotating propellers were painting their huge transparent discs as smoothly as before and there seemed to be no sign of anything unusual.

"Ohhh, shit . . . it's gone," reported the copilot as the oil pressure needle started a plunge toward the zero reading, his words more in disgust than in alarm. Dejectedly, he leaned forward to punch one of the four red buttons at the top of the instrument panel to secure the fluids to the engine and start the propellers toward their feathered position. Sergei nodded in agreement, wondering why the engine had suddenly lost oil pressure. Then, he wondered why he wondered. After all, the Bear was an old airplane with old engines. A 1956 marvel when it first became operational, it had aged like him. We have both spent too many years in the air, old friend, he mused. I have my aches and pains, why should not you? They had both become classics of the Soviet Air Force. This particular airplane had rolled off the assembly line in 1963, about the time Sergei had made major.

Oh, well, he still had three engines left and they would carry him nicely to Cienfuegos.

His confidence was alarmingly short-lived.

A sharp vibration, followed by a vicious jolt, shook the Bear from nose to tail. The turbine of number one engine had seized before it had stopped spinning, the tremendous torque wresting it loose from its shaft and hurling it through the aluminum engine casing with such force that it continued on through the nacelle and tore into the compression section of the adjacent number two engine. Sergei suddenly found himself in a completely off-balance airplane, all the power being on its right side.

The pencil-thin bomber veered violently to its left, and the F-15s peeled off for dear life.

Sergei stomped on the right rudder pedal and fought to keep his charge from rolling over out of control. The Bear reluctantly leveled and Sergei adjusted his control pressures to nurse it back to its proper heading. Without the hydraulic boost he would have been powerless; even with it, he had to reduce power on the two good engines to bring the nose back on course. The near-panic maneuver had cost him more than a thousand feet of altitude, but that was immaterial.

"The rudder!" he yelled, pointing to his quivering right leg, which had turned to gelatin under the tension of the force required. His copilot had already anticipated the command and was standing on his pedal with both feet. Together, they found a combination of rudder pressure and engine power that allowed level flight although at a reduced airspeed.

Both engines on the left side were stopped, and Sergei could see no other damage. Their cockpit emergency procedures had been instinctively prompt and explicit, and now the four giant propellers on the left side, two to each engine, were still, their blades twisted such that there was very little drag on them. The Bear would have little difficulty maintaining its present altitude, and Sergei began to calm. But the next report from his flight engineer indicated that something else could very well be amiss. The fuel indicators were showing a rapid drain from the left wing tanks. Sergei shook his head with the realization that they had to have been punctured and spilling precious fuel into the stratosphere. The engineer immediately aligned his fuel transfer valves in a vain attempt to drain from the damaged tanks into the good right wing cells.

"Give me a reading," ordered Sergei.

The engineer jotted down the quantity readings from the various undamaged tanks and passed the slip of paper forward. Sergei needed only a quick glance to confirm his fears. Before the loss of the engines, they had been well within their fuel capabilities, but now it was marginal at best. He ran the figures through his head, ignoring the calculator strapped to his right leg, and confirmed that they were going to be short of fuel. The rip in the underside of the wing must be immense to dump such a volume of fuel in so short a time. That thought led to the next, and *it* raised the hairs on the back of Sergei's broad neck. The entire wing could be endangered. Anxiously, his eyes searched outside, sweeping every square inch of wing surface to be seen. There was some vibration but no unusual flexing, certainly no more than could be expected with the jagged tears in the two engine nacelles. The wing seemed to be riding solidly enough—but he couldn't be sure.

"We're not going to make it to Cienfuegos," he announced matter-of-factly, "not even Havana. We're not going to see Cuba this trip unless we swim."

"Bermuda?" suggested the flight engineer.

"Mother of Peter, no! Besides, it's way too far."

"United States?" countered the copilot.

Sergei wouldn't even dignify that suggestion with an answer.

The copilot grinned. "I always wanted to see the States."

"Bahamas?" suggested the navigator tentatively. "We can reach several airfields there . . . Bimini? . . . Nassau?"

Sergei grunted, then spoke, "Find me someplace."

The navigator began poring over his charts, measuring distances and thumbing through his flight publications.

"Soviet aircraft, can we be of any assistance?" The voice was American and it came over the international distress frequency. Sergei eyed the pair of Eagles and seemed to consider the offer before giving a strong negative shake of his head. "Nyet," he replied over the intercom to his copilot, who he knew had a better command of English.

"No, thank you," relayed the copilot, "please stay clear and give us maneuvering room."

"Will do, Bear. Norfolk advises you have emergency clearance if you so desire."

"No," repeated the copilot, then added wistfully, "perhaps some other time."

"Understand. We'll stay with you."

The corners of Sergei's grimly set lips curled upward. The American was living up to the chivalry code of the air, offering at least moral support.

"What kind of endurance do we have?" asked the navigator.

The engineer rechecked his fuel gauges before replying. "At this rate, two hours, maybe two plus fifteen."

"About fifteen hundred kilometers," muttered the navigator to himself.

"Do we have anything in this area?" asked the copilot.

"Nothing on the surface," answered Sergei.

The navigator came up with his findings. "The only reachable islands are the Bahamas."

Sergei shook his head. There was no way he could risk letting the highly classified cylinders strapped in the bomb bay be examined by the British any more than by the Americans. "Let me see your chart," he barked.

The navigator leaned forward between the pilots and spread his aerial navigation map across Sergei's ample lap.

The mature Soviet aviator had thirty-two years of flying under his belt, most of it in the ancient Bears, and his experienced brain immediately focused on the shallow seas over the Great Bahama Bank. In some spots the water was only ten meters deep, even less near the many cays. He had landed the huge aircraft in good weather and foul, on long, wide strips and sometimes on barely adequate ones. He had landed more than a few times with an engine out and once with two inoperative. But they had been on opposite sides and there had been no great difficulty. Thus, the one thing he had going for him was his familiarity with the Bear. Why not a water landing?

"We'll put it down in international water—here, at this point." He tapped his finger on a ten-to-seven-meter area. "Contact Havana Control and give them that position. Tell them to get a salvage ship on the way."

The navigator felt his throat go dry despite his sudden need to swallow. He hadn't too many hours in the air but he knew the Bear was meant to land on nice, long, wide ribbons of smooth concrete, not water. Familiar with the notable reliability of the four-engined veteran, he had never even considered the possibility of having to ride it through a water ditching, and his charts showed numerous landing strips within their two-engine range, even if they were in the Bahamas. Still, while he might contest the old man's decision in his mind, he wouldn't dare with his mouth. If his commander said that's where he was going to put one hundred tons of aluminum and Homo sapiens, that's where he would put them. The nervous navigator hurried back and passed a hastily scrawled note to the radioman.

Sergei started a gradual descent just as the two Eagles were relieved by a pair of F-14 Tomcats from their Florida base, the Eagle flight leader raising his hand in salute as he pulled his section ahead and away from the Bear. The Tomcats slid slowly into position.

The emergency frequency crackled again, this time the voice dripping with a drawl that made it difficult even for Sergei's copilot to understand. "Tupolev aircraft, this here is ole Navy 146322, the pride of the Bad Bastards of Fightin' Sixty-Three. . . . Be advised that y'all have clearance to land at any Yewnited States airfield. . . . Would you nice commie folks like us to lead you over to the nearest wun? It's only a few miles from Disney World."

"No, thank you," responded Sergei's copilot curtly, without waiting for his commander's prompting.

"What are your intentions, Bear?" asked the Tomcat leader.

Sergei shook his head. The copilot remained silent.

"We understand, Bear." The accent had softened. "Good luck. We'll stay with you." The sarcasm was gone. Sergei knew the American airman realized that he and his crew had only one acceptable course of action. He glanced out at the Navy Tomcat driver and nodded in appreciation of the thumbs-up encouragement offered.

Twenty-five minutes later, they were passing through eight thousand feet and Sergei alerted his crew, "Make preparations for a water landing."

The Tomcat wingman dived away and swept low over the water before returning to the formation. "Bear, this is Navy 146335. The major swell system is from the southwest, long and low. Some surface chop, perhaps a foot or two. Wind eight to twelve knots from the east. Recommend landing direction, northeast, down swell and generally into the wind."

"Thank you," replied Sergei's copilot. Sergei nodded his understanding. The Tomcat pilot's evaluation agreed with his own, except he would be touching down on even more shallow water than that the F-14 had flown over. The effects of the sea and wind would be even less. As he further reduced power, the Bear became more manageable, and at one thousand feet he lowered full flaps and slowed to minimum safe speed. The two Tomcats opened to give him an unobstructed airspace. His crewmen were poised at their ditching stations, yellow life jackets strapped around their upper bodies, and each one mentally rehearsing his action to be taken when they hit the water.

Sergei eased the big bomber down to just above the surface and the huge wings pressed a large cushion of air, allowing him to fly even slower. His massive hands gripped the control yoke with the strength of a Samson, but his touch was that of a surgeon. For the last few feet, he would play the wind and the sea and the airplane like the three objects of a skilled juggler's most demanding routine, giving each equal consideration so that together all three received his undivided attention. So precise were the coordination and balance that the Bear was practically hovering.

He was lined up into the wind, and he watched the long swells pass under him. He poised the Bear a scant thirty feet above the next approaching rise of water and raised the nose. The Bear began to wallow, but Sergei was the master of the beast and he refused to allow it to drop until he willed it. It was no longer a maverick machine with a mind of its own, it was an extension of Sergei's arms and legs.

The voice of the Navy pilot returned, "You're lookin' good, Bear . . . tail skag is about five feet above the surface. . . . Try to touch down on the crest or just beyond it . . . lookin' good . . . three feet . . . there's a good one coming up with a long, flat space beyond. . . . Go for it, Ivan. . . ."

Carefully, Sergei watched the swell roll toward him and timed his next move for the instant he would be just short of the crest. With the skill and confidence of more than thirty-five thousand flight hours, he raised the nose the last degree.

The leading edge of the great wing tilted upward ever so slightly, just enough that its angle with the oncoming wind caused the flow over its curved top surface to start to break free, creating tiny eddies and burbles of disturbed air.

The Bear began to quiver, shaking the control column in Sergei's hands in protest at his efforts to fly it slower than it had been designed to fly. Far out on the leading edge of the left wing, a small metal tab lost its grip on the airflow and flapped up and down, its frantic movements triggering an irritating buzzer that sounded in the cockpit. Still, Sergei held his charge on top of the bubble as the last two knots of acceptable flying speed bled off. The wave crest slid beneath him.

The Bear stalled just as the rub plate at the very back bottom of the 155-foot fuselage began to tick the surface, and the giant bomber plowed heavily into the warm waters of the Florida Straits.

Chapter 1

July 2, 3:15 A.M.
Ramrod Key, Florida

The rain fell in vertical sheets, driven ashore by the gathering fury of a seaward tropical storm. It swept across the time-worn roof of the clapboard beach shack in waves almost as dense as those of the angry sea crashing onto the sands only a few yards away. The ancient structure quivered and creaked as successive bolts of silver lightning split the swirling clouds overhead, releasing deep drumrolls of awesome thunder that shattered the soaked air as if God himself were clearing his throat.

Little wonder the wall telephone inside the besieged shack rang unnoticed, its puny falsetto voice completely masked by the overpowering baritone of nature. Only by chance, when a chattering shutter tore loose to slam against the wall over the bed, was it ever answered. Even then, the sharp noise barely roused one of the occupants from the abysmal depths of hungover sleep.

"Yes?" grunted the disheveled man as he lifted the receiver from the wall unit with one hand and clawed with the other at the sweat-soaked triangle of kinky black hair that ran from his belly upward and around masculine nipples.

"Davey? Is that you?" came the raspy voice on the other end of the line.

"Who the hell you think it is at this time of night?"

"Night's over. My Timex says three-fifteen in the A.M. It's morning, Davey."

David Morales, second-generation Mexican-American, rubbed his dark brown eyes and belched forth the sour taste of almost-digested bourbon. Despite the sarcastic semantics of his caller, it was night inside his place.

It hurt when he squinted at the watch strapped to his left wrist. One phosphorescent hand pointed to where the number three should be; the other hand somewhere else—just where, he couldn't quite make out. He winced as a group of flamenco dancers resumed their performance inside his head, energetically tapping a staccato rhythm across his frontal lobes and down his nasal spine. With uncanny regularity, the shooting pains seemed to be determined to time themselves with the claps of thunder, which not only threatened to bring down the shaking walls of the hut but vibrated every bone in his body. Davey shuddered.

He stretched out one of his thirty-six-inch inseams and curled long, skinny toes around the frayed arm of a tattered cane-bottom chair to pull it toward him, simultaneously allowing the phone to dangle and twist itself out of its own tangles. Wearily, he plopped down into the chair with the grace of a fouled NBA forward, his free arm hanging limply over one side and his legs loosely crossed in front of him. "Okay, you got my attention. What's up?"

"I hope *you* are! We've got a live one, Davey. How soon can you get here?"

"Jesus . . . it's raining buckets. How's the causeway? I been asleep, which is what most people do at this time of night. We got a big one brewing?"

"Not as far as the weather goes. Just a tropical storm. The highway's okay. That's not what I called you about. Get your ass in here, pronto!"

"Can't we talk over the phone?"

"No way, Jose. Just come on in, and be prepared for an operation. Bring your gear."

"I'm on leave, remember?"

"Past tense, Davey. The Old Man's canceled it."

"Bullshit." Sighing heavily, Davey resigned himself to his fate. What the hell. "All right, but I'm playing this one under protest."

The phone at the other end clunked off.

It took Davey only a few minutes to shave and pull a pair of khaki shorts over his lower body. Grunting at the exertion, he raised his arms and let a faded red "I Fish the Keys" T-shirt ripple down and settle over his shoulders and chest. Fumbling his way back over to the bed, he retrieved his wallet from beneath the mattress, then shuffled around feeling for something to put on his feet. Socks were a luxury Davey conceded to the very rich and famous; he just stepped into a worn pair of blue clacks and fished his scuba gear from under the minimountain of dirty clothes that covered the sandy floor of his lone closet. As an afterthought, he ran a comb through the shock of raven hair that by all rights should have been an item in the *Guinness Book of World Records*—no two strands ran the same way. Finally, he splashed a generous portion of blue Mennen after-shave over his sharp jaw and high cheekbones. Unfortunately, his vision had cleared enough for him to catch a last reflection in the mirror over the freestanding sink in his bathroom, and he recoiled at the sunrise streaks in his eyes.

He left a note for the woman who was still asleep, sprawled face down across the foot on the bed, her waist-length auburn hair cascading forward over her head and slithering down her arms that hung off to one side. Davey resisted the urge to press his lips to the bare back of her neck, for he knew that would only rekindle a fire that had taken some hours the previous night to extinguish. He might be Mexican, with a healthy portion of Irish blood contributed by his mother, but he had to agree with the Oriental philosophy that proclaimed a woman's nape to be a most sensual place. In this case, so was the spine, a delicately diminishing procession of skin-covered vertebrae dipping down deep into an inviting valley before ascending and trailing off between the most delicious pair of buttocks he had ever stroked. The legs weren't bad, either, if one liked full, firm thighs and calves that were masterpieces of soft, compound curves. He and the woman had not left the shack for two days—they had seldom left the bed.

Even as he completed preparing himself, he let his eyes feast on the sleeping nude, her lightly tanned body a study in light and shadow in the indirect light from the bathroom. She'd be stuck without a car, and probably a bit whizzed off, but that might ensure she'd still be there when he returned. That would be nice.

His faded silver Mazda was parked only a few yards from the door, but by the time his crouched sprint had carried him to it, he was drenched. For a change, the five-year-old RX-7 started on the first attempt, and he slipped and skidded across the generous spread of thick green iceplant anchoring the sand around his shack. The one good wiper, fortunately on the driver's side, beat back and forth in a valiant but futile effort to clear away the torrent of water streaming across the windshield, giving him only momentary glimpses of the area ahead. At least, the lights worked.

Ordinarily, the drive to the Naval Air Station at Key West was an easy seventeen-minute trip, but the rain slowed him and it took twenty-five very wet minutes before he pulled into his parking place outside the Special Intelligence building.

The Marine on guard at the desk outside the entrance to the vault shook his head knowingly as Davey trotted up the stairs two at a time.

"Don't say it," cautioned Davey.

The Marine threw up his hands in mock defense but kept his intimidating smile as he pressed the release button for the door.

Davey entered and stood dripping all over the carpet in front of the Old Man's desk. "Good morning," he said, putting just enough edge on his words to indicate his displeasure at the early recall but avoiding an undiplomatic sharpness.

Someone with a weird sense of humor had taken a Buddha, wrapped him in tan wash slacks and a flowered aloha shirt, given him a clipped white beard that rose up ample jowls to almost meet on top of a sun-toughened scalp, and pulled loose the skin under the puffy gray eyes so that the bags drooped almost to the level of his flared nostrils. For good measure, the nose was pushed in even farther than one was accustomed to seeing on such a rotund figure. The Old Man was indeed an old man as far as his overindulged body indicated, but Davey knew him to be only in his early sixties with a mind that had never aged once it reached its peak, probably while Davey was still squawling for a diaper change.

"You didn't have to dress on my account," observed the Old Man, raising his eyes as if to peer over reading glasses, but he wore none. In fact, his vision was one of the most acute features about him, a source of some ego, and woe to the physician who ever suggested he might find reading more pleasant with some accommodating lenses. Consequently, he squinted a lot.

Davey collapsed into the chair off to one side of the desk. "Smitty didn't say black tie," he offered.

"Did he say 'no shoes, no shirt, no service'?"

Davey tilted his head. "I don't believe so."

The Buddha grunted and pulled a Havana from the yellow glass humidor that was the only object on top of his desk not full to overflowing, coffee-stained, or broken. Even the clipboard holding the half-inch-thick stack of message flimsies had a broken corner. The Old Man tapped the dispatch board with a crooked finger as he drew the first satisfying puffs on his cigar. "We got us a Bear down in the Bahama Bank. Ditched just before nightfall. The Coast Guard's got a C-130 over him; seems there are two rafts with nine survivors." He tossed the message board over to Davey. The series of dispatches had originated with a contact report from the Command and Control Center of the Atlantic Command in Norfolk. Several amplifying reports followed, radio messages from the F-15s and from the Navy Tomcats that stayed with him as he ditched.

"Nine floaters. The pilot did a good job," commented Davey.

"Not only that. He picked the exact spot he wanted to put that big son of a bitch down on. The Bear's under only about ten feet of water—international water," said the Old Man, giving Davey another over-the-glasses look.

"Why didn't he take it to the Bahamas? There are plenty of suitable strips. Or the States? I assume it was a bona fide emergency."

The Old Man rolled his cigar around with his tongue before replying, "He doesn't want anybody to look at that airplane."

Davey nodded. "Something on board?"

"Something or maybe someone." The Buddha shifted in his high-backed leather chair and tapped off the long white ash that had been defying gravity for the past moments. "Well, we know there's the usual stuff: classified avionics, ECM equipment, IFF code transponders, that sort of thing. But there must be something else, something sensitive he wants to be sure is salvaged—by the right people. Otherwise, why didn't he put it in deeper water, closer to rescue facilities? I don't know. I just have a feeling."

"Nuclear weapons?"

"I doubt it. But I think we ought to try and take a look."

"He was obviously headed for Castro country. They'll be coming out for him," suggested Davey.

The Old Man nodded. "Yes, but this blessed storm is sitting right in their way. You can jump up to Miami and get around it."

"Why not the military? They can use their people."

"No, the powers that be want us to take a look. Less conspicuous. The goddamned Navy would send in a twenty-ship battle group. The water's too shallow, anyhow. It takes our method of doing things."

For a flash, Davey remembered the smooth nape, delicate

spine, and soft buttocks back at his shack. They'd have a long wait. Oh, well, fate. Kismet. Que sera, sera. "I'll get started. Smitty make the arrangements?"

The Buddha belched out of the corner of his mouth and picked a speck of moist tobacco off his lower lip. "Piss poor chopper weather," he mused. "You'll have to drive. Smitty's alerted Miami. They'll have an Albatross ready. The crew will be your backup."

Davey rose and started for the door, then stopped and turned around. "I left a friend back at the shack, marooned. I may be awhile."

For the first time since Davey had entered, the Old Man smiled. "I'll see that she gets to wherever she needs to be . . . may give her my own personal service."

"You're all heart," said Davey.

"Not all of me," replied the Buddha, reaching down and giving his crotch a good squeeze. He was still chuckling when Davey closed the door.

One of the administrative people was waiting outside with a plainclothes sedan. Davey signed the custody chit and noted the plastic sign on the door: Cay Travel, Inc. He tossed his own keys to the man. "Lock up the Mazda, will you? And hold these till I get back."

It was a treat to drive a vehicle with two efficient wipers, and Davey could almost see as he passed through the main gate and headed north up the causeway. He was tempted to veer off to the shack as he recrossed Ramrod Key. The woman should be stirring by now. He shrugged. There would always be a woman. A Bear didn't drop by every day.

The sedan had a fresh set of all-weather treads, but the highway was drowning under the fierce downpour and the gusting winds rocked the car almost to the point of lifting the wheels. There was no sense hydroplaning off the causeway, so Davey slowed to a more manageable speed. The sedan settled somewhat and he was able to keep the speed to a few miles per hour on each side of the fifty-five mark.

This could be an interesting assignment. He had been with the Company for almost six years, but most of his assignments had been well below his thrill threshold. Certainly, he had expected more action when the Company recruiter had approached him during his last year in law school.

Despite the efforts of his father, who had worked the dirt of Texas fields for more than twenty years to save money for Davey's college education, he had wound up short of funds and the elusive LLD was still a financial world away. Inflation had eaten his father's savings, and Davey was facing at least a two-year work sabbatical to earn the funds for his last year of study, so he had struck a deal with the devil. The CIA funded his degree, and he, in turn, handed over his soul—for a while.

His mother had passed on a decade earlier; he would not have wanted her to know that he did not plan to immediately enter practice. Proudly Irish, she had raised her Davey in good-natured defiance of his wetback father, who had carried his own heritage from a small village near Chihuahua across a quiet moonlit stretch of the Rio Grande into Texas. Always fiercely proud of his conquistador ancestors, he had argued forcefully for a more proper Spanish name for his son, feeling that his wife's selection of David, even when pronounced as the Spanish Dah-veed, was not nearly as appropriate as Ferdnando or even Manolito. But as always, he deferred to his blond-haired, blue-eyed wife, whose aggressive Irish genes were nevertheless completely overpowered by their son's predominately Latin physique.

After two years at Langley, sitting at the Cuban desk as a junior partner in the formulation of contingency plans, Davey had finally talked his way into a field assignment. Anything to get away from the stilted bureaucracy of the headquarters staff. Even the six weeks at Camp Perry had been a welcomed change. Then, on to southern Florida and a bit of mixing with the Cuban crowd that had boated in from Mariel in 1980.

What a farce that had been. Political refugees? Bullshit. More than 100,000 of them had swarmed ashore at every bay and cove along the lower Florida coasts. Submerged in the flood of human flotsam and jetsam were some 25,000 hardened criminals, a special token of Castro's esteem for his giant neighbor to the north. So rapidly had the Cubans saturated the Miami area that the immigration people had just thrown up their hands and headed for the nearest bar. The impact was such that the feds simply could not come up with any viable method of dealing with the situation, and most of the illegals just vanished within the Cuban community. Overnight, the southernmost Florida metropolis completed its metamorphosis into a Havana clone. That's when the two-man office of the CIA at Naval Air Station, Key West, became a full-fledged substation of the Miami office, with the Old Man in charge of some thirteen agents. The quick-learning Mexican with the Irish name soon became the Old Man's protégé.

It had taken only a short indoctrination for Davey to shift his natural Latino personality and character from his native heritage to his adopted Cuban role. He had the headquarters experience as background and, with some subtle changes in his Spanish, incorporating the Cuban idioms and dropping the Mexican, he had melded nicely within the exile community.

A skilled underwater adventurer, and with no obvious means of support, he had easily found himself sought out and drawn into the underworld of the Cuban colony. Mostly small stuff, hijacking a few powerboats for coke shuttles between Miami and the shadowy ships that slowed in the night waters around the keys. Occasionally, he would be used to provide underwater security while a major transfer of merchandise was taking place. The U.S. authorities were no problem, but the competition between the Cubans and Colombians and Jamaicans was like that of the more notorious Sicilian families to the north. They derived a special satisfaction from stealing from each other.

The company had him play along; information was all they wanted until a really big fish came swimming by. But such fish, while maintaining an aggressiveness akin to that of the great white shark, were as wary as the lesser fish that were the shark's prey, and Davey had to do with little excitement and much boredom. Perhaps this foray out to examine the Bear would be a bit different. At least, as he powered the sedan through the downpour toward Miami, he hungrily anticipated a more promising assignment.

He stayed on state Highway 1 through Homestead and Coral Gables. The rain had slackened considerably despite the perseverance of the low, dirty clouds, and the early-morning traffic was beginning to build. Just south of the Miami River crossing, U.S. 41 joined the freeway, and just beyond that Davey veered off to the east, following 41 by the Goodyear blimp field and winding his way around the port of Miami until he pulled into the parking area by Chalk's Seaplane Base. The twin-engined Grumman Albatross was already in position at the head of one of the two seaplane ramps, engines ticking over smoothly at idle. One of the pilots strode to meet him.

"Hi, Davey." The man wore the blue jumpsuit of Intra-Caribbean Air, Incorporated, and he reached out for part of Davey's gear. It was only a short walk to the plane.

"Looks like a good one for a change," remarked Davey, his elated voice reflecting his enthusiasm.

The young aviator grinned and nodded his concurrence. He preceded Davey up the aluminum ladder hanging from the open waist hatch and tossed Davey's gear inside before climbing through the rectangular opening. Davey followed him into the fuselage and settled himself into the forward right-hand passenger seat as the young man wiggled into the copilot's seat in the tiny crew compartment. The aircraft commander, considerably older than his young assistant, turned around and partially leaned through the bulkhead opening to mouth a "welcome aboard" with thick, happy lips that were all but hidden behind the gay-nineties mustache. The lip cover was not quite as gray as the thin covering on the man's head. Davey leaned back in his seat, comfortable and relaxed. He liked to fly with gray-haired pilots.

The only other crewman was the plane captain, also in a blue jumpsuit but one strained by the pressure of a muscle-builder's torso. A cloth name patch sewn over his upper left pocket stated simply: Moose. Perhaps he matched the animal's build, but his movements were more those of a cat as he nimbly went about his task of securing the hatches and taking the seat across from Davey. He nodded amiably as he strapped in and gave the pilots a thumbs-up. As far as he was concerned, they were ready to go over the side.

The amphibian lumbered down the sloped ramp and settled into the water as the copilot retracted the landing gear and the pilot added throttle to head for the buoy-marked takeoff area.

Within minutes, they sped across the gently undulating waters of Biscayne Bay and lifted into the warm, moist air. The base of the rain clouds was only about eight hundred feet, and they plunged into the gray mass, riding the slight turbulence as the pilot checked his instrument alignments and engaged his automatic pilot.

Once on top of the overcast, Davey could see the towering storm sitting to the south, its center probably over central Cuba. It was big, still technically a tropical storm, but Davey guessed its ferocity was approaching that of a hurricane. Fortunately, the multilayered cumuli they were climbing above were on the outside edge of the atmospheric beast.

Within forty-five minutes they were cruising over only scattered clouds, and the blue waters of the Straits of Florida shimmered below them with the first light of the rising sun. Bimini passed off their left, the only substantial chunk of coral at the northern tip of a fifty-mile-long string of small cays—tiny white dots that led down across the paler blue waters of the Great

Bahama Bank. The Albatross rode smooth air at eleven thousand feet as they pressed south. The pilot joined Davey in the passenger compartment.

"The Bear went down here," he said, pointing with a gloved finger to a penciled X on his map. "Just southeast of Orange Cay. The Coast Guard reports indicate that the crew members have kept their two rafts over the spot, probably using sea anchors to contain their drift, or possibly they've tied themselves to their airplane."

Davey held the map in front of his small window to let the sunshine illuminate it, and studied the pencil-marked location. They should be only about twenty minutes from the position. "Any sign of surface vessels?" he asked.

"The Navy's got a couple frigates off in deep water, but they can't get near the spot. Too shallow, so they're milling around out here, five or so miles to the west. The storm edge is about forty miles southeast and reaches clear over to the southern coast of Cuba, maybe beyond, so it'll take awhile for anything to get through those seas."

"What's the plan?"

"We'll touch down close aboard; plenty of water for this bird. You can slip over the side, and we'll taxi up and offer assistance— which I assume they will refuse. We'll make sure their attention is on us while you swim over and take a look. The water's clear as baby pee, so you'll have to be careful. How long will you need?"

"If you can drop me within a hundred yards or so, I should be able to do the whole thing and be ready for pickup in about forty-five minutes."

"Check the flight deck if you can for any code books, that sort of thing."

"Will do."

"Other than that, I don't know what to tell you to look for."

"I've been briefed. We think they may have some cargo on board that is sensitive."

"Cargo? Where in hell would you put anything in a Bear? It's bound to be crammed full of electronic gear for their surveillance down our coast. Probably extra fuel tanks in the bomb bay."

"I dunno. But there is a strong indication they deliberately picked the spot for the ditching with some salvage in mind. I'll just nose around and see what I can see."

"Sounds good. We'll offer to pick them up, of course, but they've refused Coast Guard help and have given every intention of waiting for some sort of friendly assistance. Maybe they have a Soviet vessel on the way from out at sea."

"I would suspect Cuban."

"Whatever." The older man glanced at his watch. "We'll be there in another ten minutes. I'll go back up front. You can use that headset and we'll keep you informed."

"Thanks." Davey unstrapped and pulled on his wet suit. In the warm water he'd really not need it, but the thick fabric might give him some protection from cuts as he swam around and hopefully inside the Bear. After arranging his air tank and mask by the waist hatch and securing them with a cargo strap, he returned to his seat and placed the headset over his ears.

In only a few minutes, the copilot announced, "There they are." The Albatross had been steadily descending and Davey estimated they were passing about one thousand feet as the pilot pulled off more power and allowed the amphibian to drop rapidly in a low-angle dive. Peering out the window, Davey searched for the Soviet crew as the pilot made his low pass. Suddenly, they flashed by, looking quite comfortable, four to one raft, five to the other. Some were sitting on the yellow sausage sides of the rubber boats and several others sprawled on the dark bottoms. One held up a canteen and took a long swig as the Albatross passed, probably to indicate they had plenty of water. All waved and appeared unconcerned and ready to ride out any delay in their rescue.

The Bear lay right below them, its huge outline readily discernible in the clear water, the tip of its gigantic vertical tail sticking several feet above the lapping surface. That would make the depth about twenty-five to thirty feet, estimated Davey, checking the Bear data sheet provided him by the Old Man. It gave the aircraft's height as thirty-eight feet. They probably had been shooting for slightly shallower water, which would have kept the interior of the aircraft accessible from the surface and possibly even dry if the structural integrity remained, and they undoubtedly ditched pressurized. The Soviet pilot was a thinking man, no doubt about that.

The Albatross settled onto the surface with only a slight surge as it plowed through the low ground swell and slowed to an idle taxi. They had landed only a couple hundred yards away from the rafts, and the pilot maneuvered the amphibian to place it broadside to the Soviets, who were watching with detached interest. Apparently, they regarded the aircraft as civilian. As the Albatross closed to within one hundred yards, the pilot shielded Davey's exit with the hull. The plane captain swung open the hatch on the opposite side from the rafts, and Davey slipped into the water.

The shallow sea was crystal clear in the purest sense of the expression, and Davey propelled himself downward on an easy slant until he could stroke along just two or three feet above the coral sand floor of the bank. Above, the shimmering surface only slightly filtered the tropical sun, and underwater visibility was as clear as any he had ever encountered.

Most of the sea life ignored him, having had no prior encounters with such a strangely appendaged animal. To the fish of the Great Bahama Bank, Davey was a fellow fish, albeit an unusual one with four long arms instead of several thin and flappy fins. The scaleless black skin of his wet suit, with its bright yellow stripes running the length of its tubular body and out to the ends of the four appendages, was in keeping with their own brilliant coloring. With the special instinct and reflexes that prevented them from bumping one another, no matter how thickly they schooled, the multicolored water breathers flitted about Davey with an almost disdainful nonchalance as they foraged for the microorganisms that were their inferior link in the life chain of the sea. Only rarely did a fish brush against him, and then probably with intent, either to test the reaction of the huge intruder or let him know that they were not intimidated by such a weird flailing stranger.

Davey checked his wrist compass every few minutes, although the visibility was such that he could probably hold his course by a series of dead-reckoning legs, swimming from one prominent spot on the sea floor to the next in line with his intended path.

Off to his left, a pair of yellowish green sand sharks cruised into view, hugging the bottom and stirring up small cloudy contrails of sand. Warily, they started a wide arc around to his rear. Davey rolled over on his back and watched the four-footers as they, in turn, eyed him. He let his arm drop down by his right leg where he had the shocker rod stowed, but the cautious pair apparently decided there was more attractive game off to the right, and they set a steady course for a swarming school of thread herring opening frantically to the north. The excited fish began to sharply zig-zag and dart forward with amazing bursts of speed as the two miniature eating machines closed them from the rear.

Davey returned his attention up ahead, and already he could see a faint shadow, long and thin with a sharp, tapered slab rising from one end. The shadow became a gray form, then a silver tube, and finally the unmistakable fuselage of the submerged Bear. Davey could even see the large red star emblazoned on the vertical stabilizer that continued beyond the surface.

The aircraft had survived the water impact almost intact, but there was one large rip across the top of the fuselage just aft of the trailing edge of the massive wing. The Bear had broken its back. The two fuselage parts, while still joined, slanted downward from the fracture as though the airplane had settled onto a large rock. And in a sense, it had. As Davey swam closer he could see that the center of the fuselage had come to rest on a sharp outcropping of bottom coral. Weakened by the tear across the top of the fuselage, the nose and tail sections had dropped a bit farther and were resting on the mixture of hard reef and ground coral that formed the underwater mesa. As Davey approached, a frighteningly large eel, somewhat like a moray but with a vivid orange dorsal stripe running the length of its spine, wiggled from under the after-fuselage and undulated toward him, its open mouth revealing rows of tiny pointed teeth, its eyes a menacing black. Davey continued his steady stroke, wary and ready to take defensive action should the creature decide to attack, but the five-foot-long monster apparently reasoned that the larger black-and-yellow-striped thing should be observed for a while and slithered off Davey's right to sink slowly into the sand.

There was a thin ripple of oily residue rising from the crack in the airplane's back, translucent red in color, probably hydraulic fluid from severed lines within the fuselage. The tiny globules followed one another in an endless stream out of the tear, silently spreading when they reached the surface to form a widening slick.

Some twenty yards beyond the sunken Bear, Davey could see the bottom of the two rafts tethered together with yellow nylon cording that hung down in a loose loop beneath them. It was attached to another line leading down to one of the stub antennae on the top of the Bear's fuselage. The Soviets had indeed anchored themselves to their disabled craft.

Davey could also see the long keel of the Albatross jutting several feet down into the water as the pilot slowly circled the scene.

He swam toward the open emergency egress hatches raised on each side of the cockpit and pulled himself down into the copilot's seat. From there, he squirmed back onto the flight deck. Off to one side, at the rear of the crew compartment, a short ladder led down into the main fuselage. He dropped into the void and started paddling aft before becoming confused about his exact position within the long tubular structure. He had entered a narrow compartment jammed with electronic equipment. Pausing until he felt he had recovered his bearings, he continued aft. The light decreased as he approached what seemed to be a bulkhead door. He turned the dogs and pulled it open. The light returned, streaming in from the overhead tear.

He reasoned that he must be over the bomb bay, since he should be near the center of gravity of the airplane, and the crawl space before him seemed to be over a large compartment perhaps thirty feet long, with another bulkhead at the far end. He searched the deck for access panels and immediately found four in a line, each ample enough in size to permit passage of a man. Selecting the first one, he twisted the locking mechanism until the panel was free and he could place it aside. Easily, he passed through the opening, even with his air bottle strapped to his back, but once in the lower void, the light again all but disappeared. Flicking on his head-mounted lamp, he began a systematic search of the compartment. It was the forward bomb bay and it was practically empty except for two metal cylinders held by a pair of overhead racks in the rear of the space.

The cylinders were approximately eighteen inches in diameter and probably five feet long, domed at each end and securely sealed by welded seams that also anchored metal tags, which were stamped with what appeared to be serial numbers. He could not read the lettering on the assorted placards attached to the cylinders, although he could make out a lone familiar Russian word: Moskva. This shipment appeared to have originated at some Moscow facility. Some of the lettering was larger and in red, probably cautionary in nature. Davey's eyes opened a bit wider as he saw the three-bladed international warning symbol for radioactive material. Whatever was in the cylinders was hot! Yet, they did not appear to be weapons. The cylinders were most probably shipping containers. There were no fins, nor could he detect any provision for fusing. Withdrawing a pad and grease pencil from a leg pocket, he copied the Russian script as well as he could. The rest of the bomb bay was empty.

A glance at his watch indicated he had been underwater for almost twenty minutes. There was still time to examine the rest of the airplane.

The after bomb bay was empty. The Bear had a very light cargo load. He continued aft past what appeared to be a crew rest station. Starting up the tunnel to investigate the tail gunner's position, he recoiled as his headlamp illuminated a pair of wide-open brown eyes staring directly at him. The body was already white from water immersion and was starting to bloat from its interior gases. The ditching had not gone off without a price. The tail crewman had made it only halfway up the tunnel toward the nearest escape hatch before he began breathing seawater.

Returning forward, Davey searched the small galley area and pulled himself back up onto the flight deck. There were no code books, or pilots' bags, or anything that appeared to be of value. He felt a strange sense of wonder as he pushed his hand against a frame member to rotate his body, taking a final look at the interior. Bears had been operational since 1956, but he suspected he was the first westerner to see the inside of the massive machine in any great detail. Nothing really unusual, although he wished he had brought his camera to record the electronics equipment. Some of it might be the latest ECM sensors and jamming gear. He knew that the first question the Old Man would ask was where the pictures were. But he didn't normally carry a camera in his drug tasks and the matter had completely slipped his mind. Mentally, he kicked himself, saving a substantial chunk of his posterior for the big foot of the meticulous Buddha. Oh, well.

He had used less than half of his air, but there was little else he could examine or inspect. Still, the giant aluminum cave was a fascinating place. Many of his flat companions had already found cozy spots to mill around in, and they were busily gobbling up the trapped organisms and smaller fish that had floated in with the random currents and gathered in the nooks and crannies within the fuselage. Already, their excreta and the gathering of the coral animals were infiltrating every crevice within the bomber; in a few short weeks, if not salvaged, the dead Tupolev would suffer the same suffocating fate as the Spanish galleons that had plied these waters several centuries back. Ripping out their wooden bottoms on the sharp coral, they had sunk into the deeper waters off the bank, there to become encrusted with the minute organisms of the Caribbean.

Davey floated upward out of the cockpit and through the egress hatch. Hugging the sea bottom once more, he swam back along his approach course. The dark hull of the Albatross was still slicing slowly through the water, swinging wide in its arc around the floating Soviet aircrewmen. It made another complete circle before Davey could get into position for his pickup. The pilot had slowed to barely steerageway and on the next time around, Davey popped to the surface and slid along the slick aluminum side of the airplane until he reached the open waist hatch and grabbed the plane captain's outstretched hand. The man gave a surprisingly strong pull and Davey found himself hoisted aboard like a gaffed flounder.

"All done?" asked the crewman.

Davey nodded and the man said something into his headset boom mike while closing the hatch. By the time Davey had unslung his air tank and pulled off his mask, the amphibian was rearing up under full power. He barely made it back to his seat before the Albatross smacked into a series of low waves and kissed off into the air. The pilot laid the airplane over into a steep bank and made a low departure pass over the two rafts, rocking his wings. The Soviet airmen were as before, relaxed as if they had not a care and waving with all of the abandon of Sunday boaters on a calm lake.

Several miles off to the east, two U.S. Navy frigates were following each other around in a racetrack holding pattern, unable to close because of the shallows, but with all of their topside sensors rotating in a vigilant search for the Cubans who were surely on their way.

Chapter 2

Commander Ted Darly stood on the exposed port wing of the bridge and watched his LAMPS Mk. III helicopter, a brand-new Sikorsky SH-60B Seahawk, flail its way to over the USS *Bradley*'s stern and settle skillfully onto the helicopter operating pad. The pilot had already radioed that his offer to retrieve the Soviets, still floating sixteen thousand yards off to the east, had been refused, and Darly's orders were not to press the issue. He couldn't bring the *Bradley* any closer; the bank was at its shallowest in the vicinity of the downed Russians. He had watched them also refuse assistance from a civilian Albatross that was just disappearing in the northwestern sky.

Well, let the dumb bastards float forever, he reflected. He raised his glasses and checked the position of the *Bradley*'s sister ship, the USS *Voge*. Also a Garcia-class ocean escort ship, the 2,600-ton *Voge* was station-keeping three thousand yards astern.

"Coffee, Captain?"

Darly took the white porcelain mug of black brew from the messman's outstretched hand. "Thanks, Davis . . . I'd rather have a cold beer."

The young petty officer grinned sheepishly. "Yes, sir, that would be nice. Are you going to have time for any breakfast, sir?"

"No, let's skip it. It won't hurt me to miss a meal." Darly patted the slight bulge around his waist and leaned on the spray shield, sipping slowly from the mug.

The intercom inside the pilot house crackled with a report from his Combat Information Center. "Bridge, Combat. We have an unidentified aerial target bearing three-zero-zero, three-zero miles, closing."

"Any ID?" queried the officer of the deck.

"He's not squawking ... speed one-seven-five knots."

"Slow," commented the OOD.

Darly searched the bearing and in a few minutes picked up the gull-winged profile of an approaching aircraft. Radar reported the range to be twelve miles.

The youthful seaman standing the port lookout watch was also visually tracking his target with glasses. "It's another seaplane, Captain," he reported.

The aircraft was descending but seemed to be deliberately avoiding the two frigates as it headed toward the downed Bear crew.

The lookout furiously thumbed through the pages of his small recognition handbook. Triumphantly he stopped, tapping his right index finger on a three-view drawing. "It's Russian, sir! A Beriev Be-12 ... NATO code name Mail ... turboprop amphibian, sir!"

Darly had his eyes pressed to his glasses. "Cuban Air Force," he announced. "I can see the insignia." He watched the Mail touch down close aboard the two rafts.

"Can we get any closer?" he called out to his OOD.

"Wouldn't recommend it, sir. We're only five hundred yards from the shelf now."

"Very well. Keep her at five hundred yards."

The Mail taxied up to the rafts and Darly could see its propellers spooling down. The amphibian was either tying up to the rafts or dropping its anchor. Darly couldn't quite make out which, although he suspected the latter was the case. In any event, the Mail was definitely alongside the survivors.

"They've put someone in the water," reported the lookout. "There goes another one!"

"Must be going down to inspect the Bear," mused Darly. "Let's hold this position!" he called to his OOD.

A half hour passed. The nine crewmen had boarded the Mail, but the aircraft was dead in the water. As it swung with the wind,

Darly could make out an A-frame being rigged from the starboard waist hatch. There was also some activity in the water just below the hoisting frame.

"They're recovering something," he said to his lookout. "Can you tell what it is?"

The seaman leaned over the spray shield as if the additional few inches could sharpen his view. His mouth was open as he concentrated, his tongue snaking back and forth along his lower lip. The tongue stopped and his jaw dropped a bit more, this time in astonishment. "They're passing up a bomb, sir!" he reported.

Darly could also see the object. Silver and cylindrical in shape, it had the general appearance of a bomb but had no fins. It was almost as big as the men around it, but they were handling it too easily for it to be extremely heavy.

"They're recovering one of their nuclear bombs, sir!" again reported the lookout.

"No, I don't think so," surmised Darly. "It looks something like a bomb but I don't think they carry them on their runs to Cuba. I could be wrong. There! There's a second one . . . they're swinging a second one aboard."

The OOD was standing beside Darly, with his own binoculars trained on the scene. "They look like some kind of silver cylinders—maybe bombs with their fins detached."

"Could be," conceded Darly. "Let's get a message off to CINCLANTFLT. Make it priority."

"Aye, sir." The OOD stuck his head through one of the pilot house portholes and called for a radioman.

"They're starting their engines again, sir," reported the lookout.

Darly watched the Cuban amphibian slowly pull away from the rafts, which appeared to be rapidly deflating. The yellow sausage objects flattened and then disappeared. The Mail started its takeoff run and lifted into the air just as the radioman handed the OOD's draft message to Darly:

CUBAN AIR FORCE AMPHIBIAN RECOVERED SOVIET AIRMEN
021533Z X ALSO RECOVERED TWO BOMB SHAPED OBJECTS
FROM SUBMERGED BEAR AIRCRAFT X UNODIR WILL DEPART
STATION 021600Z IN COMPANY WITH VOGE AR

Darly almost dropped the clipboard as a gigantic plume of white water and speckles of debris erupted from the site of the downed Bear, followed almost immediately by a muffled sound wave that rolled across the *Bradley*, startling the entire bridge watch.

Darly watched the geyser settle.

"They blew it up, sir," muttered the lookout.

"That they certainly did," added the OOD.

Darly scribbled an addendum onto the message: BEAR APPARENTLY DESTROYED BY UNDERWATER EXPLOSION 021537Z. He scrawled his name across the release block and handed the clipboard back to the radioman.

"Get it off," he ordered.

The sailor saluted smartly and hurriedly disappeared down the ladder that led from the open bridge to the radio shack.

"Inform the *Voge* that we'll be leaving station on the hour," directed Darly to the OOD as they both returned to the closed bridge. He handed his cup to the boatswain's mate of the watch and crossed over to the navigator's chart table. "Give me a course to intercept the *Abe Lincoln*."

The navigator laid the head of his protractor over *Bradley*'s last plotted position and swung the arm around to where it lined up with a circular symbol labeled CVN-72. Meticulously, he drew several thin pencil lines and lost himself in some mental interpolation before replying, "They should be clearing the Windward Passage about now, Captain. Recommend three-five-zero to stay clear of the banks."

"That would be nice," responded Darly with gentle sarcasm and a weary smile. "Call me in an hour." Visibly relieved that their twelve-hour surveillance of the downed airmen was over, he left the bridge for his cabin.

The *Voge* closed and took a free riding station off the port quarter of the *Bradley* as the two ships swung around to their northerly heading. Their projected track would take them north of the Great Bahama Bank, then east through the two Providence Channels into the open Atlantic Ocean. After that, a turn to a southerly heading would put them on an interception course for the nuclear-powered CVN-72.

Three hundred and seventy nautical miles southeast, the Navy's newest and most sophisticated aircraft carrier was leisurely steaming northwest across the waters between Cuba and Haiti after a grueling two-week operational readiness exercise off the U.S. Navy's base at Guantanamo.

The USS *Abraham Lincoln*, a ninety-thousand-ton floating air base, manned by more than six thousand personnel, would be spending the next week exercising its air group in the southwest Atlantic as a last chore before returning to Norfolk to prepare for its premier deployment to the Sixth Fleet in the Mediterranean Sea.

Chapter 3

11:17 A.M.
Headquarters, CIA Substation, Key West

Davey sat across from the Old Man, watching him gum his cigar while the other two men at the table pored over Davey's notes on the objects he had found in the Bear's bomb bay. The heavy-set one on the right, Georgi Rasmussan, was the substation's resident Soviet expert. He looked the part: craggy face; gray hair combed straight back to form a thin skullcap over too small a head; overweight by a good fifty pounds, most of it hanging over a faded brown leather belt that squeezed his waist like a rope around a pig's belly. Being short, perhaps five-five if you stood his sparse hair on end, he was a miniature of the Old Man but infinitely sloppier. The only other occupant of the room, seated to Davey's left, was a mouse of a man whom Davey knew only as Jeremiah from Technical Services. The TS boys were a tight-lipped group and wore their mantle of dirty tricks with a weird sense of silent egotism. Want someone to have a massive heart attack? Just slip him—or her—one of the little blue pills that the TS lab puts out, each individually wrapped in a clear plastic packet and stamped with a flawless facsimile of the Food and Drug Administration's seal of approval. No traces afterward, just a pale, cold body with an obviously diseased heart muscle. Something more exotic? A real attention getter? No big deal; just requisition a package of Marlboro 100s that were kept under lock and key in that holy of holies, the TS special equipment vault. Offer one to your companion and count his puffs. You need only go to four, so even if you use your fingers for such higher mathematics you have a thumb left over. Use it to push your victim away from you and stand clear, for he'll be vomiting green bile before he hits the carpet. Oh, he won't be dead, not yet. First he has to retch his guts out and contort into a tight fetal position that pulls him into such a compact human ball he will fit nicely into a fifty-five-gallon drum. Saves you the effort of cutting off his legs. The single name Jeremiah was all Davey wanted to know about the skeleton-like human who sat supererect in his chair and wore absolutely no expression at all on his hawk-nosed, acne-pocked face.

Rasmussan finished jotting down his translation. "Most of the stuff is shipping detail: weight, handling instructions, that sort of thing. Originated in Moscow, apparently, or initially shipped from there into the military system." He glanced at Davey. "Both cylinders had the radiation symbol?"

"Yes."

"Then, whatever is in those cylinders is hot."

"Bombs?" asked Davey.

"No. Warheads, maybe. Artillery shells; torpedo heads, perhaps. They're tightly sealed if both ends are welded shut. Not quite a convenient method of packaging, even if they are nuclear. What do you think, Jeremiah?"

"Nuclear *devices*. That would be my guess. But they may be something as innocuous as nuclear medical equipment."

"Medical equipment, my ass." The Old Man's under-his-breath comment caused his cigar to roll along his lower lip and droop precariously before he rescued it with tobacco-stained fingers. "If it were something as innocent as that, they would have put that bird down on dry land and saved themselves a dunking. They very deliberately refused to consider such an option."

"But what reason would they have for carrying such things to Cuba?" interjected Davey.

"Good point," commented the Old Man with pursed lips. "And that's what makes me so curious. Castro doesn't have any activities going on that would call for that sort of thing, certainly not in this hemisphere. And the Angola fracas is a lost cause with respect to Cuban participation. It'd be out of place. Too precipitous, at best."

"Which leaves the other alternatives," offered Jeremiah.

The Old Man shook his head. "No, I can't buy nuclear medical equipment."

The outer door opened and a clerk entered. He placed a message flimsy before the Old Man and left.

The Old Man scanned it briefly, as if he already knew the contents. "They've been picked up," he announced. "Cuban amphibian. It also recovered the two cylindrical objects, then blew the shit out of the hulk as they left. The *Bradley* observed the whole thing."

"Well," began Rasmussan with a sigh, "whatever they are, they're back on their way to their original destination."

"We've alerted our people," said the Old Man. "They'll be watching for the return of the recovery aircraft. Ordinarily, it would be routine surveillance, but I think we ought to go after this one." He sunk lower into his chair as he spoke. Davey could see that he had some intuitive concern, for it was a habit of the Old Man to slump when wrestling with a mental problem, as if he wanted his enormous body to press inward and concentrate all of his energy on the thought at hand. His eyes swung over to the wall clock. Ten-thirty.

"I won't need you anymore for the moment, gentlemen," he said, obviously addressing his dismissal to Rasmussan and Jeremiah. "Davey, you stick around for a few minutes longer."

The two agency men left, and the Old Man reached down into his lower left desk drawer and withdrew a bottle of Early Times and two paper cups. He handed Davey a two-finger shot and set an equal one before himself, then capped and replaced the bottle.

"You've been bugging me for some action," he said, raising the bourbon to his nose and wrinkling his flattened nostrils.

It was a bit early for an eye-opener as far as Davey was concerned, but what the hell, when in Rome . . .

They touched cups and drank. The Old Man crushed his empty into a ragged ball and dropped it into his circular file. "How would you like to go in-country?" he asked.

Davey still had an ounce of whiskey left, and as he swirled it around in the bottom of his cup and studied the miniature golden whirlpool, he smiled in obvious agreement with the Old Man's proposal.

"You've seen the cylinders," continued the Old Man. "In fact, you're the only one who knows what they look like, since we have no pictures." He spoke the last word very slowly. Davey had wondered when the dig would come. "That Cuban airplane has landed some-where. If our people are on their toes, we'll know where within the hour. I've passed the word also to keep track. But we need someone a bit more sophisticated to bird-dog the cylinders to their final des-tination and find out just what the hell is going on. I figure you can do that. Besides, it'll do you good to work on dry land for a while. Whadda you think?"

Davey knew the question was academic. And he did want the assignment, no doubt about that.

The Old Man answered for him. "We'll put you in-country tonight. Take care of whatever you have to and be back here by five. We'll talk over dinner."

"I'm ready. I assume you sent someone out to the shack to take care of my friend."

"Smitty. He's off for a few days, anyhow."

"Then all I need is a place to pad out for a couple hours."

"We keep a room at the Navy Lodge. Go on over. I'll make arrangements for the drop."

Chapter 4

12:35 P.M.
Havana

It was good to sit, even on the hard floor. Geraldo Cordero unfolded the newspaper package, revealing a generous serving of cold chicken livers and a large hunk of bread. He smiled, remembering the meal with his wife the night before. The livers had been hot then. He was still tired from his stint on neighborhood watch, the two-to-six in the early morning period. But such things were the price of the revolution. It would be even tougher when the baby came. Sleep would be even more precious. He yawned and stuffed several of the chicken livers into his mouth.

His old thermos held only water, but it was fresh rainwater that had been bottled while still cold, and it washed down his lunch in a satisfactory manner. Life was getting better. They had a few more pesos with his promotion to supervisor and he would take his wife to a restaurant soon. After all, under the new order of equality and fairness, he, like many of his *campaneros*, lived practically rent-free. His older shack did not even require the standard six-percent-of-wages rent that was the norm for most of the housing in his village. There were actually few other financial obligations: the daily centavos for the work bus; a steady but small outlay for his tobacco; an occasional bottle of rum from his friend, who seldom charged him more than he himself had paid; and wood for the cooking stove when he could not find enough.

The Construction Ministry was expanding, and Geraldo's own responsibilities as a new supervisor for a ten-man renovation crew included the prestigious task of modernizing the interior of the rooms of the higher floors of the Icar Hotel. It was a position of some trust, for the Icar was the preferred billeting place for the friends of Cuba who came from around the world. The Soviets always held the best rooms, naturally, but there were sizable contingents of Poles and Czechs. A few Angolans, who kept strictly to themselves, and a smattering of Central American representatives rounded out the semipermanent residents.

Geraldo was still a bit leery of the latest arrivals, however. Regardless of their possible simpatico with his country, they seemed out of place. An unfamiliar ethnic trio, with olive skin and hawk noses, they kept very odd hours, seemingly returning from all-night business just as Geraldo arrived in the early morning for his long day. He reasoned that they were Arabic, for one consistently wore the checkered head cloth and colored binding band typical of pictures he had seen of such persons. They stayed to themselves when in the hotel, but Geraldo noticed that they made a point of speaking to the Russians if they paused in the hallway. Still, their faces were always angry, even when they smiled at the Russos. Geraldo could not imagine how such a people could contribute anything to the cause of Cuba, but they were quartered in the Icar, which meant they were official guests.

His hunger abated, Geraldo surveyed his morning's progress. He had finished stripping the inside walls of the stained and cracked wallboard and had removed the old decayed insulation. After lunch, he would clean up the debris, and if the replacement insulation arrived in time he could begin repacking it between the studs. The other members of his team were equally far along in their rooms, although several had a habit of slackening off if left to themselves too long. Consequently, Geraldo had to periodically interrupt his own work to check on his men. Nevertheless, it was a source of some pride that even with his supervisory duties he could keep up with the best of them.

The team was a few days behind schedule, but the Ministry had promised him two more members as soon as they were available. If they were hard workers, his team could make up the lost time in a week, surely, for Geraldo was determined to finish on time even if it meant longer hours for them all.

The last of the chicken livers were washed down with the last of the water, and he tossed the wadded newspaper wrapping onto the pile of room trash. He had time for a brief rest. The cooling rain peppering the outside of the building muffled the street noises below and spawned a light breeze, which drifted in through the window opening. Removing and rolling his shirt, he placed it as a pillow and rested his head on one of the studs while he stretched out on the floor.

A sharp noise jarred him awake, and embarrassed, he realized he had dozed off. Fortunately, someone had let something drop in the adjoining room, otherwise he might have slept away precious time. He sat up, then placed his ear closer to the bare wall that was now stripped of its sound-deadening insulation. His was the last vacant room on the floor, and several times since he had started to work in it the occupants next door had yelled at him, irritated by the noise. But this was the first time he could hear them in normal conversation. They were speaking mostly Russian, which he could not understand, but there was obviously a countryman present, for some of the conversation was in his native tongue. He listened very closely and caught the Cuban exchanges.

"It really is no concern of yours," one of the Russians was saying in thick-tongued Spanish.

"We have a right to know what they are going to do with them," replied the Cuban, obviously upset.

"It is an arrangement between them and us. You are merely providing a place of convenience for the transfer."

"That may be true, but we are in a most sensitive area. I insist that you come to my office tomorrow, and bring them also. We are entitled to know their intentions if they plan an action from Cuba." The Cuban was almost pleading.

"They will be leaving the country. There are no plans for any operations from Cuba. We are not imbeciles. We would not place our friends in such a position." Geraldo cursed as the Russians switched to their own language and had what appeared to be a short but spirited debate. There was an inflection to their voices that seemed to indicate disagreement, perhaps over the Cuban's insistence on a visit to his office.

"All right," said one of the Russians finally, "but we will talk only to Reynol. Only he is at the level within which we can discuss such things."

"*Gracias, campaneros*," gratefully acknowledged the Cuban.

Geraldo could hear footsteps crossing the room and the door open.

"*Hasta luego.*" The Cuban was leaving.

"*Hasta luego*," replied the thick-tongued Russian.

Geraldo had a healthy respect for the Russians' presence. Their financial assistance program was the difference between marginal economy and doubtful survival for Cuba; he knew that. But their overbearing attitude and sometimes compromising acts recalled too much the days his father had often spoken about, when their family was at the low end of the Batista scale and no better than nonentities in their own land. The *revelucion* had changed all that, but there were times when it seemed to him that the Russians felt no more kindly to the Cuban people than did the Batista *verdugos*, the thugs of the old days. He shared the glee when his fellow revolutionists laughingly referred to the stocky Soviets as *bolas*, for many of them did indeed resemble ambulatory bowling pins, clothed in the dull uniform of their military service and waddling along like fugitives from the bowling houses.

Geraldo was not well versed in the ways of international politics, but it was clear that after the lessons learned in the missile confrontation of 1962, the Russians had been much more careful in their development of his country as a military, economic, and political partner. The history studies during his schooling had stressed that the stabilization of the revelucion was the first goal of their Maximum Leader and that assistance from Cuba's overseas friends was necessary. After all, Cuba was the first truly free territory in the Americas, and its destiny was to lead its brothers toward the inevitable rewards of the socialist order. Even the *norteamericanos* of the Estados Unidos would eventually succumb to that inevitability.

Geraldo shook his head in self-amusement. He was getting too serious in his thoughts about the destiny of Cuba and the part played by her Russian mentors. He had much more important things to think about. There was an enormous pile of rubble to clear from the room and much work ahead of him before he could join the others on the bus and get to his waiting wife.

He scooped several large loads of the debris into his wheelbarrow and pushed it toward the outside elevator, the interior of which had been rigged with special scaffolding.

Seven trips later, the room was almost clear, and he could tell by the diminished light of the late afternoon that there was only a short time left for work. He was dirty and wet, for each trip down the elevator to empty his wheelbarrow exposed him to the rain, which although slackened from the morning downpour was still steady and sometimes heavy. His neighborhood block watch in the early morning had made his bones weary, and now after a full day's work they were beginning to ache. Only a few more loads remained and he could stop for the day. The insulation could wait for tomorrow.

As he returned down the hallway, taking care to see that the residual debris in the wheelbarrow did not spill, he encountered the three Arabs. They ignored his nod, although they did reluctantly step aside to give him passage. They were preparing to enter the room where the Russians were, and where the Cuban had visited only a short time before.

Geraldo couldn't resist resuming his eavesdropping. He carefully placed his head against the single width of wallboard that separated the two rooms.

The occupants were speaking English, obviously unable to understand each other's native tongue.

"All is well," said a voice Geraldo had not heard before. It would be one of the Arabs. "The . . . were recovered intact." Geraldo wished his English were better.

"And the crew?" asked the thick-tongued Russian.

"Also recovered, with the exception of one who was lost."

"Under the circumstances, that is good. Our Cuban friend is getting nervous. He insists we meet with his superior. I tried to tell him this is just the transfer point, but he is suspicious."

The Arab voice laughed. "This is of no concern to the Cubans."

"You forget they are the host country for this matter."

"The will of God knows not the concern of any man."

"I do not consider God to be a part of this," returned the Russian. "My concern is that the transfer goes smoothly and that we have your assurances that your plan can reflect nothing on the Soviet Union."

"Our struggle requires such action. The source of the . . . will not be revealed."

"We do not care what you hit as long as there can be no tie-in with us. I, for one, think any use is potentially catastrophic for us all. But I am a soldier, and my orders are to effect the transfer."

"Then, you should confine your comments to your responsibilities."

There was a long period of silence and some shuffling of feet.

Geraldo wrinkled his face in confusion. What was taking place in the room? What was the word he had heard twice but still did not recognize? While the conversation between the Russians and the Cuban had aroused his curiosity, this one with the Arabs aroused his fears. The underlying tone was much more sinister.

Chapter 5

7:44 P.M.
Headquarters, CIA Substation, Key West

Davey sat quietly across from the Old Man and picked at a piece of Kentucky Fried Chicken caught between two of his upper front teeth. When the Old Man said to join him for dinner, he obviously meant no frills.

Davey had slept for several hours in the room over at the Navy Lodge and was anxious to hear the Old Man's briefing, but the rotund director of the Key West substation had been almost wordless during their twenty-minute meal. Finally, he leisurely licked his fingers and wiped them and his mouth with the moist paper towelette from the red-and-white-striped fast-food box.

"It's all arranged," began the Buddha. "We'll chopper you over to Stock Island at seven. The Navy's got a nuke boat waiting and they'll take you to a spot a few miles off Bahia Honda Bay; that's on the northern coast about fifty miles west of Havana. The Cuban amphibian landed at Jose Marti International about noon and off-loaded the two cylinders at a remote side of the field under heavy guard, and then they were trucked to a National Militia bunker nearby."

"Still on the airport?"

"Yes, on the north side. At last report they were still there, and our people say there may be no way we can get a look at them unless they're moved to a less secure area. Why they didn't take them to a military installation, I don't know, unless the weather was a factor. But our man on the scene got the impression they were expecting them at Jose Marti.

"Anyhow, when you arrive at the rendezvous point you'll be picked up by a fishing boat. The skipper is one of our long-time people, Rudy Ordonez, a super-pro who goes all the way back to Kennedy's Operation Mongoose and has some very convenient ties with the founders of the old AMBLOOD counterrevolutionaries. They can get you anything you need and anywhere you need to go. For starters, they will take you to a place near the airport and you can figure your next move from there. Davey, we want to know what's in those canisters and what their eventual destination is . . ."

"Isn't it pretty risky putting a sub just a few miles off the beach?" interrupted Davey.

"It won't surface and it'll be dark. Cuban ASW is practically nonexistent. You can go out of the emergency escape hatch after they get you up to about fifty feet and make sure Rudy is there."

"He knows the coastline okay?"

"Knows it? Hell, he's the original *practico* of all *practicos,*" answered the Old Man, using the Cuban reference for underground people who made the clandestine coastal pickups.

"How about papers?"

"Jeremiah fixed up this set for you." The Old Man handed Davey a Comite de Revelucion ID card and several ration booklets along with a Cuban driver's license and two tattered envelopes that bore canceled Cuban stamps and postmarks. Inside each was a letter that further substantiated his transfer in work assignment from a cattle-breeding farm in northeastern Pinar del Rio province to the Ministry of Construction work force assigned to the Icar Hotel in Havana. The letters bore the DESA letterhead of the Ministry.

Davey raised his eyebrows as he asked, "Icar Hotel?"

"Perfect assignment. That's where the out-of-country guests of Senor Castro are quartered. By Cuban standards, a cut above the rest. Screens in the windows and all that. We normally keep one of our people employed there for surveillance, but he got transferred out from under us."

"I've been a cattle breeder? That's hardly my line of expertise. I can barely tell the bulls from the cows," commented Davey with some concern.

"Maybe that's why they transferred you to the Construction Ministry," countered the Old Man. "Besides, it's all artificial insemination. If anyone asks, you held the receptacle to catch the semen. Hardly a task requiring skilled labor."

"I'm not sure I'd want to be that close to a bull on the make."

"It's all hypothetical, Davey. What are you? Some kind of method actor who needs to know his motivation and complete background before you play the part?"

Davey feigned irritation. "No, it's just that I would feel sorry for the poor bulls. No real nooky."

"Don't worry about it. They still get their jollies. If you want to feel sorry for someone, make it the cows." The Old Man laughed so hard at his own comment that he worked himself into a coughing spell. Recovering, he wiped his moist lips with the back of his hand. "Clean out your pockets. You can leave your things here in my safe."

Davey removed his wallet and hip pocket comb. The black rubber Ace would be a conspicuous stranger in Cuba. He handed his change to the Old Man and received several assorted centavos pieces and a small wad of pesos.

After exchanging his watch for a cheap Czech brand, he slipped out of his khaki shorts and T-shirt. The Old Man started to hand him a bundle of clothes but abruptly drew it back.

"Your underwear," he said, nodding toward Davey's briefs. "I'd hate for some Cuban dolly to make you from a Fruit of the Loom label."

"They're Jockey's."

"Off."

Davey slipped them over his feet and laid them with the rest of his things. Hurriedly, he dressed. He was no stranger to nudity in the presence of either sex, but somehow, in the presence of the veteran intelligence director, he felt uncomfortably naked.

"Now, look," cautioned the Old Man, "this is a simple task. Don't overextend yourself. Once you get a handle on the cylinders and where they wind up or where they're going, get on back here. And pay attention to what our people tell you once you get there. They're all old-timers and have everything down to a routine."

Davey felt as though his mother was giving him instructions on how to cross the street on his way to school.

The helicopter wop-wopped down to the pad precisely at seven and Davey climbed into the left seat.

The gray rain clouds were still thick and low over the Keys, and the steady rain covered the Plexiglas nose of the chopper with millions of splattering blobs as the pilot transitioned to forward flight, remaining only a few feet above the surface. The sun, although low on the western horizon and completely hidden by the thick rain cloud layer, still provided enough light for visual flight, but the forward visibility was certainly restricted. Davey guessed it was a quarter mile, no more. With nothing else to do, he watched the western edge of Key West slide below them, and then they were over a darkness that Davey knew must be water. By the pilot's instruments, he could see that they were swinging around to a southeast course. At the speed they were flying they should have reached Stock Island soon after crossing the beach. Instead, the pilot held his course, occasionally fiddling with his one radio receiver.

A few minutes later, they slowed and began to inch forward through the darkening murk, feeling their way as a cat would cross a dark field on a moonless night. The sun must have set, for the little light they had started out with had faded into a blue-black three-dimensional sea of ink. Visibility was down to a matter of yards, and only the intermittent reflections of the choppy sea below them assured Davey that they weren't flailing away in some alien space.

Ahead, an even darker shadow emerged and began to take shape. Long, low, still, the shadow continued a gradual metamorphosis until its identity became obvious. A submarine. The pilot hovered over the unseen deck that Davey knew must be small and very wet. He climbed out onto the helicopter's landing skid. When it was reasonably steady and he could make out several figures waiting below him, he dropped. His landing was eased by the strong arms of a pair of foul weather–jacketed sailors. The helicopter rose and disappeared into the blackness.

By the time he was led below and shown to the compact wardroom, the submarine was nose down and reaching for Cuba. He was left alone for the first few minutes, after which he was joined by a tanned football halfback wearing the blue jumpsuit and silver oak leaves of an underseas commander.

"Welcome aboard," said the young officer.

Davey returned both the firm handclasp and the genial smile.

"I'm Don Bates. Anything you need, just yell. Coffee?" The

submariner lifted one of the two polished steel pots from the holding rings over the two-burner hot plate and poured two mugs before squeezing onto the bench seat opposite Davey. "Take us about three hours. First time?" Indicating the purpose of his question, he swept a glance around the space.

"Yes," replied Davey, "I've never been aboard a ship that was designed to sink."

"USS *Seahorse*, Skipjack class. We're old, but still pulling our weight."

"Attack boat?"

"Originally. We still carry a couple weapons, but the state of the art has sort of passed us by, so we make ourselves useful in other ways."

"Such as?"

"For the present, running errands for you spook types. Not much excitement."

Davey listened for a moment to the subtle noises of the submarine, none very sharp or definitive. Mostly hums and whispers. The low human voices that seemed to be forward were occasionally punctuated by a hearty laugh, but even that sound was softened by the background whir of the air-conditioning blowers that were keeping a constant flow of cool air circulating through the wardroom.

There was little sensation of movement through the water, although from time to time there would be a slight surging feeling as the submarine changed course or encountered a strong current shear. Davey's eyes could not pick up the motion, but his inner ear responded to the maneuvering of the *Seahorse*. The conflict between his visual and balance senses caused an uneasy feeling in his stomach, a mild but not unbearable nausea that prompted him to swallow more frequently than usual.

Bates smiled as he recognized his passenger's discomfort. "We're doing thirty knots. You'll get used to it."

"I'm sure," tentatively agreed Davey. He *was* adjusting—sort of.

"Had your dinner?"

"Yes, thanks."

"Well, help yourself to anything you find in the pantry. If you want to rest, there's a bunk in my room; first one aft, starboard side. If you need me, just give a call on the intercom. I'll be in Combat." Bates pointed to the labeled button on the sub's intercom box hanging from the far bulkhead over the table. "I'll get back with you after awhile."

After the officer left, Davey studied his ID papers and thumbed through the well-used magazines stuffing the racks of the small reading library. The *Penthouse* centerfold brought to mind his own three-dimensional centerfold, whom he had reluctantly left back in the beach shack just a scant seventeen hours earlier.

The first hour passed comfortably enough as Davey grew accustomed to his surroundings. Taking small sips of cool water seemed to effectively combat the queasy feeling in his stomach and the dryness of his throat. Either the ride was getting smoother or he was getting his sea legs.

The offgoing watch officers stopped in for sandwiches and made small talk, pointedly avoiding any questions as to Davey's identity or purpose. It was as if they routinely picked up mysterious strangers and dropped them off the Cuban coast—which, of course, Davey reasoned they did. He marveled at their professionalism; even as they ate, they did so more with purpose than with appetite: fuel the body, get some rest, and get back on duty.

The second hour dragged a bit and Davey was tempted to find the empty sack, but he really wasn't sleepy. Too much anticipation for that. Nestled in a corner of the superefficient wardroom was an extensive selection of audio- and videocassettes. Davey selected one of the smaller audiocassettes at random. Leaning back, he closed his eyes and shut out the outside world. All that existed for the moment was the music.

He became one with the world of sound inside his head, not even sensing the presence of Commander Bates when he returned and poked his head through the wardroom curtains.

The sight of the bedraggled "Cuban" slouched on the mess bench with eyes closed and head gently swaying brought forth a chuckle as Bates reached over and lifted one earphone. "No wonder I couldn't reach you on the intercom. I figured you had flaked out for a while."

Davey placed the headset on the table. "Did I miss anything?"

"No, I thought you might like a tour of the boat, but I see you've kept yourself amused. We'll be at the rendezvous point in about thirty-five minutes."

Davey checked the time on the wardroom clock. They'd been underway for just two hours. Another thirty-five minutes would make it 2130—9:30 P.M. He had figured a little more than a hundred miles for the distance. Maybe the *Seahorse* was over the hill as far as being an attack boat, but she was damn good underwater transportation, sustaining thirty knots or so.

"We'll be early?" he queried.

"Only a few minutes," replied Bates. "We've got a 2200 to 2300 window."

The submariner led Davey into central control, and at 2200 ordered the conning officer to take the *Seahorse* up to fifty feet below the surface. The noise of the compressed air blowing the ballast tanks caused Davey to instinctively grab for support, although there was no abrupt movement. Bates smiled.

"Up planes, ten degrees," ordered the skinny lieutenant with the conn.

"Up planes, ten degrees, aye, sir," responded the carrot-topped sailor seated before the plane's yoke, not missing a beat in his hearty chewing of a wad of gum.

Davey felt the movement of the deck beneath his feet, but once again his eyes failed to detect any motion. A slight bubble formed in his stomach but lasted only a moment. He watched the depth indicator and observed the conning officer order neutral planes just shy of the ordered fifty-foot depth. The *Seahorse*'s momentum carried it the remaining few feet upward, and the conning officer had the boat trimmed to lock the pointer on the fifty-foot marker of the depth indicator. The entire transition to the lesser depth had been accomplished with only a few words of command and the quiet, confident actions of Bates's crew.

Davey watched the earnest young sailors manning the various sensor equipment, some of them still in their late teens, more in their early twenties and most wearing the muted blue chevrons of senior petty officers. The Navy's elite, the enlisted professionals manned the sophisticated consoles of the complex underwater machine with an intensity that belied their youth. Hand-picked volunteers, most of them were only a few years into a career that already placed in their hands an awesome destructive power. Even now, the relatively old *Seahorse* carried a dozen nuclear-warhead torpedoes, really not much of a load when compared to the deadly nest of long-range SLBMs carried by the much larger strategic warfare boats, the Navy's big boomers. But those twelve steel cylinders, at the ready in the forward- and after-torpedo rooms of Bates's boat, still housed more destructive power than all of the armament expended by the U.S. Navy in World War II—all in the hands of men under forty.

"Contact." The sandy-haired first class sonarman manning the nearest console spoke matter-of-factly.

"Verify," ordered Bates softly.

The sailor flipped up a silver toggle switch and eyeballed a small green cathode ray tube off one side of his main console. A delicate horizontal bolt of silver lightning froze, and the sailor tweaked a small knob until the three peaks of the signal were equal in amplitude. "Verified," he announced.

"Well, looks like we'll get home early," observed Bates. "You all set, my friend?" His extended open-palmed hand indicated the way for Davey as they made their way forward to an emergency escape trunk. A black-haired chief petty officer waited for them beside the entrance hatch to the cylindrical compartment. As they approached, the chief held out a flimsy silver garment.

Bates took it and let it drop to its full length before passing it to Davey. "Put this on," he directed. "It'll keep your clothes dry."

Davey stepped into the thin oversized coverall and zipped its front. The elastic neck formed a watertight seal. With attached hand and foot coverings, the garment made him feel a trifle silly, as if he were going nitey-nite in his winter pj's. Everything except his head was covered. The chief handed him a small green oxygen bottle with a black rubber mouthpiece and an attached nose clip. There was a neck strap secured to the bottle and Davey slid it over his head.

The chief's instructions were about as energetic as a flight steward's pre-takeoff briefing. "We're easing up a bit. Once you surface, deep-six the bottle. The oversuit has a specific gravity of one-point-five, so drop it over the side once you're picked up. It'll sink and dissolve in a few hours."

"Do the taxpayers know we're being so free with their funds? Throwaway clothes?" asked Davey, nodding acceptance of the chief's monotone briefing.

The chief almost smiled. "We offer them throwaway bodies in return. Haven't heard many complaints."

"Touché. My conscience is salved," concluded Davey.

Bates touched Davey's shoulder. "I'll leave you with the chief. Good luck."

"Thanks for the ride, Skipper."

"*Por nada . . .*"

They shook hands and the submariner disappeared aft.

"All set, sir?" asked the chief.

"I think so."

The chief undogged the hatch and Davey stepped through the oval opening into the chamber. As he placed the rubber mouthpiece between his teeth, the chief leaned in. "The skipper has eased up to thirty feet. After the chamber is full and set for your egress, that green light next to the overhead hatch will come on. You open the hatch by a sharp pull on the red T-handle beside the light. You'll have forty seconds to egress before it automatically closes and reseals. Any questions?"

Davey gave a negative shake of his head.

"Take your time going up—and have fun, sir."

As the chief dogged the hatch, a rush of water swirled in around Davey's feet. It took about thirty seconds to completely fill the chamber, and as the water began to calm the green light lit. Davey gave a yank on the red T-handle and rose upward through the open hatch. The warm water was inky black, but the light from the chamber illuminated a yellow buoy line that led from an open compartment in the outer hull next to the escape hatch. It faded upward into the darkness. Wrapping his fingers loosely around the line, Davey let the natural buoyancy of the trapped air inside the oversuit lift him toward the invisible surface. He popped free almost to his waist and then splashed back down to chest depth. Immediately, he heard a hoarse call.

"Over here!"

He swung around toward the sound and could see the dark silhouette of a fishing ketch bobbing on the calm water only a few feet away.

"I spotted the buoy as soon as she surfaced," said the voice. "Welcome to Cuba."

Davey slipped off the oxygen bottle and let it drop into the depths. Less than five strokes carried him to the rope ladder slung over the port side of the boat and he climbed aboard.

"Here, let me give you a hand," said the voice and Davey felt the front zipper descend. Helping hands tugged at his sleeves as he stepped out of the coveralls. The man dropped them over the side.

"Rudy Ordonez," said the voice by way of introduction. Davey's eyes had yet to adjust to the darkness under the overcast sky after his time within the submarine, but he felt a tin cup being pressed into his hands. "Drink up, it'll remove any chill."

"David Morales—Davey," he replied, lifting the cup to his lips. The sweet, thick taste of the dark rum did indeed warm his stomach, although he felt little chill from the night sea air. The rum was very smooth, heavy with flavor, and potent with alcohol.

"Come on forward, into the pilothouse. We've got about an hour's run ahead of us."

Davey followed Ordonez, stepping over a tangle of rope and fishing gear that was piled on the deck of the aft well of the boat like so much discarded spaghetti. The catch compartment was more than half full of large silver fish, deep-bodied with large, pointed fins. Davey judged them to be tuna. As he had suspected, the ketch was running dark and Ordonez eased the throttle forward to full open as they got underway for the dark line of the southern horizon. The overage diesel sounded as if every piece within it was worn well past its tolerance, and the resultant chatter almost drowned out any chance of prolonged conversation. Davey wondered why the running lights were kept off when the engine noises could probably be heard clear over on the far side of the island.

"We're just off Honda Bay," shouted Ordonez, nodding his head toward the darkness beyond their bow.

Davey's eyes had adjusted somewhat to the night and he could make out the old man's features: short, maybe five-five, but stocky with well-worked muscle and sinew, some of which wrapped the old man's arms like the hard bulges of an ironwood tree. The old practico wore cutoff khaki shorts, and if anything, the legs rivaled the arms in athletic history, although the knee knobs stuck out like gnarled tumors, out of place on such an otherwise well-preserved body. Short contrails of white hair streamed from his head and waved in the breeze created by the boat's swift passage over the water. The front windscreen was folded flat on the top of the low deckhouse. Even in the dim light, Davey could see the crisscross of age and weather lines on the man's face, each of which bespoke of countless days on the water under a hot sun.

Ordonez sorted through the pile of cigarette butts that was overflowing the tin can lid he used as an ashtray and retrieved one of the longer ones. He stuck it eagerly into his mouth but made no attempt to light it.

"Any patrols out here?" questioned Davey.

Ordonez's reply grunt and head nod seemed to indicate an affirmative answer. A moment later, he leaned over to Davey's ear and amplified his reply, "Most of the time, but none tonight. They're working farther west. I keep track of them. We'll have to be careful once we get closer in, but this is not an unusual time to be returning after a hard day fighting the fish, and where we're going is pretty isolated. How long you gonna be with us?"

"I don't know. Just need to find out a few things."

"The cylinders?"

"Uh-huh."

The red, green, and white running lights suddenly lighted up the sea spray arcing off to each side as Ordonez hit the lights' rubber-encased toggle switch. Now the boat was noisy *and* highly visible, but Davey noticed that there were several other vessels in the vicinity, all heading toward the beach. The old man throttled back and the ketch settled in the water, steadying out at five knots. At least they would no longer have to shout.

"We're 'bout a mile out," said Ordonez.

Davey had been watching the thin black horizon line thicken until now he could see the profile of low hills running off on each side of the land mass.

"You have your papers." The old man's words were phrased as a statement but obviously meant as a question.

"Yes," verified Davey.

"Ration books?"

"Dated this month . . . partially used."

"Good. We have a car and driver waiting—my daughter, Tatiana. She'll take you by the airport and let you eyeball the shack where the cylinders are stored, then on east of Havana to a safe place for the night. In the morning, you report to a Geraldo Cordero at the Icar Hotel as an augmentee to his regular work group."

"The Old Man indicated that's the place where the foreign nationals are quartered," commented Davey.

"Yes. You'll be able to observe their comings and goings during the day, if that is a factor. You might pick up something if the cylinders mean anything to someone other than the Cubans. In any event, it's a good place to work a cover."

"This Cordero, what do we know about him?"

"Good second-generation revolutionary. Hard worker and an avid Fidelista. Don't get careless around him, although we think he's a bit naive. He's expecting two additional workers. The other one will be legitimate."

Davey wondered how he had been sneaked onto the Construction Ministry files and the fictitious transfer arranged, but it was really not his concern. The only thing that mattered was that it had been accomplished.

"We have a worker at the airport who can keep an eye on any further movement of the cylinders. If there is, we'll get word to you and you can take it from that point. As long as the damn things sit in the airport shack, no one can get near them—which may indicate that they are something special."

Davey could see no reason to mention that the contents most probably constituted some sort of radiation hazard. He busied himself searching the water ahead. They were heading into a small cove edged with random clusters of dim white lights, probably a small fishing community. He could see the running lights of other boats converging in the same area.

"Nervous?" asked Ordonez quietly.

"First time," responded Davey. "I would have thought the Old Man would have wanted a local."

"Most of our people have simple backgrounds. We can track the cylinders, but I suspect he feels the identification needs to be done by someone more knowledgeable. You, in this case."

"Uh-huh."

"Don't worry about being unfamiliar with the area. New people arrive daily and most are from the backcountry. The whole goddamned work program is so screwed up with the shifting of people around and the forming of new labor teams—worker cells, they're called—that nobody knows what anybody else is doing. The supervisors are too busy trying to meet their quotas to keep reliable records; the area coordinators are too busy falsifying reports to check on the supervisors; the program directors are too busy analyzing the last failures to plan efficiently; and the deputy ministers are too busy covering their asses to have any real feel for what is actually going on. As for the ministers themselves, they're too busy meeting with Castro and strutting around on ceremonial days. Their main concern is that they don't run out of freshly starched fatigues. So, if you don't screw up by doing something really stupid, no one will give you a second look."

They were well into the cove, holding their interval on the closest of two boats that had merged ahead of them. Ordonez held station fifty yards astern, and the small single file eased itself toward a dimly lit pier that jutted out from a darkened shed. The late night quarter moon peeking out from the broken cloud cover provided enough light for Davey to see that several figures were moving about on the pier, positioning themselves to catch the handling lines of the approaching boats. The two ahead veered slightly to the left and made the pier starboard-side-to. Ordonez had chosen the right side and throttled back to idle as his bow passed the wooden stanchions supporting the end of the pier. A skillful touch of left rudder, then a shift to the right, followed by a short burst of reverse power, and they were alongside. Davey stood on the forward deck and tossed the bow line to a shadowy figure opposite him. Only after the form wrapped the line around the pier cleat and jumped aboard did a profile of very tight pants reveal that the line handler was female.

"*Buenos noches*," were her only words, uttered through slightly smiling lips.

"*Senorita, . . .*" replied Davey as he touched the young woman's hand to help her pass aft to the pilothouse. She pointedly pulled it back and passed Davey as if he no longer existed.

"Any trouble, Father?" she asked, pressing her cheek against Ordonez's.

"No, Tatiana. This is David Morales."

She made no further acknowledgement of Davey's presence, passing him silently and leaping lightly back onto the pier. Davey followed, and they stood together while Ordonez secured the oil-cloth cover over the open sides of the pilothouse. Carrying a small canvas sack, he joined them.

"You are in good hands, Morales. I must get the catch transferred. You two go ahead."

Davey took the fisherman's hand. "*Gracias, mi amigo.*"

"Be careful, my friend," cautioned Ordonez, walking away toward a darkened shack on the far side of the pier.

Davey let his eyes watch the activity around the pier as Tatiana led him to a waiting car. The few men who had met the boats were all helping unload the smelly cargos and paid them no mind.

The automobile had come off the assembly line as a 1956 Chevrolet Nomad, but now cardboard replaced the rear side windows, the left front fender was of some other breed and fit badly, and even in the dark Davey could see that the vintage Chevy had been painted heavily with a brush, and was probably gray. The massive hood ornament, however, glimmered like new in the faint moonlight. As he eased himself into the right front seat, he could see that the metal ornament was a gilded rearing bull, obviously very virile.

Tatiana shifted into low several times before she could convince the grinding gears that there were, indeed, some spots on their perimeters where there were enough teeth for them to mesh. When she released the clutch, the Nomad leaped forward in a series of short, sharp jerks. They bumped across the sand behind a single beam of light that was so weak it seemed to want to drop under the pull of gravity, and Davey strongly suspected that the thirty-four-year-old vehicle had only rusted remnants of shock absorbers, if any at all.

Once Tatiana found the two-lane hardtop road that led away from the cove, the panting Nomad settled down into a gently undulating ride, taking the rise and fall of the highway as a small boat would ride a low ground swell. The single headlight waved its anemic beam in front of them more as a warning signal than as any kind of adequate illumination.

Tatiana drove with a concentration that ignored her passenger, and Davey could sense some hostility. While he wished to make some conversation, he wasn't sure just what they would talk about, or whether she would talk at all. He could only assume she knew where he should go. They had been traveling east along the coast for only a few minutes when they passed through a small village.

"Cabanas," she uttered. "We're about ten miles from the airport."

Davey was almost startled at her remark, which he presumed identified the town rather than the structures. He recalled seeing a "Cabanas" on a map.

"You do this often?" he ventured.

"Whenever my father needs me." Her tone indicated the short conversation was over. Davey decided to ignore it.

"You don't sound very enthusiastic."

"He is my father. I do as he asks."

"Do you know why he asks this?"

"Of course. But that does not mean I approve of it."

Davey suddenly felt the cold chill of concern. Obviously, her father trusted her, but she certainly didn't sound in sympathy with his work. Perhaps she was just an unusually obedient daughter, which would be something of a rarity insomuch as she appeared to be in her mid-twenties. He could not help prodding a bit further. "Approve of what?" he asked.

"You . . . and people like you, and what you want to do to Cuba."

"And what is that?"

Even in the night, he could see the flash of passion in her eyes. "Turn this land back into what it once was under Batista—a playground for American capitalists, a place for open graft and sin. A place of prostitution and exhibitionist sex. This was America's other self, where Mister Hyde could play out all of his horrible fantasies before returning to his stateside role as the good Doctor Jekyll. You think I am too young to know of such things? I have seen the films of Havana and the open decadence in the streets, and Caminero, the liberty port of your Navy stationed in Guantanamo where Cuban women exposed themselves in public and performed on stage for the uniformed animals of the United States..."

"Hold on! I don't deny that such things existed under Batista, but it takes two to tango, honey. Your people were the other half of the equation, you know."

"No, my people were not! The thugs of Batista were. They, with American sponsorship, created two classes of Cubans, the ultra-rich and the poverty-stricken."

"And both screwed their hearts out for the Yankee dollar."

Tatiana stiffened. "Yes. Figuratively and literally, my people did such a thing. What else can a politically and economically depressed people do?"

"I would hardly call that era's Havana social set depressed—or repressed, for that matter."

"What would you call the other ninety-eight percent of the population who fed their children dog meat and had to let them run naked in the streets?"

"And the revelucion is better?"

"You are goddamned right it is. Our people have food and education and medical care. Our priorities are in the right order. We have abolished hunger, poverty, and prostitution. We have a purpose in life, a national goal. We are a community within ourselves and do not depend on Yankee dollars for our livelihood."

"How about rubles? I seem to recall the Soviet Union's current practice of pouring their money into your country—without which you would be bankrupt, I believe. What is the ultimate difference between dollars and rubles?"

"The people of the Soviet Union are our trade partners; the people of the United States were our pimps. That is the difference."

Davey could see that the argument was taking them nowhere. "You are the product of your education and I of mine. Let's keep our thoughts on the task at hand, which incidentally strikes me as quite counter to your beliefs. Do I take that for hypocrisy?"

"Quite the contrary. I am my father's daughter; that is the way with us Cubans, unlike *Yanquis*, who have no respect for their elders. But I am also a proud member of the new social order. My father's efforts are misguided, but I cannot convince him of that. I love him and do what he asks while he lives. After that, I shall not be a part of all this."

Considering the intensity of her words, Davey wondered if she could really serve two masters, for that was what she seemed to be trying to do.

"Do not be concerned," she said, addressing his silence, "I will not betray you. It would be too easy for the authorities to use you to discover my father's futile efforts. He is old and will not be with me much longer." She paused and looked aside at Davey. "When that day comes, I will tell everything."

"And incriminate yourself?"

"No. I know what to say and what not to say. I am not stupid."

"No, I don't think you are," muttered Davey. Inside, he wondered just what he did think. "Your father has a lot of trust in you. Does he know how you feel?"

"I have told him many times. He is as stubborn as he is old."

"He is also someone who believes in what he is doing."

"The *revelucion* is complete. The old ways will never return. Under them, my father was a land baron, a good and generous one, but a master over his own people who worked his land as slaves. He shared his profits with the gringos from the north who owned all of Cuba, not with his workers and neighbors. Even my own father, in his misguided enthusiasm, ate and laughed with Batista."

Davey was growing weary of the party line, despite the interlacing of truths concerning the former American hold on Tatiana's country. He was not proud of that, but Cuba had been in the grasp of American gangsters who had treated their own country in similar fashion. He doubted that Ordonez's daughter had been taught that in her history lessons.

Tatiana had apparently also wearied of the exchange. She busied herself with guiding the Chevy through a series of left and right turns that soon disoriented Davey. Just as he felt they must be getting close to the beach area of Havana, they began to parallel the back edge of Jose Marti International Airport. She left the dirt perimeter road and they bounced across open terrain until they were next to the high wire fence surrounding the airfield. She eased to a stop and shut off the engine, and Davey watched the single headlight beam fade to a dull glow before she turned off the switch. The Chevy might have one start left.

Some fifty feet beyond the fence, on the edge of the grassed area bordering one of the taxiways, was a small wooden shack, perhaps twenty by twenty feet. On the opposite side from where they were parked, Davey could see two militiamen standing together, peering in their direction. Both were smoking, but one dropped his butt onto the asphalt and snuffed it with the heel of his boot. Expressing mild interest, he took several steps toward the Chevy.

Tatiana turned to Davey and leaned over. "That is the place."

Before he could respond, she slid across the seat, lifted her arms around his neck and pulled him to her as she leaned back against her door. "They will think we are lovers," she whispered. "Sit back and pretend you are undoing your trousers."

Davey went through the motions while Tatiana wiggled out of her jeans and laid them across the back of the seat. Then, she raised her left leg, kicked off her shoe, and let her bare foot rest on the top of the dashboard. Davey could see the guard who had started toward the car turn and motion to his companion as they hurriedly slipped into the near shadow of the shack, obviously speculating about how much they could see.

As Davey eased forward onto Tatiana, she raised her arms so they could be seen by the guards, then wrapped them tightly around his back to pull him down out of sight.

A number of things were occupying Davey's mind at the moment. Primary was the possibility of he and Tatiana being challenged by the guards, and at least told to move on. He considered that possibility slight, however. They were not on airport grounds and he strongly suspected that the two Cubans were much more interested in fantasizing about the action they figured was taking place in the front seat of the Chevy. Then, there was the chance that someone would approach the car, perhaps some type of outer perimeter patrol, but Tatiana would be aware of that and didn't seem concerned about such a possibility. There was also the chance of someone just wandering by and pausing to check if the Chevy were an abandoned car. Tatiana's upslung leg should dispel that myth. Finally, there was the feel of her body as he lay between her legs, their flesh separated only by his unzipped trousers and the filmy fabric of her underpants. That was the most disturbing thought at the moment. Just as he was beginning to succumb to an urge much more intense than espionage, Tatiana whispered in his ear.

"You touch me and I will neuter you for life."

Despite the facade, Davey was pressing heavily onto her body, and her softness and energetic movement of the upraised leg were hard to ignore. However, her words reminded him that more intimate physical contact was not part of the plan. Accordingly, there were certain involuntary physical reactions with which he would just have to live.

"When we are finished," she began in a low voice, "sit up and smoke a cigarette. Look around all you like. The fools by the shack see this sort of thing several times a night and will ignore you."

Davey continued to lie on top of her as her leg humped back and forth across the dash. Finally, she increased the tempo, let out several audible gasps, and let her leg go limp.

Davey started to sit up. She pulled him back down.

"Not yet, you fool," she admonished. "Haven't you ever made love before? Wait a moment."

Her remark touched one of Davey's sensitive areas and tempted a response. He could provide any number of testimonials to his sexual prowess. As for faking it, that was not his style. He pressed his mouth roughly over hers. Surprisingly, she returned his move, but any further adventure was met with a nasty grip of her teeth.

It was time for the cigarette. She released him and he sat upright. She raised herself and moved next to him, her head on his shoulder, her hand sliding inside his shirt.

"Touch me and I'll neuter you for life," he cautioned, smiling at the turnaround of her phrase. As he lit the cigarette, he could see the two guards returning to their post in front of the shack. The taller of the two playfully goosed the shorter one, who jumped and angrily knocked the other's hand away. Their brief stint at voyeurism was over; it was time to go back to soldiering.

"You can see that the area is too exposed to penetrate," said Tatiana, "but at least this gives you an idea of what it looks like. That is what I was told to do. What is in the building?"

Her father apparently had told her only what she needed to know to carry out her task. Perhaps he had some doubts after all about her loyalty. "Nothing important," answered Davey.

"My father leaves his bed for a bogus fishing trip and you arrive by American submarine and you tell me it is nothing important? It is the shit of the bull."

"Bullshit is the proper expression," corrected Davey.

"Bullsheet," repeated the woman, a flicker of a smile on her face. Perhaps the feel of his body on her had softened her just a bit.

She leaned back to slip on her jeans and for the first time Davey was able to assess her body. The breasts were too small and the hips too wide, but the overall effect was not unpleasant. Her best feature was her face, a delicately featured Spanish face, Castilian even, with the classical contrasts of fair skin and dark eyes. The even darker hair was cut at shoulder length. She had felt good, that he knew.

Also for the first time, Davey noticed several other cars parked along the fence. Which held lovers and which were there for surveillance he had no way of knowing. Tatiana paid them no mind. Evidently, this place was just what it seemed to be, a semisecluded trysting place for the young lovers of Havana.

Shifting her face toward the guarded shack, she continued, "If you have seen enough, we will go."

"We might as well. There's no way I can get into that shack. It's too well lighted and I suspect those two aren't the only security around here," commented Davey. The fence could be penetrated in the dark of night, but that was the only part of the problem to which he could see a solution. Perhaps if he came back during the daylight hours, he could observe the routine activity. He needed to figure out some course of action that would allow him to examine the cylinders. Obviously, he would need some sort of cover.

Back to the charade. Tatiana placed her face a final time against his while engaging the starter. The Chevy barely wheezed in response but caught its breath just before expiring and coughed to life. They backed away from the fence and she turned on the single faint headlight.

Chapter 6

The Old Man pushed himself away from his desk, sighing heavily as he arched his back in a vain attempt to relieve the pressure that was sending sharp wires of pain along stressed vertebrae. This was the second night that he had worked through, and his aging flesh was tired, not to mention the bones that gave it some semblance of support. They were hardly any better, grabbing and almost scraping against one another so that every joint in his overworked frame seemed to be just a hair misplaced, almost as if the proper twist or stretch would snap everything back into its rightful position. But such an effort was beyond him at the moment. He had tried earlier and it had hurt like hell. The pain was always with him, in bearable doses most of the time. Tonight was one of the exceptions.

Even his treasured cigars were unappealing. Perhaps some coffee would help. He grabbed the gold and black plastic server and upended it slowly over his cup. A black syrupy liquid oozed over the lip and hung down in a single sticky strand, gradually elongating until it began to pool on the brown stain in the bottom of the cup.

Snorting, he set it aside and went back to his studied perusal of the message board, reading once more the weekly summaries that came from other stations worldwide whenever they had something of interest to the Miami–Key West area. The latest stack was thinner than usual, thank goodness.

The heavily built walls of his office effectively insulated him from outside noise, but the low ticking of his wall clock, with its persistent imitation of the irritating sounds of a Chinese water torture procedure, prompted him to check the time. It was almost midnight. Davey should be well in-country by this time, perhaps even now forming some preliminary opinion as to the nature of the two cylinders recovered from the ditched Bear.

Hmmmm . . . the report from Recife contained an intriguing item. What had three Arabs been doing in Brazil? Just passing through? The report stated that they had departed for Havana early in the week. *Arabs?* That might indicate a change of pace in things. The Old Man's office had been exclusively immersed in the actions of the Cubans since 1980—mostly Castro's Cubans—and he had almost forgotten there was a world outside of his sphere of responsibility. But the report of the three Middle Eastern travelers quickly reminded him of the timeliness of the last item now habitually carried on the periodic reports from Langley: EX-TREMIST PALESTINIAN TERRORISTS HAVE REPEATEDLY DECLARED INTENT TO CARRY OUT OPERATIONS AGAINST UNITED STATES PERSONNEL AND INSTALLATIONS. REPORT ANY POSSIBLE MOVEMENTS FLASH PRIORITY. The Old Man noted that the Brazilian operator had done just that by the same message that had been sent as information to the Key West office.

Strange that his people in Cuba had not reported the Arabs' arrival. Had they entered undetected? Surely, his people could tell Arabs from Cubans. They probably even smelled different, for Christ's sake. They had better not be missed.

Why in Cuba? The naval base at Guantanamo? Langley would have undoubtedly alerted the Navy and they in turn their people at Guantanamo. The Old Man shook his head. No, action against Gitmo—as the naval base was known in military circles—was out. The Cubans would get the blame and Castro would have none of that.

Could the Arabs be considering a movement onto the continental U.S.? Security in the waters between Cuba and Florida and along the Gulf Coast was tight as a baby's ass with the recent increase in Coast Guard drug patrols and an interlacing of undercover intelligence boats. It was a difficult net to penetrate. Consequently, infiltration to the States across the Gulf didn't seem like a plausible move. There were too many much easier ways to get in. Why try to penetrate the most heavily monitored route?

Training? What could the Cubans teach the masters of international terrorism? Nothing. Of course, the shoe could be on the other foot; maybe the Arabs were there to train the Cubans. The Old Man doubted that. Terrorism wasn't a Cuban modus operandi; besides, for the moment, Castro had enough problems with his below-goal sugar crop and low prices. Things were quiet between him and the States; he wouldn't be stirring that pot.

The pain in the Old Man's back radiated around his side and down into the groin. Perhaps if he walked in his office for a moment some of the kinks would work themselves out. He stood and took several tentative steps, pressing his palms full into the ample flesh over the area of his kidneys. It did seem to feel better. He picked up the message board and continued ambling around the room.

Most of the other information in the summaries was routine follow-up material. The situation in El Salvador looked slightly better; that in Nicaragua about the same.

His mind kept snapping back to the Arabs. Their presence in Cuba made no sense at all. Castro had nothing of value to sell such people. The Soviet Union was the main supplier to the sand people and there was certainly no need for a Caribbean middleman.

He would alert his people, of course, as a matter of routine, but he wasn't scheduled for any contact with Davey unless the young agent got a handle on the cylinders. When they did talk, maybe Davey could undertake an added task: find out what the Arabs were up to. His cover already placed him at the Icar—the most logical spot to observe the Arabs.

Meanwhile, things were quiet enough for the Old Man to call it a day—a long day. He returned to his desk and washed down a small pile of aspirin with a swig of bourbon from his desk-drawer bar.

There was no way he could pull and lift the hide a-bed from the office sofa. He would just lie on top. Once he laboriously removed his shoes and propped up his feet on one arm of the sofa, the pain wasn't so bad.

Hell, he'd had it much worse in his time. Thirty-three years in the field: shot, stabbed, drugged, balls shocked—he'd had it all. So, a sore back on a lumpy sofa wasn't all that bad. No, sir. Not bad at all.

And for the moment, the Arabs could go screw themselves.

Chapter 7

July 3, 4:57 A.M.
Southeast Florida

"Duker" Davis compared the heading on his magnetic compass with that of the runway stretching ahead of him for almost five thousand feet. The black asphalt, even with the white line painted down its middle, disappeared into the predawn darkness but was still clearly outlined by the twin rows of white runway lights marking its sides. A small adjustment was needed on his electric gyrocompass. Leaning forward against his shoulder harness, he rotated the black knob on the lower left corner of the instrument to align it with the runway heading. His instructions were to fly magnetic headings.

Less than ten minutes had elapsed since he had slipped onto darkened Page Field, just a few miles south of Fort Myers, Florida, and made his way over to the unattended flight line of Page City Aviation. There, using the duplicate key he had stolen from the Piper Aircraft dealer's keyboard when he had first checked out in the Cherokee 6 two days earlier, he had climbed aboard the aircraft and taxied immediately to the runway, performing his pre-takeoff check en route. The unsuspecting Page City check pilot had given only a cursory glance at Duker's FAA Airman's Certificate and medical certification before giving him a short checkout

64

ride. Certainly, Duker was well qualified, with more than several thousand hours of light plane time, a goodly portion of it in the various orchard dusters that were a familiar part of the Florida citrus-growing industry. Of course, Duker could have stolen the plane outright, but despite his lack of aversion to anything illegal he was still a cautious pilot, and the thirty-five bucks for the twenty-minute checkout flight was of no consequence when he stood to put $50,000 in his pocket from just this one flight.

He was always running into good deals like this, and a fair number of them had been steered his way by his favorite Miami whore. Not only did the delicious Cuban amaze him with her energetic and innovative lovemaking, she seemed to instinctively know when he was running a little dry of the green and would unfailingly come up with a contact he could count on for a financial favor. Usually a short flying job, maybe something as commonplace as hauling a few sacks of grass north, or spraying a doctored load of pesticide across a competitor's orange grove, or sometimes a job that didn't involve flying at all.

Duker's six-three frame was layered with more than two hundred and ten pounds of muscle held in place by a sun-baked skin that sported a multitude of colorful tattoos across his upper body and along the outside of his biceps. His favorite was the face-up nude with outstretched legs that sprawled across his sternum, her arms pointing to his two nipples over which were the scrolled words "tit" and "tat." Next to flying, Duker had a simple list of life's necessities: drinking, making love, watching other people make love, and brawling.

The first item had cost him his Army commission and wings; the last brought him most of his nonflying pickup money. He knew how to punch a guy out with just enough finesse to keep the victim within the world of the living but make him wish he had left it, and Duker was always most discreet when protecting his employers. They liked him for that. So, with his flying, his whore, and his frequent opportunities for performing a rather primitive type of plastic surgery on strangers' faces, he had a good life. And now he was beginning to be called on for some serious-money jobs. Fifty g's for a short flight to Cuba and expenses home on Air Canada—first class—with a few days' layover in Montreal before returning to southern Florida was a piece of cake with lots of frosting. Yes, life was getting sweeter.

He opened the throttle and the three hundred horses under the cowling of the big six-place Piper accelerated him along the runway. He sucked it off at sixty miles per hour, slapped the land-ing gear handle, and reached to retract the flaps. That handle was already in the up position. No wonder the takeoff had felt like he was wallowing in a bowl of mush. Duker smiled at his oversight. A lesser pilot would have settled back onto the runway. At two hun-dred feet he leaned the Cherokee over into a steep bank and started his left turn to the south. He continued climbing steadily as he passed over long and narrow Sanibel Island and took a course that should carry him right across Fort Jefferson National Monument on the Dry Tortugas group of rocks at the end of the Key West chain. They lay sixty miles due east from the Naval Air Station there, and although he would be flying over open water, his intended cruising altitude of twelve thousand feet should provide him with plenty of visual checks on the eastern shore of Florida and the Keys. Already, as he climbed through fifty-six hundred feet, he was in the advance light of the rising sun and could make out familiar details along the emerging coastline. About forty-five minutes of peaceful dawn flying should put him over his initial departure point.

It did.

From here on, it was so long, USA—for a while—and hello, fifty grand. The Cubans wanted him low now that he had overflown the Dry Tortugas, so he eased back the throttle and let the nose of the Cherokee drop into a high-speed descent, leveling at one hundred and fifty feet on a magnetic heading of two hundred and twenty-five degrees—southeast. On that heading, he would just brush the eastern tip of Cuba, but his instructions carried the final note that he would be intercepted en route and led to his unnamed destination.

The southern U.S. radar network would pay him little atten-tion. He was going away from the mainland. Besides, he had dropped below the radar horizon and simply disappeared from somebody's screen. They might be puzzled, but with no known flight plan on file there would be no correlation with his actions. As for someone blowing the whistle on his theft of the airplane, the people back at Page Field wouldn't even be dragging in for work for another couple hours. By that time, he would be fingering a pock-etful of U.S. bills and sipping *mojitos* somewhere in Cuba.

He wasn't sure he wanted to trust the autopilot at such a low altitude, but the Piper trimmed nicely and he was able to monitor its flight while he sipped his breakfast from a pocket flask. With just a touch of light finger and toe pressure, he was able to keep the autopilot honest as he rode along smoothly in the morning calm. A few fishing boats were bobbing about on the gentle ground swell, positioned for their day's work. He was a bit concerned about Navy and Coast Guard patrol craft, but even if they spotted him they would figure he was just another Miami crazy out flat-hatting local fishermen. He'd make sure he didn't close any of them such that they could record his side numbers.

The sun was bright on the horizon and his Seiko indicated that it was the time specified for his interception, but nothing was in sight. Maybe they could not find him this low. That possibility caused him some concern; he would hate to go boring toward Cuba and have their air defense net detect him. That could be embarrassing, not to mention wet and painful should they unlimber an air-to-air bird in a moment of haste. Tired of searching ahead and to his sides, he twisted in his seat to check his quarters.

Surprise!

Riding less than fifty feet off to his left and slightly behind him was the largest seaplane he had ever seen, with a tremendously wide gull wing and twin turbojet engines turning huge propellers that were only a pilot's sneeze from his tail surfaces. The seaplane wore the dull green paint of Cuban air forces. Even as he sat, trying to swallow his heart, which had leapt up into his throat, the flying boat pulled out and forward until it flew just off his left wing tip. The right-seat pilot patted his helmeted head to indicate he was taking control of the situation and motioned for Duker to follow him. Duker had his radio set on the specified frequency but heard nothing and figured that maybe he shouldn't speak unless spoken to. At least, not yet, since the Cuban pilot had not made any hand signals to indicate a radio difficulty.

Now that he was well into this caper, he was beginning to get a little edgy. The undetected approach of the big military seaplane with its very professional pair of machine cannons pointing from its nose accented the reality of the situation. Duker could also see, now that the Cuban aircraft was alongside, that it was actually an amphibian. He had no idea the Cubans had such a machine, but it didn't take too much moxie to figure out that it was most probably Soviet-supplied. That probability added an even more sinister tint to the sight of his sunbathed escort leading him toward Cuba at a steady one hundred and fifty miles per hour.

Duker checked his watch: 6:24 A.M. It was full daylight now and he could see a large coastal city ahead. It could only be Havana. Hell, he could have found Havana without a damned escort.

The amphibian led him in a gentle climb to fifteen hundred feet, and as they crossed the shoreline, Duker could see a commercial airfield evolving from the cluster of the city. That would be Jose Marti.

"Cherokee three-nine-tango, you are cleared to land. Follow your escort aircraft."

Duker was startled to hear the call and the use of his "N" number. He should have guessed that his escort would have relayed his identification to the airport control tower.

The amphibian was landing long to give him the first part of the runway. Duker dropped his landing gear, lowered half flaps, and set the Piper down on the numbers.

"Cherokee three-nine-tango, follow your escort to parking."

He followed the amphibian onto the taxiway and they proceeded in column toward an isolated corner of the field, heading for a large open-faced military tent erected next to a small wooden shack. Just beyond was the airport boundary wire fence.

A military taxi signalman waved two green paddles and motioned for Duker to follow his signals. Duker found himself being directed into the open end of the khaki tent. Two soldiers stood by the adjacent shack and watched the procedure.

He got the CUT signal just as his wings moved into the tent, and before the propeller stopped, the taxi signalman had slung a pair of wooden chocks around his main wheels.

Duker stepped down off the low wing and was met by two men, one obviously a Cuban, and the other just as obviously not. Surprised but impressed with his VIP arrival treatment, Duker smiled at the Arab, who gave a small nod of his head in greeting.

Walking around the airplane, the Arab seemed pleased. "You have presented us with a fine craft. Come, follow me, and let us settle accounts."

I'm all for that, sheik, thought Duker.

The Arab also said something to the Cuban in a remark so low that Duker could not make it out. The Cuban looked puzzled but shrugged and walked away.

"Duker Davis," said Duker by way of introduction as they walked toward the rear of the tent. The Arab didn't seem to notice Duker's offered hand. Oh, yeh, I forgot. You guys don't shake with your right hand. Something to do with your toilet habits if I remember correctly.

They reached one of the back corners and Duker noticed they

had walked onto a large square of rubberized canvas. The Arab produced a large manila envelope and handed it to Duker.

Duker smiled in anticipation. He liked to get straight to the heart of things. Taking the bulky package, he eagerly pulled open the flap. The envelope was stuffed with U.S. bills, apparently all one-thousand-dollar notes.

"You, perhaps, should count it," suggested the Arab.

Duker let his tongue play along his upper lip. "If you don't mind. . . ." He pulled the stack of bills partially out of the envelope and ran his thumb along the edge, riffing them as he would a deck of cards. There were at least fifty. "I'm sure they are all . . ."

Duker Davis never finished his sentence. For a brief moment, he caught the shadow of an upraised blade before he felt it slice into his neck at its junction with his left shoulder. The short, broad sword sliced cleanly downward at a forty-five-degree angle, slicing through his clavicle and the edge of his scapula on its way toward his spinal column. There, the razor edge of the hardened steel severed the chain of vertebrae and the enclosed spinal cord before coming to rest in the lower right side of his chest.

The Arab held the dead mercenary upright with the sword for only the time it took him to spit into Duker's face. Then he withdrew the blade and let the partially severed body drop to the canvas. He took a small step backward to avoid the widening pool of blood.

Stooping down, he picked up the envelope and wiped his sword on Duker's shirt before flipping in the corners of the canvas and lapping the sides over the corpse.

He hardly glanced at the shocked Cuban as he left the tent. The man stood with his lower jaw slack, his eyes wide with fear.

"Get rid of the American. The arm of God has purified him." The Arab's words were flat, without emotion, as he strode away.

The two militiamen guarding the small shack, positioned as they were, could not have observed the events in the back corner of the tent. They paid the Arab no mind as he passed.

Chapter 8

7:13 A.M.
Headquarters, CIA Substation, Key West

"**T**om! . . . Tom! Wake up, you old bastard!"

The Old man refused to open his eyes. No one called him by his Christian name—except his boss, the head of the Miami station. But, what the hell, if he were there, the night was over. Slowly, the Old Man succumbed to the inevitable and pushed himself up into a sitting position. The sofa hadn't been the best of beds, but he had slept well enough. He was surprised to see that it was after seven.

Not only was his immediate superior, Felix Ariguar, standing in front of him but two others as well. Right away, he recognized the FBI headquarters representative; they couldn't seem to shake the J. Edgar Hoover image: gray suit, white shirt, unicolor tie, and a silly-ass hat. Why didn't someone tell them that men stopped wearing hats thirty years ago? Probably in his fifties, the man must be a very senior agent or maybe even one of the high mucky-mucks. Clean shaven, no fat, shoes shined, white handkerchief peeking coyly from his coat breast pocket. Disgusting.

The third man was vaguely familiar, probably someone he had seen on his infrequent trips to Langley, but he couldn't place the name or job.

Ariguar pulled up a couple of side chairs and motioned for his companions to sit before he eased himself down onto the sofa beside the Old Man.

"Tom, this is Chuck Myers from FBI headquarters. He heads a special antiterrorist division within the bureau. Ted Benson, here, is Chuck's counterpart at our own headquarters."

The Old Man studied the two intelligence agents. At least Benson showed some promise. He seemed just the opposite of the neatly groomed Fed, probably thirty to forty pounds overweight— the Old Man could identify with that—and with a face and body that were obviously neglected. Still, the remnants of a once athletic and probably physically mean physique remained discernible beneath the flowered sport shirt and tropical tan trousers. Brown cotton socks covered the expanse of his legs that ran from his blue boat shoes upward several inches before disappearing into his trouser legs. All in all, the Old Man figured Ted Benson had been around the track a few times, like himself, and was experienced, all business, and well used. As for the FBI man, he probably drank hot tea and slept in pajamas. Still, the Old Man had plenty of respect for the Feds and sometimes a trace of envy. They had scruples and they were pros, many of their field people the equal of his, and he suspected that Myers had been selected for his job because of some special qualifications that didn't require a suit and tie. The poor guy just couldn't shake the goody-two-shoes image when it came to making a field trip out of D.C., even if it was to subtropical Florida.

Ariguar had set a white paper sack in front of him on the coffee table and he extracted three cartons of coffee and several Danish pastries. Upending the sack, he dumped an assortment of packaged sugar, cream, Sweet 'n Low, and plastic spoons and forks. "I figured you hadn't had breakfast yet," said the Miami station chief.

The Old Man reached over and took one of the coffees but ignored the Danish. Holding two of the sugars together, he tore the tops off the packages, dumped the contents into the brew, and poured in one of the powdered creamers. "To what momentous development do I owe this prestigious visit?" he asked, yawning widely.

Benson, the headquarters spook, had already flipped open a manila dossier cover and arranged three eight-by-ten glossies neatly on the coffee table. They were obviously blowups of covertly obtained snapshots, cropped to show only the upper bodies and faces of three dark-complexioned men—Arabic men. Pointing to each in turn, Ariguar made the introductions, "Kamal Adwan, Youssif Daoud, and Ardeshir Zadefi. Your Cuban Arabs—or, to be technical, two Arabs and an Iranian."

"The Arabs? Palestinians?" The Old Man asked the question as much with his eyebrows as with his voice.

"Yes. The worst kind."

"Terrorists?"

"With a capital T, Big Tom," answered Ariguar. "Benson tells me they are the nucleus of a completely new splinter group of the PLO."

"Jesus, not another batch. You'd think they'd run out of names, soon."

"Ted, tell Tom what you told us on the way down."

Benson spoke slowly, almost with admiration, "You're looking at three top representatives of a superfanatical organization that up to only last week was just a shadow group we had no real handle on. They are totally suicidal, dedicated, intelligent sons of bitches."

"Jihad Islamis?" asked the Old Man. That was the only Palestinian organization he knew of that would fit such a description.

"At one time, maybe," responded Benson. Reading from a page of the dossier, he continued, "Kamal Adwan, Palestinian, twenty-eight years old. Joined Yasser Arafat's Al Fatah when he was sixteen. Originally fanatically loyal and gained a reputation as a merciless *fayadee* with above-average intelligence. His mother, father, and baby sister were killed during an antiterrorist retaliation raid by the Mivtzan Elohim—Israel's Wrath of God group—in 1983. Went on a solo killing spree for two months and probably accounted for twenty to thirty random Israeli deaths during that time. Finally curtailed by some of the more mature fayadees but became disillusioned with Arafat shortly thereafter. Felt the old-timer was mellowing and let the Americans force them out of Lebanon. There are some indications he was in on the planning of the October 1983 bombing of the American embassy. Has a perpetual hard-on for Americans as well as Israelis."

The Old Man looked closely at Kamal Adwan's picture. The face of a young man, the eyes of an ageless satan. "Weaknesses?"

Benson shrugged. Placing his finger on the second picture, he went on, "Youssif Daoud, Palestinian, thirty-one years old. One of Arafat's bright, upcoming lieutenants until about a year ago, when like Adwan, he became convinced that Arafat was tempering the

Palestinian movement with his own political ambitions. He had some early association with the Black September group, probably liaison, but as far as we know, he stayed pretty much within the operational format of Al Fatah's political goals. Orphaned at an early age during the Six Days' War in 1967. We know that he was definitely in on the Marine barracks truck bombing in Beirut. In fact, he was to be the driver until the day before, when he was accidentally wounded by a fellow terrorist."

The Old Man studied Youssif Daoud's picture. There was only hate in the acne-pocked face even though the camera had apparently caught him unawares in a casual pursuit. His black beard was heavy but short, more of an advanced stubble than a full growth. "Weaknesses?" asked the Old Man a second time.

"Women," replied Benson. "Must have a dong like a camel and uses it every night he can. Never compromises his goals, however, and has been known to kill his sex partner when suspicious of her. A real animal, not the Middle Eastern religious type we normally think of."

"Nice guy. . . ." murmured the Old Man.

Benson referred to the third picture. "Now, we know that Arabs and Persians—Iranians—have not always seen eye to eye from a religious standpoint. They're all Moslems, of course, but whereas the Iranians are mainly Shiites, most of the Arab world are Sunnites, and they spend a lot of time at each other's throats. But the Koran itself contains words that say, in effect, that enemies of my enemies are my friends. Thus, the U.S.-hating Palestinians find a ready ally in a U.S.-hating Iranian. The fact that the two people combine in their holy war against us is not unusual, even if their reasons are slightly divergent. The Arabs hate us because they blame us for the establishment and support of Israel. The Iranians hate us because they believe we are a materialistic society of infidels and unbelievers."

Benson paused to down a generous sip of his coffee. He winced. "God, that got cold fast." Disgusted, he sat the cup aside before continuing, "With that in mind, meet Ardeshir Zadefi, Iranian, forty-four years old. Ex-fighter pilot and former captain in the Shah's elitist air force. Turned against the Shah during the overthrow by the Ayatollah Khomeini's Moslem forces. Lost his flying status due to a lung wound and became an officer in the Shiite Moslem Militia. Interestingly enough, and even though a Shiite, he was one of the original group that splintered off the militia to join the Jihad Islami sect, and like the other two, is linked to the '83 and '84 bombings. In fact, he wanted to fly into the Marine barracks but was overruled."

"Weaknesses?"

"None. The man is a professional, with a solid military background—so, in some areas, he can think a step ahead of the other two—and the most dedicated of the three when it comes to religious fervor and hatred of the United States."

The Old Man looked closely at the last picture. The three faces were all beginning to look alike. Zadefi's face was hardened with early middle age, but the other two faces were just as hardened by hate and years of uncompromising combat. "God, what an unholy trinity."

"Now, this group," continued Benson, settling back into his chair, "leads an organization of more than seventy followers. They disclaim any allegiance to any other Palestinian organization. They claim to be independent and for a while they received operating funds from various oil sheiks. For some reason, that source dried up, and now they finance themselves by robbery and extortion. It is our belief that they are devoting themselves exclusively to preparing for actions against the United States, who they feel is solely responsible for the establishment and continued existence of the state of Israel and the purveyor of all the world's ills. They call themselves the New Shaheen."

"The New Shaheen?" repeated the Old Man, questioningly.

"Yes, the original Shaheen were anti-Zionist Arab terrorists who operated in the first century after the death of Christ. They particularly sought out Jewish extremists, preferred daylight for their attacks, and were most active on holidays. Their favorite weapon was the *sica*, a short broadsword, and they believed that to die during an attack was a sure ticket to eternal pleasure in the next life. In that respect, they were pre-Muhammad Muslims."

"You sound like you've done your homework," commented the Old Man.

"We all have. Chuck and I have been on this thing twenty-four hours a day for weeks. Incidentally, in the charred wreckage of the truck that was used to blow up the Marine barracks was a short, broad sword still strapped to a piece of the assassin's lower body. Symbolic, of course, but it gave us the tie-in."

Myers took up the briefing. "There's more background that we've uncovered and may give us some clues as to how they operate.

The original Shaheen had a philosophy that stressed God alone as Lord. They refused to recognize any earthly power as worthy of their allegiance. Their whole life was conducted around a frenzy of religious expectations, and as Ted indicated, martyrdom was a joyful end to this life."

"First century A.D.?" mused the Old Man. "They're reaching pretty far back for role models."

"They are trying to be the most holy of the holies," said Myers.

"And we're the infidels," chimed in Ariguar.

"So, they come to Cuba? Doesn't sound like the way they would operate." The Old Man looked at the pictures again. "Of course, if they shaved and got rid of the headdress, they might very well pass for Cubans, but not if my people spot 'em. I don't know . . . there's something here we don't . . . oh, shit!" The Old Man stood, his face ashen. "The cylinders . . . the fucking Bear cylinders."

"Oh, my God," added Ariguar, the realization hitting him with the Old Man's words.

"What cylinders?" asked Myers.

Ariguar also stood and threw his empty paper cup across the Old Man's office. Embarrassed at his loss of control, he muttered a frustrated "Sorry," but continued standing, addressing his next remarks to the puzzled FBI agent. "Remember the Bear that ditched off the Bahama Bank the day before yesterday? Tom sent one of his people on a little underwater look-see, and the agent observed two fair-sized cylinders strapped into the bomb bay, welded shut and carrying the Soviet radiation-warning symbol. Later on, a Cuban Air Force amphibian recovered the Bear's crew and the cylinders, blew up the Bear, and returned to Cuba."

"You think there's a connection?" asked Myers.

"I hadn't thought of it until now," replied Ariguar.

"What was in the cylinders?" asked Myers. "Nuclear weapons?"

"We don't know what the hell they are," replied the Old Man. "My man is in-country right now, trying to get a handle on them."

"Jesus . . ." uttered Myers, "I just thought about something else."

"What's that?" asked Ariguar.

"The Shaheen . . . they liked to strike on holidays."

"And . . . ?"

"Tomorrow," responded Myers, looking the others in the eyes, "is the Fourth of July." The words chilled the room like a sudden frost.

Benson was the first to break the silence. "You think they plan to bring whatever they have to the States?"

"Wait a minute," cautioned the Old Man. "Let's not get too far ahead of ourselves." Some of the color had returned to his face. "They may not be weapons at all, or even nuclear devices. There's some thought among my staff that they might be nuclear medical equipment or supplies." Even as he relayed the opinion of Jeremiah, his technical services chief, he knew he didn't believe it himself. But there was that ray of hope that didn't have to die until Davey made a positive identification.

Ariguar held up his hand. "We must assume the worst case. They're weapons, and we have to assume there may be a connection with the terrorists, although it may be just a coincidence. I don't think we should count on that, though."

"What would they be after? Guantanamo?" asked Myers.

"No," replied the Old Man decisively. "The Cubans wouldn't be cooperative if there was even the remotest chance of that. If there is a transfer under Cuban auspices, there's some mighty good god-damned assurances that the Palestinians are going to take the cylinders out of the country. That's my conclusion—and they're coming here, and the brazen sons of bitches are going to come right across the Gulf for a Fourth of July fireworks display, the likes of which the world has never seen!"

"Then, that's the play we're going to have to deal with," added Ariguar, obviously agreeing with the Old Man. "What kind of agent is your man, Tom?" he asked.

"Davey? Good, very good. Levelheaded, quick thinker. Name's Morales, Davey Morales."

"Davey?"

"He goes by that except when under cover. His mother was a strong-willed Irishwoman."

"Davey Morales," Ariguar let the name roll off his lips. "That's a hell of a name for a Cuban."

The Old Man grinned. "Mexican-American, not Cuban. For that matter, Felix Ariguar doesn't exactly sound like old Spain, if you don't mind an irreverent observation." The Old Man was careful to keep his smile broad as he made the remark.

"Point," granted Ariguar. "Okay, so he's a good man. How soon can you talk to him?"

"I can make arrangements."

"Better fill him in, then. Who knows what kind of time we have left."

"Davey's alert. If he sees Palestinians, his natural instincts will make the two-plus-two addition. I'll get word to him, of course."

Myers voiced what was on everyone's mind, "Well, we all know this was bound to happen, sooner or later. God knows, they've been threatening it long enough. And that 1987 excursion from Canada—that could have been the first of it had it not been for an alert small-town cop. But this—I have been praying that it wouldn't be anything like this." After a head-shaking pause, he continued, "I can't even imagine the Soviets being a part of such a thing."

"You probably think all nuns are virgins," snorted the Old Man. "This is the real world, my friend. The Soviets are masters at letting other people do their dirty work. But I'm with you. I don't think the Soviets had any idea they were setting up a nuclear attack against the United States."

"We've got things to do," interrupted Ariguar, "and so do you. Give me a call after you talk to your man. I'll get word to the southern sector people and we'll be ready for them, but let's face it, a handful of illegals get through every day."

"Three Middle Easterners with two eight-by-two metal cylinders should be somewhat easier to detect," observed Myers.

Ariguar shot the FBI man a quick glance. "They won't be flying Pan Am, Chuck."

"I know . . . sorry."

"Forget it."

"We'll have to inform the president," said Myers, "even if it's only a speculation at this time. How soon can we get back to D.C.?"

The Old Man pointed toward his desk. "Use my scramble phone for your advance call. You came down by government air, didn't you?"

"We've got a Beechcraft King Air," replied Ariguar, "but we need something faster."

"Make your call, Myers," suggested the Old Man, "then the three of you can head on down to the flight line. I'll alert the ops boss and he'll have a Navy jet ready, I'm sure. We keep an alert T-39." As he spoke, the Old Man walked over to his desk, pulled open the second drawer on the right side, and extracted a red phone, which he placed before Myers.

Myers picked up the transceiver, "This is a priority one call, scramble code: delta. Let me speak to the White House, with conference tie-ins to the Director, FBI, and Head, Special Section Charlie, CIA Headquarters, Langley."

After Ariguar and his two companions left, the Old Man made

his own call to the on-station office of the Voice of Free Cuba. He gave a coded message to the disc jockey, and within the hour a program of traditional Cuban folk songs was radiating across the one hundred and ninety miles of open water between the tall, skeletal antenna on the Key West Naval Air Station and a humble *bohio* located on the north shore of Cuba near the city of Sagua la Grande.

Inside the simple peasant's hut, an eighty-three-year-old senora of pure Castilian blood was sipping her morning coffee and rocking herself as she listened with closed eyes to the familiar music and thought of the old days. A cheap cassette recording machine lay beside her Agricola-brand radio, a gift from her grandson, who was an important member of Fidel Castro's own administrative staff. She would not only enjoy the melodies of her adopted homeland now, she would replay them later, and by so doing, feed the magnetic imprint on the plastic cassette tape simultaneously through another more interesting device, which she kept in a shoe box under her bed. The device would filter out the subliminal message that was masked to human ears by the spirited Latin music, and she would ensure that the latest instructions from her old friend at the American base at Key West reached the proper party.

Chapter 9

8:30 A.M.
Havana

Davey felt antsy. He was already more than an hour late for his first day on the job and the relic of a work bus that had picked him up at seven—and had experienced a chronically ill carburetor only fifteen minutes later—was just beginning to wind its way through the outermost streets of eastern Havana. He had to admit, however, that he had developed a great deal of respect for the old driver, who may have suffered them a sixty-minute delay but had practically rebuilt the ancient fuel-air mixture device by the side of the isolated road. The Cubans had, of necessity, become the world's most innovative roadside mechanics, keeping vehicles breathing that should have died from old age and chronic illnesses decades back. Davey mused that if they had been able to develop the same degree of ingenuity and perseverance with respect to their economic problems, Cuba would be the most prosperous nation in the Western Hemisphere. There must be a lesson there, somewhere, but for the moment it was lost.

As he rode along, grasping the back of the seat ahead of him to maintain some degree of stability aboard the bouncing bus, his thoughts relived the previous evening. He was having difficulty figuring out the daughter of Rudy Ordonez. When she had initially picked him up at the fishing village on the edge of Honda Bay, she had been antagonistic, curt, even rude. Early on, she had informed him of her distaste for Americans and her father's collusions with people like himself. During the fake lovemaking outside the airport fence, she had established and maintained complete control of the situation, even ridiculing him as he tried to make the instant adjustment to such a provocative cover for his initial surveillance of the cylinder stowage site.

She had continued her reluctance for conversation after they had left and as she coaxed the wheezing old Chevy southeast of Havana.

It had been past two in the morning, and just a few miles from San Jose de las Lajas, according to the rusted highway marker, when she had finally broken her silence.

"I have a place just up ahead. You can stay there with me for a few days as my lover. No one will question you and the work bus for the Construction Ministry comes right by it."

That remark had answered his first unasked question. Up to that point, no one had briefed him on where he would stay. All he knew was his clandestine work assignment.

Strangely enough, when they arrived at her place a few minutes later, she seemed suddenly to relax and began to treat him as an honored guest.

"Please, follow me," she said after she had steered the nose of the car up against the side of what appeared to be a roadside fruit stand, buttoned up for the night. Her room was up the stairs on the back side of the frame building and was open on all four sides to the elements. Even in the dim light, Davey could make out the sparse furnishings: a single metal frame bed in one corner, provided with some measure of privacy by a three-panel folding reed screen that isolated it from a tired sofa squatting in the center of the room. A compact cooking area occupied the opposite corner, with a two-burner hot plate, a small pantry cabinet, an old refrigerator with the evaporator and condenser housing on its top, a metal wash pan on a three-legged stand, and a four-place table with two straight-backed wooden chairs. A small three-drawer chest made up the rest of the furnishings. Her clothes hung evenly on an exposed line running diagonally across the third corner of the room. As Tatiana snapped on a low-wattage light over her bed, Davey could see that the plank floor was bare but immaculately clean, as was the entire room. Characteristic of most rural Cuban dwellings, drop shutters were raised over the four openings on the walls, to be lowered during heavy rains.

"The toilet is out back," she informed him. "Would you like something to eat?"

Davey was almost shocked at her change in behavior. She pulled two fruit-flavored sodas from the small reefer and popped off their tops.

"I don't have anything stronger," she apologized, holding one of the drinks out to him.

"Thanks, this is fine." He took a thirsty swig of the soda. Weak with flavor, it was nevertheless cold and wet and delicious after the long ride in the high humidity of the calm night. They were apparently just far enough inland to miss the sea breeze.

Noticing that she still stood expectantly in front of the refrigerator, Davey answered her previous question, "No, I'm not hungry. This is very good." He sat on the sofa and she went behind the screen.

"You can sleep there, on the sofa. It really is quite comfortable. I don't think you will need anything tonight, but there is a thin blanket in the bottom drawer of the chest if the rains come."

Davey nodded as if she could see him.

"I will call you, if necessary, in the morning. The work bus will be here by seven. It stops in front of the stand. There will be several men there."

"You live here alone?" asked Davey. If so, it would be unusual. Even though the room was small, it was customary for whole families to share such a space.

"I have two roommates—girlfriends. They will be gone for a while."

Davey looked around. There was no evidence that anyone shared the room. There were sleeping facilities only for two, unless a third paired off on the narrow bed. That thought raised other questions in his mind. Was that why she had seemed so indifferent to the touch and pressure of his body back at the airport? That would be just his luck, to live with a dyke for cover.

Soft rustling sounds came from behind the screen as she prepared for bed. Davey finished his soda and walked out back to the toilet. A worn one-holer, it had only a piece of rotating wood for a latch and smelled as if it held half of the human waste in Cuba.

When he returned, the light was out and he could see the glow of her cigarette through the cracks in the reed screen and smell the smoke.

"You don't go to sleep with one of those things in your mouth, do you?" he asked. The small two-story shack would burn like hades once ignited.

"Don't worry, Yanqui, I never go right to sleep. Takes me awhile to unwind."

Davey wondered if he detected a return of some of her earlier sarcasm. He slipped off his shoes and lay back on the sofa. Was she expecting him to make a move? Could their body contact back at the airport have stirred a more primitive emotion than the contempt she had lavished on him while they lay together in the front seat of the Chevy? She certainly had been more civil since they had arrived at her room, no doubt about that, but he had never fully understood the female psyche. Sometimes, those who wanted it the most were the hardest to get to. He peeled off his shirt, dropped his trousers, and pulled off his socks. It felt good to have bare feet again and he wiggled his toes before shoving his socks under the sofa. Lots of Cubans went sockless. The sofa was comfortable, if overly soft, but it had the musty odor of well-used, overstuffed furniture, and if the smell was an indicator of its age, it must have arrived in Cuba with the first Spaniards.

He had been lying in the silence for perhaps ten minutes with no hint of approaching sleep despite his long day when he heard the padding of bare feet and felt the slight stir of air as Tatiana passed and opened the refrigerator door. The dim light from the bulb inside softly illuminated the room, and Davey studied the young woman as she stooped and searched the inside of the refrigerator. Her ruffled-neck nightdress gave her a little-girl look, quite different from the impression her bold actions at the airport had conveyed to him. He had a sympathetic feeling that the little girl outlined in the light of the refrigerator was more truly Tatiana.

"I'm still thirsty," she muttered, sighing. "Would you like something else?" she asked.

"No, thank you," Davey replied. He sensed she was nervous, perhaps even uneasy in her role as his escort. Beneath her facade as a dedicated Cuban communist, he strongly suspected, was a confused young woman, trying to maintain her posture as an earnest young revolutionary but unable to disobey her father, whom she must love very much. And this night, with her unpleasant task bringing to the surface all of her inner conflict, she was obviously restless.

Davey remained still as she padded back to bed. Perhaps she had just wanted to talk. If so, he should have been more responsive. But there were just too many of his own thoughts racing around in his head. They had to take priority.

The better part of an hour passed before his concerns about the cylinders and how he would somehow have to gain access to them allowed the fatigue of the past twenty-four hours to coax his sweltering body into a fitful sleep.

Tatiana was up and about by six, and by the time Davey had rolled out a few minutes later, she had made her trip out back and had a grapefruit half and a cup of coffee waiting for him. Such domestic attention was completely contrary to the hostile attitude of the female who had so defiantly faked lovemaking with him the night before.

"Did you sleep?" she asked.

"Uh-huh," replied Davey, sipping his coffee and looking at his watch.

"Take your time. The bus will not be along for another fifteen minutes. I'll bring you some lunch about noon. It is customary. That way, if anything has developed and I hear from Father, I can let you know."

"You sound a little more enthused about helping me than last night."

Her demeanor abruptly returned to the frigid level of their first conversation. "I do as my father asks."

Maybe she was paranoid.

Davey dressed, cheerfully ignoring the socks he had tossed under the sofa, and joined the small group of men below.

"*Buenas dias*," greeted several.

"*Buenas dias, campaneros*," returned Davey.

"You are new," commented the one standing farthest back.

"Yes. I was just transferred yesterday."

"I see you have been made welcome," replied the man, a friendly smile and a tilt of his head indicating Tatiana's place.

"An old friend," replied Davey as they all chuckled together.

The bus made two stops before delivering Davey to the parking lot of the Icar Hotel. It was just after nine by the time he located Geraldo Cordero on the top floor.

"Well, campanero," began the Cuban, "I've been expecting you—somewhat earlier, actually." He held out a friendly hand.

"The bus broke down."

Cordero laughed. It was an explanation he could readily accept. The work buses were always breaking down. "As you can see, we are putting up interior walls and finishing the rooms as we go. You will work with me, today. Have you done such work before?"

"No, I come from a breeding farm."

"No matter, it is simple."

As they worked, Cordero asked him whether he had a place to stay, and seemed satisfied when Davey responded that he was staying with a friend. The Cuban spoke lovingly of his wife and the good fortune of him being assigned as a new supervisor. Davey responded with some remarks about his work on the cattle farm, making sure he spoke in generalities. Cordero did not seem to be curious as to details.

Davey listened carefully to the Cuban's line of questioning. There seemed to be no pattern, just normal conversational interest between two fellow workers. That was good; there was no indication that Cordero was suspicious. The other new worker arrived at their midmorning break, having missed the work bus on the other side of the city. Cordero gently chastised him and reminded him of his obligations to the revolution. The man seemed appreciative and was assigned to one of the other work teams. After their break, Davey and Cordero resumed their task of placing insulation along the outer walls of the end room.

As Cordero stooped to pick up another batten from the pile by the inside wall, he spoke softly to Davey. "Come over here, I want you to hear something."

Davey joined him and followed his lead in pressing his ear against the next room's single sheet of wallboard.

"Perhaps your English is better than mine. That is a Russian room and they have been receiving some interesting visitors."

Davey strained to hear, but the occupants were speaking too softly. "What kind of visitors?" he asked.

"Arabs."

"Arabs? Here, in Havana?"

"Yes. There is some kind of business taking place. It also involves one of our officials. I don't understand what is going on, but it sounds mysterious. I know we should not spy on our Russian friends, but it may be good to be vigilant. One never knows what service we can render to our own party."

"They're speaking in English," reported Davey.

"Yes, I gather that neither speaks the other's language. I saw the Arabs arrive a few minutes back while you were busy on the other wall."

Davey adjusted his ear position and began to catch some of the words.

" . . . for you to do . . . not a good time in . . . six or more of . . ." It was gibberish.

One of the occupants, apparently Russian, crossed the room and stood opposite Davey's ear. Davey could hear him clearly. "Then, our relationship is finished and you are on your own. I need not remind you of our previous statements concerning your operations."

"You . . . no concern . . . for the complete annihilation . . . it is . . . forward in the work of God . . ."

Davey shook his head. "I don't know what they are talking about." Inside, the presence of Arabs talking to Russians triggered all sorts of alarm flags in Davey's mind. What *were* Arabs doing in Cuba? They were speaking again. Suddenly, the hair on the back of his neck stiffened. The Russian had used the word "cylinder," but Davey missed the complete sentence. Nevertheless, it took him only a moment to connect the event of the Bear ditching and his inspection of the contents of its bomb bay with the business taking place on the other side of the thin wall. Those cylinders were being transferred to Arabic control! Try as he might, he could make no sense of the rest of the conversation. The Russian had moved back across the room, and after another three or four minutes Davey heard the Arabs leave.

Peeking around the door, he and Cordero watched the Arabs walk down the hallway to the elevator. There were two of them, in Western dress. One wore a brown-and-white-check headdress.

For the rest of the morning, Davey was tingling with concern and anticipation. Cordero made no further mention of the situation. By noon, they had completed the inside walls of the room. No more conversations would be heard unless the occupants of the Russian room held a shouting match.

It was nearly noon by the time Davey and Cordero cleaned up the debris from their morning's work. "A good first day. You learn quickly," complimented Cordero, patting Davey's shoulder.

"It isn't exactly technically demanding," said Davey with a smile.

"True enough, but it all contributes. Our foreign friends will have a comfortable place to rest once our work here is finished." Cordero surveyed the room. "Considering our late start and the fact that I had to check on our other workers, we have done well. We will do even better after lunch."

Tatiana was waiting at the bottom of the work elevator, a paper bag in one hand.

"Well, hello," said Davey, stepping off the elevator.

Cordero nodded cordially at the woman and walked away to join several of his workers who were sitting on packing crates, preparing to eat.

Davey took the sack and led Tatiana aside to a low stone wall, where they stood while he pulled out the bread and fruit. A still-cold bottle of red soda was in the bottom. Extracting it, he popped off the cap by using the edge of the wall, then took a deep swallow. "Thank you, that tastes good."

"I have some news for you," said Tatiana.

"Oh?"

"First, my grandmother, who is as antirevolutionary and as stubborn as my father, sends you a message from your control in the States. You are to be watchful for three men who are Arabic."

Her words caught Davey completely off guard. He was expecting some word of the disposition of the cylinders, not a message from the Old Man. And by way of Tatiana's grandmother? He had been told nothing of such a contact and had assumed Rudy Ordonez would be his relay. Before he had time to mull his thought around, Tatiana continued with the second part of her briefing.

"As for the activity at the airport, an American airplane landed just after dawn and proceeded toward the shack. The authorities put up a large military tent after we were there last night, and the airplane moved almost all the way into it . . . "

"Airplane?" interrupted Davey. "What kind of airplane?"

"A small civilian airplane with American registration numbers. They didn't report anything more about it, but it had only a pilot. Several hours after it landed, it took off again and flew inland."

"Did it pick up anything?"

"I don't know. There was only the pilot when it left. Immediately after that, a covered military truck was loaded with two canvas-covered cylindrical objects, then it left the airport. It has been followed and my father says it is being watched. I am to bring you there."

Davey munched on the bread as Tatiana took the soda from his hand and drank. "Leaving after only a half-day's work may create an awkward situation," he mused.

Tatiana handed him back the bottle. "It is up to you."

"I've seen the Arabs, at least two of them."

"Already?"

"They are billeted here. The two met with a couple Russians this morning, in a room adjacent to where we were working."

Tatiana waited for Davey's decision.

"I have to go, regardless. Are you certain they didn't load the contents of the cylinders on the airplane?"

"I don't know. I wasn't told."

"You have your car?"

"Yes. It is around on the other side."

Davey glanced over at Cordero and the other men. They were paying him and Tatiana no attention. There was a chance that Cordero would think of him as just a shiftless worker if he slipped away. But it would probably blow any chances of resuming a cover in the working force at the Icar.

"Go back to it. I will be there in a few minutes."

Davey continued to chew on his bread as Tatiana disappeared around the far side of the hotel. Trying not to betray any urgency, he finished the meager lunch, rolled up the sack, and looked around as if searching for a place to dispose of it. Still clutching the crumpled bag, he walked into the hotel lobby. Quickly, he made his way down one of the hallways and left by the fire exit. The Chevy was waiting across the parking lot.

"Okay, let's go," he urged, sliding into the right-hand front seat.

It took almost twenty minutes to wind through the noon street crowds and reach the southern outskirts of the city. Tatiana remained on the southern highway for another thirty minutes before swinging off onto a secondary road.

"How far away is it?" asked Davey.

"Another seventy kilometers. It is a place I know well. An old abandoned cane collection plant."

As they rode, Davey pondered the Arabic connection, if there were one. The two he spotted back at the Icar were obviously the ones the Old Man had alerted him to. Their conversation with the Russians, particularly the use of the word "cylinder," seemed to verify that. A nuclear device in the hands of the Soviets, or even the Cubans, was one thing, but in the hands of Arabs? There was an overriding chance that they were terrorists. It didn't take any great deductive ability to reason that they were being supplied with some kind of weapon to be used against Israel—or the United

States. What was the role of the airplane? It was a short-range craft. No way could they use it to return to the Middle East. That meant that they might be considering a clandestine entry into the southern U.S. But, with the push on surveillance for drug trafficking, they had little chance of flying across the Gulf undetected. The Coast Guard was even using leased Navy E-2 surveillance and control aircraft, with a look-down capability, not to mention Navy forces themselves who were augmenting the Coasties.

Did the aircraft pick up the contents of the cylinders? If it did, and he and Tatiana were on the way to where the truck had gone, they were on a wild goose chase. Empty cylinders would not tell him anything he had not already learned from his underwater surveillance. He should have insisted on a more alert watch of the airport shack. He could damn well be chasing an empty truck while the Bear cargo was on the way to God knows where. Davey didn't enjoy the feeling of being outsmarted by circumstances.

"They were sure the truck took the cylinders?" he asked.

"Two cylindrical objects, covered with canvas, was the report. Is that what you are looking for? Some type of cylinders?"

Davey recalled their earlier conversation about what was in the shack. Apparently she had not known. "Yes, there are two silver cylinders, about five feet long."

"Whatever they loaded on the truck was covered."

They were bouncing along through open country with only an occasional bohio off to one side or the other, the terrain rolling and largely unobstructed by foliage or trees, mostly sugarcane fields not yet ready for harvest. Tatiana seemed to know exactly where she was headed, ignoring some of the intersections and changing directions at others, hardly slowing as she swung from one back road to another. During the next fifteen minutes, they passed only one other vehicle, a decrepit four-door Ford, probably a 1955 model. Tatiana and the other driver exchanged friendly waves as they passed in opposite directions, Davey noting that a more apt description of the Ford would be four-doorless.

Tatiana spun off onto a cane-cart pathway and let her hands rest loosely on the steering wheel as the wheels of the charging Chevy settled into the deep ruts. The car steered itself along a dusty trail that was beginning to gently climb into low rolling hills.

They crested one of the rises and Tatiana slowed. Up ahead, Davey could see another vehicle, an ancient pickup, too rusted to reveal its original color, although there were remnants of a paint job, probably blue at one time. It was off to one side of the crude road, and Tatiana pulled the Chevy clear of the ruts to stop beside it.

"I don't see much," commented Davey.

"We walk the rest of the way."

The area was planted in sugarcane, but the stalks were low and obviously thirsty. Still, their gray tufted tops were shoulder high and provided a measure of cover as he and Tatiana climbed toward the crest of the next ridge. The early afternoon sun was just about at the broil point, and before they had struggled across many of the parched rows Davey was soaked from the outpouring of sweat. Every pore was drooling from the heat of the outdoor oven, and it took little imagination to understand the rigors of a full eight-hour day in such a sun. To add to his discomfort, the dry dirt of the scorched surface gave off an irritant that was plugging his nostrils and coating his lips. Probably dust mixed with some pesticides or powdered fertilizer. Whatever the mix, it was bitter to the taste and extremely potent. His eyes watered as though he had a severe head cold. He was just about to suggest that they stop and breathe some undisturbed air when Tatiana held up one hand and led him slowly through the cane.

Ahead, down the slope of the rise, was a small cluster of weathered shacks, windowless and facing away from them. Beside one was a canvas-covered stake truck. Davey's pulse quickened as he saw the ends of two silver cylinders under the canvas and, off to one side of the truck, a low winged airplane. He recognized it as a white Piper, probably a six-place, since the fuselage was so long and the nose seemed stretched. A long, wide swath of cleared dirt led from the airplane back across the field. A dirt runway.

There was little activity, although Davey could see several armed guards standing in the shade of the shacks. There could be others inside.

Tatiana carefully led him closer until they were within forty yards or so but still on the top of the rise and hidden by the cane.

"Tatiana?" The words hissed from the cane cover directly ahead.

"Papa," acknowledged the woman as Rudy Ordonez emerged from his hiding place.

"The cylinders are still on the truck," reported Ordonez. "There are three guards plus two others, probably one is the pilot. Several others left a short while ago in a car."

"I need to get a closer look," said Davey. "This may be my last chance."

"I don't know," replied Ordonez. "Everything is right out in the open."

Davey peered at his watch. Almost 3 P.M. "The airplane is tied down. I can see the lines."

"Down!" cautioned Tatiana as two men came around from in front of the nearest shack. They conferred for a moment before the armed guards laid down their weapons and all four men proceeded to the back of the truck. One jumped up on the bed and disappeared under the canvas. Another stood at the end of the truck, holding one end of the cylinder. Slowly he slid it backward, the other two men taking positions on each side until only one end remained on the truck, held in place by the fourth man. Together, they lowered it to the ground and pulled off the top half of the container.

"They must have opened it back at Jose Marti. The last time I saw them, they were welded shut," observed Davey.

"Look at that," directed Ordonez.

The men were lifting out a smaller cylindrical object. Davey judged it to be close to five feet in length by about ten inches in diameter. It probably weighed less than two hundred pounds, for one man surrendered his hold and ran to open the rear cargo door of the aircraft. It was on the far side from Davey and the others, but they could see the men sliding the object into the aircraft's cabin.

"Probably took out the rear seats," observed Davey.

"What is that?" asked Tatiana. A fifth man had emerged from the shack and was carrying a woman. A very stiff woman.

"It's a mannequin," stated Davey. The dummy was clothed in jeans and a flowery blouse. The hair was red. Except for the obvious stiffness, it was a very realistic figure. One of the men who had loaded the cylinder crossed around to the right side of the airplane, stepped up on the wing, and aided the newcomer in placing the dummy inside the cabin, both men letting the figure flop out of sight behind the front right passenger seat. One of the men apparently locked the door before they stepped down off the wing.

"What do you suppose that is all about?" asked Ordonez.

"Beats the hell out of me. It looks like they're buttoning up for the day."

The men were checking the tie-down lines, and the two militiamen had retrieved their weapons and were taking their positions by the left wing tip of the Piper.

The others went into the shack.

"Damn," muttered Davey. The entire area, although secluded from any main region of travel, was too exposed to allow any further undetected approach. "We'll have to wait until dark."

"Why don't I go and get us some food and water. We've got a good five hours before sunset," suggested Tatiana.

"Take your father with you," suggested Davey. He could see that the older man was strained from the loss of body water and the fatigue of the wait. Ordonez made no objection.

Tatiana leaned close to Davey. "I will be back in about four hours. Don't try anything foolish."

Davey was surprised at her concern. He shared her caution.

The sun was just beginning to slide below the horizon when Tatiana returned. Davey took one of the two plastic gallon containers and swallowed half of the water in it before saying anything. "I thought I wasn't going to last. I'm cooked."

"Here," said Tatiana, offering a slab of thick-crusted bread and a chunk of processed meat. She also had several grapefruit and a dish of greasy pork. Davey wolfed down the heavy food. It was delicious. Sucking on one of the grapefruit, he brought Tatiana up to date. "A car came about an hour ago and took two of the men away. As far as I can tell, there are only three down there—the two guards and one in the shack."

Tatiana studied the scene. "I think I can be of help."

Davey looked at her, waiting.

"After dark, I will take the car and backtrack to come down the road there by the shack. I will have car trouble and perhaps draw off the guards, or at least one of them."

"That's too risky. What would a woman be doing out here at this time of night, all by herself?"

Tatiana looked down her nose. "You think this is suburban USA? We travel safely in Cuba. I am on my way home from a day working in the city."

Davey decided not to pursue the subject. He would gladly accept any help. Besides, he had a feeling that the daughter of Rudy Ordonez could well take care of herself. "What kind of car trouble?" he asked.

"The real kind. I have a bad radiator hose. I will loosen the tape and let it leak. I will ask them for some water and help in replacing the tape."

That would be simple enough.

"All right. Let's wait until we think the one in the shack is asleep. That may cut down on the number of participants in this little drama."

Tatiana opened the other water bottle and drank heavily. "It is still an oven," she commented. "I wish there was at least a breeze." Searching the skies, she pointed to the northwest. "There are some rain clouds. If they come this way, it will make the waiting easier. We could go wait in the car. It is more comfortable."

"No, I need to make sure no one else shows up. Why don't you go on back and rest? Let's plan for midnight. Would that be too late?"

"Not if I had stayed in town with a lover."

"Good, then that's it."

"I will stay here with you."

"Listen, there's no sense in both of us being miserable. Go wait in the car."

Tatiana hesitated as if she were going to say something, but picked up her water bottle and disappeared among the cane.

The rain clouds did come their way, and by 11:00 P.M. a steady drizzle was falling, with thunder and lightning to the west displaying a vivid promise of more concentrated moisture. Davey made his way back to the Chevy and woke Tatiana, who was asleep—and dry—in the front seat.

"You look drowned," were her first words.

"I'm cooled off, that's for sure. Let's get started."

"Give me thirty minutes to get back around. I'll stop short of the shacks and they'll have to come to me."

Davey grabbed her shoulder. "Be careful. They're not stupid down there. Any sign of trouble and you get out fast. Forget about me. I can take care of myself."

Tatiana's expression softened. "I would wish you good luck, Yanqui, but I am not sure I would mean it."

"I don't need luck. I need a good distraction."

Tatiana unbuttoned a second button of her blouse. "I can guarantee I will provide that."

Davey shut the door and made his way back to his surveillance spot.

It was 11:42 P.M. when he spotted the dim single headlight of the Nomad bouncing along the road leading by the shack. The light stopped twenty yards short of the farthest structure and blinked once before expiring. Davey could see one of the guards walk out to the road and peer into the darkness. A moment later, he saw the huddled form of Tatiana approaching in the rain. She called to the guard and he trotted to meet her. They spoke and then started back up the road toward the Chevy.

Davey made his way quickly around to the far shack and used it as a shield before approaching the truck. The remaining guard was still by the airplane, under one wing, crouching out of the rain, which was now heavy. Moving slowly, Davey inched his way toward the truck and worked around the far side to the covered bed. Climbing under the canvas top, he stooped beside the two containers. One was empty, the other still welded! He knew no more now than when in the Bear's bomb bay.

The Chevy restarted and he watched the car pull up beside the shacks. The guard who had intercepted Tatiana raised the hood and looked around the engine compartment with his flashlight. Tatiana had produced a large roll of plastic tape, and the man bent over, apparently wrapping it around the faulty hose. Straightening up, he walked over to a topless fifty-five-gallon drum and dipped Tatiana's drinking bottle into it. He poured the water into the radiator. Again, he inspected the hose, and apparently satisfied, he closed the hood. Tatiana and he talked, he tilting his head and she laughing and raising her hands in animated conversation. Finally, she took him by the hand and they climbed into the Chevy.

The other guard had watched the scene with some interest but stayed under the aircraft's wing. Davey had no weapon. Fifteen minutes later, the Chevy's door opened and the first guard walked away. Tatiana started the engine and drove off down the road.

The guard under the wing crawled out and stood, his head raised and mouth open to drink of the rain. Then he ran to meet his companion. Davey watched the two of them animatedly talking, in all probability discussing the physical attributes of Tatiana. Staying low, Davey sprinted behind the aircraft and climbed onto the wing. Inside the cabin, he could see a silver cylinder laying between the two front seats. One of the second row of seats had been removed, as had both of the last-row seats. On top of the cylinder was a small red object, probably a safety cover over the arming switch. The guards' laughter made him look up. They were walking back toward the near shack. Davey tried the aircraft door, but it was locked. There was nothing further he could accomplish, and at least one of the guards would be returning to the plane at any moment. Jumping from the wing, he ran back across the road and into the cover of the cane field.

Where could they be taking the cylinder in such a short-ranged airplane? The presence of what appeared to be an arming switch alarmed him. That would indicate that the cylinders had enclosed some sort of weapon. A weapon with radioactive components. How small could a nuclear bomb be? Davey knew that there were nuclear artillery shells considerably smaller than the cylinders. But he doubted that nuclear weapons would be handled within Cuba without the presence of much more security than just a couple of armed guards.

Under the cover of the midnight darkness and the cloudy, wet sky, it was easy enough to return to his waiting place. He needed to get a look at the cylinder in better light. Perhaps in the early morning, just before sunrise, he would get another opportunity.

By 4:00 A.M. he was soaked, cold, disgusted, and sleepy. He had to seek the shelter of the Chevy, at least for a few minutes. Tatiana had returned and was waiting for him. She had him disrobe so she could pat him dry with some rags from the rear of the station wagon.

They both dozed until the first light of dawn, when the roar of an aircraft engine awakened them. Davey slipped on his trousers and ran back to his surveillance location, cursing under his breath.

The Piper was just lifting off from the dirt runway.

Chapter 10

July 4, 6:00 A.M.
USS *Abraham Lincoln* (CVN-72)

"C aptain's on the bridge."
The quiet announcement by the boatswain's mate of the watch continued a time-honored tradition. The bridge watch of the giant carrier was routinely alert and proper, but with the ship's captain on the bridge the watch became meticulously formal and very exact in its conduct of managing the world's mightiest fighting machine. The innocent small talk that helped keep the watch alert during the long night was a luxury never indulged in once the commanding officer set foot on the gray steel deck of the most holy of shipboard holies.

Captain "Big John" Flannary accepted the cup of hot coffee from the junior officer of the deck and climbed onto the tall pedestal chair that was his exclusive property. It was well cushioned, with comfortable armrests and an adjustable back. All leather, it was a plush executive chair, but not extravagant in any sense. When at sea, Captain Flannary spent more hours in that chair than he did in his bed, at his table, or in his head, combined. More than any other object on the warship, the chair, with the almost constant presence of the man who had earned it through years of dedicated service and extraordinary skills, was the crew's security blanket. No matter how rough the seas, or how dark the night, or how demanding the schedule, when the captain was in his chair, all was well.

"You get some sleep, Captain?" asked the tall lieutenant wearing the officer-of-the-deck arm band.

"Yes, Mike, it felt good." It *had* felt good. He had spent thirty-six consecutive hours in that chair, or wandering the bridge, as the *Lincoln*'s air wing went through its paces. The FA-18 Hornets, the feisty A-7 Corsairs, the bulb-nosed Intruders and Prowlers of the A-6 attack and ECM squadrons, the long-ranging S-3 Vikings, the helicopter Sea Kings of the antisubmarine warfare forces, and the dish-topped, turboprop E-3 Hawkeyes of the command and control link of the giant carrier had all been blasting off the forward end of the mighty warship and dropping back aboard on the canted recovery deck for the full day and a half that Big John had just given to the U.S. Navy with absolutely no reservations. Now, he had been afforded the luxury of eight hours of undisturbed sleep—a rarity, indeed—and was ready to resume his presence on the bridge in his twenty-four-hours-a-day role as one of the most authoritative officers in the military services, the commanding officer of a combatant at sea. Even while he had slept, every act by every man on the ship had been an extension of his authority and responsibility. His was a position of absolute command, and absolute accountability. His job was the goal of every man who pinned on those wings of gold and gave his life—and that of his family—to the United States Navy. He was the king, and around his throne was his gray castle, it in turn surrounded by a moat made up of the oceans of the world. As an absolute monarch, he had only one goal in mind: when he was called on to lead his men and machines in harm's way, he and they would be ready.

But for the moment he could sit and sip his coffee and watch the rising sun ooze slowly above the eastern horizon. This was a national holiday, and in its honor, there would be a two-hour sabbatical. Flight operations, normally underway by this time, would commence at 0800.

Big John shifted his six-foot-three, 191-pound frame to a more comfortable position, one in which he could cross his legs. The fur collar of his brown goatskin flight jacket was pulled up around his neck. There was still a trace of morning chill as the *Lincoln* plowed northward across the Atlantic. Big John liked a chilled bridge, one open to the night, or with ports aside to let in the sea breeze. A warm bridge was a drowsy bridge, a place of complacency and comfort, two conditions that had no place aboard a steaming man-of-war.

A slight ground swell was lifting and lowering the *Lincoln* with an almost hypnotic rhythm as the carrier made a steady twenty knots. There were little wind and only a few lingering night cumuli around them. That would change as the sun climbed and passed overhead. Then, the rising heat, reflected from the gently heaving water, would condense and billow heavenward as great towering white clouds, which would store the moisture until they were saturated. By late afternoon, thunderstorms would be releasing torrents of ship-drenching rain. Even with such potential, however, the weather was a vast improvement over that which had caused them to exit the narrow entrance to Guantanamo Bay at less than ten knots. Fog and drizzle and shifting winds, left over from the storm that had bathed Cuba for three days, had marked the end of their grueling operational readiness training period. Not until they had hit open ocean had the weather calmed. Today should be a good day.

The flight deck crewmen were already appearing, either walking relaxed toward the aircraft or riding the bright yellow "mules," the small tractors that they would use to position the scheduled aircraft for the first morning launch. The two-hour stand-down meant little in their unchanging way of life at sea: position the launch, launch the launch, recover the launch. A multicolored chorus of death dancers, they performed their precise choreography over and over; their yellow, red, green, brown, and blue jerseys clothing a complex mix of performers who created that most unique ballet of naval aviation—flight deck operations. They would duck past sucking inlets, crouch under screaming tailpipes, yank steel chocks from in front of straining wheels, roll away from rapidly accelerating tons of metal, and rush headlong to dive under the tail of a metal dragon as it pounced its fire-breathing body onto the only bare space on the flight deck. On occasion, one of the dancers would stand too tall and be blown over the side by a sudden burst of jet exhaust, or fail to see the end of a broken arresting cable snapping forward until he suddenly found himself standing on stumps instead of feet. Such was their performance, many of them still a year or so away from their first solid shave. Big John Flannary knew that if he ever wore stars, those kids meandering onto the flight deck, munching leftover breakfast goodies and gently jousting with one another, would deserve a lion's share of the credit. He had a son just a few years younger than those going about ship's business. When his son's day came, Big John hoped it would be in a warm, dry cockpit, not in a pair of bell-bottoms walking a slippery deck. In the latter case, he would be just as proud but much more concerned. A pilot was a trained professional, with an array of protective devices that gave him a fighting chance for survival whatever his airborne activity; some of those kids down there had only eight weeks of boot camp, a couple months of specialized schooling, and less than a half year of experience aboard the *Lincoln*. Yet, they would be expected to perform as expertly as the two-thousand-hour jet jockey strapped into his multimillion-dollar aluminum cocoon. And they would perform expertly, God bless 'em.

"Where are the *Bradley* and the *Voge?*" asked Big John.

"On station, Captain," replied the OOD. "They joined us right after midnight."

The *Lincoln* was steaming independently back toward Norfolk, although she had one destroyer, the USS *Waddell* (DDG 24), an early guided-missile ship, in company for plane guard during flight operations. *Bradley* and *Voge*, the matched pair of Garcia-class frigates, would remain with the two ships for the remainder of the cruise back to Norfolk. Not exactly a Carrier Battle Group, but it would give the four skippers an opportunity to practice steaming formations. Although Big John was senior by rank and his ship would be the guide, he was very much aware that the destroyer and frigate commanding officers were much more experienced seamen than he and probably a bit leery of a flyboy-sailor who had less overall shipboard duty than they had on a darkened bridge. With that in mind, he knew they were completely content to keep station on *him*, rather than the other way around.

At the moment, the *Waddell* was twenty-six thousand yards astern, the *Voge* off the port quarter at ten thousand yards, and the *Bradley* at thirty thousand yards and opening to the east for some independent ship-training exercises.

Big John much preferred blue water to the restricted inter-island channels and more shallow depths that had provided the *Lincoln* a passage from Guantanamo through the lower Bahamas to the open sea. A carrier commander liked plenty of open water. Right now, he had horizon-to-horizon maneuvering room and five thousand fathoms below his keel.

Some three hundred and thirty miles west lay the east coast of southern Florida. Midway between the early morning bathers at

Fort Lauderdale and the *Lincoln* sat the southern tip of Abaco Island, one of the northernmost spits of sand in the Bahamas. The *Lincoln's* air wing would be using it for mock attacks in the late morning.

On board the *Bradley*, the crew was taking a muster after a man-overboard alert. It was just a drill, but part of the procedure was a quick muster of ship's company—for the logical determination of just who it was that had fallen over the side. Commander Ted Darly was observing the performance of his officers and men from his own pedestal chair on the bridge. He was well pleased. The rapid muster had determined the identity of the "man overboard," and the motor whale boat crew had made an excellent recovery of "Oscar," the duty dummy for such drills. Darly nodded to his XO and directed "Secure from Man Overboard Drill." As the ship's routine returned to normal, he passed out of the pilothouse onto the open wing of the bridge. On the westward horizon he could see the *Lincoln* riding majestically along her northward course. The *Bradley's* bridge chronometer indicated 0655.

His crew was well trained. Every drill they had conducted since leaving their station near the sunken Bear had been executed in an excellent manner. He had worked them hard and was beginning to have guilt feelings about his early-morning drills. They really didn't need that.

"Boats!" he yelled into the pilothouse.

"Yes, sir?"

"Pipe holiday routine. Let's take a day off. The regular watch can handle anything the *Lincoln* wants us to do."

"Aye, aye, sir!"

After all, it was the Fourth of July. All they needed were some fireworks.

One hundred and fifty miles east, passing directly over the airstrip serving Eleuthera Island, ex-Iranian Air Force Capt. Ardeshir Zadefi checked his Piper Cherokee's fuel supply. He had been airborne since shortly before five and his fuel was less than half gone. If the midnight position report of his target and its projected movement was correct, he had plenty of fuel to accomplish his mission. Still, the airstrip below was tempting. He could land and refuel, which would give him additional search time, but he had no wish to be confronted by customs officials. He had no flight plan, and the silver cylinder strapped down behind and between the front seats would create an international incident, to be sure. No, he would continue on. God was guiding his hand. Reaching over, he patted the head of the female mannequin strapped into the passenger seat. Checking his charts a last time, he let the nose edge over to a compass heading of sixty-five degrees. That should do it. If he did not have visual contact with the *Lincoln* at his ETA—his estimated time of arrival—he would start an expanding square search. Additional altitude would extend his visual horizon, and now that he was considerably lighter in fuel, he could afford to climb. Raising the nose and adjusting his power, he headed for twelve thousand feet. His instrument panel clock registered 7:15 A.M. Beside him, secure under the seat belt that held his inanimate companion, lay a short, broad sword.

Big John watched the early launch being spotted. First, the steam catapults would sling the gawky E-2C off the bow of the *Lincoln* followed by a pair of FA-18s for a simulated combat air patrol sortie.

A tanker KA-6 would follow thirty minutes later and the Hornets could top off and engage in some air-to-air tactics before being recovered. The sequence would be repeated until all of the fighter jocks had an opportunity to get their jollies for the day, then the A-7s could try their hand at some masthead bombing and strafing, provided Big John could convince one of the accompanying frigates to stream a tow target.

Interwoven among the fighter and attack launches, the high-winged ASW hunters—the sonobuoy and depth charge–laden Grumman S-3s—would keep up a steady hunt for real and/or imagined submarines. They could get lucky, in which case the Sikorsky Sea Kings would join in the hunt. The water was deep and the Soviets routinely transitted the area on their way to Cuba. Thus, the game could become very realistic, and his ASW forces would get a workout in a few short hours that would be more valuable than days of exercises.

The Air Boss, a veteran fighter pilot who had held the job of Air Officer since before Big John had taken command, entered the covered bridge and gave Big John the latest revision of the flight schedule. "Everything looks good, Captain. We should get in one hell of a day of flying."

Big John clipped the sheet to a board hung before his chair. "Keep it moving, Jim. And let's have a safe one."

"The only way, Captain, the only way." Touching the front of his fore-and-aft cap in a casual but respectful salute, the commander left for his station in Primary Flight Control, the carrier's equivalent of an air traffic control tower, located just aft and on the inboard side of the island superstructure, where the Air Boss had a commanding view of all flight deck and traffic pattern activities.

Promptly at 0800, the air control E-2, its flying saucer radar housing rotating steadily, bolted off the port catapult, leaving behind it a small trail of dissipating steam and a scurry of catapult personnel who quickly rerigged the launch shuttle and prepared to spot the second Hornet. The first was already poised on the starboard catapult.

Big John watched every detail of the carefully orchestrated procedure.

The two Hornets launched less than a second apart, the flight leader first from the port side, then his wingman. By the time they had retracted their landing gear and flaps, they were a tight two-plane section pulling straight up into the blue sky. The KA-6 tanker was spotted and the flight deck personnel relaxed. They had thirty minutes of breathing time before the next launch.

"Bridge, Combat."

Big John looked back at the bridge intercom speaker as the OOD answered, "Go ahead, Combat."

"Big Eye reports a slow-moving target forty-seven miles east, closing. Designated Bogie Alpha."

"Roger, let us know when he's ID'd."

"Combat, aye."

Almost immediately, a distress call erupted from the overhead squawk box, "Mayday! Mayday! Anyone this circuit, this is Piper Cherokee three-nine-tango. Mayday! Mayday!"

The airborne E-2 responded immediately on the VHF emergency frequency, "Piper three-nine-tango, squawk seven-seven-zero-zero, ident, over."

"Squawking emergency! Mayday! Mayday!"

"That's Bogie Alpha," interjected Combat.

"What is the nature of your emergency, three-nine-tango?" asked the controller in Big Eye.

"I'm lost, low on fuel. My compass is not reading correctly."

"What's your altitude?"

"Twelve thousand feet."

"Roger, take up a heading of southwest. The island of Eleuthera will be ahead, one hundred and three miles."

"I don't have that much fuel."

"God, what a dummy," remarked Big John. "There isn't a cloud in the sky and he must have passed more than a half-dozen islands to get way the hell out here."

"What is your endurance?" came a second question from the E-2.

"Fifteen, maybe twenty minutes . . . I see a ship! I see an aircraft carrier ahead. I can make it to the carrier!"

"Stay away from the carrier, three-nine-tango. He is conducting flight operations."

"I can land on the carrier!"

"Negative, three-nine-tango. I will lead you toward the nearest land."

"I will land on the carrier. I have my wife and small child with me. We cannot survive a water landing."

Big John could see the Piper, high and to the west, heading straight for the *Lincoln*.

"PriFly, are you monitoring this?" asked Big John on his intercom.

"Yes, sir."

"Can we take him on board?"

"That depends on him, Captain. The cant's clear, but you can see we're spotted all around it."

Big John shook his head. The canted landing deck was clear, but his air wing aircraft were solid along the inboard side and the first third of the outboard side. He had no idea as to the Piper pilot's ability. "Get all personnel away from there and rig the barrier. He sounds like he's going to come down whether we like it or not." Inside, Big John knew there was a chance the Piper could make a successful landing. There were thirty-five knots of wind over the deck and the light aircraft would only be going sixty knots or so at touchdown. With such a slow relative landing speed, twenty-five knots, any reasonably efficient pilot had a fighting chance to pull it off. Of course, a reasonably efficient pilot wouldn't have allowed himself to get into such a foolish predicament. Big John could see the two Hornets coming up behind the Piper, undoubtedly under the control of Big Eye. They had dirtied up by dropping their landing gear and lowering full flaps, but they would be unable to slow sufficiently to keep station on the Cherokee. They eased by, eyeballing the Piper, and Big Eye reported in.

"Home Plate, Dipper One reports occupants to be a man and a woman. Child could be out of sight in rear seat."

Big John could see the barrier rise, the khaki straps of the interwoven net ballooning aft under force of the relative wind. The Piper was on a left downwind, wheels down, in good position. Just prior to coming abeam the approach edge of the landing deck, it started a turn-in. The pilot was using full flaps and power to slow his aircraft. He seemed to know exactly what he was doing. Big John watched the ready Sea King helicopter lift off and take its plane guard station aft of the *Lincoln*.

"Hell, he looks like he's been out here before," remarked the OOD. "A perfect lineup."

The Piper seemed to hang in the air for a moment, then settled toward the ramp. Big John noted the relative wind was thirty-seven knots, right down the deck. Nose high, power cut, the Piper touched down between the first and second wire and stopped just short of the barrier.

"Let's get him off of there and clear the deck. We've got airborne," ordered Big John.

The first man on the wing of the Piper was a yellow-shirted plane handler. Two others grabbed the wing tips and a fourth stood by with a pair of Hornet wheel chocks.

The yellow-shirt opened the Piper's door and stared straight into the lifeless eyes of the female mannequin. Puzzled, he looked across at the pilot, who was holding a small black box in his outstretching left hand. His right hand was resting on a large silver cylinder strapped between the seats.

"This is a nuclear weapon and I am holding a remote detonator, which is activated by a dead man's switch. If, for any reason, I release it, or my hand is forcibly removed from it, we will all be in the center of a nuclear explosion."

The yellow-shirt was confused. "Sir, I . . ."

"I release this and we all die! Do you understand?"

"Yessir."

"Get me your captain. I will speak with no one else."

The yellow-shirt backed down the wing, holding out his hands. "Don't anyone come up here! Chief!" He dropped off the wing in front of an older yellow-shirt. "He says he has a nuclear bomb. He wants to see the captain."

"Holy shit! Let me talk to him."

"No! He says only the captain. He's crazy, Chief. That's a dummy woman, and I saw the bomb."

"Get one of the Marines. We'll shoot the son of a bitch."

"No! Get the captain! He's clutching a dead man's switch."

The chief looked at the dark eyes peering back from within the Piper's cabin. "Tell him the captain's on the way."

Big John had watched the yellow-shirt climb down and excitedly talk to his chief. Picking up his binoculars, he searched the Piper's cabin. The woman was not moving. Hell, she was a dummy! And the man had his right arm between the seats, resting his hand on a silver cylinder. What in hell was going on?

The flight deck officer burst onto the bridge. "Captain! The pilot claims he has a nuclear weapon! He wants to talk to you."

"My God, I've got a whole flight deck full of people and no one can overpower him?"

"He has his hand on a dead man's switch, Captain. If he releases it, or we force it off . . ."

"Jesus . . . let's go!"

By the time Big John arrived at the side of the Piper, the Marine security guards were present, their weapons at the ready, but they were being held back by the yellow-shirted chief.

"Everybody keep calm," cautioned Big John. "Don't try anything. Let me talk to him." Climbing onto the low wing, he opened the cabin door. "I'm Captain Flannary. What do you think you are doing?" Big John could hardly keep his eyes from the pilot's right hand, which was pressed down over the red lever on a small hand-held black box.

"I know exactly what I am doing. Select two men to assist me. I will go to the flag bridge and we will talk."

"We will do nothing of the kind. This is an American Navy combatant, in international waters. If that thing is a nuclear weapon, you are committing an act of piracy."

The pilot replied calmly, "This *is* a nuclear weapon, Captain, and I am fully prepared to discharge it if you do not do *exactly* as I direct. You do not have a flag on board, therefore I will be led to the flag bridge and we will talk. I will not give this instruction a third time." The man glanced down at the cylinder.

The man apparently had a military background, perhaps naval, and he was obviously a Middle Easterner.

"All right. We will do as you say. Just be careful with that thing. Whatever you are after I am sure can be worked out."

Zadefi smiled. "I doubt it, but we must try, yes, Captain? I will need two men to carry the weapon."

Big John turned and spoke to the men gathered below. "I want two men to help with this cylinder. The man accompanying it is not to be harmed or even threatened. That is a direct order and I want it passed throughout the ship immediately. We will do exactly as he directs. Chief, give me two men. The rest of you clear the flight deck."

The chief selected an athletic-looking fellow yellow-shirt. Together, they replaced Big John on the wing. Slowly, with agonizing care, they extracted the cylinder through the rear cargo door and started across the flight deck. The chief led, carrying the front of the cylinder. Zadefi stayed a pace behind them, his eyes shifting warily, in his left hand a short sword, in his right the black box. Big John could see the depressed dead man's switch. There was no way anyone could reach out and grab the box before the man could release his grip. "Stay several paces behind me, Captain. Any closer and I release the switch—and pray I do not stumble," Zadefi said wryly as they started across the flight deck for an open hatch at the base of the island. Big John followed, his mind somewhat boggled by the fact that his ship was being commandeered by only one man with a small sword—and a nuclear weapon.

The ladder to the flag bridge was steep and narrow, and it took the small group five minutes to reach the covered outside wing of the bridge. Finally they passed inside and placed the cylinder on the chart table. The yellow-shirts hastily left.

"I am Ardeshir Zadefi. I am a soldier of God, a member of the New Shaheen Palestinian group for the reestablishment of Palestine and the elimination of the Jewish and American states."

"That is a big order," answered Big John. "You are also a military man?"

"Yes. I was a member of the Shah's forces, the air force, before the demise of that devil."

"I thought as much. You brought the Piper aboard like a veteran."

"That is of no consequence."

"I suppose not."

"Listen carefully. The time for execution of my orders is only as long as I can stay awake and keep my hand on this detonator switch—and I am very tired. You will contact your president and tell him of this situation. He will agree to do four things: first, the Jews will release all Arab prisoners; second, he will agree to pull out all American military personnel from the Middle East; third, he will cut off all contact with the state of Israel; and fourth, he will provide himself as a hostage to our group, to be held while negotiations take place for the occupation of Israel by Arab troops."

"That is ridiculous, and you know it."

"Is the death of every man on this ship the price you wish to pay for testing this situation?"

"Oh, I will do as you say. But the president will not agree."

"No? What did you do when your hostages were being held in Iran? Or even the few in Lebanon? You did nothing that would risk their lives. Here, you have more than six thousand souls to consider. This is a complete American city, Captain. I should also tell you that this is only one of several weapons we have in our possession, so this is only the first situation you Americans must deal with."

"It will take time."

"I am prepared to wait—a reasonable time."

"Until you tire and release the switch?"

"Yes, but we can provide for my rest."

Big John wondered aloud, "How?"

"There must be a compartment on this bridge where the admiral can sleep. I will occupy it, provided it is closed off and lockable. While inside, you cannot approach me without my detection. If you do, I will detonate the weapon. You will not know when I am sleeping or when I am awake. I will also require that the ventilation system be plugged. You will have food brought and placed in the compartment. If we must wait, Captain, we will wait, but not any longer than I say."

"How long is that?"

"For the first replies to my conditions, six hours. Then, I must have the compartment for my use. When I consider the delay inordinate, I detonate the weapon."

"Then, I must go. I have many things to do."

"Yes, but I remind you. I will be sitting here with my hand on the switch—for six hours. Any attempt to attack me will inevitably result in my release of the switch. You do clearly understand that?"

Big John nodded. It was quite clear.

"One other thing, Captain. You may continue normal operations if you like. Even let your aircraft and flight crews leave the ship—you cannot evacuate your crew. And if your pilot officers wish to abandon their shipmates, that is the privilege of cowards. Interesting, isn't it, the small ramifications of this situation?"

Big John pointed to the intercom box. "You can contact me on this. I will be on the bridge."

"Six hours, Captain."

* * *

"All right," said Big John. "We have to come up with a plan to deal with this." He spoke to the small group around him, his XO, the CAG (carrier air wing commander), his Damage Control Officer, his Operations Officer, and the Air Boss. "Communications has relayed this nut's demands. I've ordered our three escorts to clear our area and we'll stay well out at sea. CAG, I want the air wing off."

"They're not going to want to leave."

"Then they'll be committing suicide. It's an order. That way, it is my responsibility. It's one of the few practical things we can do. Save some lives. Forget the consequences."

"Every man who leaves this ship will have it on his conscience if this doesn't work out."

"They'll be alive because of obeying my order. There is no disgrace in that. We have almost six hours to get them all off." Big John addressed the XO, "Fred, I want every seat on every airplane filled, draw lots if you have to, but no ship's company officers."

"Aye, aye, sir."

"Now, what can we do with this madman?"

"Maybe we can slip something in his food," offered the Air Boss.

"It's a thought. But we have to make sure it acts instantly. We can't give him time to realize something is going on."

"We can cheat when we plug his air-conditioning vents. Maybe slip him something that way," suggested the Damage Control Officer.

"Get the doctor up here," ordered Big John. "I don't know. Anything we try has terrible risks."

"Can we rush him and grab his hand and hold it on the switch until we can knock the shit out of him?" asked the Air Boss.

"He won't let us get that close," replied Big John. "We probably missed our opportunity when we were helping him carry the weapon to the flag bridge. I looked very closely at how he was holding it. One sudden move, unless it caught him completely by surprise, and that would have been it."

"Can we see him well enough on the flag bridge to get off a shot if he walks away from the damned thing?" asked the XO.

"No way," replied Big John. "Where would you put a marksman without him seeing him? At low angles, we could see only his head and have no idea if he were holding the switch or resting with it de-armed. Too big a risk."

"Is there any way to interrupt the firing sequence once the switch is released?" asked the Damage Control Officer.

"Who knows?" answered Big John. "I suspect that once it is armed, detonation is instantaneous when the switch is released."

"Maybe that's it!" exclaimed the Air Boss. "Did you see an arming switch? If we could throw it back to safe before he released the switch . . ."

"I looked for one on the way to the flag bridge. There is a small cover plate on the top of the cylinder. It looked like a flip plate, but I have no idea what is under it," responded Big John. "Besides, now that he is on the flag bridge, there is no way he will let us approach the weapon."

"I'll alert the air wing." The Air Boss spoke the words without any enthusiasm. A thought seemed to suddenly come to him. "Suppose this cookie wants the aircrews to leave and doesn't have a real bomb. He just wants to make it appear that our moral fiber is so thin that we'd desert our people to save our own skins! Maybe this has a propaganda twist rather than being a real threat. Where would they get a nuclear weapon in the first place?"

"God only knows, but they sure as shit have one," answered Big John. "Get the air wing off the ship."

The Air Boss walked away. The Air Wing Flight Surgeon walked in.

"Doctor," began Big John, "do you have something we can put in this guy's food that will knock him out, instantly?"

"We can knock him out, but not instantly."

"How much time?"

"It would depend on him, his constitution. Maybe five seconds after it hits his stomach, maybe less, probably more. It would be lethal."

"So, we bury him at sea," observed the XO.

"All right," concluded Big John. "For the moment, fix him something, Doctor. He won't eat for a while, probably. We'll have to play it by ear when the time comes, but have something ready."

"Why not in his drink?" offered the doctor. "You swallow something to drink all at once and fast. You don't have to chew it and maybe get suspicious or just swallow a bit at a time with a slow reaction. Gulp it down and it gets to your stomach fast."

"Wait a minute," interrupted the XO. "Why not a diuretic or something even stronger, a jumbo Ex-Lax for example, to give him a bad case of the runs. He might not take that detonator into the head with him. There's another head on the opposite side of the bulkhead. We wait until we know he's in there and rush him."

"Through a locked steel door? I don't think so, besides this guy is a smart bastard. Where he goes, that little black box goes," commented Big John.

"Let me work on the food or drink angle," decided the doctor.

"Whatever you think is best," agreed Big John. "Just make it potent."

The Executive Officer spoke, "Captain, what about the crew? We need to tell them something."

"Tell them we have a nut on board with a bomb. What else can we say? There were too many people around that airplane. The word's all over the ship by now. They're good troops. They'll stay calm."

"Even when the air wing flies off?"

"I'll talk to them first."

"Why not use the boats? The survival rafts? Hell, we can practically abandon ship with that idiot closed up in a compartment!" The Damage Control Officer was elated.

Big John thought a moment. "That's an idea but I don't know how feasible. We've got six thousand men on board. That would be one hell of an operation to pull off. In any case, start to work on it. You'll have to brief through the department heads, down through the division officers and senior petty officers. Play it as a quiet abandon ship, to be executed on my order, let's say when I call for all hands to pray. That will be the signal. When I call on ship's company for prayer. . . . I don't see how it could work." Big John shook his head, then sighed. "But if he holes up, there is some chance, perhaps. It won't hurt to think about it . . . all right, here's the plan. We get the air wing off. We try to poison the bastard, but only if it's foolproof. Failing all else, we delay him until he takes to his compartment, then we look for an opportunity to haul ass. We can alert our three escort ships to close in and pick us up."

Even as he spoke, Big John knew such a plan was completely unrealistic. Even if they could abandon ship, with six thousand men it would take the better part of an hour, more than likely two, for the men to be recovered and the rescue vessels to get out of range of a nuclear explosion. If it came to that, he would stay on board and keep Zadefi engaged in negotiations. At least it was a plan and it bought them two things, time and hope.

Five hours later, the last aircraft departed the ship. Big John entered the flag bridge. "Can I come in?" he asked, directing his voice toward the chart room.

"Yes."

Zadefi was still standing by the chart table, holding the dead man's switch.

"The president has not replied to your demands. He is considering them, but such things take time. You know that."

"We do not have time. I do not believe you have even informed your immediate commander, much less your commander in chief."

"I have informed him. I talked with him, personally, by satellite."

"You are lying."

Big John did not like the change in Zadefi's demeanor. He was nervous and irritable. Undoubtedly tired, possibly hungry. "We need to keep our wits about us. Let me bring you something to eat. We can ready your compartment. The admiral's sea cabin has no openings and is lockable."

"You ordered the aircraft off."

"It was your suggestion."

"I stand by it. My work can be done with those of you who are left."

Big John took a step closer, but made sure it was not a threatening nearness. "Let me send for some food. I want you to remain alert and not do this thing because of fatigue or despair. The president *is* considering your demands. He must consult with others, the Israelis, our other allies."

Zadefi's eyes were glazed. His breath was coming in short spurts. "God is good," he stated. "I am his servant."

"So am I. So are most of the men on this ship. We all love our God, your God. It is the same."

"Then one of us is evil, for we cannot serve the same God."

"We do, believe me."

"We can't. It is an impossibility."

"There is only one God. We both believe that. We both are the children of Abraham."

Zadefi straightened his back and stood erect. "Then, let us allow God to decide which of us is his faithful servant."

He removed his hand from the dead man's switch.

Chapter 11

"Captain! We have a flash message coming in from the *Bradley.*"

The OPCON—Operational Control—Duty Officer dropped the half-eaten doughnut beside his coffee cup and hurried over to the descramble printer. The message was just clicking off as he peered down at the emerging message draft:

> 041940Z JUL
> FLASH FLASH FLASH
>
> FROM: USS BRADLEY
> TO: CINCLANT
>
> SUBJ: NUCLEAR EXPLOSION
>
> USS LINCOLN (CVN-72) VANISHED IN NUCLEAR EXPLOSION
> 041933Z X USS BRADLEY USS VOGE USS WADDELL UNDAMAGED X
> HAVE ASSUMED OPCON AND PROCEEDING UPWIND OF POSIT
> 26-41N 73-50W X NO SURVIVORS NO DEBRIS X WILL CONDUCT
> RADIAC SURVEY X REQ YOU ADVISE ALL SHIPPING REMAIN 100
> MILES CLEAR OF ABOVE DATUM AR

"Dear God in heaven . . . the bastard did it." There was a chilling quiet in the space, broken only by the gentle whirring of air-conditioning blowers. The four-striper picked up a red telephone.

"Admiral, this is the OPCON Duty Officer. The terrorist just detonated his weapon. We've lost the *Lincoln*."

Pause.

"Captain O'Connor, sir," replied the CDO, identifying himself.

Pause.

"The surface escort vessels are undamaged. *Bradley* has assumed OPCON. They're starting a radiac sweep."

Pause.

"DEFCON THREE, Atlantic Command area, aye, aye, sir."

Pause.

"*Bradley* reports no survivors, Admiral. The *Lincoln* has disappeared."

Pause.

"I understand, sir. The watch has the messages ready to be released." The Duty Officer looked up at the stunned men and women around him and gave a thumbs-up signal. Several hurried away. The others remained.

"Aye, aye, sir."

Captain O'Connor replaced the telephone in its cradle. "You all know the procedure. Watch augmentees will be on the way immediately." As his personnel returned to their duties, O'Connor returned to his desk. Tears clouded his eyes as he swung angrily and knocked his coffee cup clear across the room.

"I'm sorry," he apologized.

A female chief petty officer handed him a freshly filled cup. "We all feel the same way, Captain. No apology necessary."

Chapter 12

6:48 P.M.
Sugarcane Field in Central Cuba

"They're all getting into the truck!"

Tatiana raised herself and leaned forward to sight down Davey's outstretched arm. The three men remaining at the site of the Piper takeoff were climbing into the cab of the truck. Davey could see the shaking of the tailpipe and the puffs of gray smoke as the driver started the engine.

"Come on! We have to follow them!" Quickly pulling Tatiana to her feet, Davey led the way back through the tangled cane to the Chevy. Not wishing to tackle the many idiosyncrasies he knew the battered car to have, he retook his customary place in the front passenger seat. Tatiana jumped behind the wheel and twisted the key. There was a brief murmur, then a series of clicks. Nothing else. "No...," said Davey in utter disgust. The tired battery was giving up its soul to wherever dead batteries go. Tatiana sat back and turned off the key. "We have to push," she said.

"On a dirt road, in ruts?"

Tatiana tried the key again. The clicks phased themselves out.

Davey was out of the car and placing his shoulder to the grill. "Push in the clutch. If we can get it back far enough, maybe it'll be on the downslope." Instead of heeding his exact instructions,

Tatiana placed the gear lever in neutral and hurried around to help him push. "The wheels will stay in the ruts," she announced. Together, they hit the Chevy like a pair of NFL linemen. The car gave way and rolled backward. Digging their feet in, Davey and Tatiana strained every muscle in their bodies, moving the Chevy down the ruts. After twenty feet, the road sloped and the car began to have a momentum of its own. "Now!" shouted Davey, continuing his short choppy steps. Tatiana raced around the open door and jumped into the seat. "Clutch in! . . . Reverse!" shouted Davey.

"Ready!" returned Tatiana. The Chevy was moving well backward, careening against the sides of the wheel ruts. At Davey's affirmative nod, she let out the clutch. The Chevy bucked and threatened to stall. She pushed in the clutch and let it out again. The Chevy bucked again, coughed, and roared to life!

Davey ran downhill, chasing the Chevy, until he could open the door and climb in. Tatiana continued backing at breakneck speed, skillfully guiding the bouncing Nomad into a clearing large enough to permit a turnaround. Throttle to the floor, she slung the Chevy down and around the knoll on which they had maintained their lookout and skidded onto the road that doubled back by the shacks. They passed them going fifty miles per hour and accelerating despite the fact that the neglected hardtop was far from an acceptable high-speed roadway. The Chevy pitched and twisted as Tatiana fiercely guided it along, swerving abruptly from side to side in a valiant attempt to ride the smoothest surface. They had gone three miles with no sign of the truck when they came to an intersection. Tatiana hit the brakes. "Which way?" she asked.

Davey stared at the three directions leading from the intersection. They had a one-out-of-three chance of selecting the correct one and there was no time to ponder the unfavorable odds. There had to be some indication of which road the truck took. Davey climbed out of the Chevy and studied each alternate surface. As he stood there, he heard Tatiana call out, "Look!"

Coming at them from ahead was the truck! Davey stepped to one side as it sped back to the intersection and made a sharp turn to take the right fork. The soldiers inside the cab recognized Tatiana with a hearty wave.

"They took the wrong road!" exclaimed Davey. "Let's go."

Tatiana swung to the right and followed the truck, staying as far back as they dared.

Five miles later, the road turned into a clay washboard and

narrowed. Tatiana didn't want to push the ancient vehicle faster than fifteen miles per hour, as it would simply shake to pieces.

"We can't lose them," cautioned Davey.

"We can't go any faster," replied Tatiana. "The road is just too rough."

The truck had also slowed but was gradually pulling away. Davey lifted himself from the seat to ease the pounding. Tatiana swung the shaking Chevy from side to side as she tried to seek out the least rough portion of the road. They topped a small rise and Tatiana braked to a stop. A half-mile ahead, the truck was turning into a small military compound. There were several large tents, a number of vehicles, and several orderly rows of small personnel tents.

"Do you have any idea where this road leads?" asked Davey.

"No, but we are getting into the backcountry."

"That's a small camp."

"Perhaps they are on maneuvers," suggested Tatiana.

"I don't know. It looks like it has been there for a while."

"I'm not sure we should get any closer."

"Can you remember where we are—with relation to where we first saw them?" asked Davey.

"We can draw ourselves a map."

"All right. Let's backtrack, marking our mileage until we get back to where we spent the night. I must speak with your father. I need to get a message to my control."

"In the States?"

"Yes."

"When I left earlier with my father, he was going to my grandmother's house." Shrugging, Tatiana added, "Sometimes, she works with him."

"Would he still be there?"

"I do not know. But her house is much closer than going all the way back to Honda Bay."

"Let's go to your grandmother's."

The central highway of Cuba was a misnomer. Two-laned, it at least showed signs of cursory care, and in stretches it was wide and smooth enough for relatively high speed, but to call it a central highway was a not-so-subtle form of exaggeration. They sped northwest, back toward Havana, passing little traffic and watching their speed whenever militia vehicles were on the road. Davey was surprised that they could travel with such freedom. Tatiana did not seem to be at all concerned about their passage from central Cuba toward the city of Sagua la Grande. A few miles west of Santa Clara, Tatiana guided the Chevy north onto a secondary road. Twenty-five minutes later, they passed through Sagua la Grande and on north toward the coast. The modest dwelling of Tatiana's grandmother sat on a high knoll with a view of the coastal village of La Isabela, thirteen miles farther on. Tatiana parked in front of the bohío, and a strikingly handsome woman, despite her obviously advanced years, appeared in the open doorway. Tall, maybe even close to six feet, with a crown of carefully arranged white hair, the regal grandmother of the daughter of Rudy Ordonez smiled broadly and reached out to embrace the younger woman.

"My Tatiana!" Even as she hugged her granddaughter, she peered over Tatiana's shoulder at Davey. "You are Morales," she announced to herself.

"*Si senora*," replied Davey, taking her outstretched hand lightly. She stood with chin raised, not with disdain but with pride in her heritage. She was of noble and pure blood and a gentleman caller had certain obligations upon being presented to her. Davey raised her hand and touched it to his lips. "Senora," he repeated, lowering her hand gently and taking a step backward. He would remain silent until she opened their conversation.

"Papa? Is he here?" asked Tatiana.

"No, he stayed for only a short while. He has gone back to Honda Bay to wait for contact from Senor Morales. He has a message. But, I have it also. It came through me."

"This is my grandmother, Dona Ordonez," said Tatiana belatedly.

"I have a message for you from Thomas," added Dona Ordonez, holding herself very erect.

Davey had heard that form of address so seldom, it took him a moment before he realized she was speaking of his mentor, the Old Man, back in Key West.

"Come inside," invited Dona Ordonez. "Rudy expected you to proceed to his place. But no harm is done. I will tell you."

They followed the woman inside. She offered them chairs and then a cool citrus drink. Davey could taste a mixture of lemons, grapefruit, oranges, and sugar.

"You are to proceed to the American Naval Base at Guantanamo," said Dona Ordonez.

Davey was surprised that the Old Man had anticipated his

request for instructions. The substation chief could not yet know of his failure to keep track of the cylinders. What could have come up that precipitated his recall? "I should like to talk to him," requested Davey.

"That is not possible without traveling to my son's place. I have only reception capabilities here. There is an irregular schedule. I suspect the message will be repeated, however, later on in the evening." As she spoke, Dona Ordonez directed Davey's attention to her table radio from which radiated a complex classical guitar rendition.

"You receive messages over that?" asked Davey. Such a method of clandestine communication seemed painfully risky.

Dona Ordonez nodded. "Yes. I have a recorder. When certain music is played, I turn it on. Within the subsequent music is submerged a message. I also have a device that replays the recording without the cover music. You are surprised to see such an old woman with such a modern device?"

"I take exception to your description of yourself, Senora." Davey could not have chosen more gracious words. Dona Ordonez tilted her head in gracious acknowledgement of the compliment. "Your young gentleman is a person of manners, Tatiana. You would do well to remember him the next time you visit me with one of your Fidelisto friends. *I* shall."

Davey could see the slight stiffening of Tatiana's back as she dutifully replied, "Yes, grandmother." The defiance she displayed with respect to her father was not present in her voice.

"Would you like to hear the tape?" asked Dona Ordonez.

"That is not necessary, but I do not know of any arrangements for my recovery."

"Tatiana will drive you. Papers are being prepared, so you must wait until morning. You may stay here. It will be a pleasure to entertain a young gentleman at dinner. I have few opportunities for such an evening. I want to hear about yourself, your family, your work."

"Grandmother, you entertained one of my gentleman friends only a week or so ago."

"Gentleman friends? The man would have eaten raw pork off the floor had I served it so."

Tatiana took the rebuff silently.

"You must excuse me. I must send word to my son that you are here and that arrangements are being made. *Senor.*"

Davey stood as Dona Ordonez walked outside, climbed aboard

an ancient bicycle, and pedaled energetically back toward Sagua la Grande. "We should drive her," he exclaimed.

Tatiana laughed. "She will make better time on her bicycle. Besides, she prefers it. Says it keeps her young."

"She is indeed that. A striking woman."

"Yes. If this land ever had any dignity before the revolution, it was because of people like my grandmother. She raised me, along with my father of course, after my mother died. I was three. She is my mother."

"I suspect she does not take any great deal of satisfaction from your political persuasion."

"None whatsoever. But she does realize that the overall good of the country is better than during the days of the Batistas. She was not a contented woman during that time, either. Her pride sees only Spain, and that is what she wishes Cuba to be, knowing full well that it is only a dream that will die with her and her kind. Cuba was never destined to be a new Spain. I think she was disappointed when she first came here as a child, and has lived her life in that disappointment with a dignity only one of her blood could manage. For that, I love her very much."

"You are of her blood."

"Diluted twofold. First, by the American who was my grandfather, and then by the black who was my mother."

"The plot thickens. You are part American?"

"A part I do my best to disown."

"Your grandfather, who was he?"

"A sugar merchant. An executive. I remember him. And I believe he was a good man and a good American—a contradiction of terms, of course."

"Of course."

"I remember his warm lap and large arms that used to hold me as he told me fairy tales and stories. Grandmother worshipped him."

"It must have been quite a loss for her—I assume he is gone."

"He died when I was ten. An accident. After the revolution, he stayed here with grandmother, one of the few of your kind who did. He became a field worker, of course, which was a hard life for an old man used to the comforts and privileges of an American executive, especially one who lived in Cuba. He died in the sugarcane fields, crushed under a tractor."

"I'm sorry."

"Yes." Tatiana stared vacantly out the open doorway. "She still prays to him, as if he were here in this house."

"Perhaps he is. Who are we to know?"

"He is dead."

"She called my superior by his first name, Thomas. Do they know each other?"

"Yes. I have heard her and my father talking many times about the old days. Your superior apparently worked with or for my grandfather for many years, here in Cuba. They were very close, from what I understand. Perhaps that is why my grandmother keeps up this crazy role she plays in your intelligence network. It makes her think she is still close to my grandfather."

Davey began to have a deeper appreciation for the dilemma Tatiana must be in. She had a great love for her grandmother and her father and yet was a product of the revolution.

"If you would like to rest, I have things to do," offered Tatiana. "I do not think it wise to go outside. Your presence here is already known, naturally, but those who have the responsibility for such things will not approach us in the house of my grandmother. She is still a person of influence and respect among her neighbors."

Davey noted the significant change in Tatiana's manner of speaking. Gone were the phrases of the revolution, even the frequent reference to campaneros—comrades—which would have been her term for the people of Sagua la Grande. Her suggestion to rest was a good one. He was very tired from the all-night watch and the travel back to Dona Ordonez's bohio, and there was nothing he could do but wait.

Sometime during his sleep, Dona Ordonez had returned and with her granddaughter had supervised the preparation of their dinner. She took her place at the head of the table as a queen would host her royal court, dressed in Spanish finery of deep blue, her mantilla a crown of matching lace, positioned on her head by exquisite combs of stained ivory and draped over her shoulders with obvious care. Tatiana had changed into a dress of flowers and pleats. Davey sat to Dona Ordonez's right, freshly scrubbed and appropriately attired in the white shirt, string bolero, and unborn calfskin vest provided him. He tried not to feel embarrassed at finding a pair of silk socks with the stack of clothing beside his bed after he awakened. Tatiana's grandfather must have been very close to his build and size.

In keeping with her emphasis on the importance of entertaining a gentleman who knew his obligations toward a Spanish lady, Dona Ordonez had engaged one of the locals to serve the meal. The young woman did so with the grace and familiarity of someone who had performed such a service before.

The dinner extended for more than two hours, with both Davey and Tatiana enthralled by the stories of Dona Ordonez. After-dinner coffee was taken at the table, and Davey declined the offer of the traditional cigar. It was a rare evening within Castro's Cuba.

It was a full day's drive, three hundred and seventy miles, from Dona Ordonez's bohio to the town of Guantanamo. Considering the state of the central highway, the inordinate delays in arranging for gasoline at the midpoint of their drive, and the security checks that occurred at the towns of Camaguey and Victoria de las Tunas, outside of Holguin, as well as on the open highway as they approached Guantanamo, ten hours for the trip was not unreasonable. Davey's papers were in order, testifying as to his work assignment change from the Construction Ministry to the American Naval Base at Guantanamo as a yard worker. Tatiana's papers, equally well forged, identified her as his wife and adviser to Young Pioneer cells. Tatiana traveled in a skirt and blouse, and at each checkpoint she would unbutton the top two buttons of her blouse and arrange her skirt casually above her knees. Davey doubted that the militiamen even bothered to read their carefully prepared documents, invariably handing them back promptly with a gracious smile to Tatiana and an envious look at Davey. What a man, they figured, to have such an assignment, to join the Cuban work force on the American base, and to sleep with such a woman every night. He must be a high intelligence agent, probably one of the Maximum Leader's handpicked few.

Their overnight stay in Guantanamo was unpleasant to say the least. They shared a one-room hut with a family of four who were part of the Ordonez network, Davey sleeping on the bare floor and too near one of the openings. During the early-morning hours, he received an unwelcome bath, courtesy of the night rains. By daylight he was cold, wet, and hungry. Walking outside into the glaring morning sun erased the first two discomforts, but a bowl of lukewarm goat's milk and a slice of coarse bread did little for the third. Tatiana drove him to the assembly point for the workers who made their daily entrance into the Guantanamo base.

"Our soldiers will check your papers here. Then you will file through the gate you see on the far side, and the U.S. Marines will check your papers a second time. If there is any question at the American checkpoint, and there should be none, just tell the Marine you must talk to Captain Overholt—that is our code word."

"Tatiana, I don't know if I will be going back to Key West or what, but I want to thank you for what you have done for me—for us."

"I will be here when your shift returns. If you are not here, I will return every day for a week. By that time, we will have some message to tell us what has happened."

"I am truly grateful. You risk a great deal."

Tatiana smiled, more pleasantly than he had seen her do so before. "I do as my father wishes. We should kiss now, my husband, as I see you off to work."

Davey was surprised to find her lightly moistened lips soft and receptive to his. He took the bag lunch and fell in line with the other men and women. Tatiana walked away.

The Cuban soldiers meticulously examined each man's papers but paid no particular attention to Davey. As he entered the American compound, he was surprised to see the degree of battle readiness displayed by the Marines. All were in full combat gear. Light machine gun squads were set up covering the security gate area, and walking patrols could be seen monitoring the fence areas.

The Marine checking his papers looked at him, apparently checking his face with the picture on the Cuban work permit. "Step over here, please," he directed. Davey followed his pointed arm and stood aside while the others continued passing through the checkpoint. After the last Cuban had passed, the Marine returned to Davey. "Come with me, please," he ordered, and approached a master gunnery sergeant who had been observing the routine. He handed Davey's papers to his sergeant and they spoke for a moment. The sergeant motioned for Davey to join them.

"I believe you wish to see Captain Overholt—is that correct?"

Davey wasn't sure what the sergeant was asking but he remembered Tatiana's caution that, should there by any problem he should ask to see Captain Overholt. That was the buzzword and the sergeant had preceded him in its use. "Yes, I believe I do."

"Come with me, please."

Davey followed the sergeant and climbed in the staff car beside him. Only after they drove off and were well away from the gate, heading toward the central area of the base, did the sergeant turn and look at him. "Cigarette?" he offered.

"No, thanks," replied Davey.

"They're waiting for you at the base command and control center," the sergeant continued.

"They?"

"Our base commander and several people from the mainland."

"Do you always maintain this degree of combat readiness?" asked Davey.

"Only since the explosion," replied the Marine. "We're at DEF-CON TWO."

"Since what explosion?"

The sergeant looked at Davey, puzzled. "You don't know, do you? I forgot, you've been hiding out since the fourth."

"That I have. What is this all about?"

"The nuclear explosion that took out the *Lincoln*. Two days ago, just to the east of Eleuthera. You didn't know?"

Davey felt his stomach go sour. "Jesus, no."

"A goddamned terrorist blew it up. Turned ninety thousand tons of metal and men into vapor and hot steam. She went down in a thousand fathoms of water, what was left of her. . . . Here we are." The sergeant stopped in front of a sandbagged entrance to an underground bunker. "Here we are, sir," repeated the Marine. Davey could hear the voice but not comprehend the meaning of the words. In his mind's eye he could see the Piper aircraft lifting off from the dirt strip in central Cuba. That must have been the start of the attack. And the contents of the cylinders were nuclear bombs! The vision of the red arming switch came back. But how, even with such a weapon, could one light aircraft sink the world's mightiest warship?

"Sir, you okay? This is where they want you."

Davey looked at the sergeant with blank eyes. "Thank you."

One of the two Marine sentries opened the door to let him pass. Inside, there was only one way to go, down an inclined hallway to a single door. It was locked. He pushed the buzzer.

"Take a step backward and face the overhead monitor, please," came a detached voice. "Raise your face a bit, please."

Davey looked up at the television monitor. There was a loud buzz and the voice returned, "You may enter, sir."

The Old Man was waiting on the other side of the door.

"I just heard," exclaimed Davey. The Old Man took him by the arm and led him through one of the doors lining the chamber.

"It's hit the fan, Davey. We're just a short hair from going face to face with the Soviets. DEFCON THREE stateside, TWO here."

A Navy captain, several commanders, and three civilians sat around a conference table. The Old Man made the introductions as Davey took a seat beside him. "Captain Ronney; Commander

Jason, Operations; Commander Partleigh, Intelligence; Felix Ari-
guar, Miami Station Chief; Chuck Myers, FBI Special Terrorist
Unit; and Ted Benson, our counterpart to Chuck. Gentlemen,
Davey Morales."

Davey returned the nods as the Old Man continued, "Davey, on
the Fourth of July, two days ago, an Iranian terrorist landed a small
Piper aircraft on the *Lincoln* by claiming to be a lost pilot with his
wife and child on board. He had one of the two cylinders in the airplane and that afternoon succeeded in detonating the weapon.
The *Lincoln* and all hands were lost, although the air wing had left
the ship. We're shit short of time so I can't give you all the details,
but we know the weapon was one of the ones you were assigned to
locate and identify, we know the Soviets provided the weapon, and
we suspect Cuban authorities cooperated in the transfer of the
weapon to the terrorists. In forty-five minutes, Captain Ronney has
a classified conference call with the National Command and Control Center and we need to know what you can add, if anything."

Davey looked around the table. The eyes of the others were
locked on him as he began to speak. "The cylinders were delivered
to military security at Jose Marti International Airport. They left
by truck on the third, along with a Piper Cherokee Six aircraft, and
were tracked to a remote field in central Cuba. I was able to examine one of the cylinder covers at that location and got a brief look
at the contents of the other. It was a smaller cylinder, silver in
color, but it was dark and I didn't get a chance to examine it in any
detail. I observed the Piper take off on the morning of the fourth,
and followed the truck with the remaining weapon when it left. I
had no way of knowing where the aircraft was headed. . . ."

"We understand that, Davey, and to set things in the proper
perspective, we know there was nothing you could have done about
the situation."

Davey could feel his eyes moisten. "I could have maybe
stopped the airplane . . . I had no idea . . . oh, God, I'm so sorry. . . ."
He felt the angry shudders come from his belly and shake his
chest. Standing, he clenched his fists. "I saw them! I saw the airplane leave! We followed the truck with the second weapon until it
entered an armed compound. I had no weapons."

The Old Man stood and grabbed his shoulders. "It's all right,
Davey. There was nothing you could have done."

"I didn't even get a chance to make a report."

The Old Man eased him into his chair and poured a glass of
water from a plastic decanter. "Drink this," he directed.

"I'm sorry," said Davey, shaking his head in despair. "I apologize for losing control." The water calmed him.

"The truck in the compound, do you think it is still there?"

"Who is to say? Dona Ordonez was going to relay to Rudy the location of the camp, and I asked her to tell him to resume the surveillance. I didn't know until I got to Gitmo what had happened."

"Did you see any of the other faces of the Palestinians?" asked the Old Man.

"Yes, although not clearly. One was outside on guard, the other in a shack near the plane. I could probably identify them. There were a couple Cuban guards also. I have seen them earlier in Havana, at the Icar."

"We know who they are," responded the Old Man. "We believe the one who blew up the *Lincoln* was an ex-Iranian Air Force captain by the name of Zadefi. He was the only one pilot-qualified. We have identities on the other two, both Palestinians. They're from a new group and call themselves the New Shaheen."

"The New Shaheen?"

"Yes. They've taken their name from the first Palestinian terrorists who operated almost two thousand years ago."

Davey could only swing his head from side to side, overwhelmed by a feeling of failure.

"Is there anything else you can tell us about the weapon, or the two men?" asked the CIA man, Benson.

"No."

"Do you know of anyone else who might be able to identify them?"

"A girl—a young woman, Tatiana Ordonez. She's the daughter of Rudy Ordonez, who picked me up from the sub." Thinking back to Tatiana's luring of the guard into the Chevy, he continued, "She may have seen one of them very close up."

"Where were you when you received my instructions to report here?" asked the Old Man.

"At her grandmother's house."

"Dona Ordonez," indicated the Old Man to the others. "Davey, we're going to have to send you back. Rudy's people are trying to relocate the second cylinder. The two Palestinians must be killed at any cost before they can get the thing out of the country."

"The Cubans know about this, surely. How can they continue to condone such an action?" asked Davey.

"The Cubans are in the middle and scared shitless we're going to invade. And we may. The president is considering that right now."

"But everything is so calm outside the gate. It's a normal day."

"Only the Cuban authorities know what has happened. Castro has clamped down on any media revelation, although I suspect the news is leaking all over as we speak here. The atmosphere when you go back this afternoon may be drastically changed. Things are happening very fast."

"The Soviets did this," stated Davey. "What are they saying?"

"They are saying that they disclaim any knowledge of any weapons being provided the Palestinians."

"I saw them in the Bear! We have proof!"

"No, we have only you. Unlike the Cuban missile crisis of 1962, we have no pictures to present before the world. The Soviets say we are trumping up the whole thing to mask an accidental explosion of a nuclear reactor at sea."

"That can't happen!"

"We know it; they know it; but the poor bastards walking the streets of the world don't know it. For the moment, we're outvoted."

"I can't believe this," muttered Davey.

"Believe it," spoke Captain Ronney. "In addition to putting all military bases and units on the alert, worldwide, the president has ordered the Mexican border sealed, and the Gulf of Mexico is under a full wartime surveillance effort. All U.S. ports of entry, air and sea, are closed. Coastal states have had their State Guards federalized and those troops are assisting the Army in patrolling both coasts. Canadian authorities have placed all of their ports of entry under military supervision. No one enters without positive and very personal identification. The United Nations Security Council is in emergency session and condemning the United States for a war scare. The Soviet Union has vetoed an attempt by the United States to call for a United Nations force to be used to threaten the PLO, Syria, Libya, and Iran with immediate military attack unless they act to identify and recall the two remaining terrorists. Israel is posed to attack Syrian forces in Lebanon and elsewhere if given the slightest encouragement. Now do you believe it?"

"Gentlemen," said the Old Man, "I don't think we can do anything more here. If I may, Captain, I would like to try and plan for Morales's return in-country."

"Certainly. We will relay the contents of this discussion to Washington, although it will be of little help, I'm afraid. You may use the lounge for your business if you desire. There are provisions there. I would like to speak to you, Mr. Ariguar, once you have finished among yourselves."

"Thank you, Captain," said the senior CIA agent as he and the Old Man indicated to the others to follow them into the adjoining room. They arranged themselves comfortably on the several motel-style chairs and sofa.

"Davey," began the Old Man, "the three of us are returning to D.C. when we're through here. We have a meeting with the director and possibly with the president's staff, maybe even the president, for a briefing on the cylinders and what we know about them. I think I can cover that little bit since we don't know one hell of a lot. I intend to tell the director that you have gone back in-country and if you can find the other two Shaheen people you will kill them. I will also be telling him that there is a pretty damned slim chance of that. But, it is the obvious course of action for us to take. Ordonez can provide you with weapons, and if the damned bomb goes off in the process, Cuba takes the hit, not the U.S. Any heartaches with that?"

"I'm not a terminal operator, you know that. But I sure as hell welcome the chance to make up for losing the first cylinder. If they're there, I'll get to them. To be frank, however, I don't relish fooling around with the device."

"That's understandable. Now, the Cubans are worried about U.S. reaction, but that doesn't change their overall objective. If they are in contact with the Shaheen, they will insist they leave the country and provide any assistance necessary, I'm certain. Actually, I strongly suspect they're already gone."

"Where? They aren't stupid enough to try the overwater route north into the States."

The Old Man walked over to a wall map of Cuba. An old Mobil Oil roadway map, it was faded and dated, but of such a scale that it displayed most of the Gulf and Caribbean area. "Here at La Fe," he said, pointing to the extreme western tip of Cuba, "there are plenty of fishermen willing to take the Shaheen across the channel to the Yucatan Peninsula—it's only a hundred and fifty miles. If they went directly to La Fe, or one of the other fishing villages on the tip, they would have gotten there and made their way into Mexico before we ever reacted to the loss of the *Lincoln*. I suspect the Arabs have plenty of money, and the poorest of the poor—of Cuba and Mexico—don't have any day-to-day realization of what's going on in the world. Their life revolves around the next peso, so the Shaheen can go underground for as long as it takes. Putting you in-country is just insurance in the event they are too dumb to already have made that move. You know, of course, security will be tightened all over the island, so the risks are higher, but what the hell, you make good money."

Davey failed to see the humor.

The door to the command center opened and Captain Ronney leaned in. "The Cubans are recalling all of their nationals. We're herding them up, now. Is your man going back?"

"Yes," replied the Old Man.

"I wouldn't advise it," stated Ronney, shaking his head. "They'll give every returnee a very thorough check under the circumstances now."

"How are your papers?" asked the Old Man.

"They haven't given them a second thought so far, but if they check with the Construction Ministry, I don't know."

"You'll have to make your way clear back to Rudy."

"Tatiana is supposed to be waiting for me."

"How much time do we have, Captain?" asked the Old Man.

"As I said, we're loading the trucks now. I don't think it would be smart to have one of the workers show up at the gate in a staff car."

"Okay, Davey. Sorry we can't give you more guidance—just play it by ear. And remember, those bastards undoubtedly intend for the next weapon to be detonated in CONUS. If we can keep them in-country here, we've got them."

Davey stood and looked at the others. The risks he was taking by going back through the gate were written on each face. He had the distinct intuition that they figured they were looking at a dead man. "I'll be in touch," he said, squeezing past Captain Ronney.

Outside, the truck was waiting and he joined a half dozen other Cubans, cleaning people, and yard men who worked in the unclassified section of the command post. The truck was full by the time they reached the Cuban gate. Davey fell in among the others as they filed past the Marine guards and reentered Cuban territory.

"Darling. . . ." Tatiana was waiting just beyond the Cuban militiamen checking the returnees' papers. Davey nodded and smiled.

"You are a Construction Ministry transferee?" asked the militiaman.

"Yes."

"Just within the past two days?"

"Yes."

"Where were you working before the transfer?"

Davey hesitated. Should he say the breeding farm or at the Icar? "Havana."

"Who was your immediate superior?"

"A campanero Cordero." Keep your answers vague and simple, Davey, my boy, he remembered being advised.

"Is the woman with you?" said the soldier, eyeing Tatiana.

"My wife."

"Both of you come with me."

Tatiana quickly joined Davey and took his hand, her eyes telling him to be silent. They followed the soldier. "Don't worry," she whispered, "I have a phone number that will spare us further interrogation."

Don't worry? Davey could already see the ugly little black holes that were the business end of the rifles of a firing squad.

Chapter 13

July 8, 5:13 P.M.
Soviet Union Embassy, Havana

Colonel Vladlen Mikhailovich Plotnikov stared out the window of his office within the special GRU—Chief Directorate of Intelligence of the General Staff—*residentura* section of the embassy. Although he could not quite see them, he knew that the white sandy beaches stretching eastward from Havana were peppered with small figures, some inert, taking the late-afternoon sun, others moving about like a scurry of black ants searching for a tidbit to take back to their nest. Ordinarily on this day, he would have been down there with them, enjoying the stimulation of firm female bodies in brief swimsuits—all in conformance with standards set by the revolution, of course—or taking vibrant strokes through the surf, which was quite gentle at the moment. There were never a lot of people on the beaches, certainly no numbers to compare to the crowds that threatened to sink the sands along the Russian Riviera, where the lush hills of Crimea faded out into the chilly waters of the Black Sea.

Plotnikov was using the quiet time to review his brilliant career—and the sudden turn of events that threatened to result in Siberia being his terminal assignment. Perhaps the best days had

129

been during his first commissioned duty with the Spetsnaz—the special units that were the elite of military sabotage and forceful reconnaissance. As a young Spetsnaz lieutenant, he had been at once a free soul and a strict disciplinarian with a fierce sense of duty and loyalty. His rapidly developed reputation and skill had early on marked him as a candidate for a higher calling within the Tenth Chief Directorate of the General Staff. There, he had been highly instrumental in providing weapons to the Soviet Union's surrogate fighters, the Cubans and Africans and Central Americans. Within the Tenth Directorate, he had found his niche while still a major: a career in the GRU, the military intelligence arm of the Soviet Union.

Tapped for the supersecret unit—no one officially requested such prestigious duty, it would have been presumptuous—he had undergone his final training under the auspices of the Second Chief Directorate of the General Staff and had spent the required time at the GRU headquarters facility known as the Aquarium, a little-known and highly classified complex next to its own Khodinka Airfield. Even he did not know its exact location. But etched in his mind's eye were the glass central tower of the control building, the fortlike wall surrounding it, the central entrance to the complex—which was never opened—the restaurant and hotel that opened onto the airport, "The Colony" living quarters for active-duty GRU instructors and retired GRU officers, the Space Research Center, and the crematorium. The crematorium was the only way out of the GRU, and then only when you died or betrayed your office; in the latter case, you entered the ovens fully conscious.

Those had been heady days, the days within the walls of the Aquarium, made so by the realization that you were a member of an intelligence organization superior even to the KGB in terms of martial arts expertise and military responsibility. During the rigid training under the auspices of the First Faculty of the Military-Diplomatic Academy of the GRU, Plotnikov had honed both his profession's intelligence skills and his own personal skills of interrogation and killing. "Puppets"—condemned criminals used as live targets for realistic and quite lethal combat training—had fallen by his hand easily as he absorbed his lessons without the slightest twinge of conscience. He had finished at the head of his class and had won early promotion to the rank of colonel, bypassing numerous comrades and the customary time-consuming career path. He became the elite of the elite, not only serving as a senior officer of the General Staff but taking his place as a foreign service officer, the most trusted of all. Even among that group, there was a caste system, and his assignment to the embassy of the Soviet Union's most prestigious Western world satellite placed him high on that privileged list. It was because of his reputation for efficiency and flawless performance that he had been given the special responsibility of overseeing the transfer of the two nuclear devices to the small Arab contingent that had purchased them from the Soviet Union. And he had screwed it up royally. The lowest lieutenant in the service would have formed some doubts about such a transfer taking place in Cuba. Obviously, the Middle East would have been the logical place; *anywhere* in the Middle East. True, he had not been in on the planning, just the execution, but even so, he should have raised questions. Now, it was obvious. The terrorists never had any intention of stockpiling the devices. They were intended from the very beginning for use against the Americans. And he had helped preposition them. The fact that he was only one of many duped by the Arabs was of little comfort at the moment.

Now, the name Vladlen Mikhailovich Plotnikov was at the top of the Kremlin's what-the-hell-is-going-on list, and at any moment, Gen. Viktor M. Gigiyashvili, the tough Georgian commander of the Second Chief Directorate of the General Staff, would come barging through Plotnikov's office door, teeth bared and aching for a big chunk of Vladlen's posterior. A fellow member of the *nomen-klatura*—Party members who held the most prestigious posts within the Soviet Union—Gigiyashvili had been Plotnikov's mentor for many years. The fact that both he and Plotnikov were nomenklatura of the Central Committee, the highest of the high, made the current situation as sensitive as any could ever get, and it didn't help matters that Gigiyashvili was the first non-Russian to hold the prestigious post of commander of the Second Chief Directorate; his Russian comrades were always after his skin. And it was a time-honored custom that when a general officer got the sack, he rode the train to Siberia surrounded by his trusted associates and special protégés.

To add insult to his injury, Plotnikov was painfully aware of the amusement his counterparts in the KGB were taking from his predicament. Even the ambassador, the public head of the Soviet mission but within the private walls of the embassy subordinate to the two senior KGB and GRU officers, would take comfort should Plotnikov be summarily removed from his post. And that was a distinct possibility.

Even though Plotnikov fully expected it, the sudden opening of his door startled him as the full figure of General Gigiyashvili strode in.

"Comrade General," greeted Plotnikov with more than a little apprehension.

Gigiyashvili was alone and angrily shut the door behind him. Plotnikov tensed for the inevitable. It never came. Instead, Gigiyashvili's countenance softened and he grabbed Plotnikov's shoulders and pulled the younger officer to him. "Vladlen, my special student, you never cease to amaze me."

Plotnikov stood stunned. "I don't understand."

"First, we drink. Have you ever ridden one of those damnable Tupolev bombers from our homeland to this place? A more uncomfortable airplane I cannot even imagine. Every bone in my body aches. I have not slept in twenty-seven hours."

Plotnikov poured the vodka. Gigiyashvili raised his straight to his mouth, threw back his head, and reached out with the empty glass. Plotnikov refilled it.

Gigiyashvili downed half of it before taking Plotnikov's chair behind the colonel's desk. "The bastard Palestinians put one over on us." Plotnikov took immediate comfort in the general's use of the first person plural pronoun. "But their strike at the American carrier is a stroke of genius. Do you realize how hard it would be to sink an American carrier? We would use a whole task force or submarine flotilla. And a dumb Arab, all by himself, accomplishes the same task. Incredible."

"Excuse me, Comrade General, but I thought you would be furious."

Gigiyashvili glanced over at the closed door. "Officially, I am. But, unofficially, I congratulate you for being an unwitting party to this coup. Not that we don't have a most severe problem. The Americans are making war noises, but it is only a blowing of their noses. They have no proof that we were involved, and it is a fact that we did not intend to be involved in such a thing. But now, we must use it for the opportunity it presents. Sit down, but first pour me another. I intend to sleep well this night."

Plotnikov filled the general's glass and set the bottle within his reach. "The Americans are hopelessly confused as always," Gigiyashvili continued. "They know a soldier of Islam has struck them, but they don't know who sponsored him. In fact, they recognize that no one sponsored him! The Palestinians and Iranians have so many fractured groups of idiots that legal determinations of responsibility are impossible. The Americans want to hit the Cubans, for they know our comrade Castro had a hand in this, but there were no Cubans directly involved in the attack. For a giant to squash a midget because he can't catch the mosquito that has just inflicted a painful bite would be only an exercise in frustration and do nothing to dissuade the mosquito from biting again. As for making big noises against us, the loss of one warship is not worth a nuclear exchange, although the loss of more than six thousand men is an emotional strain. Traditionally, however, the Americans are ineffective in their response to such things—but they are not stupid. Fortunately, to complicate their internal matters, they are sensitive to world opinion, which at this moment is screaming at them to calm down and talk about this thing. Ha! This could not be better if we had planned it this way!"

Plotnikov poured himself a refill.

"The Israelis are like mad dogs on a weak leash. This is the perfect excuse for them to strike. Rise up to the defense of their benefactor! Yet, deep down within their own intelligence circles— which arc among the world's best as you and I know so well—they realize that an all-out conflict with the Arabs would have to involve massive American support, and while the American people are most sympathetic to providing that support because of the loss of their six thousand sailors, the American leaders know we will back our friends in the Middle East. So, the test of Israeli and American wills can only weaken their dependence upon one another. It is a massive disagreement, with the injured party—the Americans— restraining the friend who wants to take revenge in a rather self-serving way, of course. It is beautiful. We shall never see another dilemma as unique as this one."

The vodka seemed to be stimulating Plotnikov's thinking of the general's arguments. "But, Comrade General, there is another weapon. If the Palestinians manage to detonate it on American soil, I fear there will be no holding back either the Americans or the Israelis. I seem to see a much greater danger in this than you— with all due respect of course."

"And that is exactly why I am pleased to have you here in the middle of all this. You see correctly." Gigiyashvili's eyes narrowed and his glee vanished. "We must stop the Palestinians, for that very reason."

"The Cubans are already searching for them."

"And they won't find them. The clever devils are surely gone from this island by now."

"Then our comrades in the KGB must know where they have gone."

"Oh, they do, Vladlen, my young friend. But the responsibility for the recovery of the remaining weapon remains with the GRU. I have obtained permission to reassign you as my personal representative in doing just that. You may have to go to Mexico. You may have to go to the United States. Either way, you will enter as a member of our diplomatic corps. Once in-country, where you go and what you do will be your prerogative. Instructions to our people have gone out to render you all assistance. I want you to track down the Palestinians and get that weapon back. I need not tell you that even an idiot who sees it will recognize it as a Soviet product. The General Secretary has no intention of seeing pictures—or the actual weapon itself—paraded before the Security Council of the United Nations."

"Why would the Palestinians do that?"

"Oh, I'm not talking about the Palestinians. If they have their way, they will detonate the damn thing. But if the Americans somehow get their hands on it—that is what we must prevent. We are talking about a very volatile situation, literally and figuratively."

"I can go any time, Comrade General."

"Good, Vladlen, and I expect you to move as soon as we pinpoint the whereabouts of the weapon. I am sure that it is out of Cuba." Gigiyashvili reached out with his glass, and Plotnikov poured. Downing the liquid in a single swallow, Gigiyashvili pushed back his chair and stood. "I have a brief meeting with our ambassador, then we will pay a courtesy call on Comrade Castro. Keep yourself at the ready. I would suspect that by morning we will have come across the trail of the Palestinians. You might like to pack some things."

"I will either be here or at my quarters, Comrade General."

"That will be satisfactory." Gigiyashvili slapped Plotnikov soundly on the shoulder. "You are like a son to me, Vladlen. It would grieve me deeply to see your ashes rise up out of the great smokestack of the crematorium. That is the price we pay, you know, for failure." For the first time since the conversation began, there was no good humor on the face of the commander of the Second Chief Directorate of the General Staff.

Plotnikov cared for a few impending actions and placed the directives in his outgoing basket before leaving, the last-minute actions taking a full fifty-five minutes after Gigiyashvili left. In front of the embassy his faithful Lada awaited him. The small, squarish four-door sedan was not a prestigious vehicle within the Soviet Union, but here in Cuba it was the envy of every Cuban nursing a forty-year-old Ford or Chevy. Out in the fresh air, clear of the dark confines of the GRU quarters within the embassy, Plotnikov felt a fresh freedom. He was going into the field and that was where a man of his calling did his best work. If it were Mexico, he would obtain the necessary papers at his embassy in Mexico City and simply pose as a photojournalist. Fluent in Spanish, Portuguese, and German, the latter so instilled in his training that he spoke the other two with a German accent, he would be an East German journalist preparing a story on the poor and exploited peasants of Mexico. If his destination were the United States, he would simply switch sides and be a West German reporting on the good life of democratic America. Neither destination would be entirely new to him.

One of the few of the Soviet diplomatic corps to have his own Cuban dacha on the beach, he pulled the Lada out onto the sand and walked inside his residence, taking special care to deactivate the alarm system. He would leave it off, for tonight he would entertain a guest.

First, he prepared his travel bags in the event of an urgent call. Then, he straightened up his quarters, which were already a model of military neatness. He placed the wine in the cooler and checked to ensure that his Soviet housekeeper had prepared the smoked salmon. She had. An appetizing-looking tray, wrapped in clear plastic to preserve the moistness of the fish and the juice of the lemon slices that outlined the salmon, sat in the refrigerator.

By 7:00 P.M. he had taken a quick swim, bathed, shaved, and double-checked to ensure that the fresh linens on the bed had been lightly scented. By 7:30 P.M. he had set out the salmon and the wine on the low table in front of the picture window. At 7:42 P.M. there was a light rapping on his door. He opened it.

"Tatiana, my love. I have missed you this past week. Come in and tell me what mischief you have been up to."

The daughter of Rudy Ordonez entered and kissed Plotnikov on the cheek and then full on the mouth as he pulled her to him and slid one hand down to grasp the firm flesh of her buttocks.

Chapter 14

July 9, 3:22 A.M.
Havana

Tatiana lay with her head on Plotnikov's chest, exhausted yet not at all sleepy from their marathon lovemaking. Plotnikov had not stirred for more than an hour. The night was finally cool, the sea breeze softly breathing across their bodies. For the first time since they had become lovers, she felt concerned. She knew the man resting under her head was a Soviet intelligence agent. All embassy personnel were intelligence agents. And as such, she expected him to be less sensitive, less emotional, less sentimental than other men she had known. That would not have bothered her. But, within their personal relationship, he was generally kind and gentle and considerate. Still, there was a submerged streak of cruelty that she had only tasted up to now. After awhile together in bed, he became almost impersonal, treating her body as if it were just a thing rather than the revered object of his love. Thoroughly aroused by that time, she always responded to his demands, but it was a different encounter, almost animal-like, and he sometimes spoke Russian words that she did not understand but were clearly derogatory in tone, as if he were cursing her. Tonight, for the first time, there had been pain.

He had yet to ask her about Morales. After Tatiana's considerable persuasion and threats, the Cuban guards back at Guantanamo had reluctantly contacted Plotnikov's office and he had vouched for her and her "husband." That had been a serious consideration, and she knew he must be at least curious and perhaps suspicious that Morales was another lover. If so, she would have suspected him to be more jealous. Whatever Plotnikov was thinking, Morales was now safely back at her father's house, and hopefully her duty with the American was over. She did not want to tell Plotnikov the real identity of Morales—that could be too dangerous for her father and grandmother—but she yearned to tell the Russian that she had not been with another lover. She would never be unfaithful to the Russian, not now that she was carrying his child.

There was another very serious concern. A packed suitcase lay on the table in the bedroom. Was Plotnikov being transferred? She had wanted their relationship to deepen to the point where he would consider taking her back to the Soviet Union. It would be the ideal way out of her dilemma. Her firm belief in the concept and future of revolutionary Cuba was in direct conflict with her sense of duty to her father and grandmother, and when they found out she was pregnant by one of the *bolas*, there would be a great scene. She had to do something, soon.

It was only when she was with Plotnikov that she was at peace with herself. A life with him and their child in the USSR would remove her from the conflicting obligations that sometimes threatened to rip out her insides. The past days with Morales were a prime example. Her father was demanding too much of her.

The pager on the bedside table began a constant, irritating series of beeps. Plotnikov awakened immediately and slid from under her upper body to turn it off. She felt it best to feign sleep. Immediately, he walked into the living area and dialed a number on the phone. Curious, she slipped out of the bed and stood in the shadows beside the door.

Plotnikov was speaking in Russian. She could not understand the words, but his inflections and tone betrayed a serious conversation, perhaps even an argument. At one point, he was obviously being interrupted as he tried to speak. He became irritated and argumentative. Finally, with much nodding of his head, he seemed to arrive at some agreement with the caller. He even seemed to be pleasantly excited as he closed the conversation and hung up.

Tatiana turned and started for the bed. Her foot caught on an unseen cord and the bedside lamp crashed to the floor. Plotnikov was in the doorway looking at her. He said nothing until he crossed over, picked up the lamp, and placed it on the table. "Are you all right?" he asked.

"Yes."

He gathered her in his arms. "I am sorry the pager awakened you. I have an assignment."

"You must leave right away?"

"Yes, but perhaps not for too long."

"Vlad, I want to go with you."

"That is impossible. I told you, I have an assignment."

Tatiana pulled Plotnikov tightly against her. "You're not coming back, I know it." Her tears wet his chest.

"Don't talk like that. Of course I'll be back. It is just temporary. My main assignment is here."

Tatiana felt her world slipping away from her. Plotnikov had an important position in Cuba. If he was being called away in the dead of the night, something was very wrong. She loosened her grip on his back. She must tell him, now. "Vlad, I'm carrying your child." Her words were too abrupt and urgent. This was not the way she had planned to let him know.

Plotnikov let his arms slide around from her back and he gripped her upper arms. "You said this would not happen. I trusted you."

"I love you, Vlad. You must take me and your child with you back to the Soviet Union where there will be a decent life and . . ."

Plotnikov shook his head. No, this must not be. The GRU did not mind a discreet affair. That was the nature of man. But the regulations were quite specific when it came to breeding with Cubans. That placed the agent in too vulnerable a position. Certainly, marriage was out of the question; there would be no taking Tatiana and the child back to the Soviet Union. General Gigiyash-vili was already exercising heroic tolerance in giving Plotnikov a chance to redeem himself by recovering the remaining weapon. To have a Cuban woman surface at this time, demanding a mother's rights, would mean an instant end to his career. "Are you sure?" he asked.

"Of course. I want to go back with you—as your wife."

"No. I mean, are you sure you are pregnant?"

"Yes."

Vlad stepped back and ran one palm across her belly. "It does not show."

Tatiana smiled. "It is only a matter of weeks. It will show soon enough."

"The man at Guantanamo. He is the father."

Tatiana let her anger at the remark narrow her eyes and give them a fierce sparkle. "No! I was there because of conditions over which I had no control. He was no lover. You are my only love, Vlad. Do not insult me so."

"Who was he?"

"It is of no consequence."

It was Plotnikov's turn to be angry. He had been more than gracious by not inquiring more into the Guantanamo incident. "I did as you asked because of our relationship. I took your situation on faith. I cannot do that now, not in the light of what you have told me. It *is* of consequence. You will tell me, now." Reaching out with both arms, he roughly grabbed her.

"You are hurting me," pleaded Tatiana.

Plotnikov lightened his grip but held onto her arms. "Tell me!"

"The man is an American agent, here on a special assignment."

Plotnikov let his mouth open for only an instant before resetting it to talk through his teeth. "An American agent? You are working for the Americans! You have used me! What have you done? What have you told them?"

Tatiana saw something in Plotnikov's eyes she had never seen before, not even at the height of his rough lovemaking.

"No! No! You must understand. I have told the American nothing. Please, let me go! Let me tell you."

Plotnikov released his grip.

There was no other way out now. Tatiana knew that to speak would be to risk betrayal of her father. But the life within her had to have its chance. She would fight anyone for that. "Members of my family sometimes assist American intelligence agents. It is a harmless activity, the act of old people who have not resigned themselves to the revolution."

"Go on."

"My father is old. I love him and I am his only child. He will die soon. I must do as he says. I do not want to break his heart . . ."

"Tatiana." Plotnikov's voice was soft, caring. "You are rambling. I am not interested in your father. Ninety percent of the old Cubans have not reconciled themselves. They are not important. The American is."

"He is here to find out the nature of some cylinders . . ."

Plotnikov's interest suddenly became very acute.

". . . and I have been escorting him and providing him cover."

"Escorting him where?"

"To the airport and in the backcountry where we saw the cylinders being loaded onto a small airplane."

"When? How long ago?"

"Several days ago. The airplane left with one of the cylinders and we tried to trace the other, but it was taken to some sort of armed compound."

"Military?"

"It was not Cuban military. It was an armed camp of some sort."

Plotnikov now knew how the Palestinians had removed one of the devices from the country. How they had subsequently used it to destroy the American carrier was still a mystery but irrelevant. Further tracking and recovery of the second device was the assignment just given him, and the intelligence relayed by the phone call was compatible with what Tatiana was saying. The Palestinians were known to have been in central Cuba prior to the attack on the carrier, and then they disappeared. The Soviet intelligence community within Cuba was certain that the Palestinians were no longer in-country and had unconfirmed reports that they were in Mexico.

"What were you and the American doing at Guantanamo?"

"He was ordered to report there. I do not know what happened while he was on the base."

"His name?"

"Morales. Davey Morales."

"He used his own name?"

"That is the name he gave me."

"CIA?"

"I do not know."

"CIA," Plotnikov declared quietly. "They know about the devices. But, how?" he wondered aloud.

"Please, Vlad, my father is an old man. Do not let me betray him."

"I am not interested in your father. He and his companions are your Maximum Leader's concern. I have no wish to do him harm." Plotnikov knew what he must do, and his words were spoken to reassure the young Cuban woman who stood naked in front of him, her eyes moist and confused with fear and despair at the choice she had just made.

"You have been honest with me. For that, I will reconsider our situation. I must go on this assignment. When I return, we will talk of the child and perhaps I will ask permission to take you with me when my tour here is over."

"Oh, Vlad, I love you so. Thank you. Thank you."

Plotnikov kissed her on the neck, letting his hands lightly roam her lower back. "It is all right. Calm yourself. I have a small amount of time left. Let us not waste it."

Tatiana turned to go back to the bed but Plotnikov held onto one arm. "Wait, why not a swim first? We are already undressed for it!" Teasingly, he slapped her bare bottom and grabbed her hands.

"Vlad, I would really rather not." Tatiana could not understand his sudden change in mood.

"Come on. We'll wash away those tears."

Tatiana did not want to go swimming. She wanted to go back to bed and have Plotnikov cover her with his body and fill her with his passion. Even his roughness would assure her of his love. She made one feeble last protest, "At this time of night? Vlad, you are sometimes crazy! We would freeze!"

"Not once we are in the water. I will see that you are not cold. You know that. Come on, it will be a different way to say good-bye."

"Good-bye?"

"Only for a while, as I said. I will bring you something when I return."

Together, they ran to the edge of the lapping surf, Tatiana somewhat reluctant at first, but squealing with delight as they entered the night-cooled water. Plotnikov pulled her to him and they clung to each other, alternately submerging themselves and rolling in the surf. They finally stood in water neck deep, laughing at their foolishness.

Tatiana felt him harden. "Vlad, let's go back to the house."

"Hush, silly one," said Plotnikov softly, letting one hand slide down across her belly, his fingers probing her rapidly swelling genitalia. "Let me make love to you," he whispered.

Tatiana responded as soon as he touched her. She raised her legs and wrapped them around his waist, the buoyancy of the water lifting her effortlessly to receive him. Plotnikov partially squatted for a moment, and as he rose abruptly Tatiana felt him plunge inside her. Gently at first, she matched his rhythm with rotary movement of her pelvis. Then, as her arousal became all-consuming, she met him on even terms, opening herself wide as he achieved maximum penetration. Their coupling became more intense and she felt his hands grasping her buttocks with a fierceness that would have frightened her had not her orgasm arrived. Involuntary spasms arched her back and she stretched out her legs to heighten the sensation. "Vlad . . . oh, we'll be so happy, Vlad."

Her climax had never been so intense or lasted so long. She

was stretched almost horizontal as Plotnikov continued his relent-
less thrusting.

Even as his own orgasm began, Plotnikov looked up and down
the beach. There was no one. He did not like being forced into what
he must do. Gasping, he felt the rising surge of indescribable pleasure overwhelm him and almost erase his purpose. But as soon as
it passed, he lunged farther forward, keeping himself tightly locked
inside Tatiana. They disappeared beneath the waves and he used
his full weight to push her toward the bottom. Tatiana struggled,
confused for only a moment before the awful realization of what he
was doing drove her into an immediate panic. She pounded on his
back and head. He countered by grabbing her arms and pinning
them to her sides, forcing her to use only her body in the struggle
beneath him. She tried to use her teeth, but she was already out of
air and swallowing water. Plotnikov turned her around, locked her
arms in front of her, and bent her torso forward. Holding her in that
position, he regained his footing and stood, his head just out of the
water, his body straining against her desperate attempts to free herself. But there was no way she could break his grip. Her struggle
weakened. There was a final, violent jerk of her body and then a
series of shudders, each one weaker than the previous. Then she was
still. Plotnikov held her under the water for several more minutes,
keeping her limp body bent double at the waist. Once more checking the beach, he carried her back into his beach house and slipped
on her string bikini, shaking his head in disappointment at such a
waste of erotic beauty. Carrying her back into the water, he swam
several hundred yards downcurrent and released the body.

Returning to his bedroom, he dressed and gathered her things
along with his suitcase. Hurriedly, he walked to his car. He stopped
the Lada opposite the waters where her body would be floating, got
out of the car, and made his way down to the sand. Arranging a
beach towel, he placed her clothes in a neat pile beside it. Before
reentering his car, he took a final look down at the beach and
beyond at the dark water. She should not have been unfaithful to
him—and she should not have allowed herself to become pregnant.
That was an unforgivable mistake. There was no way that he could
have allowed himself to be trapped into such a marriage. He had
been fond of her, but not at the expense of his career in the GRU.

Davey Morales sat in the open doorway of the house of Rudy
Ordonez. It was just too hot to sleep, despite the fact that Ordonez
lived on the edge of Honda Bay, where there should be some breeze

working in from seaward. There was just enough to carry the smell of fish but not enough to cool his moist skin. It was almost dawn. Already, the first tinge of new-day light was bleeding over the eastern horizon. Tatiana was probably just as restless back at her place over the fruit stand near San Jose de las Lajas. Davey also wondered how Geraldo Cordero had taken his walking off the job after the first day. He must have reported it. In any event, Davey felt very fortunate to be away from Guantanamo. Tatiana had a powerful friend somewhere. That phone call had resulted in an immediate release of them both, no questions asked.

It was difficult to place in the proper perspective the guilt he felt about failing to intercept the *Lincoln* weapon. Adding to his misery was the fact that his efforts since then had failed to yield a clue as to the whereabouts of the remaining two Arabs and the weapon. His failure to perform had cost six thousand Americans their lives. He did not intend to ever fail again.

Further random searching in Cuba was pointless. That he knew. The terrorists obviously enjoyed some Cuban military support and, if they had wanted to leave the country, they would be out by now. If only Rudy would return. The old practico had left shortly after midnight, promising to make contact with Key West and see if there were any instructions for Davey. It was almost light enough to read when Ordonez returned.

"The Old Man wants you to go to Mexico. He says they have reports that the Palestinians may have escaped across the Yucatan Channel. God only knows where they'll hole up, but that's what they'll do, in my estimation, until things cool down a bit."

"It'll be difficult getting off this island," observed Davey.

"Maybe not. Aeromexico flies into Jose Marti twice a week. The Old Man wants you on tomorrow's plane. With the state of emergency that Castro has declared, they won't care what foreigners leave as long as the proper papers are shown. And with the invasion scare, there will be Mexican nationals leaving. We will just have to see that you're one of them."

"You people seem to have a full-time printing mill going, the way you turn out papers."

"We've got a problem this time. Mexican nationals carry a special passport. We've not seen one close enough to be able to reproduce it. We'll have to figure a way to get you on the plane without one."

"How will you do that?"

"I don't know yet, but I have several people working on it. We have a few sympathizers working at the airport in nonsensitive positions, but they are not too anxious to risk something like this. The problem is that the plane will be fully booked. Even if we get you on board, there remains the problem of a seat—and the passenger list will be closely checked. There is another factor. The Mexican community is not large and most of them know each other quite well."

"How about a boat across to Yucatan? Isn't that the most probable way the Palestinians escaped?"

"I have some people working on that, also, but it may not be feasible or desirable. Assuming you get past Cuban and American patrols, which are now quite heavy since the U.S. went on their alert, you will have to enter Yucatan blind—at least until you can make contact with one of your people to find out if there are any leads as to the terrorists' location. It is best you go to Mexico City and have access to all of the intelligence facilities of the embassy until a lead turns up. After that, travel within Mexico should be relatively simple."

"Do Palestinians have support in Mexico?"

"Hell, everybody has support in Mexico if they have enough pesos. The peninsula is riddled with *banditos* who will do anything. There is very little effective law community in the outlands, although the larger towns are safe enough. Tourists are all over the area visiting the Mayan ruins, but they stay pretty much in groups. Otherwise, nobody gives a damn about anybody."

"Can I get to Yucatan and then to Mexico City?"

"Our organization is very thin in Yucatan. I don't know about other CIA presence. I can't guarantee any assistance. You can have some Mexican papers, no problem: driver's license, lottery tickets, and so on, and pesos. But you would be on your own as far as travel."

"That doesn't sound too bad."

"It may be what we have to do. But let's wait until we see what our friends have accomplished. I have requested a briefing tonight."

"Here?"

"No. Much too risky, with the block wardens all over. We'll go fishing today. It is my normal routine. After dark, we should be able to meet just inside the bay with no patrol interference. We often meet that way, to drink a few beers and exchange talk about the best fishing areas and just relax after the work of the catch."

"I'm not much of a fisherman."

"Then come! I'll make one of you."

✳ ✳ ✳

The morning sun was halfway to its zenith when the Soviet Air Force Ilyushin Il-76 cargo transport started its descent into Mexico City. On the flight deck of the big jet, almost a perfect copy of the U.S. Lockheed C-141 Starlifter, Vladlen Mikhailovich Plotnikov stood watching the flight crew's routine as they guided the aircraft down through scattered clouds. They were passing through twelve thousand feet when the plane commander, sitting in the right seat and acting as the copilot for his other pilot, looked back at the colonel. "Comrade, it might be advisable for you to strap yourself in securely for the landing. Andrei has been known to bounce halfway down the runway before I must take control of the aircraft from him."

The younger pilot spoke in his own defense, "You can stand on your hands, Colonel, and my landing will not even affect your balance."

As both pilots laughed, Plotnikov added, "I think I will strap in."

The landing at the high-elevation airport was as smooth as any Plotnikov had ever sat through, and the young pilot was openly gloating as Plotnikov left the flight deck and entered a waiting staff car. Within minutes he was in the GRU residentura of the Soviet embassy, being briefed by his Mexico City counterpart.

"We believe the Palestinians entered the Yucatan Peninsula early in the morning of July fifth at the fishing village of Punta Allen. Inquiries there have revealed that two men with a crated cargo box about the size of the device arrived and hired one of the locals to drive them from the village. They indicated that the box was a burial box of a Mexican national who had died at sea. The villager was later found on the road to Valladolid with his throat cut, his pickup abandoned just south of Merida, which is a tourist city near the northwestern tip of the peninsula."

"When was that?"

"The pickup was discovered on the afternoon of the seventh."

"They could have gone much farther within that time frame. That means they stopped for some reason."

"To hide the device?"

"Perhaps. Or to hire someone to provide them with services, transportation, a hideaway, protection. How thorough has our surveillance been since that time?"

"Two men, even non-Latins, could have escaped our detection if they did not have the device with them. It would be hard to take along unnoticed. We have searched every village on the peripheral

road along the west coast and uncovered nothing. You should realize that there is some bandito country on the peninsula, with most
of the inland roads going to the ruins. Some isolated farmers in the
backcountry. Peasants on the lowest economic scale."

"...who would welcome exchanging shelter and privacy for
even a few pesos."

"Yes."

"If they backtracked, where could they have gone?"

"They would have gone clear back around the tip of the peninsula, back through Puerto Morelos and then south."

"Why not cut across the peninsula?" asked Plotnikov, looking
at a wall map of the area.

"They could have, but most of those roads are traveled by the
tourist buses, as I previously indicated. There are a few others, but
they are practically trails and are often washed out and nonexistent despite the red lines you see on the map."

"Then I will start at Merida. The police may have a lead. I will
need a rental car. I have my own identification documents."

"The town police, like so many in Mexico, are probably corrupt
and could have been bought off, but I agree it is a starting place.
The car is already arranged. Will you eat before you leave?"

"No, I can eat on the airplane, assuming there is an immediate
flight. I have only a few minutes of preparation to make."

"Aeromexico leaves in just over an hour. You are already
booked to Merida. Our complete staff and field people are at your
disposal, of course."

"I expect that."

Not only was Davey Morales not a fisherman, he was not much
of a sailor on this particular day. Despite his expertise at underwater work and his many hours spent on small craft, Ordonez's
boat and the seas off of Honda Bay had combined to give him the
ride of his life. Ordonez took it all in stride, as if his rugged body
was without a stomach, throat, or mouth, the three organs Davey
was ready to cut out of himself.

"My God, how do you take all this?" asked Davey, not really
caring if he lived or died.

"This is a bad one, I admit, but it is my life. I have sailed many
days like this. You adjust after a time. We will not catch many fish,
however."

"What a shame," commented Davey, leaning over the leeward
lifeline for the umpteenth time.

"Why don't you go below and try to lie down for a while? I will head back toward the bay and perhaps find smoother waters. We can wait there until nightfall."

"Feel free to bury me at sea," said Davey, making his way down the hatch that led to the small galley and sleeping area. Lying prone did help, and after an hour Ordonez had the boat in slightly calmer water. Davey dozed until the hard slaps on the hatch cover woke him up.

"It is time! I have the other boats in sight," yelled Ordonez.

Davey sat up, pleased that the nausea seemed to have disappeared. He was still weak, and grabbed a hunk of bread, deciding to risk his stomach rather than his energy. It stayed down.

Back up on deck, Davey could see that they were just inside a breakwater on the southern end of Honda Bay. Rudy Ordonez was dropping his bow anchor, and two other boats were approaching in the early night. Davey's watch read 9:18 P.M. The two boats tied alongside Ordonez's ketch, and several of their crew came aboard. Everyone sat in the afterdeck well as Ordonez passed around rum in paper cups. All the men were within five years, one way or the other, of Ordonez's age.

"I think we may have a way out for your man, Rudy," offered one of the fishermen, the captain of the nearest boat, a tall man of perhaps six-four. "One of the names on the flight list is Davey Morales, courtesy of our contact in the Aeromexico office."

"You used my real name?" exclaimed Davey.

"Why not? If your name has been brought to anyone's attention, say because of your quick departure from your assigned job at the Icar or the detainment at Guantanamo, it will not have been passed around for such small matters. As far as the Aeromexico authorities in Cuba know, you are just one of the aircraft reconditioning staff—a nameless face among their employees. We do have one difficulty and that is your passport. We don't have one."

"How do we get around that?" asked Davey.

"We can't run you through outgoing customs, so we have made arrangements to have you board the aircraft as soon as it arrives. As one of the plane cleaners. Stay on until they start to load, then off with the coveralls and into one of the restrooms. Come out when you hear the others boarding and take a seat—there will be one vacant."

"And at the other end?"

"Your embassy knows you're coming. They will identify you as an American citizen and will intercept you at customs. It is all arranged. The necessary Mexican authorities all will have received compensation. So, by confusion on this end and graft on that end, you should have no difficulty."

Davey permitted himself an observation. "I have always been under the impression that our organization in Cuba is very thin and barely effective. You people seem to do anything you want."

"Only in small matters, our friend. Getting necessary papers, moving people in and out, that is not difficult. But as for any effective action such as deep penetration intelligence, sabotage, elimination of undesirables, we must turn to Miami and Key West. We do not have the expertise, and if any of us are caught there would be widespread retribution. So, from time to time, a person like yourself is sent in and we do what we can. And you are right, we are spread thin and are barely effective, and I would add that when we are gone, there will be no more like us," answered the tall fisherman.

Davey nodded.

"Any questions?"

"I assume Rudy knows how to get me onto the airport."

"Oh, yes. And when you get back, you might tell the Old Man that we could use some more funds. You are a costly operation. A few thousand dollars doesn't go as far as it used to, and the one thing we can't print is American money."

Davey watched the ground drop below him as Aeromexico Special Flight 122 lifted off from Jose Marti Airport. Every seat on the airplane was full, but no one seemed to give him a second glance. The profusion of excited chatter was muffled by the padding and stuffed seats of the passenger compartment, and his seatmates seemed content to merely acknowledge his presence with friendly nods and arrange themselves more comfortably for the three-hour flight to Mexico City.

It was hard not to think of Tatiana. With more time, he suspected her attitude toward him would have softened. It was interesting to think of what may have developed. They had worked well together, despite her reservations. But now that he was leaving Cuba, that was all over and certainly of no consequence when he thought of what his failure to intercept the cylinders had cost. Six thousand lives, a capital ship of the U.S. Navy, his country now at a very nervous alert. He had to agree that the Palestinians were long gone—somewhere—and although Mexico was the logical place, there were others. Why not the Caribbean? Central or even South America? An offshore pickup ship?

And where did they intend to use that second weapon? That was really the only important question.

An embassy courier was waiting for him when he disembarked, and with quiet efficiency herded him through customs. Once they were in the main arrival concourse, the man handed Davey a sealed envelope. Davey ripped it open and removed the single page. The typewritten message was a relay from the Old Man:

Davey:
We have strong evidence that our subjects entered the Yucatan Peninsula and have passed through Merida. Proceed at once and contact Lolo Alvarez, chief of police. We are concentrating on area.

It was signed with the Old Man's customarily scrawled "T," and a penned note was added:

Rudy advises Tatiana drowned while swimming off Alerco Beach near Havana. Sorry. We owed her.

"I have your ticket, sir," said the courier. Davey didn't hear him. His mind was on the young Cuban woman in the ruffled nightdress. Drowned? How? Why? He felt a great sadness. She was so young and so full of fire. So devoted to the revolution and so loyal to her family. A troubled soul who deserved much more than an early death. Davey couldn't shake the idea that she had not drowned by accident. It just didn't fit. Not Tatiana, the resourceful and fit daughter of Rudy Ordonez.

"I have your ticket, sir," repeated the courier, holding out a brown envelope and a small carryall bag.

Davey took them without replying. In the envelope was an Aeromexico folder, his authentic ID papers, and some Mexican currency. The bag would have clothes.

"I'll check in when I get to Merida," he said listlessly to the courier.

"Yes, sir," the man replied.

Within the hour, Davey was back in the air, headed for the Yucatan.

Chapter 15

July 11, Dawn
Central Caribbean Coast of Belize

The eternal surf continued its thunderous pounding as it rolled across the great barrier reef of the Caribbean. Second in size only to the massive protector of Australia's northeast coast, the reef churned the blue water into a white froth that sparkled iridescently, reflecting the first rays of the morning sun. Sixty miles to the west, the coastline of the new nation of Belize, nestled just south of the Yucatan Peninsula of Mexico, was beginning to experience predawn light. The occupant of the thatched shack that was the lone structure on the stretch of sand twenty miles south of Belize City was just starting his morning ablutions.

"In the name of God!" intoned Kamal Adwan, his first words of the new day coming softly and with reverence. Dipping cupped hands into the gray clay bowl of seawater that sat on a tripod of bound sticks, he rubbed his palms together, making sure that the water flowed over every inch of the skin. He dipped his hands again, and then a third time. Leaning forward, he rinsed his mouth also three times, ensuring that each time he snuffed some of the water into his nostrils. He washed his face, deliberately proceeding from his hairline down to his neck, around to his chin, and up the openings of his nostrils. Taking another cupped palm of the water, he massaged his beard, allowing the water to rinse out any dust and food particles. Once more, he washed his hands, up to and including his wrists. Leaving them moist, he rubbed his head and ears, again going from forward to rear and onto the nape of his neck and upper back.

Lifting the bowl, he placed it on the floor of the hut and stepped in with each foot before squatting on a straw mat and cleansing his feet and ankles, meticulously cleaning between his toes with his fingers. Twice more, he repeated the act of washing his feet, then stood on the mat, his face raised toward heaven. "I witness that there is no god but God, the Unique, who has no partner. I witness that Muhammad is His servant and His messenger." Walking outside, he picked up a small twig, stripped it clean, and chewed it until the exterior was covered with tiny burrs. With it, he cleaned the spaces between his teeth, and rubbed the chewed wood across their surfaces.

Facing east, Adwan raised his arms until they were at the level of his shoulders. "Allahu Akbar!" (God is most great.) His eyes searching toward the first light of the dawn, he continued,

In the name of God, the Merciful, the Compassionate.
Praise be to God, the Lord of the Worlds,
The Merciful One, the Compassionate One,
Master of the Day of Doom.

Thee alone we serve, to thee alone we cry for help.
Guide us in the straight path
The path of them Thou has blessed.
Not of those with whom Thou art angry
Nor of those who go astray.
Amen.

Having recited the obligatory first passage of the Koran, Adwan added a short verse from the last part of the Holy Book in a low but audible voice. Then, leaning stiffly forward, reaching with his hands for his knees and keeping his back straight during the inclination, he repeated, "Allahu Akbar!" He held his inclination for a moment before raising his head to continue, "God hears those who praise Him. My God, Our Lord, to Thee be praise!"

Next, he stood erect, his countenance serene, his demeanor quiet. After a moment of meditation, he dropped once more to his knees and fell forward.

"Allahu Akbar!"

Prostrate, he touched his forehead and nose to the sand, his palms flat upon the surface beside his ears and aligned with his head toward Mecca. He made certain that his feet were perpendicular to the ground, the ends of his big toes touching.

"Glory unto Thee, my Lord! I have wronged myself and done evil! Forgive me! In my zeal, I have let my pride overcome my wish to do Thy will, and in my soul I take false comfort from the vanquishment of Thine enemies. Guide my feet and make firm my hand that holds the sword of the Lord! Allahu Akbar!"

Twice more, he prostrated himself and recited the holy prayers, finally ending with,

Unto God be all salutations, all things good, all things pleasing, all benedictions. Peace be upon Thee, O Prophet, and the mercy of God and His blessings! Peace be upon us all, and all righteous servants of God. I witness that there is no god but God, the Unique, without partner. I witness that Muhammad is His servant and messenger.

Looking straight east toward Mecca but tilting his head slightly to the right, Adwan concluded, "Peace be upon Thee."

The tip of the sun sparkled above the horizon.

Returning to the hut, he opened a bottle of water and drank thirstily. The bottle was still upended when he heard the car approaching. It stopped at the end of the road, which did not quite reach the hut. Relieved to see that it was their rental vehicle, he watched Youssif Daoud open the door and step out.

Adwan waited for him to approach. "You are taking great risks, going into the city," he commented.

Daoud shrugged. "I am a man of God on a holy mission. Nothing will happen."

"Have you abandoned the law of the five prayers? You are transgressing against the teachings of the Qu'ran. Why do you do these things? How can you be a soldier of God and not follow His law?"

"I do follow His law, my brother, just as you do. The Qu'ran admonishes us against unjustifiable killing, does it not? And yet we kill, sometimes indiscriminately, for by doing so we prove ourselves fervent defenders of the law. You have finished your morning prayers, have you not? And in them, did you not proclaim peace to all? *Peace?* Kamal. Is that what we are about?"

"Yes, in the ultimate. It is not the same with fornication."

"Oh, that is it. We can disobey and kill for our purpose, but not fornicate!"

"You know the Qu'ran as I."

"I do, indeed. And I have made the hajj, Kamal, the holy pilgrimage to Mecca. I have seen the sacred Ka'bah and kissed the Black Stone of Abraham before completing the seven walks around the Ka'bah. I have stood at the Mount of Mercy at Arafat, where the last prophet preached his final sermon, and I have said my prayers to Allah before the tomb of Muhammad in Medina. I have made the pilgrimage for Allah, I kill for Allah, and I fornicate for Allah."

"You blaspheme!"

"No, I fornicate only with infidels. Is that any more blasphemous than killing them? Is giving them pleasure more of a sin than killing them, Kamal? Do you know where I have been this night? I have been in the sleeping compartment of an American tourist, an infidel of the highest order. We fornicated, Kamal, and then I slit her infidel throat. God is most great!"

"That is an excess of wine talking. Even there you sin. If you have done such a thing, the authorities will be after you and our holy mission can be compromised. You will not go into town unless I say so. No more! Already, you may have gone once too often."

"Unless *you* say so? What will you do, Kamal? Kill me?"

"Yes."

"That is our solution to everything, isn't it, my brother? Kill. We are very good at it. I am tired."

Adwan watched Daoud walk unsteadily into the hut. His drinking and womanizing were becoming worse. The man could not be a true believer of Islam. But he was one of the deadliest of Islam's soldiers and for that reason Adwan would let him live—for a while. He called after Daoud in a loud voice, "If you have any respect for the sacred law, you will cleanse yourself—now! Youssif! You are unclean! You have been with a woman, Youssif! Do not abandon the teachings of Muhammad!"

Daoud entered the hut without replying.

Adwan felt cursed. With the exception of Daoud's attitude and careless behavior, their mission was going exactly as planned. The transfer of the two weapons in Cuba had gone off flawlessly. Zadefi's strike at the *Lincoln* had been successful beyond belief. Adwan could visualize the response of satanistic America, which had to be in a state of turmoil with the government desperately striving to react properly against the threat and the people vocally criticizing everything the government was doing. That was the way of Americans, so fiercely independent that they found great difficulty in uniting in a single course of action. Without a doubt, the two political parties in the American Congress would be blaming each other for the state of affairs that allowed simple peasants of the Middle East to engage and destroy elements of the world's mightiest and most sophisticated military machine. In their pursuit of things material, they could not see the simple truth that it was a triumph of those who were believers in the one God over a society of materialists. The ultimate end, the triumph of Islam over the West, was inevitable.

Adwan took great comfort that their escape from Cuba had gone as planned, as had their entry into Belize. God was surely guiding them. Formerly British Honduras, the colony was a perfect place to hide for a while, either a few weeks or several months if necessary. The tiny country was uncomplicated politically and easygoing with respect to border security. As for the heritage of the people, the Belizeans were a mixture of Creoles of African descent, Black Caribs—Afro-Indians from the eastern Caribbean—mestizos of Spanish and Indian blood, sharp-featured Mayans, Europeans, and a scattering of Chinese and Lebanese. It was the presence of the latter group that had made Belize the choice for their hideaway—Adwan and Daoud could easily pass as Lebanese. There was another bonus since neither he nor Daoud spoke Spanish: the official language was English, with Spanish a second albeit a frequently spoken tongue.

The thatched hut had been acquired months in advance of the operation and was in a place of natural seclusion, being just beyond the mangrove swamps south of Belize City, the main seaport of the tiny nation. Adwan had seen no other human since their arrival.

As for their weapon, it had been safely buried back on the Yucatan, easy enough to retrieve when their mission was resumed. For now, they would wait until their contact in Mexico visited them and laid out the plan for their entry into the United States. That would be Ahmad Labidi, a member of Mexico City's small Muslim community and a fervent supporter of the Palestinian movement. He should also reveal to Adwan and Daoud their target city in America.

Adwan was not comfortable with inactivity, and the morning wore on very slowly despite a refreshing breakfast of fresh fruit and a swim in the warm waters. Noon prayers were a comfort. After them, Adwan walked south along the beach and exercised by clearing away washed-up debris and making minor repairs to the hut. His companion slept away the day but woke to join Adwan in an evening meal of fish and corn. Adwan wanted to argue with Daoud about his conduct and impress upon him the danger it was to their security, but he knew the man to be stubborn, and words seemed to have little effect. He said his evening prayers alone. Daoud watched him while sitting on the sand a short distance away.

They had retired for the night when an approaching automobile swung beams of light across the front of the hut. Adwan woke Daoud quietly and they grabbed their personal weapons, staying out of sight as the car's lights were extinguished and a single individual approached. Daoud slipped quietly out of the rear of the hut and worked his way around behind the approaching figure.

Stopping a few yards from the hut, the man called, "Kamal! Youssif! It is I, Ahmad! Ahmad Labidi! Are you there?" Adwan could see Daoud barely five feet behind Labidi, his weapon pointed at their visitor's head. Labidi almost jumped out of his skin as Daoud spoke. "Do not turn around. Walk into the hut."

Adwan lit the small kerosene lamp and recognized their accomplice. "*Labbaika-Alluhumma, Labbiak!*" (Here I am, O God, at Thy command, Here I am!) said Adwan, using the greeting normally reserved for entry into the Islamic pilgrim's state of concentration on the precious visit to Mecca.

"Labbaika-Alluhumma, Labbiak!" responded Labidi.

The three sat at the small table that was the main feature of the hut's meager furnishings.

"It goes well!" began Labidi. "We have struck a mighty blow."

"God is great!" replied Adwan. Daoud remained silent.

"I see you are settled," continued Labidi. "Were there any problems?"

"None of any consequence. Our weapon is buried where no one will find it. Crossing the border into this place was routine. We have funds and seclusion. How long must we wait?"

"That is uncertain. The Americans have instituted a rigid control around their borders. Mexico is cooperating but they lack the coherence and sophistication to properly patrol their own land. There is still danger, of course, and you must not move around at all. Into town for provisions, perhaps, but that is all. We researched this place quite thoroughly before establishing your sanctuary here. It is off the tourist path, and even the local people have little need to come down through the swampland. There are much better recreation and fishing beaches elsewhere. If you do encounter anyone, pretend to be Lebanese settlers."

Adwan looked pointedly at Daoud, who remained expressionless.

"I suspect there will be an intense period of concentrated effort to discover where you have gone, but that will pass. When things then become more routine, I will have transport arranged to take you from here and north to the border. We are working on your crossing arrangements."

"We are anxious," spoke up Daoud, much to Adwan's surprise. His companion had seemed almost detached from the conversation.

"Yes. But patience is the virtue we must practice, for as long as it takes. We must allow the Americans to think that the threat has passed."

"Our contacts in the United States? They are not in jeopardy?" asked Adwan.

"Some, as you would suspect. There are many brothers in America, concentrated for the most part in several of the larger cities. Students and operators of small businesses. Well established, many of them now citizens. They are under intense scrutiny, of course, and hardly any are sympathetic to our methods of warfare. Fortunately, our fellow members of the Shaheen brotherhood have been able to merge themselves with such communities and are quite safe. The next few weeks may be a difficult time for them, but a quiet one for us. In their haste and panic, the Americans will undoubtedly take steps against American Muslims that will create further divisions within their society. They are a strange people. We will use that division to our best advantage, a lesson we have learned from the Godless ones in the Soviet Union. It is Allah's plan, is it not?"

"How will we cross the border?" asked Daoud, leaning forward with more apparent interest.

"That is undetermined at the present. We have several sites in mind and you will be informed before you leave here. There are two conditions before we move farther. The Mexicans must tire of checking travelers and become lax in their efforts. The Americans must convince themselves that the threat has lessened and loosen their border patrols. They will not discontinue them and they will never be as sparse as they were before, when the main concern was illegal Mexican entry. But they will eventually stand down from their present maximum effort, and when they do, we resume the operation."

"Can we go around by sea?"

"No, definitely not. For one thing, we would need a very capable boat, and offshore surveillance is one of their strongest efforts at present. The Gulf is saturated with American patrols and the southern coasts of both sides are heavily patrolled. We would have to go as far north as perhaps Seattle or the New England states. That would not be practical. There has been some discussion of flying into Canada and penetrating from the north, but the Canadians are fully cooperative with the Americans and even if we could get you two in, we could not disguise the weapon."

"Then we shall be patient," observed Adwan.

"There is another matter. The Russians are in a state of rage over our use of the weapon against the Americans. They say it is a devastating breach of our contract with them. Frankly, they are worried that matters between them and the Americans can escalate out of control."

"The Americans know the weapons are Russian?"

"Somehow, they do. I was called into the Soviet embassy and they are furious. They demanded we return the remaining weapon. I informed them the weapon has been taken back to our land for use as a deterrent against the Jews. I do not think they believed me. So, to add to our problems we can expect the KGB—and the GRU—to be searching for you as well as the Americans."

"The Godless ones would do well to worry," stated Adwan. "God waits to use our hand against them after we defeat the Americans."

"Here is my address in Belize City. I have a room at the Han Guest House, toward the end of Queen Street. It is north of the Swing Bridge and on the right just before you come to the American embassy. I will be watching for any increased activity at the embassy, although I do not think the Americans have any feel for our possible presence in this country. It is thus a precaution and I will inform you if I feel there is any threat. Meanwhile, we will have no contact unless it is vital that you speak with me. The owner of the Han is Chinese and speaks only Chinese, so this is my room number and a key. If I am not there, wait for me. But remember that to enter the city is to expose yourselves."

Adwan and Daoud walked outside with Labidi and watched him drive away into the dark night. "We must heed his advice,

Youssif," said Adwan. "Our only trips into the city must be for necessities."

"I agree, my brother, but my necessities are more than yours. Do not concern yourself."

Adwan was tempted to reply but kept quiet as Daoud reentered the hut. The light inside faded and was gone. Adwan walked to the water's edge and sat. The new day was already arriving although dawn was still several hours away. Labidi's visit had been reassuring. Things were under control.

The night birds were soaring overhead, their squeaky calls punctuating the steady sound of the gentle surf. Adwan peered skyward at the cloudless night and the millions of stars sparkling overhead, their incredible distances from Earth reminding him that he was seeing their light as they appeared millions of years before. The vastness of the universe was a source of great wonderment to him, and the contemplation of such things was his only relaxation. But even that, tonight, could not erase his concern over Daoud and his loss of faith. He had twice reminded Daoud of his obligation with respect to the daily prayers. The *shari'a*—the law—provided that if a brother Muslim neglected those prayers, he was to be reminded three times. If he still omitted them, through negligence, then it was right and proper to kill him, for he had become an infidel. Adwan's thoughts were confused. What was his greater obligation? To ensure that their holy task was carried out?—and Daoud was quite vital, perhaps indispensable, to that— or was he obligated to carry out the specific provisions of the shari'a?

The peaceful stars overhead offered him no answer.

Back at the Yucatan-Belize border city of Chetumal, Vladlen Plotnikov shifted uneasily on the uncomfortable wooden bench in the crude passenger waiting area of the Batty Brothers Bus Service terminal, impatiently waiting for the 5:00 A.M. departure to Belize City. With nothing better to do, he reviewed his notes. There was the sighting of the two strangers at the Yucatan fishing village of Puerto Moreles on the morning of July 5 and their "burial box" for a deceased companion. There was the commandeered pickup, subsequently found near Valladolid, and the owner's hacked body found south of Merida. A strange sequence, but not entirely illogical. He had no doubt that the Palestinians were holed up somewhere not far from their point of entry. Forcing the pickup driver to take them through Merida had probably been a ruse to throw any followers off track. Then they had doubled back through Merida after killing the pickup's owner and driven toward Valladolid. Why they abandoned the pickup short of there was a mystery, and what mode of transportation they used from that point on was unknown. They would not have holed up in the immediate area since it was Mayan ruins country and there were frequent tourist buses and other travelers.

He put himself in their place. Mexico would certainly respond to the United States' request for help in tracking them down. The quickest way out from the Yucatan—over land—would be to head for Guatemala or Belize. There were ample KGB people in Guatemala; they could cover that area. But there were no Soviet agents in Belize. That small, stable country had little to offer for the advancement of the revolution and was of no strategic importance, the approach to its coast hampered by the extensive barrier reef. And there was an inherent feeling in his gut, a feeling that had been honed to a fine edge by many years of investigative work within the GRU intelligence agency, that yelled "Belize" with a very loud voice.

Departure time finally came and Plotnikov suffered through the four-hour ride to Belize City with an assortment of Indians, two impeccably dressed Englishmen, a Spanish priest, and a small flock of chickens, several of which had the run of the bus. Where to stay was no great decision. The Han Guest House was only a short walk from the bus terminal and it was clean and centrally located. Unable to communicate with the Chinese manning the desk, Plotnikov merely held out a handful of bills. The Chinaman took several and gave him a key. By the time he had washed up from the ride, it was after 11:00 A.M. and his stomach was reminding him it had gone without nourishment since the previous evening. Finding a decent and reasonable restaurant was a challenge. He finally settled for a small seafood establishment near the Swing Bridge.

It was clean, and the waiter, to his astonishment, was actually Arabic and quite efficient. The broiled snapper was from the morning catch and complemented with an orange yam that was stringless and delicate. As the waiter brought him coffee, Plotnikov amiably asked in English, "You are Arabic?"

"Yes, sir. Lebanese. Are you on holiday, sir?"

"Yes and no. I am a journalist," replied Plotnikov, touching his camera bag.

"Oh, that must be an interesting profession, sir."

"Are there many Lebanese here in Belize?"

"Only a few of us, sir. It is a very nice place."

"That would be an interesting aspect to my assignment. I didn't expect to find any Middle Eastern people here. Is there somewhere you gather after work or for relaxation?"

"Oh, yes, sir. My brother runs a coffeehouse on the south end of Queen Street. It is very small and not in the most desirable area, since it is near where the fishermen off-load their catch. Here is my brother's card. He would welcome you."

"Thank you. I shall look forward to a visit, perhaps this evening."

"Thank you, sir."

Plotnikov finished his coffee leisurely. A walk around the central city and an inquiring stop at the one-room police station finished off his afternoon. The police were most cooperative, suggesting several areas where he could shoot representative pictures and talk to the local people. It was a pleasant constabulary, and the desk officer confirmed that their crime rate was well below that experienced in neighboring Mexico. In fact, the only major consideration under investigation at the moment was the murder of an American tourist woman. Someone had cut open her throat. It was a rare crime and a shameful one, but she had been most indiscreet in visiting one of the seamier parts of the city after dark.

As Plotnikov reentered the Han, he arrived at the desk to pick up his key just as another guest walked away. The man was dark and with the features he had just observed on the Lebanese waiter. Perhaps there are but a few Lebanese in this country, but in the last few hours I seem to find them wherever I go, thought Plotnikov. He spent the remainder of the afternoon and early evening studying a map of Belize. The small country covered less than nine thousand acres, with its northern border adjacent to the Yucatan, its southwestern border separating it from Guatemala, and its eastern border the Caribbean coastline. There were only two cities of any size, the one he was in and Belmopan, the capital, situated almost in the geographical center of the country. A decent highway ran from the Mexican border south through Belize City and then inland to Belmopan. Other than that, there were only a few roads, mostly leading south parallel to the coast. The Maya Mountains formed a natural topographical division, starting just southeast of Belmopan and swinging gently to the southwest toward Guatemala. Inland from them were a number of farm villages, several rivers, and lots of open but very rough terrain. Seaward from the Maya Mountains were several smaller ranges and a series of foothills.

Fishing villages dotted the bays and coves, but much of the coast was swampland. There were some offshore islands, notably Ambergris Cay to the north and the Turneffes due east of Belize City and out beyond the barrier reef. He had noted in his walk around the city that limited boat service was available to the offshore cays. Finally, he noted that the country's international airport was just outside Belize City.

He summarized his thoughts. Belize was an excellent place to find seclusion and wait out the first frantic days of the American response to the nuclear destruction of their aircraft carrier. But the Palestinians would not box themselves in. The offshore islands were out—they would have no avenue of escape other than by boat if the islands were searched. And that would be too conspicuous. Belmopan was too exposed. As the capital, there would be an alert international community. Also in Belize City, where the American embassy was located. Too much action. Inland there were ample open country and overland escape routes into Guatemala and back to Mexico.

Plotnikov, however, if he were running, would have preferred the coast. And the northern section of the coast provided three avenues of evasion if a hideaway were threatened: by land, over the narrow and isolated roads; by sea, out through the gaps in the barrier reef; and by air, by exodus through the Belize airport. Following that premise, he would want a place secluded on the beach, near a passable road, and within a reasonably short drive to provisions Belize City and the airport. His eyes examined the map. The Sibun River was only eight or nine miles south of Belize City. It ran to the Caribbean and there were no roads with bridges across it. He would want to stay north of the river. The only other reasonable possibility was on the coast, forty miles farther south. In between there and Belize City were the Sibun, two large lagoons, swampland, and no roads. Forty miles was a bit far, and the circuitous road network actually required driving more than a hundred miles. So the coastal area just to the south of the city but north of the river looked very intriguing. Tonight, at the Lebanese coffeehouse, he would make some inquiries.

Plotnikov was surprised to find the coffeehouse full and noisy with patrons, all men, and almost all Lebanese. He presented the card, and the waiter's brother welcomed him graciously and seated him at a small table near the back wall. Those around him turned and inquired as to his purpose in Belize. They offered him friendly suggestions on where to sightsee, but none invited him to share their table. That was just as well. Plotnikov would just as soon pick those with whom he wished to speak. The conversation around him was Arabic, so he would pick up nothing by idle listening. The coffee was strong and black, very close in viscosity to syrup, and the date cookies placed before him on a plate were not to his taste. Everyone was smoking, and the few lights in the place gave the swirling smoke emphasis and exaggeration. There were three heavily curtained windows on the sea side of the room and two curtained doorways, which he assumed led back to the kitchen and toilet.

The recorded music stopped and there was a general shifting of chairs. When the music began again, a weak spotlight fought its way through the smoke and accented one of the two curtained doorways. A veiled and heavily skirted Arabic female appeared and began a mildly sensuous dance, her body completely covered but with such thin cloth that her movements gave full form to her torso and legs. The men murmured in approval as she swung and swayed around the tiny clearing in the center of the room. Plotnikov could see only her eyes, but if they were any indicator of her beauty, the Lebanese men of Belize City were deprived of little of their culture. He was quite content, being in the back where he could observe the comings and goings and study the faces of the patrons.

As the woman danced, the owner came to his table and sat with him. "You are a student of Middle Eastern culture, perhaps?"

Plotnikov smiled. "No, I am a photojournalist, here on an assignment. I work for a magazine in East Berlin, *The Peoples' Eye*. I fear it is not very well known here, but my editor thought an article on this country would be unusual and attractive to our readers."

"That is most interesting."

"As I mentioned to your brother, I was somewhat surprised to see a Middle Eastern community here."

"We go back to the times of the British, although our numbers are small. It is a good place to live. A beautiful country, actually, and very reasonable in its services to its people. My grandfather worked for an English civil servant."

They sipped their coffee and watched the dancer.

"She is very talented," commented Plotnikov.

"Yes, the daughter of a cousin. During the day she is a loan officer in one of the banks. We try to keep our customs and traditions alive."

"Do you have many visitors? Countrymen, who travel here?"

"No, hardly ever, except for an occasional relative from our homeland. But that is very rare. We are too many generations removed now, and there is such turmoil back there. I think we are mainly forgotten."

"I see."

"The only hard part here is our life goal to travel to Mecca on the holy pilgrimage. It is very expensive and few of us live that well."

Plotnikov ached to ask if there had been any newcomers to the community but thought it best not to abuse the Lebanese hospitality by too many questions. He would come back and, after gaining the man's confidence, he could use him well, perhaps to ferret out the two Palestinians. Fellow Muslims, they would be seeking brothers for prayers.

"Do you have a mosque here?" asked Plotnikov.

"No, we are too small a gathering. But we have hopes, even plans."

"I wish you well, then."

"Thank you. If I, or any of us, can be of assistance to you in your work or your personal needs, it would be our honor and pleasure."

The woman was ending her dance and backing gracefully through the curtains.

"I must attend my customers. God be with you, my friend."

"And you," replied Plotnikov, standing to return the owner's embrace. It was a few minutes before midnight and a number of the men were leaving. Plotnikov sat to finish his coffee.

The dancer emerged in Western dress and spoke with several of the men before departing. As she left, a late arrival entered and was ushered to a table on the opposite wall. Plotnikov gave the man only a cursory glance as he rose to leave and was halfway across the room before the subtle familiarity of the man's profile struck him. It was Youssif Daoud! He wheeled—and stared at an empty chair where only a second before the man had been seated. The curtains leading to the toilet were moving. Plotnikov raced across the room and burst through the beaded cloth, reaching inside his shirt for the Tokarev 7.62mm automatic tucked under the waistband of his trousers. Before he could extract it, a charging body caught him in the midsection and drove him back into the main room.

Plotnikov twisted and drove his clenched hands up between the man's legs. He felt the strong arms loosen in reaction to the pain, and he followed his blow to the groin with a driving fist into the face of Youssif Daoud. Again he reached for his weapon, but Daoud countered with an open palm across Plotnikov's face, his fingers digging deeply into the GRU agent's eyes. Plotnikov yelled in pain and forced the hand away, twisting it sharply up and around to concentrate the force of his move onto the shoulder muscle of Daoud. The Palestinian grunted loudly as Plotnikov forced him to the floor.

Blood from the savage eye gouge clouded Plotnikov's vision. They rolled across several chairs, knocking them aside and spilling a table backward onto several of the onlookers. Plotnikov drove the tips of his extended fingers deep into Daoud's side below his rib cage, then caught the Palestinian with a vicious karate chop to the side of his neck. Arms outstretched, Daoud rushed the GRU agent and threw him against the back wall, driving his knee into Plotnikov's stomach. Plotnikov countered with a swinging right hook, which brought an outcry of pain from Daoud as he was knocked backward.

Plotnikov dove and tried to pin the Arab's arms to his sides, but Daoud squirmed free and drove a foot into Plotnikov's side. Plotnikov could hear the rib crack as well as feel it, but he continued to grasp for the Palestinian, managing to throw him off balance and back onto the floor. Daoud yelled in fury and rolled frantically away. Springing to his feet, he faced Plotnikov with bared teeth. In his right hand he held a blade of steel. Plotnikov reached for his automatic. It was gone, apparently dislodged during the struggle. He took a firm stance in front of Daoud and waited. The Palestinian lunged and Plotnikov stepped into the thrust, twisting as he did so to place his back toward Daoud and grabbing the knife arm with both hands. Using Daoud's own momentum, Plotnikov bent sharply forward, pulling Daoud across his back and slinging him against the wall. Daoud whirled around, his outstretched arm arcing blindly toward Plotnikov's midsection. Plotnikov leaped backward, the blade missing him by only inches. Daoud was momentarily off balance, and Plotnikov leaped forward, grabbed Daoud's knife hand, and twisted it with all of his strength. The knife clattered to the floor.

Daoud screamed a curse and dove for the knife. Plotnikov fell on top of him and the knife scooted farther away, accidentally propelled by Daoud's grasping fingers. Daoud rolled frantically and managed to slip through Plotnikov's grasp. Plotnikov stood, only to catch the full force of a chair that Daoud slung into his chest. He toppled backward, out of breath, and fell hard against the wall, his head snapping back against a brass ornament. His last vision was a blurred impression of Daoud stooping down to pick up the knife.

Most of the men had fled. Only two in a far corner and the owner remained, all frozen in fear and shock at the brutality of the sudden fight. Sucking his breath in great gulps, Daoud bent over the Soviet agent and raised the knife. But the shrill ring of a police whistle stopped his downward thrust.

Daoud leaped over the debris and ran through the curtained doorway that led to the back of the cafe. Still breathing heavily, a mixture of saliva and blood bubbling in one corner of his mouth, and his right arm held slightly raised to ease the pain, he hurried from the coffeehouse.

Kamal Adwan nervously paced the beach, frequently glancing back at the road that ended only a few yards from their hut. Youssif Daoud had been gone for more than two days.

What could have happened? Adwan wondered. Surely, the idiot knows the risks he is taking—for the both of us—by such exposure. Two days! There can be no excuse for this! Dear God, give me the wisdom to resolve this issue that is jeopardizing our holy mission.

Disgusted, Adwan stooped and picked up a handful of pebbles. One by one, he threw them into the boiling surf. There must be a storm offshore. The seaward horizon was dark and the waves rolling up on the sand were much more violent than any he had observed up to now. However fierce that storm at sea, it does not match the fury in my heart at you, Youssif, thought Adwan.

The anger almost brought tears to his eyes as he continued to toss the tiny rocks into the water, his frustration made even more so by their light weight, which made an angry throw almost impossible. He wanted to fire them at the water with the force of bullets and let their impact dissipate some of the tension that had his stomach tied into a series of overlapping knots. If I had the car, Youssif, I would be away from here! But you have that, also. Where are you with our automobile, Youssif? fumed Adwan silently. For a brief moment, the thought of an accident occurred to him. Could he be misjudging his brother? No. This was too typical. Youssif was with a woman and probably drinking.

This is the last time, Youssif. The next will bring the wrath of God in the form of my hand. The shari'a provides for this. But what anguish it will be for me. You are my brother. Why can't you regain

the faith that took you so steadfastly through those early years?
Thoroughly out of patience, Adwan dropped to the sand and sat.

What is that? he wondered. Several hundred yards down the
beach, toward Belize City, he could see a figure hugging the grass
line but definitely approaching. Alarmed, he jumped to his feet. The
figure raised a hand. Adwan squinted to see better in the glare of the
afternoon sun. It was Daoud! Adwan ran toward the plodding figure.

"Youssif! Where have you been? Where is the car?" shouted
Adwan as they met. "What is wrong with your arm?"

Daoud's right arm was held in a sling made from a piece of his
shirt. The upper portion appeared swollen. "I have injured it. It is
nothing."

"You've had an accident?"

"No, I've had no accident," spat back Daoud. "It was the bastard Plotnikov. He almost caught up with us. I am certain that he
was after our weapon."

"Plotnikov?"

"Yes, Colonel Plotnikov, our Cuban contact for the transfer. I
tried to kill the bastard but the police came."

"No! Youssif, tell me! What exactly has happened?"

"I was in the coffeehouse. Plotnikov was there also. I spotted
him as he started to leave, just at the time that he spotted me. We
fought and I ran."

"There were witnesses?"

"Yes, the coffeehouse was full. But they are all brothers. I ran
and made my way south along the beach. I holed up during the day
and walked by night."

"Where is the car?"

"Where I left it, on Queen Street. I didn't want to go back to it
in case someone would see me and make the connection. It is safe.
No one will notice until you can get in and pick it up."

"The police will find it! Stupid!"

Daoud grabbed Adwan by the collar with his good hand. "No,
Kamal, there are cars parked there for days. All you have to do is
get it!"

Adwan reached up and removed Daoud's hand. "How is your
arm?"

"Bruised, but I don't believe broken. I can still move everything. It is just swollen and hurts when I let it hang."

"Come on into the hut."

Daoud followed Adwan.

"Lie down."

Daoud flopped on his bed. Adwan poured water into the clay bowl and started to bathe Daoud's shoulder. "The cool water will help," said Adwan.

"You had better go get the car," admonished Daoud.

"How? Do I walk out to the road and flag a passerby? Hail a taxi? One reason this place is so appropriate is that the road is so little traveled. How do you think it will look for me to be seen?"

"You must go into town the way I came. By the beach."

"A two-day walk?"

"Something less. You are not injured and as sore as I."

"But just as wanted! The police will be watching everywhere."

"We cannot leave the car there too long. It will arouse suspicion."

"Can any of the witnesses identify you?"

"By sight, yes. I have been in the coffeehouse several times before. They all saw the fight start, although the light was low."

"We may have to leave. You have compromised our mission. Youssif."

"They are all brothers under our God. They will not turn me in."

"You talk as a child. They are citizens of a foreign country, removed from our struggle. They will not jeopardize their position by shielding you. The police already have a description. You can count on that."

"But," interrupted Daoud with a wry smile, "do we not all look alike to westerners? We have the same color skin and the same brown eyes and dark hair and beards."

Adwan shook his head in disgust. "They will identify you."

Daoud twisted on the bed and made an effort to sit up. "What is that?" he asked, raising himself to peer outside through the open window spaces.

Adwan heard the noise at the same time and leapt over to the other side of the room reaching underneath his mattress to get his weapon. A car was stopping at the end of the road. It was Ahmad Labidi. He ran toward the hut. Adwan met him at the open entrance.

"Is he here?" shouted Labidi.

"Inside, on the bed."

"Fool!" cried Labidi, rushing in and standing over the half-sitting Daoud. "There is a manhunt on! The police will be coming here! Fool! These people do not take such violence lightly."

Daoud started to get up. Labidi struck him with an open palm, knocking the weakened Daoud back onto the bed. Instantly, Daoud recoiled, then leapt to his feet, his blade in his hand. Labidi merely stuck the nozzle of his revolver into Daoud's chest.

"That is your solution?" screamed Labidi, pointing at Daoud's knife hand. "No, my brother. You have done enough."

Daoud stood transfixed with rage. The barrel pressing into his skin was an insult. "You must pull the trigger, for I intend to kill you." The knife started forward.

Without hesitation, Labidi sent a .357 Magnum slug into Daoud's body, the force of the oversized round tearing a bloody tunnel through the man and carrying a great chunk of bone and flesh with it as it exited his body and spent itself in the far wall. Daoud lay half on and half off the far side of the bed, his hand still clutching his knife. Labidi walked around and put a second round into his head. "We have to get you out of here," he said to Adwan.

Adwan looked down at his companion.

"You have regrets?" asked Labidi.

"None," announced Adwan. "I would have had to do it to him if you had not come. He was getting completely out of hand."

"We are better off without him. But we will miss his expertise. Nevertheless, the will of God has been done. We will give him a proper burial. Perhaps his soul will receive the mercy of Allah, the only One."

"We have time?"

"Yes. The search is concentrated in the city. It will be awhile before they get out this far. The urgency of the situation is no cause for us to abandon our responsibilities to our brother, no matter how far he has strayed."

Lifting Daoud back onto the bed, the two men prepared his body. Using the remainder of the water from the clay bowl, they washed him and cleaned him of blood. Adwan took a sheet from his bed and tore it into three sections.

"Wrap him. I will dig the hole," instructed Labidi. Adwan began winding the three pieces of cloth around Daoud as Labidi went outside.

"We have no lote-tree leaves or camphor, Youssif," murmured Adwan as he wrapped, "but that will make little difference in your appearance before God. I cannot cover your sins, my brother. I cannot walk before your bier, as would be the custom, for there is only me and Labidi, but this minor transgression of our customs is necessary." Finishing the last of the three wrappings, Adwan lifted

Daoud and carried him outside. Labidi was back by the bush line and still digging.

"Someone will eventually find him," stated Labidi, "but it will be awhile, and there is nothing to tie him to us."

Adwan rolled the corpse into the shallow pit.

Chapter 16

July 13, 1:40 P.M.
Merida, Yucatan, Mexico

Merida, built on the site of the ancient Mayan city of Tiho, sat a short distance inland from the north central coast of the Yucatan Peninsula. Reminiscent of its Spanish namesake, it originally featured the orderly, lime-covered houses characteristic of its sister city in Spain, and the current counterparts glistened in the bright sun as Davey looked down from his arriving Aeromexico aircraft.

It was only a few minutes' ride from the airport to the central district. Davey gazed with interest at the shops with their wares overflowing onto the streets as his taxi threaded its way through the heavy pedestrian traffic to police headquarters.

Inside, Captain Lolo Alvarez was waiting in his office. A man of gargantuan proportions, his presence behind his desk made the piece of office furniture seem more the size of a coffee table. Davey estimated that Alvarez grossed out at around three hundred pounds—and as much as a quarter of that could be his smile. He and the Old Man would have trouble being in the same room together.

"Welcome to Merida, Senor Morales," greeted Alvarez, making a brief effort to rise but apparently deciding the courtesy could wait. He settled for a friendly wave toward the only other chair in his office and leaned forward to lift a large bottle of soda from his desktop. "Manalo!" he yelled toward the outer office. "Bring Senor Morales something cold to drink." Already anticipating the call, the officer entered the room and handed Davey an orange drink. The liquid was flaked with ice crystals and strong in flavor. Davey downed half the bottle without pausing.

"That hits the spot. It's hot as hades here," remarked Davey.

"Yes, we're too far inland and we bake in the sun during such long days. The nights are little better. Ha! The richest man in Merida has the soft drink company. Ah, but one gets used to it. I may have some good news for you."

"Captain Alvarez, I could use some."

"Please, you call me Lolo."

"And it's Davey, here."

"Good, Davey. Life is so full of formality. People should be friends together. Our time is so short, we should enjoy one another. But, in my business, and yours, we see so many people who do not understand this. There is not enough love, Davey," Alvarez raised a finger in emphasis. "The world is full of bastards like these Palestinians we are after. They must be terrible people. How can they justify mass murder such as their attack on your aircraft carrier? I will never understand such a thing."

"The good news, Lolo?" prompted Davey.

"Yes. You probably did not realize it, but here in Merida we have an impressive number of Lebanese and Syrians. Their community is certainly small when compared to the overwhelming majority of ethnic Mayans who populate Merida, but they still number some twenty-five thousand persons. And they are, in good measure, decent people who have adapted thoroughly to the friendly atmosphere of this fine place. Overall, this is a happy and very contented city, and you will not find equal hospitality in all of Mexico."

"I had no idea there were Arab types here."

"Now you know, and I think that such a factor was known by your Palestinians. That is why they have come here, Davey."

Davey's heart skipped a beat. He had expected a lead, yes, but Alvarez's statement was much more than that.

"You know that for a fact?"

"Well, not for a fact, exactly, but let me tell you. Since we received the alert from the national authorities in Mexico City, I have put several of my officers on full-time duty in the Lebanese-Syrian section. We get outsiders from time to time, usually visiting relatives or friends, and they stand out, of course. Mayan and Arabic features are certainly different, although the coloring can be quite the same. And our other minorities are Indian or more cosmopolitan Mexican mixes. We have been watching three strangers. One of them is very close in appearance to the Palestinian identified in the alert circulars as Kamal Adwan."

"Why haven't you picked them up?"

"They arrived with no baggage or boxes or anything. We assumed that you want the weapon also. So, we wished to wait and see if anyone or anything else turns up. And when we heard you were coming, that reinforced our decision to keep them under surveillance. If you wish them apprehended, we can do so anytime."

"No, I think your decision is supportable. We need the whole package. And there is a possibility that others have joined them and have the weapon."

"You know, of course, about the murder of the man near here? We believe that, for a while, the terrorists were using his pickup truck. We found it abandoned just outside of town."

"Yes, that is one of the things that puts us in this area."

"We strongly suspected a tie-in and closed the peninsula as best we could at that time. Then, when we were unable to come up with any leads, we figured they had managed, somehow, to avoid our roadblocks and searches. But I just had a feeling in my gut that they would keep this place in mind for future use. Your authorities have informed us that the United States is most probably their ultimate destination. If so, and they were still in Yucatan or south of here, then they might use Merida for a further staging point. Again, and I apologize to all of our decent and law-biding citizens, I thought of our Lebanese and Syrians. This is a different world, today. It may be that the Palestinians have sympathizers here. So we waited. And I think our wait has paid off."

"Are you sure you can keep the strangers under surveillance?"

"Yes. I would recommend that we wait another twenty-four hours, just in case anything develops that could lead us to the weapon. If it looks like Adwan is trying to leave before that happens, we will bring him in. Does that meet with your approval?"

Davey knew that the one thing he did not want was for the other terrorist to be alerted by a premature arrest of Adwan and make off for parts unknown with the remaining weapon. "I agree, but I'm not sure we should wait any longer than the twenty-four hours."

"Then I will get you settled. If anything at all happens in the interim, I will have an officer come and get you. Otherwise, we meet again this time tomorrow. I will give you an update on Adwan's actions and we can decide if we should pick him up or wait longer."

Alvarez gripped the edge of his desk and forced himself to stand. Before moving, he circled his waist with his hands, tucking in his shirt and hitching up his trousers in order to swing his gun belt back into a more proper position. Leading Davey from the room, he accepted another soda from his office clerk, Manalo. "Another?" he asked Davey.

"No, thanks. I'll wait until I get to a hotel."

"I have a room for you at the Hospedaje Bowen. You will find it comfortable. The rooms are very clean. There is an arcaded patio for leisure thought, or meditation, or whatever. It is very close and they keep cold bottled water for gringo stomachs."

"That I will appreciate. But, perhaps, I should drop off my things and we go to the Lebanese-Syrian section. You could point out the location of Adwan." Davey was having difficulty contemplating an idle day when the terrorists could be so close.

"I am sure that you are most anxious, but it might not be wise. For one thing, I am known to everyone." Alvarez patted his rotund stomach, which was stuffed now beneath the steering wheel. "Recognizable by sight, of course. We do not wish to be too visible, I would think. I have undercover officers on the scene and they have instructions to take Adwan if he attempts to leave the area. I think we should give any others a chance to appear. It is your decision, however, Davey. I can make arrangements to take Adwan any time you wish. Within minutes, if you desire it."

It was not hard to detect the reluctance with which Alvarez was making the offer. The big Mexican obviously wanted both the terrorists and the weapon, as did Davey. A bit more patience would not be out of place.

"The hotel will be fine, Lolo."

"I will have an officer with a car at the hotel around the clock. All it will take is a brief call and we can move."

Davey took dinner in his room. Just as the last rays of the sun were leaving the well-tended courtyard of the hotel, he received a call from the Old Man.

"Davey, I just got off the horn with Alvarez. He gave me your number and filled me in on things. How do you feel about the situation?"

"I don't like the wait, but I have to admit he has a point. It would be preferable to wrap this up with one apprehension."

"I agree. State has asked Mexico City to provide some federal backup, and agents should be there by dawn or so. It may be that Alvarez is waiting for that."

"He didn't mention it to me."

"Pride, maybe. He'd like to make the bust with local troops. The Mexican feds will bring Adwan, and hopefully his companion, to Mexico City, where our people will take custody and bring them to the States. Just hang in there, Davey. It can well be over in a few hours. We're subordinate in this thing at the moment. We don't want to piss off the Mexicans. It's their show."

"I understand. But I won't hesitate to make some mighty strong recommendations. We can't let this opportunity slip away from us. I'm already going bonkers sitting here in this room."

"I've made a few inquiries. Merida is okay, one of Mexico's better communities. And Chief Alvarez has a good reputation. His troops are reasonably honest and they come down hard when they have to. I think they can handle this, but keep an eye on them, anyhow."

"You can bet I'll do that. I think we should go in even if no other suspects have arrived."

"You're on the scene. It's your call, Davey. Just remember the diplomatic angle."

"I'm not sure diplomacy is the key consideration when we have a couple of crazies walking around with a nuclear weapon."

"Point well made. I'll back you in whatever you decide."

Sleep was out of the question. It was an effort just to lie nude on the bed and try to get some rest. The long, hot night was made little better by the feeble efforts of the overhead fan, although if Davey positioned himself exactly underneath it, his perspiration rate slowed to a trickle.

A disturbing knock on the door prompted him to look at his watch—3:21 A.M. He rolled off the bed and pulled on his trousers. "Yes?" he queried.

"Senor Morales, it is officer Mendoza. Chief Alvarez orders that we are to join him *muy pronto.*"

Davey slipped on a shirt and rammed his feet into his shoes.

Within four minutes, he was following Mendoza into the police headquarters building. Lolo Alvarez offered him a .357 Magnum. "I am sorry. We have nothing smaller."

"I have my own," said Davey.

The room was full of uniformed police officers and several people in street clothes. Alvarez was right. Davey could see nothing smaller than the Magnum. Three of the men carried the powerful revolver and four others had M-16s. One carried a submachine-gun, probably an Uzi, and the rest had shortened double-barreled shotguns.

Alvarez continued, "One half hour ago, two men arrived at the place of Adwan. With them they had a large crate. Since then, there has been much activity. The lights have been on and there are two cars parked in front of the house with waiting drivers. I think now is the time."

Alvarez led the way from the building and squeezed himself into the car still being driven by Mendoza. Davey crawled into the back. The others piled into three other vehicles, none of which had any markings. Hurriedly, but without any sirens, the convoy made its way along the east side of the central plaza, Alvarez bowing his head and crossing himself reverently as they passed in front of the cathedral. A right turn carried them into one of the less-cared-for sections of Merida, and several intersections later, Davey watched the two cars immediately behind him peel off down side streets. A bit farther, and Mendoza flicked off the lights and slowed to a stop. The car behind them did the same.

A few minutes later, at the next intersection, a light flickered three times. "The outside guards are taken care of," announced Alvarez quietly. Mendoza let the car ease forward. Alvarez whispered, "If you wish, Davey, take my men from the car behind us and cover the back. We will take the front and the others will space themselves around the house. I will try to call them out."

"Wait," cautioned Davey. "If they have the weapon and we give them any time to react, they could set the damn thing off. We sure as hell don't want that. I think we need a powwow here."

"Powwow?"

"American Indian talk, Lolo. A conference. We need a plan."

"Alright, Davey. I agree. Mendoza, go around and bring back one of the men from each of the cars."

Mendoza trotted off quietly and Alvarez leaned against the side of the car, wiping the sweat from his head and neck with a large, soiled handkerchief. "The heat never lets up. Sometimes I think I will move to the coast and just be a fisherman."

The four occupants of the car behind gathered around Davey and Alvarez. The little group remained quietly by the car until Mendoza returned with two of the others. Alvarez looked expectantly at Davey.

"We need to time our entry—everyone in at the same time. Lolo, you and your group in the front, me and my folks in the back, and the others in as many windows as we can use." Davey had observed that the houses around had open windows and most had no screens. "How about the windows on the other side? Screens? Curtains?"

"Wide open, but curtains. We couldn't see inside, but most of the lights are on," offered one of the men with Mendoza.

Davey studied the house. It was identical to several others in the block. "I wish we knew the room arrangement," he mused.

Alvarez supplied the details. "Most of these are identical. Living room in front, probably one small bedroom off a side hall that leads to a kitchen."

"Pardon me," interrupted one of the men, "we don't want to shoot each other. If they fight us, it will be very confused in there."

"Everyone take a handkerchief or tear a strip from your shirt. Tie it around your head. Anyone without the strip, we shoot," ordered Lolo.

Simplicity. Davey had to admire Alvarez's prompt and logical answer. "Good. Lolo, we go in on your command. A whistle?"

"I don't have a whistle. We don't use whistles."

"Lolo," exclaimed Davey, "all policemen have whistles."

"Not in Merida."

"How do you stop people or get their attention?"

The Mexican goliath grinned. "We shoot into the air."

"Okay, but we all have to be ready to move instantly. Lolo, give us three minutes to get into position."

"Three minutes, Davey. Everyone have that?"

"One other thing," added Davey. "If we can take them alive, this is preferable. There could be other groups and we'll need to interrogate them. But don't hesitate to use whatever it takes. These people are fanatical killers. Protect yourselves."

A chorus of nods responded, and the group split up and began surrounding the house.

Alvarez's shot split the night air with an ear-assaulting crack that must have been heard as far away as Mexico City. Davey and one of his men, shoulder to shoulder, hit the back door after a six-foot run, and it split into three pieces as it burst open. Even as they entered the empty kitchen, shots rang out from the front area of the house. One of the occupants came running down the hall. Davey could see he was unarmed, and he braced himself to make the intercept, but just as the man reached the doorway a shot rang out to Davey's left rear and the man stopped in his tracks, his chest blown away by the shotgun blast. A second man appeared, this time armed with a handgun as big as a cannon. Davey fired, and the man pitched forward. Davey's shotgun-wielding companion leaped over the twitching body and raced toward the end of the hall. Davey heard several short bursts of automatic fire that momentarily overrode the sharp reports of handguns. Then the booming shotgun blasts stopped, followed by a chorus of triumphant yells. By the time Davey reached the front of the house, Alvarez was turning over bodies and checking faces. So much for taking anyone alive.

"This one, Davey. Take a look," said Alvarez.

The man was Middle Eastern, quite possibly Lebanese or Syrian or maybe even Palestinian. But he was not Adwan. Davey's shoulders sagged. "That's not him."

"He looks like the picture," responded Alvarez.

There was a resemblance, but Adwan's features had been ingrained too deeply into Davey's mind from his countless examinations of the pictures provided by the CIA antiterrorist people. "Sorry, Lolo. No sale."

Alvarez slammed the man's head down sharply on the floor. "The crate?" he wondered aloud. "Where is the crate?"

Several of his men went into the small bedroom. "In here!" one of them called.

As soon as Davey saw the crate, his last hope was gone. It was barely four feet long, although the cross-sectional dimensions were about right. One of the men ripped off the top. It was packed with plastic bags of white powder.

"Snowmen," announced Davey dejectedly. "We just busted a snowhouse. Shit."

Alvarez pulled open one of the ziplocked bags and touched his tongue to a finger-dipped sample. "This is the very first time in Merida. I wonder how long it has been going on." Methodically, he roamed the bodies, examining each face. "Colombians. Two of these evil men are Colombians. I would bet my star on it. I am stunned. A Lebanese-Colombian cocaine waypoint here in our Merida. We have no drug problems. We will put an end to this." To accentuate his disgust, he turned toward one of the fallen men who had let out a low moan and put a bullet into his head. "I am sorry, Davey. It looked like your matter."

"I'm sorry, too, Lolo. But it wasn't a wasted effort."

"No. I'll have Mendoza drive you to my office. You must wish to make a report to your superior."

"As soon as I can."

Back at Alvarez's desk, Davey called the number that the Old Man had given him the last time they had spoken. The Old Man displayed little emotion despite his words of condolence, "I'm sorry, Davey, but I'm not too surprised. We have a hundred other reports. Everyone in Mexico has spotted our Palestinians. If all of the reports are true, we're looking at a thousand Arabs, all looking like Adwan."

"I'm back to square one here."

"Not for long. Some of the fair-haired boys in the national center have been feeding all sorts of proposals into their microchip intelligentsia and have come up with probability figures—ain't that a kick in the ass? We're letting little speeding electrons whose only talent is reading a combination of zeros and ones give us areas of probabilities. And you, Davey my boy, are right in the middle of the hottest area. Two possible sightings had been made over at Villahermosa. Grab a car and get over there. One of our people is already on the scene. Take a look at his evaluation and we'll go from there."

"I'm not anxious to shoot it out with any more powder hustlers."

"Understood. But we just have to go on what we have. I may have something further for you by the time you get over there. Regardless of how all this looks, I am beginning to see some tiny bit of order coming out of the chaos."

"On my way."

Chief Alvarez walked in as Davey replaced the phone in its cradle. The disappointed police official was holding a big half-eaten orange in his right hand. "What will you do next?" he asked.

"I need to get over to Villahermosa."

"Take Mendoza's car," offered Alvarez, lowering his super-obese torso into his chair. "Leave it with the department over there. We'll never find any of the rental people this time of morning. Can I buy you breakfast, Davey? We've both a long day ahead of us."

"Thanks, Lolo, but I'll just swing by the hotel and get my things. I appreciate the car."

"I have to go over in a few days. I'll bring it back."

Merida was predawn quiet as Davey made his way back to the Hospedaje Bowen, the only people on the streets the cleaners and trash collectors. Unlike some other Mexican towns, Merida was meticulously clean, and the early-morning effort was a daily occurrence. Davey had a feeling that Alvarez's pride in his city was fully justified. But now, the big Lolo had a new problem, one that love certainly could not solve. "There is not enough love, Davey," the police chief had stated at their first meeting. But that big gun belt was Lolo's alternate weapon and his actions back at the snowhouse had shown that he had no qualms about using it. American law enforcement could use a few Lolos, thought Davey, as he passed through the outskirts of Merida and headed for Villahermosa.

Chapter 17

"Davey! Get your ass over to Belize City—pronto!" The Old Man's words were clear and unmistakable, despite the background static in the telephone. "I think we're finally onto them! Check into the embassy. They'll fill you in. How soon can you get there?"

"Belize City?" repeated Davey Morales, puzzled about the order.

"In Belize. You *do* know where Belize is?"

"Yes, of course. But I just arrived *here*—within the hour. What the hell's going on? I'll have to check flights and see when the next one is. I haven't even investigated our leads here."

"Forget all that. This one looks good. Positive ID, Davey. The Belizeans and Mexicans are cooperating fully and have sealed their borders."

"We have made contact?"

"No, not yet. That's why I want you over there ASAP. Don't waste time. Charter a plane if you have to."

"I'm on my way, but I'm feeling like I'm going around in circles."

"It's all part of the game, Davey. I should be there within

twenty-four hours. Do what you can, but no apprehension unless absolutely necessary. The police will give you all the help you need to keep them contained. And don't forget, they've still got one weapon with them. We need to figure out a plan. God help that little country if the bastards set off the nuke."

Davey felt like he was in the middle of a replay of the fiasco at Merida. "I'll see you there." Davey hung up. Jesus, this is ridiculous, he thought as he dialed the travel desk in the lobby of the nearby Hotel Manzur. There was an Aeromexico flight leaving at 5 P.M.

Davey resigned himself to the next leg of his search. Waiting to board his flight, he tried to make sense out of the rapid developments. Obviously, despite the Old Man's previous comments, the search in and around Tabasco had failed to verify the previous leads, as had efforts in the neighboring state of Chiapas, just to the south. Other American and Mexican agents were concentrating in Campeche and Quintana Roo. The state of Yucatan, where everyone figured the terrorists had entered Mexico, had been scoured thoroughly, the murdered pickup driver and the abandoned pickup near Merida being the only possible clues to the actions of the Palestinians. After the raid with Alvarez, he had been ready to concede that the two Arabs had either made their way farther north or were holed up tightly along the Guatemalan border. Now the Old Man's orders seemed to indicate a pretty positive contact in Belize. God, I hope so, he thought. Ever since his arrival in Mexico City, courtesy of the Mexican airlift out of Havana, and his briefing at the embassy, he had been on the road, asking questions and showing the glossies of the two Palestinians in cafes and petrol stations and car rental agencies—he, and several hundred other agents.

The Aeromexico Boeing 727 was airborne at 5:26 P.M. and the flight took only forty minutes. By 6:45, Davey was being briefed in the office of the resident CIA agent, Phil Donovan, at the American embassy in Belize City.

"Night before last, there was a fight in a small Lebanese coffee-house down on the other end of Queen Street," began Donovan. "A European and an Arabic person. Maybe Lebanese, maybe not, but not a regular member of the Lebanese community here. The European was roughed up and the Arab escaped. The police started a routine investigation but immediately called us in when several witnesses indicated that the Arab looked like one of the Palestinian terrorists, possibly the one called Daoud. The man had been in the coffeehouse three times before but had stayed to himself. They had noticed him and were a bit aggravated when he made a pass at one of their dancers. They are all Muslims and don't take kindly to such things, even from one of their own. Anyhow, not having anything else on the Arab, we're running a check on the European. He claims to be an East German photojournalist."

"Is he in custody?" asked Davey.

"Yes, the local police are holding him."

"You know where the Palestinians are?"

"No. But we believe that they are still here, in Belize, and there is a good chance they are either in the city or very near by."

"Any papers on the European?"

"Yes, all in proper order. There was one rather interesting thing, however. We searched his hotel room—he is staying at Han House—and we found some notes written in Russian."

"You did say East German?"

"Yes. And there is another revealing piece of evidence. During the struggle, a small-caliber automatic was lost by the European, a 7.62-millimeter Tokarev automatic."

"Russian."

"Known as a favored weapon by the GRU. It's small, easy to conceal, and at close range lethal enough."

"Could I see his personal effects?"

"Sure." Donovan pulled a camera case and a plastic bag of personal belongings from his office closet.

Davey examined the contents of the camera bag. "He isn't a professional photographer," he announced, looking up at the agent.

"Oh?"

"Only one camera. Five rolls of film, all the same speed. No professional could achieve the versatility he would need with just that. He'd have three or four cameras and assorted film."

"All the more reason to believe he is GRU—or KGB."

"My guess is GRU."

"Why?"

"Let me answer that with a question. How active is the KGB in Belize?"

"Nonexistent, if you ask me. I'm the lone Company man and there is absolutely nothing here for me. I just pissed off the director or I wouldn't be here. We haven't been keeping a full-time surveillance."

"Well, they could have sent a man in, but my guess is that the

Russian followed the Palestinians from Cuba. The Soviets have their ass in the crack over this one. They want the bastards as much as we do—almost. It was their military's screwup in transferring the weapons to the wrong people, and it will be the military's responsibility to recover the remaining weapon. That means GRU. And the Aquarium graduates are clever, more so than the KGB in my estimation. The Palestinians probably weren't too hard to track out of Cuba, and the leads from Punta Allen and Merida and Valladolid directed the man here somehow. I'm afraid he was more on top of this than us. It's a perfect tie-in. The coffeehouse Arab has to be one of the terrorists, probably Daoud."

"The police are conducting a citywide search, aided by some of the militia. The locals are pretty uptight over this. This little hideaway country has very little violent crime, but just a few days ago a tourist, an American woman, was raped and her throat cut. Then, this coffeehouse incident. The Arab tried very hard to use a knife."

"There could be a connection."

"How?"

"Daoud likes to pump out his testicles regularly and has been known to kill his sex partner afterwards. He's a Muslim in name only. It all fits."

"God, we could be getting close, Morales."

"That means we have to be very careful. Who's in charge of the search?"

"The chief of police, Jerry Smythe-Hall. English, from one of the old colonial families. Very competent. Has a small force, augmented by two companies of militia."

"All right, let's pull off the militia."

"Sure?"

"Definitely. That's too many people without the proper sense of what is really going on. If they stumble onto the Palestinians and try to take them, it could be Mushroom City."

"Let's go down and talk to Jerry."

Chief Smythe-Hall was on the phone when Davey and Donovan arrived. Smythe-Hall motioned them to sit and finished his conversation. Hanging up the phone, he extended a hand toward Davey. "Morales. Phil said you were on the way," said Smythe-Hall, tilting his head toward the local CIA rep. "That was the officer-in-charge of my command center. We set up at the Belize Hilton—more phone lines."

"Anything new?" asked Donovan.

"No. My guess is they are not in the city. We're starting a search south, along the coast."

"Any positive ID on the European?"

"No, nothing yet. The magazine that he says he works for is nonexistent. We are tracing his passport. The prints and photo match. If you ask me, he's Soviet. The gun, the notes in his room, they point to that."

"Our conclusion, too. Possibly GRU."

"We don't hear much about those fellows."

"That's the way they play it."

"I would suppose so. Tea?"

"No, nothing for me," interjected Davey, seeing his companion give a negative shake of his head.

"We've tried not to alarm the populace any more than necessary. They know we're looking for an armed felon and that he is Arabic. We have been saying Lebanese. We did have to show the photos of the Palestinians to people, without identifying them, of course. But the man in the street is not completely naive and the paper has followed the crisis since the loss of your warship. The thing we don't want to do is panic the terrorists."

"We agree fully with that," responded Donovan. "Davey thinks we ought to scale down our force now that the city has been pretty well covered. A matter of control."

"I agree. I think we should give the impression that the man has probably escaped the immediate area. It will help stabilize things. Oh, yes, I almost forgot. We have uncovered the presence of another Arab, but he doesn't fit the description of the two terrorists from Cuba. A guest of Han House, a hotel just down the street. He has also disappeared, and a search of his room has revealed nothing. And a final note. We have impounded an abandoned rental car that we believe was issued to one of the terrorists."

"Excellent," complimented Davey. "Everything points to this being the place. How secure are your borders?"

"I would be lying if I told you they are sealed, especially to the west. Lots of rough country there. But we have patrols on all of the roads and several aircraft and helicopters at our disposal."

"The European, where is he?" asked Davey.

"We have him under protective custody in the police infirmary."

"Can we talk to him?"

"I would think so. He has a hairline crack in one rib and a nasty eye gouge but no serious injuries," replied Smythe-Hall.

"Would now be convenient?"

"Yes, yes, of course. Come with me." Smythe-Hall led Davey and Donovan through a small holding-cell area and into the infirmary. There were three beds and in the far one Plotnikov was trying to sit up. "Here, let me help you," offered Smythe-Hall. "How do you feel?"

"Thank you. I'm feeling much better now." Plotnikov patted the adhesive tape wrapping that was around his rib cage. "I would like to return to my hotel."

"We have your statement. I see no reason why you must remain here; however, you have undergone a rather traumatic experience. You are most welcome to remain overnight and rest under our medical supervision. There will be no charge. You are a guest in our country and we feel responsible," offered Smythe-Hall.

Plotnikov nodded. "Thank you, but I would prefer to return to the hotel." His eyes were fixed on Davey and Donovan.

"Perhaps you would not mind talking to these gentlemen from the American embassy," suggested Smythe-Hall. "This is special consul Donovan and Davey Morales."

Plotnikov tried very hard not to let his surprise and wariness show as Donovan and Davey offered their hands in turn. Davey Morales? Tatiana's Morales? wondered Plotnikov. He could not believe that such an astounding coincidence was taking place. "Gentlemen. What can I say to you?"

"You are a professional photojournalist?" asked Davey.

"Yes, mostly free-lance. I'm here on an assignment for an East German magazine."

"A magazine that does not exist," prompted Smythe-Hall.

"What is the speed of the film in your camera bag?" asked Davey.

Plotnikov looked perplexed. "Four hundred. I only shoot ASA four hundred. It covers various light conditions and is good for action."

"But very grainy when blown up. Not a typical all-purpose film," countered Davey.

"What are you trying to say?" asked Plotnikov.

"You are not a professional photographer. Your film is four hundred, yes, but it is standard tourist grade and not a typical single-speed choice for a professional. You are Soviet. We found evidence in your hotel room. What are you doing in Belize?" asked Davey.

"Chief Smythe-Hall, am I being charged with anything?" asked Plotnikov, ignoring the question.

"No, sir, you are not. But I do have confidence in Mr. Morales's statement. Please answer his question."

Plotnikov threw back the sheet. "No charges, no questions. Please leave me to dress."

Smythe-Hall's proper British slipped a notch. "If I wish, I can charge you with creating a public disturbance and hold you for as long as it takes. You will answer Morales's question or I shall escort you to a holding cell."

Plotnikov studied the three men's faces. If there was one thing he had learned as a young Spetsnaz trooper it was that there was a time to become aggressive and turn a deteriorating situation into an advantage. That philosophy had not changed with his passing years in the GRU. "I am a Soviet citizen and would like to consult with my embassy here in Belize."

Davey smiled. Things were looking up. He decided to lay everything out on the table. "You were fighting with a Palestinian by the name of Youssif Daoud, a known terrorist who had just entered this country illegally from Cuba."

Plotnikov pursed his lips, then let them retract and widen to match Davey's Cheshire cat grin. "You are CIA."

"And you are GRU," countered Davey.

"Ha!" exclaimed Plotnikov, slapping his thigh. "We are such professionals, are we not? Chief Smythe-Hall, may I talk with Mr. Morales alone?"

"We'll be right outside," stated Smythe-Hall. Donovan followed him from the room. Plotnikov let his legs dangle over the side of the bed. Davey drew up a straight-backed wooden chair.

Plotnikov studied Davey's face with some intensity. It was time for boldness. "What were you doing in Guantanamo?"

Davey's head instinctively cocked to one side. "How do you know that?"

Plotnikov timed his answer to allow his surprise statement to have full effect. "Tatiana. I am the one she called. My name is Colonel Vladlen Mikhailovich Plotnikov of the Soviet Army. You and I are after the same thing, the remaining cylinder."

"And Tatiana?" queried Davey.

"She is a friend, a very close friend of mine—and the revolution."

"She is also dead."

"What?" Plotnikov tried very hard to look shocked.

"Drowned."

"That is terrible. I was just with her."

"I don't know the circumstances."

"She was a very good swimmer," mused Plotnikov. "Perhaps she developed cramps or something."

"Or something. Did you two have a thing going?"

"A thing?"

"Were you lovers?"

"Oh. Yes, we were lovers and comrades. She was very useful to me at times, and I could perform some small favors for her. The Guantanamo thing is an example. She later told me about you. That is why I asked to speak with you alone. We have both come very close to the Palestinians. Together, we can catch them. I know their personalities."

"That's a switch. The GRU working *with* the CIA?"

"In this most serious matter, yes. You and I know what those fanatics intend to do with the remaining weapon. If they succeed, not only will there be a terrible loss of life, but a great rift will develop between our countries. It is not time for that. We have not intended such a thing. The Palestinian devils have betrayed every man and woman on this earth. Desperate problems call for desperate solutions. You and I must work together."

"*Glasnost?*" asked Davey almost sarcastically, but even as he made the remark, he knew the Russian was right.

"Something like that," responded Plotnikov.

"I agree. Can you get dressed?"

"I am fine. Give me a few moments."

Davey left Plotnikov and joined Donovan and Smythe-Hall. "That is a very remarkable man," he began.

"Soviet?" asked Donovan.

"Down to his tippy toes, and he's GRU. He just plain came out and identified himself and suggested we work together. He knows the Palestinians and probably had something to do with the weapons transfer. I suspect he's on somebody's list for a first-class ticket to Siberia unless he finds the second weapon. That could be a big plus for us."

"What do you think?" asked Donovan.

"I agree. Soviet intelligence is as deeply into this as we are. We may each come up with pieces of the puzzle that fit. Hell, if ever we needed both abilities, it's now. Chief Smythe-Hall, will you hold off on any charges?"

"Of course. I admit this is an unusual but most proper course of action. We will do whatever we can to cooperate—excuse me."

Smythe-Hall interrupted the ringing of his phone by picking up the receiver. "Yes? Where? Are you sure? That's bloody well good work. Don't disturb anything. I'm on my way." Placing the hand unit back in its cradle, he turned toward Davey, his smile almost wrapping around his face. "They've found Daoud."

"Where?" asked Davey, rising to his feet.

"A shallow beach grave, about twenty miles south of here."

"Grave? He's dead?"

"Yes. Shot in the chest and head. Shall we go?" asked Smythe-Hall, obviously pleased with the work of his men.

"Yes," replied Davey, heading back toward the infirmary door. "Let me get my partner!"

"By all means," added Donovan.

Standing on the beach sand in the waning minutes of twilight, Davey followed the beam of Smythe-Hall's flashlight and looked down at what was left of the corpse's face. There was enough remaining for a reliable ID. It was Youssif Daoud. Plotnikov agreed.

"One down, one to go," muttered Smythe-Hall.

"Not quite," added Davey quietly. "The one at the Han is probably with Adwan, taking Daoud's place. Adwan can't handle the weapon by himself."

"Yes, of course," agreed Smythe-Hall. "We must have just missed them. I'm no coroner, but this body is fresh, no more than a day old. How about the hut?" asked Smythe-Hall of the police sergeant standing with them.

"We're going over it now. The man was apparently shot inside on one of the beds, dragged or carried out here, and buried."

"They were in a hurry. Shallow grave, poorly covered," added Smythe-Hall. "The road leads only one way, back toward the city, but there is an intersection that leads west to Belmopan. There's a good chance they've gone in that direction. Sergeant, get on the radio and alert the patrols."

"I already have, sir."

"Good. Shall I assume then, Morales, that your identification is positive?"

"Colonel?" asked Davey, turning to Plotnikov.

"I am certain," repeated Plotnikov.

"All right, Sergeant. You can have the body removed. We'll go take a look at the shack. That solves the cafe fight problem," declared Smythe-Hall.

"And, I suspect, that of the American woman," suggested Davey. "This man was a known sex criminal, as well."

"Sergeant, have a sperm and blood comparison made. Then I can go home to Mrs. Smythe-Hall this evening and have my gin with a clear head. Perhaps we can resume a proper way of life."

Davey and Plotnikov both picked at their breakfast back at the embassy. Neither was hungry. Donovan sat with them, sipping coffee. The prior evening's search of the shack had revealed nothing. The two Palestinians, Adwan and the one from Han House, were undoubtedly quite anxious to put a lot of distance between themselves and Belize City. It was obvious that the shack had been intended as a long-term hideout. It was well stocked with food. So that meant the mistake by Daoud had put a crimp in their plans.

Davey could only wonder how complete the Shaheen network was in Central America. Logic dictated that their presence there, whatever the number, was just as a support task force for their U.S. operation. But, how sophisticated *was* their plan? Up to this point, they seemed to have thought of everything. Except the behavior of Daoud—that was a slipup of the first order. With their kind of over-all smarts, they would avoid Belize City and points north. The only other road, and that was a mostly gravel one hardly suited to high speed, was to Belize's capital city, Belmopan. And from there it was only fifty kilometers to the Guatemalan border. The embassy map showed that portion of the country to be wild and sparsely settled. Unless the two Arabs wanted to fight their way through forests and cross the wide Usumacinta River at the border, they'd have to stay on the roads and head even farther south. What were they driving? "Phil, the one at Han House, did he have a car?" asked Davey.

"Yes, rental records show a Land Rover," answered Donovan.

"Shit, they can go anywhere."

"What are you thinking?"

"The border with Guatemala. Suppose they beat it south along the road out of Belmopan and took off cross-country?"

"Possible. Depends on where they picked their spot. In some places, they might make it. In others, they won't get more than a few miles off the road. Also, and may the heavens grant us this favor, there are some backcountry Indians who aren't really friendly toward outsiders. They could wind up as Arab stew for some isolated village."

"Cannibals?"

"Well, not in the strictest sense, but they have been known to feast on man-sandwiches in the past."

"That would serve the bastards right." Davey was tempted to get an embassy car and search down the road to Belmopan and beyond to the border. Someone might have seen the Palestinians if they had gone that way. In the same thought, he realized that the route was already heavily patrolled. He wouldn't accomplish anything. No more wild goose chases. His pride was already dented. Plotnikov had outperformed him and damned near caught the Palestinians. What leads had he been in possession of that Davey had been without? Probably inside Cuban information. At least there was some comfort in the knowledge that he and the Soviet were in the hunt together. At this point, it was almost immaterial to Davey as to who stopped the terrorists. Just so they were stopped. "What do you think, Colonel?"

"They could have gone south or west, but I think not. I think they are running scared now, and will do one of two things—either abandon their mission or head straight north for the United States. My money would be on the latter course of action."

"Are there other Soviet agents in Belize?" asked Davey.

"No, none who are of any consequence. I can make some calls and perhaps come up with something."

The phone rang. Donovan answered it, listened for a moment, muttered "Thanks," and hung up.

"They snookered us, Davey," said Donovan.

"What do you mean?"

"The Land Rover. Jerry Smythe-Hall says they just found it on the beach south of the city."

"Damn."

The thirty-foot fishing ketch was under full sail and riding a gentle swell system inland of Ambergris Cay, the northernmost protuberance of coral that marked the end of the hundred-sixty-mile-long barrier reef off Belize. At the wheel was Henry Ruiz, a fisherman out of Belize City. Aimed at his back was a .357 Magnum revolver, held steady by the right hand of Ahmad Labidi.

"Head to seaward," ordered Labidi, pointing eastward.

Ruiz swung the wheel to take them north of the cay and out off the Yucatan coast.

Kamal Adwan stirred and sat up on the pile of canvas he had been using as a buffer between him and the moist deck of the ketch. Yawning heavily, he shook the last remnants of his nap from his head. "We're going out to sea?" he asked.

"Only off the coast. We will land back at Punta Allen, where you made your first entry into the Yucatan. That is the one place where they will no longer be looking for you."

"Very clever," commented Adwan, recognizing the good sense of Labidi's decision. God was still with them, guiding their hand. Acquiring the ketch had been risky. To do so, they had driven the Land Rover up the beach to the outskirts of Belize City and commandeered the ketch just as Ruiz was putting out from the port. Such a tactic had carried many dangers, but oftentimes the last place one looked for fugitives was the obvious.

Lowering his voice, Labidi continued. "While you have been resting, I have given much thought to this change in plans. We will reenter Mexico and duplicate your first movements. I will phone our contacts in Mexico City and arrange to have them move up our schedule. We will have to take a car, as before, recover our remaining weapon, and work our way north. Then, we must prepare to cross the border into the United States."

"Is it not too soon? The Americans are still on a very high level of alert."

"We have no choice, I believe. They are on our trail, but probably think we have headed inland. I don't think they will give much thought to us going out to sea and heading back north. The Americans will receive the reports of our presence in Belize and feel that we are being pursued there, with many days before we would plan to go north to the border. We, of course, will do just the opposite. The crossing site has long been selected and some arrangements have been completed. There is no reason we cannot effect a surprise. The American border vigilance may even be relaxed, with them thinking we are busy eluding authorities in Central America."

Adwan stood and stretched. "I like it. It is the will of God. I feel it."

Chapter 18

July 16, 8:00 A.M.
Situation Room, White House

The President of the United States strode into the Situation Room waving his right hand palm down to stop the others before they could rise to a full standing position. "Please, everyone, keep your seats." He lowered his athletic frame onto the leather wing chair at the head of the table and leaned forward, hair still damp from his morning swim, the moisture confusing the generous crop of gray with the original light brown. "I've just been talking to Malenkatov. He assures me that the Soviet Union will continue to give every cooperation and assistance to our problem."

The secretary of defense grunted. "Certainly he will, now that the *Lincoln* is at the bottom of the Atlantic."

The president cut his defense secretary in two with a flash of deep blue eyes. "I buy his explanation, although we cannot condone the original intent of the transfer—but our immediate task is to locate the remaining weapon. John?"

John J. Julian, director of the CIA, was the president's senior in age by a decade, and had very little hair on the top of his head—gray, brown, or otherwise. He pursed his lips, causing his full mustache to lift up around his lower nostrils. "Our latest confirmed position of the terrorists is in Belize, as you know, Mr. President. We damn near had them. In fact, we did get one, already dead. We believe that there are still two of them and our best information is that they have gone inland, possibly into Guatemala, possibly into Mexico. The authorities of both nations have been most cooperative and they have every available man combing their countries. In all candor, I must add that the Guatemalans have a limited and unsophisticated internal security system and the Mexicans know very well that their own constabulary is susceptible to bribery in many areas, particularly the farther you get away from Mexico City. But their national police and intelligence services are not that bad. They may very well come up with something."

"Meanwhile?" The president's forward-leaning posture had not changed.

Julian continued, "We have our borders with Mexico and Canada sealed with the military. Our coasts are under the surveillance of the Coast Guard and the Navy—but I should defer to Dan."

The director of the FBI nodded. "Julian is right. We're sealed tight. For the first time in our history we have a continuous military patrol around the perimeter of the United States. Our own agents, of course, are all on duty and we're beating the bushes nationwide."

"Hawaii?" questioned the president.

"And Alaska as well, Mr. President."

The president leaned back in his chair and rubbed the tops of his thighs with his palms.

"In-country aliens?"

"We have around-the-clock surveillance on all aliens of Arabic origin."

"The fucking Iranians are not Arabs, Dan . . ."

"We are all over them, too, Mr. President. I just used a generality."

"I'm sorry—forgive the Anglo-Saxon lapse—maybe we should round them all up. Our people are in a badass mood. The situation in San Francisco last night is just an example."

No one offered any comment. Three dead and seven injured Iranian and Arabic students in a city known for its tolerance were mute testimony to the mood of the American people.

"Mr. President. . . ." The speaker was General David "Duke" McLean, U.S. Army, Chairman of the Joint Chiefs. "We have our joint antiterrorist team on alert at Bragg. General Filippo has aircraft on alert and ready to take them wherever they're needed."

"Put them in Denver. It's more centrally located. They're too many hours away from the West Coast," directed the president.

Julio Filippo nodded, scribbled something on a notepad, and handed it back over his shoulder to an aide. The blue-suited major hurriedly left the room. "They'll be at Buckley Air National Guard Base in Denver ASAP, Mr. President."

"Who's the team leader?" asked the president.

"Schuyler Petroviny."

The president smiled. "Still?" Everyone knew Schuyler Petroviny, colonel, U.S. Marine Corps—forever a colonel, USMC—a professional with absolutely no tact but with a Medal of Honor won long ago at a place called Dong Hoi. Overage in grade but the physical and mental equal of any two men half his age, Petroviny was a born combat leader, a veteran of more than thirty-three years in special operations, and in the last decade an antiterrorist specialist who had bloodied his knife in covert activities in more than eight mideastern locations. Making him the team leader of Joint Task Unit Sierra may have prevented him from wiping out the entire Palestinian underground. Perhaps, thought the president at the moment, we should have let him be. "Petroviny—what kind of name is that?" wondered the president aloud.

George Abrams, the president's chief of staff, entered and placed a blue folder before his superior. The president glanced up before flipping back the cover. "Might as well sit in, George. Another head can't hurt."

"Yes, Mr. President," replied the chief of staff, taking one of the vacant chairs behind the president.

"Stupid bastards." The president shook his head as he closed the folder. "We've got some more dead Arabs in New York, Lower East Side. What were the bastards doing walking the Lower East Side? *I* don't even walk the Lower East Side." Looking up, he questioned, "Should we round them all up and put them in camps?"

His chief of staff leaned forward. "Three of them were American citizens, Mr. President. The other two, professors at Montreal University, were from Saudi Arabia but were Canadian citizens. Do we lock up our own people?"

"Like the Japanese during World War II?" added the secretary of defense.

The president shook his head. "No, of course not. God, this whole thing gets complicated. Who the hell are the bad guys and who are the others and who are who? You know what I'm going to do? If those sons of bitches get into this country, I'm going to declare martial law and we'll mobilize. That's pretty goddamned extreme for two shitty-ass terrorists, but we're talking nuclear weapon here and I'll seal every building and house and put troops in the street if I have to."

The secretary of state, Kenneth Parish, lit up a cigarette. "Damn," he said quietly. "I've been off these things almost six months."

General McLean smiled at Parish. "Hell, Ken, you're like me. Our livers will go before our lungs." Turning toward the head of the table, he let the smile fade from his face. "Mr. President, if you agree, I think we should assume that the remaining terrorists will attempt to carry out the rest of their mission, which I believe is penetration of our borders and the destruction of a major military installation or maybe even a city. We need to have an instant plan ready to go the moment they show up—assuming we aren't able to intercept them."

"I agree," stated the president. "We need to be prepared with a counteraction, a program for keeping the people calm, and a definite plan to keep the press informed and controlled. That's our domestic chore. We have an international crisis, also. You know the mood of Congress. If that Soviet weapon is detonated on our soil by Arabs, I'm not sure I can—or want to—go against the prevailing opinion, which will most certainly be to strike back. Therefore, I intend to turn the internal problem over to the vice president. As of this moment, Terence, you will meet with whomever you decide and have a plan on my desk by this afternoon."

Terence Shinn nodded.

"Mr. President, you mentioned 'strike back.' At whom?" asked the secretary of state.

"For starters, Libya, Iran, Syria, and Lebanon."

The men around the table stared straight ahead, none changing expression and only Duke McLean moving. He reached over, took Parish's cigarette, and touched it to his own, all the while confining his gaze to the eyes of the secretary of state.

"Invasion, Mr. President?" asked the secretary of defense.

"No. I don't intend to sacrifice a single foot soldier to those bastards. We go nuclear."

"Mr. President . . ." The secretary of state didn't even get his third word out before the president held up his hand.

"These people have taken it upon themselves to start a nuclear war. The attack on the *Lincoln* was the first half of a nuclear strike. The second half will be an assault on our own soil. We will treat them the way we would treat any adversary who launches a nuclear strike against the United States. Any problems here?"

"Lebanon, Mr. President?" queried the secretary of state. "We have Christians there. Friends."

"Lebanon is no longer divided as a nation. It is thoroughly Palestinian controlled. If we have any friends there, they should have left before now. I'll recall our troops that are part of the UN peacekeeping force and advise everyone else to do the same. In fact, the order has already gone out. I am quite serious and I think the American people will back me up."

"I don't usually play this role, Mr. President, but let me be the devil's advocate for a moment," CIA Director Julian began. "If we launch an all-out attack as you suggest, world opinion will consider it a devastating overkill. How do we handle that?"

"We have been slaves to world opinion too long. What kind of support have we received from our friends? The French, for example. The United Nations, if you want to consider world opinion. What has the UN done for us?"

"Britain, Italy, West Germany?" continued Julian.

"I concede their help. They will just have to understand."

"The Soviet Union?"

"This is the one time we have them on the defensive. My firm thoughts on the Soviets are that they will applaud our action. The Muslim world has them lined up after us. Moscow won't say so publicly—it's too good an opportunity to condemn us. But it will be all politics, no action.

"For the moment, I think we are getting ahead of ourselves. I have told you what I intend to do and I have done so deliberately to give you time to evaluate my support among the American people and the Congress. Just keep uppermost in your minds and actions that we can avoid this awful thing by intercepting the remaining terrorists. That is our immediate task. And Terence—"

"Yes, Mr. President."

The president rose. "Ken and I have a meeting with the Israeli ambassador in fifteen minutes. We will be discussing Israeli participation in whatever action would be precipitated by our failure to intercept the terrorists. The remainder of my morning schedule is full, but it is to be interrupted whenever you deem it necessary, Terence. I want a report by three this afternoon as to what our plan is."

"Yes, Mr. President."

"Gentlemen. . . ."

All rose as the president left the room, closely followed by his chief of staff and the secretary of state.

"If you can all give me a few minutes, I would like to brief you on my immediate plan," requested Terence Shinn. "Please feel free to comment. As of this moment, I am forming a special team to handle the domestic side of this crisis. I have sent for Colonel Petroviny. I would like also to have Chuck Myers."

The director of the FBI nodded in agreement.

"Also Ted Benson from your group, John."

"You got him," responded the director of the CIA.

"That gives me two antiterrorist specialists and a counterforce team. I'll provide clerical help from my staff and a press officer. Who else should I have?"

"Liaison officers from each service," recommended General McLean.

"I'd like to add two people," requested the CIA director, "my substation chief from Key West and Davey Morales, our agent who has been with this thing since the Bear ditched."

"*Excellent.* Anyone else?"

"It depends on how large a team you want," commented General Filippo.

"Absolutely no more than called for. The smaller the group, the better. If I need additional help, I'll use the appropriate team member to coordinate service and agency assistance. I want them to have full power to requisition whatever forces I need. No chain of command, just me through them to whomever I want. And I want operators, no staffers. I'll see that all of you are kept informed, of course. I will assemble the team here in D.C., except for Colonel Petroviny. He goes back to his men in Colorado as soon as we have a common meeting of the minds. We will be on twenty-four-hour alert until the terrorists are apprehended. Let's see, that will make ten people plus clerical; no more than two of those. So, we will need air transportation at the ready around the clock for a dozen people with perhaps an extra seat or two for the unforeseen. And I want the fastest aircraft you have."

"Where will the team members stay, sir?" asked General Filippo. "I will need to position a helicopter. The aircraft will be at Andrews."

"For the moment, with the terrorists still outside the country, it is a CIA operation. We'll bunk at your headquarters, John. General, have the ready helicopter on the CIA pad."

"Yes, sir. It'll be there within the hour."

"How soon can I have the team assembled?"

"You say Petroviny is on the way. My two people from Key West will be here within four hours," responded the director of the CIA, looking around at the others.

"We'll pull your military liaisons from the Pentagon," added Duke McLean.

"Good. I will be depending on you people to keep me updated on our latest estimate of where the terrorists are and what we are doing about it. Until they gain entry to this country, and God forbid that, I must depend on you. I want to be briefed this afternoon at two-thirty, just before I see the president, and I want the team assembled at Langley by then. Any questions?"

No one answered.

"Any heartburn about anything?"

The room remained silent.

"So be it. In the event you come up with something we've missed, you have direct access to me. Until the two-thirty briefing I plan to be in my office. One last thing. I will make no announcement concerning this evolution, and I am sure the president will not. That is your guidance. Let's do what we have to do, keep it quiet, and if any word leaks out I can assure you that every person in this room, including myself, will be removed from governmental service. Every citizen in this land is already acutely concerned. We don't want any panic. Business as usual, and get those goddamned people before they get us."

Shinn questioned each man a last time with his eyes, flicking them from one to another. All sat mute. They were good people. When the test came, he couldn't be in better company. But may the test never come, he prayed to himself as he left the room.

Chapter 19

"**G**ood morning." As he spoke, Davey rose and held out his hand toward the familiar bulk entering the room.

The Old Man looked like he had been awake all night, and most probably had. He had arrived at the airport only a few minutes before. "Davey," he muttered, giving his young protégé a nod of his head but ignoring the outstretched hand, reaching for the coffee-pot instead. "I can never sleep on a damn airplane. There's always that background slur of engine noise and air pressurization that sounds like somebody breeding lizards beneath your seat." He sat and drank heavily of the coffee. "Christ! That'll wake me up! What do they brew this from?"

"They like it strong."

"Hummmpph—well, the bastards are still one step ahead of us, eh?"

"Afraid so. We were close," declared Davey.

"Where do you figure they've gone?"

"Well, until late last night, we figured south toward Belmopan and over into Guatemala."

"You come across anything?" asked the Old Man, reluctantly taking another sip of his coffee.

"No, but I assume Donovan has filled you in on the latest development. We have a new ally, a Soviet colonel."

"Ain't that a kick in the ass! Yes, during the drive from the airport he covered that, plus the finding of Daoud's body."

As if on cue, Plotnikov entered with Donovan. Davey made the introduction. "Sir, this is Colonel Vladlen Plotnikov. Colonel, this is . . ."

"Name's not important. If you have to call me something, Tom will do," interrupted the Old Man.

"It is my pleasure—Tom."

"Glad you're here with us. We were just about to have an old-fashioned skull session," added the Old Man.

"Skull session?" inquired Plotnikov. The term was strange to him, but almost instantly it became self-explanatory. "Oh, I understand. That is an interesting way to put it."

"Getting back to Daoud. So, we got one of the sons of bitches, or more properly, Adwan got one for us. What's your guess as to where they have gone?"

"Originally, they had a Land Rover," began Davey, "but we found it later on the beach. They either abandoned it for another vehicle or they've doubled back north."

"Hmmm." The Old Man poured himself a second cup of coffee. "Well, we don't have much in Guatemala. Our people have been alerted, of course. I don't feel too confident that that's where they are. They're crafty sons of bitches and they've obviously got this thing pretty well laid out in advance. We may have surprised them here in Belize, but I'll wager they have a contingency for just about anything that happens. We're going into the ninth inning on this thing and I keep feeling we already have two outs."

"You think they're still heading for the States?" asked Donovan.

"Without a doubt," immediately responded the Old Man. "And I'm not sure we can stop them. We're so damn pissy-ass complacent. Just before I left the Keys, I was on a conference call with the director and he put me on hold halfway through the conversation to check on a guest list he'd given his secretary for an evening party at Langley. We're busting our guts chasing a pair of nuke kooks around Mexico and the director is more concerned about who plays kneesy with whom at a dinner table." The Old Man looked sternly at his coffee. "This stuff is really bad."

"Let me order a fresh pot."

"No, that's all right. Chances are it's my taste buds. My tongue feels like it's sticking up a rat's ass. So what do we do?"

Davey looked at Plotnikov. "Maybe the colonel has an idea."

"I do, but I would like to defer to Tom for the moment. You people seem to have a firm grasp on the possibilities."

"Well," concluded Davey, "I don't feel we'd be very productive searching at random. I'd have to toss a coin to see where we should go next."

"I agree," said the Old Man. "Besides, the Mexicans are getting a bit touchy about all of the *americanos* roaming their highways and byways. The director wants us to scale down our effort and concentrate on a plan if the bastards show up in the States. I phoned him when I got in this morning and told him we'd missed them. I'm not sure the next move is up to us. We will continue our surveillance operations, naturally, but anything in the States is really outside of our responsibility."

"That's never stopped us before," commented Davey with a grin.

"Well, we play the game, Davey, we play the game." The Old Man rose and studied the wall map of Mexico and Central America.

"You see 'em anywhere?" asked Davey.

"They're there, somewhere. You know, I used to play a bit of football in my youth. College. Really loved it, still follow the Dolphins. We had a coach who was straight off the berry farm, had trouble just putting together a complete sentence in conversation. But when he worked a chalkboard during a game, he was a genius of the unexpected. My senior year we were undefeated—God, that's a long time ago—and we did it all with the unexpected. You know, we had the best goddamned pass offense in the conference. A quarterback with an arm that could put a football up a cat's twat at fifty yards. And receivers who were as good open field runners as they were catchers. We went all the way to the conference championship on that arm and those receivers. And you know how we won the big one in the closing seconds?"

"No."

"An end run, Davey my boy. For fifty-four goddamned yards. With fifteen seconds on the clock. Caught the other team all over our receivers on the other side of the field. I don't know what ever happened to the coach, but I suspect if he were here now and coaching those Palestinians, with our defenses covering everything that moved in the secondary, he'd call that same play." As he finished speaking, he tapped his finger on the waters just east of northern Belize.

"You think they've gone back to sea?" asked Donovan.

"That could explain the abandoned Land Rover," declared Davey.

"We've got patrols out there," added Donovan.

"Beyond the three-mile limit, yes," amplified the Old Man. "And with that bodacious reef, maybe farther out than that. How about just hugging the coast and heading north?"

"It's a thought. Where would they land, assuming they plan to reenter Mexico?" asked Plotnikov.

"That's a good question. There are plenty of places: inlets, bays, coves. The question is: are they executing some sort of contingency plan? They've shown every sign of having this thing well planned."

"Of course, they may have stayed inland or gone into Guatemala as I mentioned. They're damned clever."

"The Land Rover could have been a plant," added Davey.

"They may have done that, too," agreed the Old Man. "Well, for the moment that's not our concern, although I intend to have the embassy relay to the Mexican authorities my hunch. They can act on it or piss on it, either one. Okay, colonel, you have heard my thoughts. We'd like to hear yours."

Plotnikov joined the Old Man in front of the map. "I know nothing of American football, but I agree with your reasoning. I would add one other thought that reinforces it. The terrorists are driven by one overriding motivation: to strike their next blow on the soil of the United States. They already have accomplished a significant attack. I believe their success against your warship and their fanatical religious fervor will overshadow a more prudent course of action. They will head directly toward America. No side trips. No detouring through Guatemala. Just go north. And it is that overconfidence that we can exploit."

"By?" interjected the Old Man.

"By acting as boldly as they will act. I suggest that Morales and I put our heads together with the latest information we have from the field, determine our best estimate of where the Palestinians intend to penetrate the American border, and take a position to intercept them."

"That's a wild ride," commented the Old Man. "What if you are wrong?"

"Then we are no worse off than we are at this moment," replied Plotnikov. "We can go in only one direction, and I like the idea of stopping your—how did you say it?—your end run."

"All right, it's decided. Just before I left to come down here, the director called me. Davey, our orders are to go to Langley, you and me. We're going to be part of a special antiterrorist operations group under the leadership of the vice president. The search down here will be turned over to the Mexicans. We'll still provide assistance, but on an as-requested basis. Someone in Mexico City got his nose bent out of joint with us more or less barging in like we owned the place. Some leftist probably put a burr under the Mexican president's saddle. Of course, now that Colonel Plotnikov has presented his thoughts, I'm going to leave you here for one last effort. I don't want to pull you back to the States until we've lost our chance down here to stop the bastards. Just play it low key with the Mexican authorities."

"That's fine with me," decided Davey. "This is the place to stop them, not after they've gotten to the States."

"Good. Tomorrow, there's an early-afternoon flight direct to D.C. I'll be on it. Meanwhile, is there anybody in this godforsaken place who can make a decent Bloody Mary? I need breakfast. Damn! I figured we had 'em this time and they've slipped away again." The Old Man turned to Plotnikov. "Colonel, we're glad to have you on board. Obviously, this thing transcends any differences we may have for the moment. I'm going to depend on you and Davey to stop these people."

"We have a better chance together, sir."

"I'll take some comfort in that. For the moment, I suggest you contact as many of your sources as you can. Davey and I will do likewise. We'll also check with the Mexican authorities. I have until tomorrow afternoon to help in any way I can, so unless something drastic happens in the meantime, let's meet back here this evening, say seven?"

"I will be here," agreed Plotnikov. "Meanwhile, we have a consulate in the city: you may reach me there."

The Old Man watched Plotnikov leave the room. "The man's a good thinker. Isn't afraid to stick his neck out. I like that. Well, Davey, let's get to work. First order of business, I suppose, is to contact Mexico City and see what they have—if anything."

Chapter 20

July 17, 3:00 P.M.
Oval Office, White House

"Coffee, Terence?"

"No, thank you, Mr. President."

"All right, where do we stand?"

"I have just come from a briefing of my team, sir. I spoke with Colonel Petroviny at the completion of the session. His people are on station at Buckley Air National Guard Base in Denver and they have their own assigned aircraft. We'll keep them on continuous alert until we hear something that would justify a stand-down. Meanwhile, they can be anywhere in the contiguous United States within three hours."

"Good. Do you have everybody you need?"

"Yes, sir. The chief of the Key West CIA substation and his action agent, David Morales, will be here before six, which is the time of our next meeting. The service chiefs have assigned three liaison officers, all good operators, and have given them carte blanche authority as long as the Joint Chiefs are kept informed as to what's going down. I have taken Charlie Kelly from my own staff as press officer. He's sharp, knows how to be discreet, and is well liked by the press corps."

"How about a command center?"

"For the moment, at Langley. We've got worldwide communications capability, and Julian is providing watch officers around the clock. We've got an alert helicopter on the CIA pad and an Air Force C-9, reconfigured for team use, at Andrews Air Force Base. Also a backup duplicate."

The president nodded his satisfaction. "I had a good meeting with the Israeli ambassador. In fact, it was an excellent session. If nothing else, the use of the nuclear weapon against the *Lincoln* has forced us all to reevaluate our courses of action. As for Ambassador Akamir—have you ever met him?"

"No, sir, I have not."

"Well, Yukev Akamir is the first ambassador who seems to have a very firm grasp of his prime minister's personal attitude as well as his professional one. Also, he has the ability to make decisions, within limits of course, but decisions that have always been one step up the ladder until now. I think for the first time we have a prime minister, an aggressive ambassador, and a Knesset majority who speak with one voice. And it is interesting to see their new attitude. We may even have a chance at solving the Palestinian problem. Of course, at the same time, we may have to sit on the Israelis a bit. They're shit-hot ready to launch all out against Libya, Lebanon, and Syria, which in the overall picture would be counterproductive at this point."

"I don't see how that would solve the Palestinian problem."

"No, of course not. That is not what I'm saying. What I was referring to is their willingness, in earnest this time, to discuss a surrender of territory while at the same time maintaining a very aggressive attitude in the light of our problem."

"They are considering giving up the West Bank? The Gaza Strip?"

"Perhaps not in their entirety. And I'm not referring to a physical surrender, but a political one, with certain fail-safe provisions of security."

"Forgive me, Mr. President, but aren't we straying just a bit from our immediate problem?"

"Hear me out, Terence. You know this situation has all sorts of ramifications, not the least of which is the direct threat against our own soil. And incidentally, I'm worried—not to change the subject—but I don't think we can take any tighter security measures without my invoking emergency powers. Thank God this isn't an election year; at least we seem to have bipartisan support on the Hill. What do you think are our chances of catching the bastards before they try to get in-country?"

Shinn had been disturbed by the rambling sequence of the president's thoughts and was glad to return to the more immediate problem. "Good, Mr. President. We know, as of just a few days ago, that they were in Belize and most probably now are somewhere in Mexico or Central America. Our intelligence people have the area saturated, and the Mexican government is giving unprecedented assistance. I don't see how the Palestinians can penetrate our southern border. I really don't."

"That leaves the coasts and Canada."

"No way Canada. Their ports and airfields are sealed tight with police and military. Every person entering is subject to a personal identity confirmation and search. We have the same strict measures here."

"Have we counted out Hawaii and Alaska? I feel uneasy about the possibility of a strike at the islands or Alaska."

"Well, to get to Hawaii they will require long-range transportation, and we can readily monitor arrivals. Basically, the same is true of Alaska, although there is quite a bit of rough country that we don't cover except by air. Frankly, I think that both states are secure. We have the same security conditions there as here, also. It's too much of a long shot for them."

"Any thoughts that they may have called it off?"

"No, Mr. President, absolutely not. I believe the fanatical bastards have a well thought-out plan. They found the *Lincoln*, so they must have known from some sort of intelligence network where it was steaming. The acquisition of the light airplane—it was stolen from a southern Florida airfield—was preplanned. They had a hideaway in Belize already arranged for. If one of them had not gotten into that fight in Belize City, we'd have little idea where they are. That was a slipup, so they are fallible. I believe also that they have compatriots here in the States who will assist them in trying to penetrate our border. That has to be part and parcel of their scheme."

"They made political demands from the *Lincoln*. Do you think that is still their overriding purpose?"

"Undoubtedly. Perhaps they have a series of these attacks all getting underway. Who knows? Their ultimate aim has to be political, of course. A Palestinian state and the elimination of the Israeli state—those are their goals. But we do have one ace in the hole."

"What is that?"

"They have only one weapon. This is not enough to bring us to their bargaining table, even if they succeed in using it."

"I don't know. We could be talking a couple of million American lives here. The Navy reports that the weapon that took out the *Lincoln* was seven times the force of the one we used at Hiroshima. God! Isn't progress a goddamned wonderful thing? In 1945 we had a bomb that was the size of a dump truck and it took the combined efforts of several thousand people to just get the thing delivered on target. Now, a pair of skinny Arabs are carting around the equivalent of seven such weapons with their bare hands. And it's damned near small enough to hide in their raunchy undershorts! We've come a long way, Terence."

"Yes, sir. That we have."

The president stood and walked over to the love seat in front of the office fireplace. Shinn joined him and poured two coffees from the silver decanter. They sat side by side, turned slightly to face each other.

"Akamir says they are willing to resume the West Bank talks," explained the president. "They are willing to include not only the PLO but selected leaders of the splinter groups, including this Shaheen faction. He says that the prime minister is willing to reopen negotiations for an Israeli-Palestinian Jerusalem and seriously consider the political return of the Gaza Strip and the West Bank—for starters."

Shinn's cup froze two inches from his mouth. "What brought this about?"

"I believe the prime minister has read the use of the nuclear weapons by this Shaheen group exactly as I have."

"And that is?"

"We're not just talking a Palestinian problem here. We're talking the whole goddamned Moslem world. Remember, it was an Iranian Moslem that took out the *Lincoln.* So, there are two forces, joined together, and each requiring careful and deliberate action; but fortunately for us one is dependent upon the other for success. Only a few years ago, back when the rock-throwing incidents were squashed, we might have had a chance to deal with just the one force, the Palestinians. But then, the Israelis were too pissed off. Anyhow, they got things back under control. Not that I blame them, exactly. Hindsight is so one-hundred-percent pure.

"But now, the entire complexion of the peril has changed. You know what I received at the intelligence briefing right after my meeting with the ambassador? An estimate from the combined intelligence communities that there is unprecedented solidarity within the Moslem world—hell, every fifth person on this planet is Moslem—and the PLO. Anyhow, the consensus is that there is a holy war pending that makes everything we've seen thus far pale by comparison. I'm not a literal Bible person, but it seems to me we're on the brink of the chaos every preacher since Moses has been yelling about. Yet, there is hope."

The president declined Shinn's offer of more coffee. Instead, he stood and rested one arm on the mantel. "To begin with, you know as well as I that not all Moslems believe as the Shiites do, and certainly not as the extremist Shiites. If they did, we would already be engulfed in a religious world war. The Iranians and the Palestinian fanatics, including these Shaheen, are greatly outnumbered by their more rational brethren. The Palestinian question just happens to be the catalyst that gives combined terrorist groups the coincidental support that makes them the dominant threat at the moment. Most of the Arab world as we know it—the Egyptians, the Saudis, the Kuwaitis, the Jordanians, all of the modern civilized Moslems—outnumber the fanatics who think the United States is actually the realm of the devil. They are in sympathy with the Palestinian dilemma, true. But solve that problem and we might very well calm the Arabs and in turn solve the Shiite problem with their help. We must take away from this unholy alliance their one shred of respectability—their argument for a Palestinian return to a traditional homeland."

"And this reflects the Israeli attitude?"

"Absolutely. The Israelis see this alliance between Palestinians and extremist Shiites and their accessibility to nuclear weapons as a completely overpowering threat. We, the United States, are at risk now. And in the interest of our survival, we may very well place the survival of Israel secondary."

"We would abandon Israel? To appease the terrorists?"

"No. Tel Aviv knows we would not do that. But they also know that a worldwide terrorist effort, using suicidal nuclear tactics—which seems to be their new method of operation—can escalate into a worldwide guerrilla war. And Israel could be the first casualty. The Arabs have never succeeded in defeating Israel with organized military forces. But with concentrated terrorist tactics and weapons of mass destruction, it's a different ball game. To refresh your memory, neither have we ever been defeated by organized military forces, but one of the reasons we sure as hell got kicked out of Vietnam was paramilitary tactics that bordered on terrorism."

"It was a political decision, Mr. President. We could have accomplished our task if we had enjoyed the support of our people."

"A political decision based on the fact that we were getting our ass kicked by a bunch of primitives who didn't even have a navy or air force. Can't you see the terrible lesson? We were licked by an ideal we couldn't counter. People die for ideals much more readily than for causes. And the lesson applies here. We either come up with a political solution to the Palestinian problem or we face a worldwide idealistic cause that goes one hell of a lot deeper than a Palestinian homeland quest."

For a long moment neither man spoke. Then the president slowly shook his head and let a half smile crawl across his face. "What ever happened to simple old communism? That we could cope with."

Shinn sat back on the love seat. "Oh, it's still around, Mr. President, as you well know. Just waiting in the wings."

"That's the other complicating factor to all this. The weapons are Soviet. Yet, Moscow is vehement in their argument that the devices were intended as counterbalances to the Israeli nuclear arsenal. They claim that they have half the KGB and GRU out in the field trying to catch the bastards. As for their argument, I'd like to believe them, but I've never known them to be that naive—or that stupid. So we have that problem. There's a very delicate balance here. On one end of the scale is a rationale that tells us to proceed as we are and chalk up the weapons acquisition to just what the Soviets claim it to be—a foul-up. On the other end is reprisal. And that could lead to a great tragedy. Do we want to risk nuclear war with the Soviets?"

"You know the answer to that as well as I, Mr. President."

"Yes. So, I have a problem. And you have a problem. I will use every aspect of this office to get the Israelis and the Arabs reengaged in some form of dialogue on the Palestinian problem. Ultimately, I am also responsible for the security of this land and the safety of our people. You will have to continue to be my action officer on this, and you have full authority to act in my name. Just remember, Terence, I must constantly know what is going on. You make the decisions and I'll back you up. If we let the terrorists succeed in striking against the people of the United States, we will have failed in our most important responsibility. But, if we can handle this one step at a time, we can count on our pictures being in every history book between now and eternity."

"And if we don't?"

"No problem. There won't be any history books."

Adwan and Labidi stood in the pilothouse with the Indian fisherman, watching the lights off their port bow flicker in the clear night air. They were approximately three miles from land. Labidi motioned for Adwan to step clear.

"Is that Punta Allen?" asked Labidi.

"Yes," replied the Indian.

"Shouldn't we slow? Aren't there shallow areas around here?"

"No, it's clear water all the way in."

Adwan could see Labidi's hand slowly shifting his revolver around the Indian. The shot severed the man's spinal column just below his skull. Labidi stepped over the body and cut the throttles to idle. "Help me get him over the side," he requested. Together, he and Adwan rolled the corpse over the gunwale into the water. "We'll be long gone before he floats ashore," announced Labidi flatly. "Take the helm."

Adwan carefully avoided the slick blood on the deck and shoved the throttles forward. The scene was familiar to him. He had initially ridden toward Punta Allen on just this course only ten days back. Only that time he had been with Daoud.

Chapter 21

7:00 P.M.
U.S. Embassy, Belize City

D avey, Plotnikov, Donovan, and the Old Man sat at a small table, facing the wall chart of Mexico. In the chart, at the villages of Misantla and Poza Rica on the lower east coast, were two red pushpins. Another marked Coyuca de Benitez, on the opposite coast just above Acapulco. A fourth stuck out from Zacatecas, in the middle of the country, and a fifth at Ciudad de Valles, just inland from Tampico.

"There have been three other reported sightings, but they are all still in the Yucatan," began the Old Man. "I think we have to discount those. There is no way the bastards have stayed there. Now, the way I figure it, they have either gone out of the country or we need to evaluate those five possible sightings we have marked. Colonel, you want to go first?"

"Yes, certainly. My sources are responsible for the reports from Coyuca de Benitez and Ciudad de Valles. In both cases, our people showed the photograph around and received identifications of Adwan. However, the reports are only two hours apart, and the distances are such that one report has to be an error, if not both. The report from Coyuca de Benitez placed the Palestinian with a woman. At Ciudad de Valles, it was a lone man purchasing food. Therefore, I say we disregard the western report."

"That seems logical," agreed the Old Man. "What do you have, Davey?"

"The other marked locations are the best of eight reports. We were able to discount five because of circumstances. In one instance, the suspect was buying several bottles of tequila and smoking a cigarette, hardly indicative of Adwan. That sort of thing. Of the remaining three, Misantla and Poza Rica look good. In both instances, there were two suspects and they were in an Isuzu Trooper four-wheel-drive vehicle. The Mexican computer spit out the theft of such a car back at a small village on the Yucatan Peninsula. Not too far away, the bodies of two Americans were discovered in a shallow grave. Both had been brutally carved up and the Mexican police have been able to tie them in to the vehicle."

"Zacatecas?"

"A reliable report. Two men bought gasoline at a small station. They were driving a sedan and one appeared to be Arabic or at least Middle Eastern," amplified Davey.

"Do any of the other reports mention a vehicle?" asked the Old Man.

"No," answered Davey.

"How about timing?" asked Plotnikov.

"The three east coast reports are all within a feasible time frame," answered Davey.

"What have the Mexican authorities done about the reports?" queried the Old Man.

Davey deferred to Donovan.

"In each report that we received, a follow-up search was instituted, but nothing came of it. All suspects just disappeared," reported Donovan.

"Colonel?"

"Our people were several hours behind the sightings, and the suspects were gone. But there is a pattern," replied Plotnikov.

"Yes, look at Highway Eighty-five," directed the Old Man. "It runs through or near the three sightings of Misantla, Poza Rica, and Ciudad de Valles, and runs north all the way to the American border."

"Laredo?" questioned Donovan. "You think they may be planning to cross at Laredo?"

"Possible," replied the Old Man very slowly, "but not smart— and these bastards are smart."

"Brownsville?" offered Davey.

"Why a city?" interjected Plotnikov. "I would think they would avoid such areas."

"First things first," continued the Old Man. "We have to decide if the three sightings are sufficient to take action on."

"I say most definitely yes," urged Davey.

"It's the best we have," added Donovan.

"Colonel?"

"The reports are consistent. There is *someone* out there heading north in a rough-terrain vehicle."

The Old Man chewed his lower lip. "All right. Let's assume they are going north on Highway Eighty-five. We put roadblocks at Ciudad Victoria and Monterrey."

"It may be too late for Victoria," suggested Davey, "considering the time of the reports."

"Maybe, maybe not," suggested the Old Man. "It wouldn't hurt. Donovan, get on it."

Donovan left the room.

"There is something we're not seeing here," said the Old Man. "It's too cut and dried. With all of the devious progress they've made thus far, a straightforward shot up a main highway doesn't seem in character."

"Let me offer something," broke in Plotnikov. "They know there is a manhunt on and must assume that one of their faces, at least, is known. So, they will figure on being spotted from time to time. But, if they can move fast enough, they can stay ahead of the reports. At the same time, I believe they want to leave a pattern of travel. That will cause us to concentrate in the wrong area. They may, in fact, be traveling north on Highway Eighty-five for a while, but they will branch off somewhere, and that somewhere will be at the point that they head directly for their penetration of the United States."

"You would think that some of the road patrols would have picked them up by now," suggested Davey.

"You forget, Davey, that we aren't talking Texas Rangers here. The Mexicans are not set up for this type of thing with the sophistication we're used to. I don't want to bad-mouth them, for they are giving us outstanding support. I just think the Palestinians are outsmarting them."

The three men looked back as Donovan hurried into the room.

"We just got a report of a Mexican cop being shot on Highway Eighty-five just north of Ciudad Mante. His last radio call was to report he was stopping an Isuzu Trooper for failing to yield a right of way!" reported Donovan.

"How long ago?" quickly asked the Old Man.

"Within the hour," answered Donovan, "and the cop was killed with an automatic weapon."

The Old Man stood and approached the wall map. "We're running out of goddamned time," he murmured.

"The Mexican police are swarming to the area," added Donovan.

"Coahuila," said the Old Man very quietly.

"What?" asked Davey.

"Coahuila," repeated the Old Man, only this time his word was strong and final. "That's where the bastards are off to. It is the worst badass country in all of Mexico. Hot as hell, bare as the Sahara, and as tough to cross as Death Valley. Just right for a couple of Arabs who grew up in the same type of terrain."

Plotnikov looked closely at the area. "It is large. There are a number of places they may try to cross. It looks like very rough country."

"Donovan, call the airport and get a charter. I saw several Lear jets there when I arrived. Corporate aircraft, probably American. Commandeer one if you have to. I want Davey and the Colonel out of here tonight. Is there an airstrip at Monclova?"

"I don't know," replied Donovan.

"If not, get them into Monterrey. There is bound to be a chopper there. I want them in Monclova ASAP."

Once more, Donovan hurried from the room.

"I've got to get back to the States before tomorrow afternoon. Surely we can get something out of southern Texas, an Air Force jet from San Antonio or something from the Navy at Corpus. You two, start moving out! I'm going to call Langley."

"Wait, wait," pleaded Davey. "So, we go to Monclova. What then?"

"Assuming you get there ahead of the bastards, take 'em. Figure out your own time frame and fall back toward the border if you have to. But don't go all the way to Texas. We'll have troops there, all along the border. Search and destroy, Davey boy. We're on their ass!"

Plotnikov grinned broadly. "I like the way you move, Tom!"

"I'm very seldom wrong when I play my hunches, Colonel. I just want you and Davey to go up there and kill those sons of bitches."

"It's dark out there," commented Davey, pressing his nose against the small circular cabin window in the side of the Lear jet.

Plotnikov glanced at his watch. Only a few minutes before midnight. The pilot assured them he would have them in Monterrey by one in the morning.

Davey leaned back and tried to relax. There was nothing he could do at this point. Donovan had called the American embassy in Mexico City. They assured him they would have a police chopper waiting at Monterrey. It would be another hour to Monclova. The town police would already be alerted.

Plotnikov sipped on a plastic cup full of cool water. Vodka would have been better. Outside his window, he could see only the inky black of the Mexican sky. His thoughts returned to Tatiana. There had been good moments between them. He sighed. From what Morales had told him, her body had already been found. At least she was not still floating in the warm water off Cuba. Her beauty would have faded fast in such an environment.

The chopper was waiting at Monterrey. And the chief of police of the small town of Monclova was waiting at the pad behind the jail as they landed.

"Mr. Morales?" he inquired.

"Yes," responded Davey, "and this is my associate . . . Mister Plotnikov." He had almost used the Russian's rank. That might not have been wise.

"Please, senores, come inside. I have a message for you."

The only other occupant of the jail was the night clerk. The four cells were empty.

"After you left Monterrey, the authorities there relayed a message to me. They received word from the American embassy in Belize instructing you to proceed to Allende. I have written the exact instructions down." Picking up the paper, the chief continued, "Donovan relays orders from your superior to proceed at once to Allende. The suspects may try to take a secondary road out into the open country of Coahuila—why would anyone want to do that?" the police chief added suddenly. "That is the most terrible country. The suspects, these are the terrorists?"

"They very well could be," replied Davey.

"I will alert my force! This is sudden for us."

"Are you able to furnish us with a car?"

"Yes. It is already set aside for your use. I apologize that we do not have something more better for you, but this is a very poor area and we do not receive the latest equipment."

The chief of police was a master of understatement. Davey and Plotnikov found themselves being ushered to a surplus military jeep of unknown vintage. "I have provided weapons for you," he stated proudly. A pair of very dirty Soviet AK-47s lay on the floor behind the front seats.

"Think you know how to use one of these?" teased Davey.

"I will manage," replied Plotnikov, examining one of the weapons. "I suspect my automatic may be a better weapon. These probably have not been fired in years."

Davey jumped behind the wheel. "A map?" he abruptly cried out. "Do you have a map?" he asked of the Mexican.

"No, senor, there is only one road north, there across the plaza. Highway Fifty-seven. It is one hundred and ninety-two kilometers to Allende."

"Can you call ahead for us," asked Davey, "and let the authorities know we are coming?"

The Monclova police chief smiled awkwardly. "There are no authorities in Allende, senor. It is a very small place."

"Great," muttered Davey, grinding the gears until they dropped into low. "We're on our own, Colonel," he called as they pulled away from the Monclova jail and started down one side of the town plaza.

Plotnikov held onto the rusted jeep with both hands. "Ride 'em, cowboy," he yelled with a broad grin and the worst Texas accent Davey had ever heard.

Chapter 22

L abidi replaced the leaking hose on the rusted gasoline pump and paid the young Mexican boy who manned the simple two-pump gasoline shack on the northern outskirts of Allende. Adwan had remained seated inside of the Isuzu Trooper. The rugged four-wheel-drive vehicle had been acquired in the Yucatan village of Oxkutzcab by the simple act of luring two homosexual archaeology students away from their diggings by a promise of Middle Eastern variations in the classic one-on-one position favored by such males throughout history. Never before had Labidi and Adwan taken such pleasure in disemboweling degenerates, the use of their knives all the more satisfying with the realization that the two gay young men were Americans. From Oxkutzcab, the two Arabs had driven to the burial place of their remaining cylinder and substituted the two American bodies.

The drive north had been extremely tiring. Avoiding the major highways had added several days to their time, and the constant bouncing along the twisted secondary roads had created pain in every bone, joint, and muscle in their bodies. They had stayed east of Mexico City, roughly paralleling the Gulf Coast as they made their way northward. From Pachuca, they almost threw caution to

the winds and followed National Highway Eighty-five to Mon-
temorelos. But the sight of increasing Army patrols along the highway had prompted them to branch once more eastward to bypass
Monterrey. Up to now, their roughest stretch had been from La
Gloria, a mere eighty-one miles south of the Texas city of Laredo,
to Crucera Juarez. Their map showed a gravel road; in reality,
there were only sand and dirt with twin wheel depressions that
formed a trail northwest. But there had been one distinct advantage to their circuitous routing. Since departing the Yucatan, they
had encountered Mexican authorities only once, a single *policia*
waiting for *turistas* just outside of Cadereyta, east of Monterrey.
The officer had stopped them for excessive speed. ("Unfortunately,
senores, the sign that drops the fifty-kilometer limit to fifteen has
been overturned by a windstorm. The speed limit, of course, is still
in effect.") The man had not questioned their tourist cards or international drivers' licenses, both identifying Labidi and Adwan as
Lebanese scholars. He merely returned them without comment,
and after only a short discourse on how Mexico valued its tourist
trade but must regretfully enforce its traffic laws—for the common
good—he had unhesitatingly accepted a handful of pesos as ample
compensation for the violation.

As Labidi wheeled the Trooper away from the gas shack,
Adwan checked their map. "There," said Adwan, pointing ahead
and to the left, "State Road Twenty-nine. That is correct? Watch
out for that car!"

A battered 1956 Chevrolet coupe had pulled out in front of
them.

"Fool," cursed Labidi, shaking his fist at the short Mexican
peering over the steering wheel and navigating the Trooper around
the windowless Chevy. "Yes," he continued, "we have fifty kilometers and then we will test this fine vehicle to its utmost. This will be
our last stop. Should we eat?" As he spoke, he pointed to one of the
few town buildings. The clapboard structure had a weathered sign
lettered "Cantina" hanging over its open door. Sitting in front was
a battered and rusted jeep.

"We have food with us," idly remarked Adwan, studying the
map. "Let's keep going. Fifty kilometers?"

"Just beyond Zaragoza. We head northwest."

Adwan searched the map again. "There is nothing there."

"Ah, but there is. Sand and low hills and dirt and ground
bushes—but passable."

"There are no landmarks."

"It is like our land. We will use the crests of the hills to determine our course. I have driven this way before. It is all part of our plan. From here on we will see no one until we are ready to enter the land of the infidels."

"We are going to just drive into the United States?"

"No, of course not. You will see. Indulge me for just a while longer. Our entry into the country has been well planned."

"I do not believe our good fortune. We have only been challenged once."

"This route has been long determined and test-driven several times. We anticipated that the Mexican authorities would set up roadblocks at major intersections, with little patrol in between. So, you and I have avoided those places."

"And seen lots of Mexico," remarked Adwan. "It is really not too unlike our own country. More greenery, of course, But dry and hot, and cold at night. I do not care to sleep to another dawn on the ground."

"Sleep in the vehicle."

"Impossible, as you know." Adwan sat silent for a while, watching the featureless countryside pass. "But it is a good place for prayers. Out here, in the open, I can feel God."

"He is our guide and our protection, my brother."

Inside the cantina, Davey and Plotnikov were finishing a bowl of green chili.

"There goes a car!" exclaimed Davey, jumping up and running to the door. Through the dust, he could barely see the rear of an old Chevrolet laying a thick black cloud of oil vapor. "Just a local," he uttered, returning to the table. He washed down a large spoonful of the chili with a thirsty swallow of cold beer. "Thank God they have refrigeration, but I'd kill for a glass of safe water. I hope this chili's safe. This would be a bad time to a catch a case of the runs."

"Yes," agreed Plotnikov, "I thought some of the Cuban food was hot, but this is something else. I love peppers, but in this mixture the taste is destroyed. I suppose it is just right for you, yes?"

Davey grinned and wiped his nose. "Perfect. Clears out the sinuses. Sort of a Mexican Dristan. I'm getting tired of trying to sleep in that jeep, though. You would think they would at least have a spare room somewhere around here. If we had known, we could have asked the chief for a couple of blankets and slept on the ground."

"Did you see the things crawling around on the ground?" prompted Plotnikov. "I prefer our transportation."

"I think that Chevy is only the third or fourth car we've seen passing through."

"I don't believe this is on the tourist route," commented Plotnikov.

Fifteen minutes later, they finished and walked outside. Davey waved at the young boy attending the gasoline shack several buildings away.

"Did you see the car, senor?" yelled the boy.

"Yes," answered Davey, then aside to Plotnikov added, "Must have been an event."

"I was coming to tell you, like you asked, but I think maybe you see it when it passed the cantina."

Davey's brow wrinkled. "What does he mean? I told him we were looking for an Isuzu." He yelled back at the boy, "That was an old Chevy!"

The boy shook his head. "No, senor, it was a Trooper, just like you said!"

The boy's sentence was like a starter's gun. Both Davey and Plotnikov took off on a dead run toward the station. "What? We only saw the Chevy," countered Davey.

"No, senor, the Trooper stopped and filled up with gasoline. There were two men."

Davey had Adwan's picture out by the time he and Plotnikov reached the boy. "Was this one of them?"

"Si. You showed me the picture before."

"Let's go, Colonel! They've got a twenty-minute head start on us!"

It was twenty-two minutes by the time Davey and Plotnikov had the ancient jeep cranked up and roaring at its top speed out of Allende.

"The Old Man, that uncanny bastard," observed Davey.

"Old Man?" asked Plotnikov, raising his voice to be heard over the noise of the engine.

"Tom. My boss. He goes by the rather nondescript name of the Old Man within the community. You and he make a great team! He called the end run and you suggested we put all of our apples in this one barrel, Allende! We were right on, Vladlen! Only we sat in the cantina like a couple of gringo tourists."

"Oh." Plotnikov reached behind him and grabbed one of the AK-47s. He wiped it with an oily rag that he had retrieved from under his seat, then he examined it. Apparently satisfied that it was in working order, he wiped off the other and placed it between

the seats for Davey's use. Within minutes, they had passed
through the village of Morelos and were approaching Zaragoza.
Davey was able to keep the speedometer pegged at ninety-six kilometers per hour—sixty miles per hour—but the road wouldn't
tolerate any higher speed. He wasn't sure that the jeep had a
higher speed. He braked hard in Zaragoza to skid to a halt beside
a woman and a small child.

"Excuse me," said Davey in Spanish. "Did another car pass
this way a short time ago?"

The woman took her child's hand and backed away. Davey
repeated the question.

"*Sí.*"

"Were there two men in it?"

"*Pienso dos.*"

"Was it a square, tall car with lots of windows?"

"*Sí.*"

"*Gracias, senora, muchas gracias.*" Davey floored the acceler-
ator. "I was afraid they might have left the road."

"This is terrible country."

"Yes, but remember, the Old Man said they would head into
open country. We're only about thirty miles from the border. If
they're going into the boonies, it should be soon." Davey kept his
speed below sixty kilometers as he and Plotnikov scanned the
shoulders of the road. "Look!" he cried, braking hard. Leading off
from the left shoulder were two deep, curving ruts: wheel tracks.
"They left the road here; there is still sprayed sand on the asphalt
where they swerved off the hardtop."

"Let's go."

The jeep might have been capable of sixty on the highway, but
in the sand they would do well to reach two-thirds of that speed.
"They will pull away from us in the Trooper," observed Plotnikov.

"Yes, but the bastards will leave a clear trail. We'll catch up with
them." Davey lifted his left hand from the steering wheel and grabbed
the side rim of the windshield. That way, he could raise himself
slightly and soften the severe blows of the hard seat as they pounded
their way toward central Coahuila. The late-morning sun was almost
overhead, but the canvas top of the jeep afforded them some shade,
and their passage through the scorched air created a steady breeze
around them. That helped some. Ahead, the tracks led across the
rugged terrain in a series of dips and shallow climbs while winding
their way northwestward. Scrub oak and mesquite peppered the desert floor, but the tracks remained generally clear of them.

"This way has been driven several times before," yelled Plotnikov.

"Yes! Keep a sharp lookout in case they have left it."

They topped a small rise and could see well ahead. "No dust. Nothing," observed Davey.

"They had twenty minutes on us and have probably gained a few more. They could be twenty, maybe thirty kilometers out in front of us," replied Plotnikov.

Well, thought Davey, the tortoise caught up with the hare. He would keep driving the hellish road clear across Mexico if he had to.

Kamal Adwan was convinced that the sharp edges of his pelvic bone were about to slice through the skin of his buttocks. For the past two hours, the pounding of the firm seat of the Isuzu against his thinly fleshed rear had progressed rapidly from irritation through discomfort to downright pain as Labidi forced the Trooper across the endless sand of Mexico's most barren state. They had been in and out of the abrupt foothills of the Sierra Madres and had followed several parched riverbeds, always working their way northwest. Retracing their route in his mind, Adwan figured they must be getting close to the American border. After leaving Allende, they had followed the highway north to just beyond the village of Zaragoza. There, as he had promised, Labidi had taken off cross-country. At first, they had easily steered northwest across salt-saturated desert floor. Within a few hours, however, that relatively smooth stretch of four-wheel-drive passage had given way to ball-shaking vibrations as they followed the waffled bed of the San Radrigo River westward. Even for one born and raised in Arabian deserts, the high Mexican desert was punishing and demanding. Adwan's body was threaded with a thousand aches.

"Drink some more water," suggested Labidi, reaching down and retrieving a felt-covered canteen from beneath his legs. There were at least six more in the back, two of them already empty.

Adwan unscrewed the cap and filled his mouth, moving his tongue and cheeks to wash them of the sand. When he finally swallowed, he could taste the grit. The second mouthful went down cleanly.

"We are almost there. Think of me . . . I have driven this route seven times before to establish our camp and ensure that I would need only the sand and sky to tell me the way. We are in the middle of a harsh, foreign land, Kamal, but it is a land I know well by now.

Just ahead, over one more short stretch of hills, is our destination. You will be pleased, for we will have time to rest and renew ourselves with prayer. And then, before this night is over, we will be in America. How does that sound?"

Adwan nodded, ashamed to admit that the heat and discomfort had robbed him of a small measure of faith. Atonement would be due. Muhammad, he prayed silently, forgive my impatience and intercede for me. God is great and you prepare a place for me at his feet. The prayer did not help. "We have to stop," he complained. "I have to have a few minutes away from this pounding."

"Very well," conceded Labidi. He had to admit they had been pushing hard. He let the Trooper slow down but kept it in the tracks as it stopped. Adwan crawled out and stretched his arms and rubbed the small of his back. Labidi joined him. They had stopped on the crest of a small hill. Together, they walked ahead a few yards, then started back to the Trooper. Labidi grabbed one of the canteens and tipped it to let a small amount of the water wet his face. Adwan did the same.

"This feels good," said Adwan.

"My behind is still vibrating," admitted Labidi, laughing, "but we are getting close to our destination."

Adwan walked to the side of the car path and began spraying urine on a large clump of mesquite. As he did so, he let his gaze wander around the surrounding desert and back over the crude roadway over which they had just traveled. "Look, my brother, back there!"

Labidi shaded his eyes with one hand and stared east. A small cloud of dust was rising. He squinted to better focus his eyes. There was no wind. The narrow dust cloud was slowly forming and dissolving at a steady rate. "It is a car!" exclaimed Labidi. "Someone is following us! Can you see it?"

"Only the cloud, but it is moving toward us."

"How can this be?" wondered Labidi.

"Maybe it is just coincidence," offered Adwan.

"I have never seen anyone on this path. I made it myself with repeated passages. It goes nowhere, except to where we must be. Somehow, my brother, we are being followed. Come!"

Labidi let the Trooper glide down the slope of the hill. "Grab your weapon," he ordered as he stopped the car. "We will go back to the top. They will not see our vehicle until they hit the crest. At that point, we will put a quick end to their folly." Adwan ran behind him as the two men took their positions off to the right side of the roadway. Lying flat under the cover of the scrub oak, they would not be seen.

Davey felt as if he were encased in a dust cocoon. The poor aerodynamics of the jeep were such that both he and Plotnikov had been breathing and eating the foul dirt since they left the asphalt. Plotnikov had covered their weapons with the cloths he found under his seat. Ahead was a small hill, and Davey pushed harder on his foot pedal to keep their speed up as they bounded upward. Just as they topped the rise, the Trooper came into view. Davey shifted his foot over to the brake as Plotnikov pointed ahead. "Look!" cried Plotnikov.

Even as Plotnikov yelled, a vicious volley of automatic fire broke out from the hilltop ahead. Davey stomped on the brakes as he turned the steering wheel sharply away from the direction of the gunfire. The high-g jeep began a rapid roll, throwing Plotnikov along the outside of the turn. Davey had only time to grab his AK-47 before leaping from his seat. He hit hard and kept himself rolling until he was in a slight depression. Cautiously raising his head, he could see two figures perhaps fifty yards away. He took careful aim and squeezed off several rounds. Both figures dove and rolled out of sight. Davey grunted in disgust at the settings of the Soviet rifle's sights. They were useless.

A burst of fire sprayed sand all over him. He rolled farther down into the depression and took stock of his situation. The jeep was on its side a good thirty feet away from him. Beyond were the Palestinians. Plotnikov was nowhere in sight.

"Vladlen!" Davey called.

Plotnikov heard the call but there was no way he could answer it. His body was twisted around the rough trunk of a large scrub oak and he could taste the warm, moist salt of his own blood. There was little strength to move but he could raise one hand to his stomach where the awful pain was. His clothes were soaked with a thick, oozing fluid. He had taken more than one of the sudden rounds.

"Vladlen!" came Davey's call a second time.

Plotnikov opened his mouth but no sound came. He knew his eyes were open but he could see only vague shapes. One was standing over him. "Morales?" he mouthed.

"This one is still alive," a muffled voice said in Arabic.

Plotnikov was fluent in Arabic as well as Spanish. That was one of the reasons he had been selected to oversee the transfer of the weapons. The Arabic words were music to him. He tried to grin. He had been right. He and the American had intercepted the terrorists. General Gigiyashvili would be very proud of him, maybe even give him a decoration. He could go back to Cuba and get Tatiana. No, Tatiana had taken advantage of him. Yet, she was so beautiful. She was stooping over him now and he could see her full lips. But they were pale with no color, and a green slime was dripping from them. Seaweed. I'm sorry, Tatiana. There was no other choice. You know that, Tatiana, my career... Plotnikov neither heard nor felt the round that entered his brain.

Davey heard the single shot and knew he was alone. The depression around him was apparently a dry creek bed and led away from the road to eventually reach another small hill. He very carefully raised himself and peered over the rim of the depression. Nothing. Crouching, he ran down the creek bed toward the hill. There, he would have the high ground.

"Can you see him?" asked Labidi.

"No. He is over on the other side of the road."

Labidi studied Plotnikov's form. "We got one."

"The other seems all right. We'll have to work around behind him."

"No," objected Labidi. "We can't take any chances. If one of us is hit, our mission will be jeopardized. Cover me."

Keeping the jeep between him and the last position of Davey's gunfire, Labidi made his way to the overturned vehicle. The hood had sprung open. Quickly, he reached inside and yanked off the distributor cap and the ignition wires, then retraced his path to rejoin Adwan. "We will leave him out here to die. There is no way he can follow us on foot. And there is no hope of anyone coming along. We have a schedule to keep. If we delay too long, it could mean we would miss our rendezvous. And I must say again that we cannot take any chance on one of us being wounded or killed."

Slowly, taking advantage of the rises and falls of the terrain, the two Palestinians returned to the Trooper.

Davey lay as still as he could, listening for any signs of movement. He felt more secure now that he had reached the back side of the hill. Staying on his belly, he crawled upward until he reached the top. Leading with his weapon, he pulled himself between some mesquite and chanced a look down at the road. He first saw the jeep and Plotnikov lying beside it. He let his eyes roam the area from which the attack had come. There was no movement anywhere. He was ready to slide back into his cover when he heard the whir of the Trooper's starter. They were leaving! Davey jumped up as the Trooper pulled out and sped away. He emptied his clip at the car but could not see where his rounds went.

"Shit."

He half-ran, half-stumbled down the hill and hurried over to Plotnikov. The Russian was dead, his chest and face shattered. Davey tried to roll the jeep back over onto its wheels but it was too heavy. As he started to close the hood, he saw the bare points and rotor of the distributor. And the spark plug wires were missing. Even if he could right the jeep, he would be going nowhere. At least it provided some shade. Reaching inside, he retrieved a canteen. Fortunately, he and Plotnikov had filled it with bottled water as an emergency supply and he had recently eaten. He could last for a few days. But who would be looking for him?

Two hours later, Labidi and Adwan passed over the last hill and swept down into a wide ravine, following it northward until it became deeper and more narrow and the sand became slightly less dry. Their ride smoothed. The desert scrub became more dense alongside their route and they could no longer see their side horizons. They were following a deep dry wash, one that could easily become the bed of a roaring river should the towering cumuli behind them continue to build and release their moisture. They were within feet of the tent before Adwan saw it, so cleverly had Labidi pitched it on the side of the dry wash. Scrub brush was arranged over its top, and Labidi wheeled the Isuzu against the left bank.

"Help me cover it. The American helicopters of the border patrol sometimes approach. But we are still twelve miles inside Mexico, and they have yet to come close enough to inspect this area."

Together, Adwan and Labidi covered the Trooper with scrub before entering the tent. It was double walled, Arab fashion, to provide an insulating layer of air, and although not of Arab design, modified in the ways of the desert people. Openings were cut in the sides near the top to allow warm air to escape, and the canvas bottom was covered with multicolored Mexican throw rugs. The dry wash formed a natural channel for the mild breeze stimulated by the not-too-distant budding thunderstorms. Adwan experienced instant relief as they sat and gathered their thoughts.

"This is a terrible place to establish ourselves," said Adwan.

"When those clouds relieve themselves, everything will be swept away, including us if we are foolish enough to remain."

"This tent has been here for six weeks. The clouds approach every day as they do now. But before they mature, they swing east. This is the one constantly dry wash in the whole area."

"It has seen water. That is evident."

"True, but the Mexican who first brought me here assured me that the normal progression of summer flash floods reaches this area no sooner than August."

"Someone knows of this place? Is he trustworthy?"

"Completely."

"How can you be sure?"

Labidi's lips formed a mock pout. "If you doubt me, we can walk a few paces to the east and you can ask him. The shovel is just outside."

Adwan rolled backward, convulsed with laughter. The tension of the past days flowed from his body. "Beautiful!" As he rolled on the rugs, he thunked against a trio of fifty-five-gallon drums. "We can wash! You have provided enough water for us to wash." He stripped off his shirt and kicked away his trousers. "Never have I felt so soiled. The sands of our Palestinian desert may sting and cling to our bodies, but they are nothing compared to this abomination. And Western clothing in the desert! One is better off naked." Abruptly, he sat up. "I just thought. Should we leave our weapon in the car?"

"Of course. It is well covered, and if we should have to get out of here in a hurry, moments could be saved."

"You are not that confident of the Mexican's words, then?"

"I am not speaking of the flow of water. I am concerned with intruders. Not very likely, perhaps, in this isolated hellhole, and we will be here only a few hours. But the weapon is better off where it is."

Adwan removed his underpants and walked naked from the tent. "You did a good job with the brush. They will not see us from the air. But ground traffic?"

"Believe me, nothing crosses this surface this time of year."

Adwan recalled his rough and extremely hot four-hour ride as he retreated to the relative coolness of the tent. "I believe you." Removing the cover from one of the water drums, he plunged in his head and then stood erect to let the cooling liquid drain down his body. Wadding his shirt, he wet it and began bathing his body. Labidi stooped and retrieved a thin telescopic pole from behind a pile of boxes. Extending it, he guided it through the slits in the twin tops of the tent and connected the cable at its bottom to a radio unit. Then he inserted an audiocassette into an open receptacle on the face of the unit and shoved it shut. A single pull of the rope started the portable Honda generator and, after checking the power output, Labidi flicked on the radio's master switch and set the output selector to the tape transmit position and the speaker switch to the monitor position. Lively mariachi melodies filled the tent, causing Adwan to turn and grin broadly while drying himself.

"Mexican music, my brother? I must confess some bewilderment."

"Yes, Kamal, Mexican music. Selected pieces, arranged in a specific order, and played for our friends who are only twelve miles away at this moment."

"It is our pickup signal!"

"Of course. Since the middle of the month, the ears of the Shaheen in America have been waiting for this music. It was planned that they would not hear it until the first of August, perhaps later, but the business with Daoud in Belize has upset that timetable. And the attempted interception back there has decreed an additional urgency to our plan. We have contingencies for just such a situation, however."

Adwan finished rinsing his trousers and undershorts and walked outside to spread them on the slopes of the tent. Returning, he sat down on the rugs. "I think it is time you told me what will happen next."

Labidi was removing his own clothes. Tossing them into the drum and splashing water over his sand-encrusted body, he nodded. "Yes. Let me get the map."

Adwan heard the door of the Isuzu open and slam shut. When Labidi returned he held their map case. Dropping beside Adwan, he selected one of the folded sheets and spread it before them. "You have been harassing me to tell you this since we left Yucatan, but if we had been intercepted, it is possible the authorities could have extracted the plan from one of us. No distrust intended, Kamal, but the less you knew, the better. It would not have been good to have jeopardized any future operation should this one fail. Even I do not know of our ultimate destination. My purpose is to get us across the border. Here, where I have penned the circle, is our camp. And this irregular body of water ten miles to the north is an artificial lake formed by the damming of the Rio Grande."

"Amistad Reservoir," read Adwan aloud. "It appears quite large."

"Yes, and it is the main recreational area for this part of the American state of Texas. There are small boat piers and fishing camps and much activity."

"We are crossing the lake?"

"In a manner of speaking. First of all, it is heavily patrolled, even in ordinary times. Mexican nationals have tried to use it for crossing illegally into America. On this side of the lake, just to the west of us, is a Mexican national park. Now, of course, there is the added dimension of military augmentation along the entire southern U.S. border—except for this section of the lake shore. This area is too barren to cross easily, and helicopter patrols can survey it with little difficulty."

"Yet, it is where we are going to cross? A heavily populated and patrolled area?"

"It is a perfect place. Despite the tension due to our successful attack on the American warship, the people continue with their set ways, even while their soldiers look for us."

"We are crossing by boat, then? I don't see how we can do that undetected. There must be patrols on the lake."

"Yes, but normal ones. Fishing and game patrols by paramilitary wardens who are primarily interested in the observance of fishing and boating rules. There is no military presence on the lake."

"But surely the wardens also keep a lookout for illegal crossings."

"Definitely. But they will be of no concern to us. We will not be on the lake."

Adwan cocked his head. Puzzled, he ventured a wild guess. "Under it?"

"Ah! That crossed our minds. But better than that. You recall the tactic used by Abul Abbas's group in November of 1987?"

"The raid out of Lebanon—against the Israelis at Kiryat Shemona. Who does not remember that daring feat? Three hang gliders were used and—we are crossing by hang gliders?"

"Better than that. The state of the art has improved. In response to this music, at ten o'clock this evening we shall be joined by two very light aircraft—ultralights they are called. They are nothing more than aluminum tubing and cloth with a small motor for propulsion. But for our purposes they are ideal. Each will carry two persons. In our case, you will ride on one with a pilot. I will fly the other with the weapon. The pilot whose place I take will break down this camp and return in the Isuzu to the Mexican interior. We may have occasion to use this plan again, so we will remove any traces of this staging point. These very small aircraft can fly at four or five thousand feet with no difficulty. The motors are muffled and at that altitude they will not be heard on the lake, even during the night when we make our crossing. There are always boats on the lake, patrols or early fishermen. Their noise will help mask ours."

"You mentioned the helicopter patrols."

"Yes, and they go on during the night, also. But they are low and looking for people on foot. We will be well above them and they certainly will have no chance of hearing us, or seeing us. We use no lights, and the engine exhaust is covered."

"Radar," suggested Adwan. "Surely, there is radar coverage, for commercial airliners if for no other reason."

"That is the only radar. There is no military surveillance coverage of the southern border. And there are no regular air routes, except for occasional commuters into the town of Del Rio, here just to the south of the lake. Besides, there is a confusion factor present, confusion for the Americans. There is an air base just outside the town. A training base for American Air Force pilots. While they normally are not flying at the hour we will be crossing, the appearance of a strange blip on the air center's radar is not unusual and presents no threat to their air traffic. This is almost all a restricted area for military training flights, and the military has only approach control radar. Our tiny cloth airplane will not make much of a radar signal, anyhow. At best, it will be an intermittent target that will appear only when we climb, and disappear when we descend. If anything, they will think it is a helicopter return. Our speed will be only seventy miles an hour or so. If we are detected, we may even appear as a boat on the lake. It is foolproof."

"Ten o'clock they will arrive? How will they find this place? To show a light would certainly invite investigation."

Labidi reached over and lifted a small yellow hand radio from its box. "This is a standard emergency locator transmitter, the kind small aircraft carry. It is designed to be activated by crash impact and sends out a continuous signal for homing purposes by a rescue party. It can be manually turned on as well, and we have changed the frequency crystal to a common communications setting so that activation will not alert rescue centers. The aircraft coming from the far side of the lake will home in on this transmitter. When they are overhead, we will turn on the headlights of the Isuzu. There is a landing clearing next to this wash, and we will have the headlights facing away from the lake. At this distance, nothing will be seen from the ground, and unless a patrol helicopter is exactly in the right position, nothing will be seen from the air. Even if the light is detected, the American helicopter will not enter Mexican airspace and will note it only for future correlation with any other suspicious sign."

"The pilots can land at night?"

"The landing speed is only thirty kilometers per hour—a fast walk, Adwan. And they need only a few hundred feet at most. There is only one worry. We must not have much wind, for the little airplanes cannot tolerate heavy gusts. That is the only possible deterrent. And if tonight is windy, we wait until tomorrow night."

Adwan could only admire the plan. It was well thought out and ingenious in its concept—unless there was a full moon. "What about the moon? Could we be seen against such a light?"

"This time of the year there are normally scattered clouds during the time of darkness. The thunderstorms break down after the sun sets and the remnants drift until sunrise, when the returning warmth causes them to rebuild. The moon is in its first quarter, but it should present no light to speak of."

"Where will we land"

"There is a hardtop road that leads from an isolated complex of boat docks north toward the highway. We will be five miles beyond the docks, and the road is quiet at our time of landing. We have signals arranged and can delay if need be until there is no traffic. Perhaps an early-morning fisherman driving to his boat. We can work around that. We have rehearsed. We need only two minutes of uninterrupted time to effect the landing and transfer the weapon. There will be someone waiting to take the aircraft inland, or we can abandon the aircraft in an emergency. That would be undesirable, naturally, for their discovery would arouse suspicion, but we will have been long gone."

"It sounds as if we have prepared for as many eventualities as we can."

"I am sure of it. Now, I must wash my clothes. After prayers we can eat and rest. The Mexican music will continue to serenade our friends and any others who may chance upon the frequency. An hour before the aircraft are due, we must be up and make preparations."

Adwan walked outside and studied the thunderstorms. They were at their most energetic stage, and erratic bolts of silver lightning were splitting and streaking aimlessly through the dark blue areas of heavy rain angling down to the desert. Just as the Mexican had advised Labidi, the storms had worked east and presented no threat to the dry wash where Adwan stood. A very pleasant chill was crawling over him; just twelve miles to the north lay the United States. He and his brothers had promised the Americans they would come. Stone-still, he listened to the thunder—great rolling vibrations of invisible energy that reached down from the heavens and passed through his naked body, leaving with him a feeling of sensual pleasure not unlike that he experienced at the moment of sexual climax. Even though the clouds were several miles away, the winds spawned by the movement of the unstable air flowed outward and followed the dry wash, refreshing Adwan with their cooling breath. An involuntary shiver rippled through him. There was a spiritual force present. Almost in concert, the earth-jarring bursts of thunder became deeper and more frequent. Enraptured, Adwan turned to face the land across the unseen lake. The thunder became a constant crescendo of raw energy, vibrating through his body until it seemed a part of him. But the thunder was more than that; it was as if an angry voice was roaring from the heavens and proclaiming that the time for Palestinian justice was at hand. Adwan dropped to his knees as he realized that he was hearing the voice of God warning the infidels that a great storm was coming.

Chapter 23

6:00 P.M.
Command Center, CIA Headquarters,
Langley, Virginia

Vice President Shinn looked down the rectangular table. At his left sat Chuck Myers of the FBI; then Ted Benson, CIA; Capt. Pete Duncan, Navy liaison; and Col. Fred Thompson, Army liaison. At the foot of the table sat Tom Padina, the Key West CIA station chief more popularly known as the Old Man; then up the right side Col. Joe Fisher, USAF liaison; and finally at Shinn's right, his press officer, Charlie Kelly.

"Colonel Petroviny should be back with his troops by now," began Shinn. "I assume everyone knows everyone. I met with the president at three and briefed him on the team and our intentions. He has given us his unqualified support and absolute permission to take whatever steps we feel necessary as the situation develops. All of you are aware of our basic problem but I think we should ensure that each of us has a complete grasp of the picture. For that reason, I'd like to start with Tom Padina, the CIA station chief at Key West. His office had the initial action on the event that started this whole hot ball of wax. Tom? Where is Mister Morales?"

The Old Man felt uneasy being addressed by his given name.

His associates routinely called him the Old Man or simply failed to accord him any form of address. But he recognized the stature of the people around him and forced himself to observe the amenities. "Mister Vice President. I took the liberty of assigning Morales to a last-minute effort to intercept the terrorists. Because of rather unusual circumstances, which I don't believe we should go into at this time, he is working with a Soviet intelligence agent. Together, they are tracking down a strong lead in northern Mexico. Should I go on with my briefing?"

"Yes, of course. Mister Morales will be joining us later, I presume?"

"I would think so, sir, if his lead does not work out."

"Then, proceed, please, Mister Padina."

The Old Man's briefing was thorough, starting with Morales's initial inspection of the ditched Bear and continuing on up to the discovery of Daoud's body in Belize.

"Thank you, Tom," acknowledged the vice president. "I believe that brings us all up to date. Did Morales get a good look at the objects either in the submerged Bear or in Cuba?"

"Not a good look, but enough to identify the weapon if it surfaces. I would say it is probably about five feet long and ten to twelve inches in diameter," replied the Old Man.

"The Lincoln reported that the device brought aboard was just shy of five feet long and approximately ten inches in diameter, and also that the Iranian hand-carried a remote-control detonator with a dead man's switch," added Captain Duncan. "He also reported that the device itself appeared to have some sort of master arming switch."

Shinn looked at the Navy officer with admiration. The captain had obviously done his homework.

"Can one man carry it?" asked Charlie Kelly.

"Certainly two can," answered the Old Man. "I suspect one would have difficulty, however."

"They call themselves the New Shaheen. Do we have a detailed profile on them?" asked Army Colonel Thompson.

Benson gave the same ID briefing he had given to the Old Man on his visit to Key West just after the Bear ditching.

Thompson continued, "Since the loss of the Lincoln we've gone to a very tight security mode. Do we really think they can penetrate into the States? I guess that's a stupid question. We have to assume they may. Sorry. How about in-country help?"

"Chuck?" relayed Shinn.

"We know that there are members of various radical groups in-country. Some we have had under tight surveillance. Most we have already picked up. We have full-time coverage on a number of sympathetic and fellow-traveler groups. I think we would be rather naive not to assume that the whole operation is thoroughly preplanned. With that in mind, we have to assume that there are members of the New Shaheen already here. We just may not know who they are or where they are. It's like the Navy's antisubmarine program—they can easily track the noisy ones, but it's that goddamned quiet son of a bitch that's the problem. My gut feeling is that he's out there and there's just no way we can cover every square inch of the continental United States any more than the Navy can cover every cubic foot of ocean. And I use the singular figuratively; there can jolly well be dozens of the bastards already in place. By themselves, they can create a bit of havoc before we can zero in. But we can contain them if it comes to that. Our worry is that that's not their plan. They want to use the weapon. Why kill a few hundred people when they can look at the possibility of a million or more casualties? The weapon is what we have to keep out of this country. And they can't just walk in with it slung over their shoulders."

"Not to get ahead of ourselves, but what is the Soviet position in all this?" asked the USAF liaison officer, Colonel Fisher. "They provided the weapons."

Shinn answered. "You all know, of course, that the Soviets immediately contacted the president and urgently gave their support in catching the terrorists. They claim the weapons were intended only as an Arab counterbalance to the nuclear capability of Israel. I am sure that each of you has been directly concerned over the readiness states and alert conditions that have affected your own services. Still, the president believes the Soviets but would agree with all of us that it was an incredibly stupid act. There are probably lots of heads rolling around in the dark halls of the Kremlin."

Benson added, "We do know that one of their military intelligence people is now in Mexico helping us track the Shaheen."

"Which for the moment," interrupted Shinn, "is of little concern to us. The president will handle the international ramifications of the situation, and they are complex. We must concern ourselves with our charge: to deal with the terrorists if they do surface here, God forbid. I will give you my thoughts, then the floor is open.

"We have Petroviny and his team on station at Buckley Air

National Guard Base in Denver. We are not that centrally located, but for the time being I believe we should stay right here where we have worldwide communications and can keep on top of the pursuit effort by the intelligence community. Our task is to utilize Petroviny and his team according to any domestic situation that could develop should the Shaheen penetrate our borders. In broad terms, it will be up to us to sanitize the area around the threat, provide guidance and information to the press, and approve or disapprove any actions of the antiterrorist assault team. We will provide the on-site command and control. Obviously, if such a situation develops, and there is a nuclear threat to the land and people of this country, the president will be busy exercising his international options and will rely on us for local control of the threat."

There was absolute silence around the table. Shinn's words reinforced the thoughts of those present—that the seriousness of the threat would affect events far beyond the borders of the United States. Shinn continued, "We will be unable to isolate ourselves from international developments, but we must try to keep them in perspective. A little prayer that they don't get out of hand would certainly be in order. There have been some late developments. The PLO has requested an immediate meeting with the president. Just as did his predecessor, he has refused, and to emphasize his frame of mind he has alerted a carrier battle group positioned off Libya and has passed demands to the PLO that they assist in locating the remaining weapon. Great Britain and the commonwealth nations have all declared their intent to assist the United States in whatever way they can. Typically, France has been silent, as have most of the NATO countries. Interestingly enough, Yugoslavia, Poland, Turkey, Greece, and Italy have all declared support of any reprisal actions we may care to take concerning the loss of the *Lincoln*. Israel has gone to a complete wartime alert, anticipating an American reprisal strike against Libya, Iran, and Syria. In short, gentlemen, there is considerable pressure on the Arabs to help stop the Shaheen, but whether it will impress or inflame them remains to be seen."

Chapter 24

10:00 P.M.
Extreme Northern Coahuila, Mexico

Silhouetted in the dark night like a giant black moth seeking the light of a flame, the first air machine materialized out of the sky. It passed over the Trooper to drop suddenly into the bright beams of the headlights and land roughly twenty yards ahead of the vehicle. The second aircraft followed and touched down in the tracks of the first. Both turned and taxied back to where Labidi and Adwan were waiting. Labidi turned off the Trooper's headlights as the pilots cut their engines.

"Ahmad!" called out the pilot of the first machine. Labidi rushed forward and the two men embraced. The second pilot walked first to Adwan, and after a moment's hesitation they too wrapped their arms around each other and made their introductions.

"I am Kamal Adwan."

"And I, Muhammad ben-Ali, my brother." The huge out-stretched hand was as warm and friendly as the wide smile that even in the night revealed teeth white as sea sand. Adwan was not a little man, being almost six feet in height, but he had to raise his eyes to return ben-Ali's greeting. "It is a good night for us," continued ben-Ali.

Adwan examined ben-Ali's machine. As Labidi had foretold, it was indeed constructed of blackened aluminum tubing with wings and empennage encased in taut black cloth. The three wheels were spoked as if they had been taken from bicycles, and the one holding up the nose, apparently steerable, was linked to the pilot's rudder pedals by steel cables. There were two hard plastic seats, side by side, and a rudimentary instrument panel perched on a single support in front of the pilot's position. Stubby, leather-wrapped control sticks rose in front of each seat. The shoulder-high wing was held rigid by a spiderweb of cables that ran from an overhead center stanchion and then from the bottom of the wing to the fuselage tubing. Safety-wired turnbuckles provided the proper amount of tension. Mounted on the trailing edge of the wing, precisely on the centerline of the skeletal fuselage, were a two-cylinder opposed engine and a wooden pusher propeller. Ahead of the engine was a small fuel tank, and tightly braided control cables ran from the engine to a throttle device bolted to a supporting member outboard of the left seat. Adwan shook his head in amazement.

"We are flying to the land of the great satan in these metal mosquitoes?"

Ben-Ali, a giant of a man with deep weathered lines etched in his face and a monumental nose worthy of a Saudi Arabian sheik, slapped him hard on the back and practically roared a response. "These machines are our tickets to paradise, my brother. They will take us wherever we must go and do so with a stealth unmatched by any other craft. Do not belittle them, for the Americans with all of their multimillion-dollar interceptors and detection devices will see and hear nothing. If we wished, we could fly to the capital city of Washington and land on the White House lawn."

Labidi and the other pilot had already started unloading the weapon from the Trooper. They carried it over to one of the ultralights and set it on the ground. The pilot unbolted the right-hand seat and set it aside. Together, he and Labidi lifted the weapon and strapped it into the seat's place, tying each end securely to a section of fuselage tubing. As the four men walked toward the dry wash, Labidi discussed with the pilot the details of breaking down the camp and returning the Trooper to the interior of Mexico. From their conversation, Adwan reasoned that the pilot was not a stranger to the country. It took only a few minutes for Adwan and Labidi to gather their small packets of personal things and their hand weapons. While they did so, the other two Arabs struck the tent and began rolling it for loading on the Isuzu. The water drums were rolled outside but left upright and filled.

"You must go. I will finish this," urged the pilot staying behind.

Labidi, Adwan, and ben-Ali hurried back to the two ultralights, and Adwan followed ben-Ali's instructions as they manned their machine. Fastening his seat belt and shoulder harness, Adwan observed, "We are sitting out here with nothing around us!" Ben-Ali handed him a cloth helmet and goggles.

"You will enjoy this. Not only are we about to accomplish a most vital phase of our plan, we are to experience the thrill of the birds themselves." Reaching back over his head, ben-Ali gave a strong jerk on a rope handle, and the little two-cylinder engine sputtered to life. As they taxied into the bright beams of the Trooper's reactivated headlights, Labidi started the second machine and followed, waiting patiently to one side while ben-Ali began his takeoff.

Adwan was pressed back into his seat, and startled at the leap of the fragile craft into the evening air. Nose high, it climbed like a homesick angel. Ben-Ali started a gentle turn and within the first minute the lights of the Trooper were behind them. Adwan caught his first glimpse of the large Amistad Reservoir, the surface of the water shimmering dimly under the faint illumination of the quarter moon. Irregular in shape, with long wiggly fingers reaching in all directions, the man-made lake was several miles across. Along its banks Adwan could see the scattered lights of fishing camps. The surrounding terrain, however, was practically invisible, reflecting hardly any light from the partly cloudy skies. The slipstream held him back in his seat, but with the goggles protecting his eyes he could see well and he looked around for Labidi. The tiny aircraft were using no lights and he could see nothing.

Their passage through the air was hauntingly quiet, the engine noise muffled to such an extent that he could hear the wind rushing across the wing support wires.

Ben-Ali continued to climb, and the lights below became silver pinpricks, occasionally even disappearing as wisps of low scud clouds slipped beneath the ultralight. Adwan had no idea how high they were or how fast they were proceeding, but the ride, despite his initial apprehension, was no more harrowing than his first experience on a motorcycle. He still retained some concern, however, that there was probably the better part of a mile of sky between him and the unseen ground. Seated in the extreme front of the aircraft with nothing ahead of him except the control stick and rudder pedals, he was being thrust through black space with no visible means of support. He gained some measure of confidence by twisting and looking back over his shoulder to watch the outline of the wing, although after a few minutes he began to notice its flexing as they rode gentle currents of air over the reservoir. He wasn't certain that aircraft wings were supposed to bend up and down like that.

Ben-Ali held up a small box. "Observe," he said, pressing the button on top of the box with his thumb.

A flash of orange light erupted from the surface of the lake and lit the sky with its unexpected brilliance.

"The mark of Allah!" called ben-Ali above the muted noise of the engine.

Adwan could see several sets of green, red, and white running lights as the few boats on the lake speeded toward the source of the explosion.

"Our diversion," added ben-Ali.

Then Adwan understood. In addition to the precautions of a superefficient engine muffler and high unlit flight, ben-Ali had obviously arranged for a boat of explosives to be positioned on the lake and detonated by his hand-held remote-control box to further draw the attention of the patrols from the sky. As they flew on, Adwan could see the flames of a burning boat and the circling wakes of those who had gone to investigate. Straight ahead, from the north, he could see the spotlight of a rapidly approaching helicopter and watched the machine ease to a hover upwind of the scene of the staged accident.

Ben-Ali pointed ahead and directed Adwan's attention to a bright cluster of lights on the far edge of one of the fingers of the lake. "Our checkpoint! A small camp, well lit with floodlights. The road we seek runs from there into the night ahead. We are on course!"

Adwan's eyes were becoming accustomed to the dark, and by leaning over he found that he could read the two dials on the small instrument panel. They glowed green and white under a dim light. Ben-Ali had steadied the craft at four thousand feet, and the airspeed needle was vibrating at the fifty-mile-an-hour mark. Adwan wondered if radar beams were sweeping across them; even if they were, the tube and cloth structure would reflect precious few. He wondered about the bulk of his and ben-Ali's bodies before deciding that air traffic control radar was probably not that sensitive. Ignoring further concern, he continued to search the sky and finally located Labidi slightly below and off to their left. From Adwan's vantage point, Labidi's craft was outlined by the lights of the activity on the lake, but Adwan doubted if those who chanced to look up would see anything at all. He felt secure and was becoming accustomed to the movement of the ultralight despite its erratic response to every whim of the wind. Theirs was a good plan—simple, but ingenious in concept, and obviously well thought out.

As they approached the camp lights, Adwan realized with some excitement that he was in American airspace. Even if something went wrong now and he were to die, it would be with the comfort of knowing that three Palestinians with a pair of unsophisticated—simple, actually—aircraft had succeeded in penetrating the airspace of the world's greatest air power. Such success must be an omen of good things to come.

They passed right over the fishing camp, and ben-Ali began a gradual descent, reducing the power of his engine until the exhaust was but a whisper. With the bright lights behind him, Adwan could see nothing but black ahead, but he had noticed that ben-Ali had checked his watch just as they passed over the camp and was apparently timing their progress inland. As they proceeded farther away from the lights, Adwan could begin to make out terrain features below. They were over what appeared to be mainly level land with some low rolling rises and much scrub brush. By straining, he believed he could make out a straight, narrow road running directly ahead of them. He guessed their altitude to be about half of what it had been during their crossing of the lake.

Ben-Ali tapped Adwan on the shoulder and pointed ahead and down. At first, Adwan could see nothing except the blotchy contrasts of the earth below, but then he saw three very faint green lights. They were in a row and positioned on the side of the road perhaps a kilometer ahead. Abruptly they changed into a pair of red lights. Almost immediately Adwan understood why. Far ahead, the headlights of an approaching vehicle appeared. Ben-Ali held his altitude and circled until the unwelcome vehicle passed behind them to the south and the three green lights reappeared.

Ben-Ali resumed his letdown and passed over the lights at an altitude of only a couple of hundred feet. Adwan could see that they were over a white, beetle-shaped vehicle. As they passed overhead, the vehicle pulled out into the middle of the road and turned on its headlights. Ben-Ali immediately banked steeply into a left turn. When he had completed a circle he was behind the vehicle and lined up with the road as well as being very low to the surface. They passed over the white vehicle so closely that Adwan felt tempted to reach down and let his fingers drag across its top. Ben-Ali cut the engine and raised the nose of the ultralight as they floated down onto the black asphalt, straddling the yellow-dashed centerline. They rolled forward for almost a hundred meters before ben-Ali swung the craft around and started back toward the headlights. Labidi had landed just behind them and was also reversing his course. As they approached the vehicle, Adwan could see that it was some sort of small tanker truck, with two cylindrical tanks mounted longitudinally, side by side, behind the cab. By the time ben-Ali braked to a stop beside the other ultralight, Labidi was already untying the weapon. A shadowy figure rushed up to Adwan.

"Hurry!" Strange hands reached out and assisted him in unfastening his safety harness, then guided him as he was pulled at a dead run toward the truck. A voice prompted him: "Underneath there is an access hatch, on this side. Crawl up into the tank. It is empty and there is a light inside. Also a ventilation port. You will have an uncomfortable ride, but it will be safe."

"The weapon?" asked Adwan, resisting the push of the hands to drop him down to the asphalt.

"We will care for it. Do not worry. There is room for two of you inside but not the weapon. Hurry! Someone could approach on the road at any second."

Adwan crawled under the truck and pulled himself up and into the empty tank. Labidi was pushing his legs and followed quickly. The hatch slammed shut and Adwan could hear the tightening of bolts. There were blankets in the tank and he and Labidi arranged them as thin mattresses. The light was battery powered and as soon as they were settled, Adwan turned it off. "That was fast," he commented.

"I told you, we would have only a minute or two to make the change," Labidi replied.

"What will they do with the weapon?"

Adwan could not see Labidi but he could *feel* his partner smile. "We are in the right-hand tank of a propane fuel truck belonging to Del Rio Propane, Incorporated. Del Rio is a small border town some twenty miles south of here. The left-hand tank is full of propane and has fully working gauges. Our tank registers 'empty,' of course. On the other side are stands for two smaller propane bottles. One is already in place. In the other stand, the weapon will be strapped and locked into place. Right now, our driver is placing placards on it that identify it also as a propane tank. Our weapon, Kamal, will be carried in the open, right under the noses of the Americans!"

Both reached out to steady themselves as the truck lurched forward and accelerated to its cruise speed.

"The ultralights will be flown to a nearby field and abandoned. We are on our way, Kamal! We are on our way!"

"On our way where?"

"That, I have not been told."

Ben-Ali breathed more regularly now. The second set of lights that had appeared to the north just as they were finishing securing the weapon were approaching but still a quarter mile ahead. As they closed, he could see that they belonged to a pickup truck with its fishing boat in tow, most likely on its way to the Amistad Reservoir. Ben-Ali already had the propane truck up to forty miles an hour as the two vehicles passed. The dashboard clock revealed the time to be 11:23 P.M. Excellent. Seven miles ahead was State Highway 277/377.

Within ten minutes he reached the intersection and turned north. Somewhere within the next twenty miles he would reach the U.S. border patrol roadblock. They varied it from time to time, but it was usually between the road from the reservoir and the branching of the two highways. There would be no problem. Ben-Ali had been driving the same route, Del Rio to Amistad to San Antonio, three times a week and varying the days, for the past six months. He was well known to the officers, he and his little white propane tanker, and as much a part of the routine as their search for illegals entering from Mexico. They would be more vigilant tonight, perhaps, and augmented by several members of the state guard, but no more suspicious.

Twelve miles along 277/377 ben-Ali saw the red flares and slowed. Only one car was ahead of him as he entered the marked lane. As usual, the border patrol station wagon was parked off to one side, down a slight incline, but for a change there were two figures in the rear seat behind the wire-partitioned driver's compartment. Ben-Ali assumed them to be Mexicans as he flipped off his driving beams and eased forward. The officer ignored his outstretched arm and driver's license, which along with the name on the door of the truck, identified him as Angelo Nitti, the owner of the small propane company in Del Rio.

"Good morning," said the officer as he painted the inside of the cab with his flashlight beam. "You're right on schedule tonight, Angelo."

"Punctuality is a virtue."

"See anybody back along the highway?"

"No one, but I see you have had some business."

"Yes. Poor bastards just came walking right up the road. Said they were told to go to the red lights for further transportation. Some redneck prick ripped them off, for sure. Makes our job simple, but next time across, they'll be wiser and we won't see hide nor hair of 'em."

Ben-Ali watched the two soldiers approaching casually from their radio jeep by the side of the road. One walked around the truck, giving it a cursory inspection, and nodded to ben-Ali as he rejoined his partner.

"How is your hired help working out?" asked ben-Ali, tilting his head toward the troops. The border patrolman stuck his head partially into the cab. "National guardsmen—hell, those terrorists could pass right in front of the dumb bastards and they wouldn't suspect a thing. Probably activated schoolteachers or plumbers or something."

"The hunt is still on?"

"Oh, yeah. Kinda scary, isn't it?"

"I don't think they'd come this way."

"Wouldn't pay. We know all the regulars and would snap 'em up in a second." Stepping back from the truck, he waved ben-Ali on. "Well, you have a good one."

"You, too. Thank you." Ben-Ali waved to the guardsmen as he switched on his lights and drove on.

The Texas night was still warm. The evening thunderstorms had dissipated early and denied the night their cooling showers. Ben-Ali waited until the lights of the roadblock passed from his rearview mirror before gliding onto the shoulder and stopping. Leaving his parking lights on, he stepped from the cab, stuck an unlit cigarette in his mouth, and walked around by the disguised ventilation port to the dummy tank. "Everything all right in there?"

"Yes. Why did we stop?" came back the muffled reply.

"Border patrol. No problem. They're always there, looking for illegal aliens from Mexico. As soon as we reach the interstate, one of you can come up front."

"It is not bad in here. We get some road fumes. They were not suspicious?"

"No. They know me and the truck."

"God is great."

"And most certainly, not American," muttered ben-Ali as he flicked away the cigarette and returned to the cab of the truck.

At the point where 277/377 split into separate highways, ben-Ali swung right to follow 377. It would be ninety-eight miles to Interstate 10. State Highway 377 followed a winding path across the low hills of southern Texas, working generally northeast through sparsely settled country. Ben-Ali was quite relaxed and comfortable despite the firm ride of the truck, but he looked forward to the intersection at the town of Junction. There, it would be safe to stop for a cooling drink. Just past the town was a rest stop, where either Labidi or Adwan could leave the cramped tank compartment and join him in the cab.

The road had been recently resurfaced, and the smoother ride was beginning to lull him dangerously toward sleep when he topped a small rise and came unexpectedly upon a cluster of rotating red and blue lights. Ahead, partially blocking the highway, were three military vehicles and a number of soldiers, one standing directly in the center of the road and holding up his hand. Ben-Ali cursed. This was no border patrol looking for wetbacks. He had driven this same route each time and had never encountered any signs of surveillance. He had no choice but to stop. The roadblock was strategically placed just over the rise so that oncoming traffic would be upon it before realizing what was there. To turn around would be a very suspicious act. Ben-Ali once more slowed and braked to a stop at the signal of an armed sergeant.

"Would you shut off your motor and step out, please?" The sergeant really was ordering, not asking. Ben-Ali did as told.

"May I see your driver's license?"

As the sergeant examined the license, several of the other soldiers began walking around the truck. One dropped to his knees and searched underneath with a spotlight. The sergeant compared the license picture with ben-Ali's chiseled face and noted the repetition of the name on the door. "Anyone here speak Italian?" he called.

Hearing no answer, ben-Ali grinned and replied, "I speak it— *atu capice?*"

The sergeant's expression did not change. "You're out of Del Rio?"

"Yes. My tank farm is there."

"Which way did you come?"

"From Amistad Reservoir, up 277 and onto 377."

"Did you pass the border patrol?"

"Yes, of course. I make this trip three times a week."

One of the soldiers was tapping on the propane tanks and examining the gauges.

"Let me see your invoices."

Ben-Ali reached inside the cab and retrieved his delivery sheets, all dummied but authentic in appearance.

"I thought this was butane country," speculated the sergeant.

"Butane and propane. The campers seem to prefer propane mostly."

"Where are you headed now?"

"To the interstate and San Antonio, then back to Del Rio."

The sergeant handed back the delivery sheets. "Have you passed anyone on this road?"

"Several cars, back the other side of Rocksprings." Ben-Ali tried to reverse the tightening of his muscles. The soldiers were professionals and thorough. Ben-Ali wondered if Labidi and Adwan could hear any of the conversation.

One of the soldiers spoke up. "The left tank reads full, Sarge. The right's empty." He was standing in front of the upright weapon!

"We'd like to see in that tank. Is there an access panel?"

Ben-Ali had seen the soldier look under the truck. There was a good chance he had seen the hatch. Now would not be the time to lie. "Yes, underneath. It will break the seal of my tank."

"It has a pisspot full of bolts, Sarge," added the soldier.

The sergeant thought for a moment. "You say you're a regular on this route?"

"Yes, three times a week usually."

"Can anybody back at the border patrol checkpoint ID you?"

"Yes, they know me."

"Check it out, Shannon," the sergeant ordered, and one of the soldiers hopped into a radio jeep. A few minutes later he reported, "ID's verified, Sarge. He's a local."

Stepping back, the sergeant apologized. "Sorry to have detained you, Mr. Nitti. You're free to go. We can't take any chances."

"I understand. It is good to see such vigilance. It makes me feel better."

"I would try and do my traveling in the daytime over the next few weeks," suggested the sergeant.

"Thank you, I will do that." As he pulled away, he noted the sergeant recording his vehicle license number and giving some instructions to the soldier in the radio jeep. The license was valid and registered to Del Rio Propane. A check with the state highway department would reveal nothing suspicious. But, for the first moment since they had landed on the reservoir road, ben-Ali felt a little unsure of himself. If the authorities carried the vehicle check far enough, they would find at the Del Rio Propane address mostly empty tanks and no personnel.

It was an hour to Junction, and ben-Ali pulled into an all-night fast-food store and stopped in front of the gas pumps. Filling his tank, he paid inside and picked out a six-pack of cold sodas before driving off. He popped open one can and drank as he entered the on ramp to Interstate 10. Traffic was normal for this time of the morning, moderate but nothing like the vacation traffic during the daylight hours. The Army roadblock troubled him, not that he was worried they would later become suspicious. But if the roadblock had been unexpected, there could be other surprises. It was still two hours to San Antonio. Reason dictated that the back roads would be getting most of the attention from the military. Interstate 10 was a wide-open, well-traveled highway, and at this point a hundred miles from the border; he doubted that surveillance would be that deep. But there could be spot checks anywhere.

There was a small rest stop just beyond the Mountain Home turnoff, or rather it was what the state of Texas called a rest stop—a couple of picnic tables and wooden steps across the fence to an open-air toilet. Originally, ben-Ali had planned to stop there and at least let Adwan and Labidi out of the dummy tank for a breather. The ventilation port provided a measure of fresh air but not enough to cool the space adequately. By now, they most certainly were cramped and stiff and sticky wet with sweat from the warm night. But the unexpected appearance of the Army checkpoint made such an act too risky. Three men in the front of a small tanker truck, even considering the hour and modest traffic, might arouse suspicion should he be stopped again—and Labidi and Adwan had no papers. His two compatriots would have to remain entombed until he reached Kerrville. There they would be switching vehicles. He checked his watch—2:43 A.M. Another forty minutes to Kerrville. Still, he should at least check his two companions. Once more, he pulled off the shoulder and stood by the ventilation port.

"How are you riding?" he asked.

"The ride is not bad, but it is as hot as the sands of hades in here. How much farther?" asked Labidi.

"Forty minutes. Then we will be changing vehicles. Can you make that?"

"Of course, but keep the vehicle moving. We need the flow of air. We heard some of the talk at the last roadblock. They sounded more professional."

"Army troops. That is why you must remain concealed until we reach Kerrville. There could be another patrol."

"Do not worry about us. We are fine."

Ben-Ali jumped back into the cab and resumed his course for Kerrville. Being able to drive at sixty-five miles per hour on the interstate reduced his estimated traveling time, and at 3:16 A.M. he steered onto the Kerrville off ramp. Within a few minutes he found the side road he was looking for and followed it until he reached an abandoned farmhouse. Behind it was the prepositioned black step-van. Stopping the tanker truck beside it, he hurriedly crawled underneath and removed the bolts holding the entry hatch in place. Labidi and Adwan scrambled out and stood in the fresh air, sucking in great gulps of the Texas atmosphere. They were dripping with perspiration and smelled strongly of body odors. Both spread their legs and began relieving themselves against the weathered boards of the farmhouse.

"I thought my bladder would burst," exclaimed Adwan, sighing in pleasure at the release of pressure within his body. "But we felt quite safe."

"Then you did not hear the Army sergeant consider examining the inside of the tank?"

"No! He did?"

"Yes," replied ben-Ali. "It was close. If they had not been able to check my ID with the border patrol, I fear our excursion would have ended right there. We would have been in a very awkward position. My weapon was under the seat, but you two could not have been effective, I'm afraid. They recorded the vehicle license as we drove off. If they follow through far enough, they will become suspicious. But it will be too late. We will have reached our objective."

"Which is?" queried Labidi anxiously.

"The city of San Antonio, just forty-five miles down the highway. Come on, let us get the weapon inside the van and I will fill you in as we ride. You will be much more comfortable. Also, I have some cool drinks in the tanker cab."

"San Antonio. I have heard of that place. It is very large, is it not?" asked Adwan.

"Yes, but let us be on our way. You get the drinks from the truck while Ahmad and I transfer the weapon."

After placing the cylinder inside the van on a pad of furniture wrapping quilts, ben-Ali mounted the driver's seat and they headed back for the interstate. Adwan sat in the right seat and Labidi rode in the rear of the van, leaning forward as ben-Ali described their target city.

"San Antonio is in the south central part of this state of Texas, a large cosmopolitan city of more than one million people when you consider its outlying areas. It is a transportation hub. A great American shrine is there, the old Fort Alamo, where the early settlers put up a heroic defense against the Mexicans before Texas became part of the United States. Many of the city's people are of Spanish and Mexican descent, and there is a very large military population due to a number of military bases in or on the outskirts of the city. Many of the devils who have struck us and our friends in Lebanon and Libya and Iran are actually here now in this place, honing their skills to attack us again, you can be certain. So, if our negotiations fail, it is a lucrative target.

"We picked San Antonio because it is the first large military-civilian complex we could reach after crossing the border. At the same time, it is far enough inland that the emergency patrols generated by our successful attack on the warship ignore it. Surveillance is concentrated much closer to the border—as we have seen tonight. I have been in the city many times in the past months on my trips from Del Rio and Amistad, and it is business as usual with the inhabitants. The Americans are a complacent people. There has never been a modern war on their soil. Also, in the city we have been able to move around unnoticed. Our Mediterranean features are not that much different than those of the Latins. My twelve years of Italian operations have fitted me well for the role I have played these past months, setting up this penetration. There are also some Lebanese in San Antonio. It is perfect for us. You will see."

Adwan found himself waking fully after the tiring confinement in the tanker truck. They were speeding along one of America's premier highways, closing on their target city with ease. Despite the early-morning hour, as they proceeded toward the city, traffic was gradually increasing. The highway itself was wide and smooth and engineered for high-speed passage, winding its way among the low hills of southern Texas. Adwan marveled at the apparent wealth of a country that not only could afford such a highway, but boasted an equal one going in the opposite direction. He had studied the map of the United States and also knew that such superhighways crisscrossed the entire nation, but the great distances involved were in contrast to the size of his own land, where they would already have crossed their traditional Palestine homeland several times over. He could not believe that the highway was not patrolled by the military, thus the appearance of a police cruiser parked in the median strip prompted a comment. "There, that is a police car," he said, tapping ben-Ali on the shoulder.

"Radar. The patrol cars have special radar sets to check the speed of traffic. He is only a traffic policeman. We will see more as we go along. But I have noticed no increase in patrols, and as long as we observe the speed signs we have no worry."

"I cannot believe we are unchallenged."

"We have blended in with the others. To that police officer back there we are just another piece of the routine traffic. He has no reason to suspect us. Also, if you have kept track of our directions, we are approaching San Antonio from the northwest, not from the south, which would be the expected route for those coming across the border. By crossing at the Amistad, we have managed to circle east and approach our objective from the least-expected direction. I would suspect the highways entering the city from the south are patrolled."

"Still, I am in amazement."

"You are accustomed to the wartime posture of our own land, where there are the military and other authorities even in the alleys. It is different here. We are going to change that, Adwan. After this first strike of the New Shaheen, this land of infidels will realize that it is no longer impervious to the terror and tragedy we have lived with all of our lives. The American Zionists will find considerably less sympathy for their support of Israel when their Gentile friends realize how vulnerable they are to the great will of Allah. We are making history, Adwan, as the advance force of millions of our brothers who will support us in this most holy of wars. And by our actions alone, we may see the restoration of our homeland. It is an accomplishment almost beyond the comprehension of our minds. We are blessed—and we must not fail. We have the opportunity to unite all of Islam. I truly believe that our time has come. You can see the signs in our successful penetration of this once-mighty nation. Americans are a degenerate people and lack the will to stop us."

"I am anxious for the details of our operation, ben-Ali," interjected Labidi. "My task was to arrange the border crossing and then participate in whatever the operation required of Adwan and me. I am ignorant of what we will do when we reach San Antonio."

"We will first refresh ourselves at a motor hotel near our specific objective. After we have rested, we will meet with the other two operatives who will join us for the final phase. Then you and Adwan will be thoroughly briefed. In keeping with our tactics so far, you need know no more at this moment, but all will be revealed this day, for tomorrow is the day the jihad comes to America. And soon I will be able to point out our specific objective."

It was 5:00 A.M. but still dark as the van followed the interstate into the first outskirts of San Antonio. Adwan and Labidi took in as much of the view as they could, constantly switching their gaze from side to side as the highway took them deeper into the city. Frontage roads paralleled the interstate, providing access to roadside businesses, quiet in the predawn hours but nevertheless brightly lit with their multitude of neon and incandescent lights. The gaudy mixing of the entire spectrum of colors gave a carnival atmosphere to the unending rows of shops and stores in the city's outlying business areas, which reinforced Adwan's disdain for the capitalistic society of America.

Adwan was peering ahead, trying to see the skyline of the central city, when he first saw in the distance a brightly lit dome atop a thin shaft, towering high above any adjacent building. The dome was fat, half as thick as it was wide, with inwardly sloping sides, sporting a crown of white lights. On top of the dome was a small cupola and from it rose a single antenna pole, also lit, and capped with a flashing red beacon. They were not yet close enough for him to make out further details, but the object was obviously a landmark of San Antonio. He had seen only one other structure similar to it, the Cairo shaft, a slim monolith that rose more than five hundred feet into the Egyptian sky. Even considering the distance of the object, the tower ahead seemed taller than the Cairo shaft, and certainly the dome was much larger as it overhung the slim shaft by at least twice the shaft's diameter. "Look at that!" Adwan exclaimed. Labidi was also studying the object.

"The Tower of the Americas," announced ben-Ali with considerable emphasis on the last word. "That, my brothers, is our specific objective."

The tower slowly dropped from view as the interstate passed

into a low area. Within a few minutes, ben-Ali swung right onto the Commerce Street off ramp and wound his way through the central area of the city until they were within a block of the tower. He eased across a side street and entered the parking area of La Quinta Motel. Steering the car behind the main front wing, he parked opposite a side entrance. "We have arrived," he announced. "Wrap your weapons in the cloths and come." He locked the van, then led them past the motel swimming pool into the lobby. They took the elevator to the third level and walked to one end of the wing. Ben-Ali softly knocked on the door of room 301. Adwan heard the locking chain being slipped loose, and the door opened.

"Welcome, my brothers, to the new land of the holy war," greeted the figure in the doorway.

A second occupant was also waiting. Adwan recognized both as Shaheen brothers, Khahid Aswar and Hosni Haidari, the latter an Iranian comrade of Ardeshir Zadefi, the martyr of the attack on the *Lincoln*. Embracing, all excitedly spoke of the success of Adwan and Labidi's entry into the country with the second weapon.

"Daoud? Where is Daoud?" asked Aswar.

"He will not be with us. He was lost in Belize," replied Labidi quickly, signaling to Adwan with his eyes that the matter was best left with that.

"We have much to speak of," continued Aswar. "We have been here for seven days and all is ready in our minds and hearts. You must first eat and rest. Has the weapon been removed from its container?"

"No," replied Adwan.

"Then, Hosni and I will see to it. We also have the adjoining room, 303, and 302 across the hall. There is food, and afterwards you may rest. We will meet for noon prayers and then go over our plan. Ben-Ali, I recommend we strike as soon as possible. If all goes well, we can aim for late tonight or early tomorrow. It is God's will that we are here together. Let it be thus God's will that we show the infidels the wrath and might of Islam and the determination of the Palestinians."

"First, we must talk of the tower." Aswar spread a large drawing of the Tower of the Americas across the bed and laid beside it a guidebook. The cover featured a nighttime photograph of the tower, brightly lit and reaching high into the sky.

"The important thing to know is that once we have control over the domed cap of the tower, we are invincible. Nothing will be able to reach us and, with the weapon as our threat, nothing can attack us. This is the third-highest tower in the world, and the level we will be on is six hundred feet above the ground. The roof is up another fifty feet and the antenna reaches even higher.

"Consider the shaft, sunk sixty-three feet below the natural level of the ground and anchored with twelve hundred cubic yards of concrete and one hundred and ninety tons of steel. On top of that foundation was poured another seventeen hundred and eighty-five cubic yards of concrete to form a base cap ninety-two feet in diameter and eight feet thick. The shaft consists of a multifinned cross section and it is flawlessly formed by reinforced poured concrete. Provisions are made around the shaft for three exterior elevators, spaced one-hundred-and-twenty degrees apart. They face outboard and have a large viewing window in their exterior wall. Inside the shaft are two stairways for emergency use, and they wind all the way up to the top. The elevators may be operated manually or automatically, but are normally operated manually so the operator can ensure they are not overloaded by an anxious public. Around the bottom of the shaft and the supporting buttresses is a glass enclosure. It provides protection and also access to the admission ticket office, two of the three elevators, and the two stairways.

"The shaft is capped at the top by this three-level domed structure. The lowest level is a restaurant that revolves slowly. Next is a lounge area and another restaurant section, which is stationary. Finally there is an observation level that is also glass-enclosed. There we will establish ourselves. There is an outside walkway that extends around the perimeter of the observation level. Inside the observation space is a small souvenir counter, a walled-in security office, and toilets. There are normally from three to five security personnel on duty during the hours of access by the public, which are from ten in the morning to eleven at night, every day. The security people are not armed in any way. There is also an operator of the souvenir stand and sometimes an additional elevator operator when two or more are in use. Otherwise the security people operate the elevators and patrol the observation level.

"The doors to the two stairways are kept closed, although they are not locked, and an alarm will sound if they are opened. They are steel and have a small viewing window in their upper half. Access to the outside observation walk is by several stairwells, which drop down five feet or so and lead outside. The outside access doors are lockable. Questions thus far?"

"The outside walk. There is a railing, yes?" asked Labidi.

"Yes. A solid wall extends upward for two and a half feet, then there is a strong fence of vertical stainless steel rods, spaced perhaps six inches apart and extending upward for maybe six feet. The tops are pointed and curved inward and there is an open space approximately eight feet high from the top of the fence to the bottom of the roof dome."

"And there is three-hundred-and-sixty-degree visibility?" further inquired Labidi.

"Complete visibility around the level. Also from the rotating restaurant level."

"Is there roof access?" asked Adwan.

"Yes. There are access hatches. Many antennae are on the roof."

"The elevators. They go right up into the observation dome?"

"They start off from the glassed base, climb the exterior of the shaft, and have stops at both the restaurant and observation levels."

"Is the restaurant level accessible by stairs from the observation level?"

"Yes."

Looking around at the others and detecting no more questions, Aswar continued, "One of the beautiful things about the top dome is that there is one thousand gallons of stored water, enough food—for the restaurant, normally—for a long stay, and all the facilities we will need for an extended occupation."

"Communications?" inquired Labidi.

"Telephones. Radios—walkie-talkies."

"The electricity could be cut off from below?"

"Yes, if we permit it. Even without it, we can stay to the limit of the provisions."

"We could be isolated there," stated Adwan.

"Exactly. That is our purpose."

"How do we counter assaults?"

"The weapon is our ultimate counter. But first, we blow out a section of each stairway and lock the elevators at the observation level. The tower exterior cannot be climbed; besides, there is the dome overhang, which cannot be transitted. We have an unobstructed view of the entire city. Even helicopters cannot approach us without being detected. The tower will be assault-proof for us. Remember, we have the weapon with a dead man's switch. Any attack on the tower and the weapon is detonated."

"We will also have hostages," added ben-Ali.

"Yes," confirmed Aswar. "I recommend that we assault the tower tomorrow morning. There is one security guard in the tower overnight. At about eight in the morning there is an influx of the security detail for the day, usually five men, several cleaning people, and apparently two to three advance people for the restaurant. I propose we take them all and add what we can. They will be our bargaining chips for concessions and negotiations. For our ultimate objective we have the weapon."

"Can we see the military bases from the tower?" asked ben-Ali.

"Some. With glasses we can see some of them and there are telescopes on the observation level. We also have an unrestricted view of the central city's main road arteries and of the downtown area."

"There are no tall buildings near the tower?"

"That is another advantage for us. We are at the highest point in the city. The nearest level, the top of the Marriott Hotel, is a hundred feet or so lower and is probably a thousand feet away. Maybe more."

Ben-Ali walked over to the window and drew back the curtains. Across the way, beyond the buildings facing the motel, the Tower of the Americas jutted skyward, a formidable monolith of gray concrete and steel, its greenish brown cap high above any surrounding structure. "It is perfect," uttered ben-Ali. "Once we have control, nothing can be done to us, and all of the city will be under our will. Whose choosing was this? I will kiss his feet and sing his praises to the end of my days. Surely this shaft has been ordained by God to be our tower of prayer and promise. Yes, the Tower of the Americas shall become the first minaret of the Shaheen in America, and from its enclosed dome we shall be as muezzins, calling upon worldwide Islam to join us in this first blow of the downfall of the land of the great satan! I feel it. I am impatient! We should take it now!"

"You must restrain yourself, my brother. There are several hundred, perhaps a thousand at its base at this hour. I propose that we stay with a quieter hour, for it is our plan to take the tower before anyone knows we are present. The first sign this great city of America will see is the flag of the Shaheen flying from that tall antenna," announced Aswar.

"We have a standard?" Adwan was beside himself with joy.

"Let me show you something first." Aswar opened the closet

and extracted a cloth-wrapped object. It was long and thin. Laying it on the small reading table beside the window, he gently unwrapped the cloth, exposing a rust-eaten blade, barely recognizable but instantly inspiring to those in the room, except for Adwan, who was seeing it for the first time. "This came from our land, the land of the Gaza, where almost two thousand years ago the first Shaheen waged their holy war against the Jews. It was found during an excavation by one of our people working for the Israelis. We have no way of knowing for sure, of course, but in our hearts it is the blade of a special broadsword. Adwan, you may well be gazing in awe at a sacred sword of the Shaheen."

Adwan leaned down and placed his lips against the rust. "Can it be?" he wondered aloud.

"If we believe it, why not?" answered Aswar. "At the very least, it is a symbol of our heritage and determination. That ancient blade may well have tasted Jewish blood, just not enough of it, for the devils have survived. But they will not survive the present-day sword, the one we have down in the van. That is the real sword of the Shaheen, Adwan. And this is our standard."

Aswar unfolded a large rectangle of cloth. It was similar to the flag of the Palestine Liberation Organization, having three wide horizontal stripes, the top green, the middle white, and the bottom black. A red triangle reached out from its staff side. And in the middle of the flag, positioned with its tip upraised, was the red silhouette of a broadsword. Around its blade was the spinning-atom logo of a nuclear weapon.

The walk from the motel to the tower area took Kamal Adwan the better part of thirty minutes, but it was late evening and the oppressive heat of the day's sun had been wafted from the city by a confused mixture of air currents generated by the afternoon thunderstorms. The clouds had deteriorated into puny heirs of their mature selves and were scattered sufficiently to allow Adwan to enjoy his stars as he approached the plaza around the base of the tower. Beyond the greenery was a plate of rocked concrete and stoned walkways that surrounded the glassed-in base of the shaft. An artfully spaced series of greened-bronze streetlights provided soft illumination, and a number of high-backed benches accented the design of the walkways. The hills formed by the leveling of the central area were faced with a series of narrow stone steps, and a cascade of clear water covered the facings.

It was close to 10:00 P.M. and Adwan was glad he had persuaded the others that he was entitled to a late-night reconnaissance of the tower exterior. People were still about, some standing in small groups, gaily talking as they looked up the brightly lit shaft and relived their moments at its top. Others were slowly walking from the area, cautiously watching the darting children who were expending their last moments of energy chasing each other and swinging on the lampposts.

Adwan had remained within the shadows, but now he walked out in the clear and raised his head to examine the tower. As he studied the shaft and became absorbed in the form of the structure, particularly where it provided paths for the elevators, he failed to notice a small running form, who smashed into his legs with some force. Her balance lost, the girl grabbed Adwan around the waist for support, then quickly backed away, embarrassed.

"Excuse me," she apologized.

Adwan immediately regretted that he had ventured too far from his initial vantage point, but could see no harm done. Looking down, he was captured by the beauty of the little girl's eyes, large brown orbs, almost iridescent as they reflected the lights of the tower. Their owner was barely three feet tall, and Adwan judged her to be about seven or eight years old. Her thin form gave inadequate support to the light cotton dress that was gathered loosely at the waist by weak elastic. It was covered with brightly printed wildflowers. Her hair was shiny black and neatly braided into a single tail, which dropped down her back to her waist. She was barearmed and barefooted, and Adwan could see that her skin, like his, was olive, but it was the wide-open eyes that held his own. They were Palestinian eyes, bright with the innocence of childhood but inexplicably marred with a terrible underlying sadness, as if the joys of her childhood had been often tempered with disappointment or hurt. Adwan wanted to stoop and sweep her up in his arms and hold her close and give her the comfort of his concern.

"I didn't see you," she continued defensively.

"It is all right. I did not see you. I was looking up at the tower."

"Did you go to the top?" asked the child.

"No—I am going up there tomorrow."

"You can see the whole city."

"That is what I have been told," responded Adwan.

"I have been to the top. I could almost touch God."

"Yes, I would think so."

"Do you speak Spanish?"

"No, just English and my own tongue."

"I didn't think so. You don't look Mexican. I am Mexican. Mexican-American. I speak Spanish *and* English. Would you like me to teach you some Spanish?" asked the child eagerly.

"That is very kind of you. But should you not be getting back to your friends, or your mother?"

"My mother went to the toilet. I'm waiting for her."

"Perhaps you should go look at the waterfalls. They are very pretty, and your mother can see you there. You should not be over here with me."

"You look lonely."

Adwan let his eyes drink in the innocence and beauty of the girl. She was the universal child: Mexican, American, Israeli, Palestinian. "Do you live here in the city?" he asked, looking back up at the tower.

"Yes. We walk over here to see the lights of the tower."

"You walk? You must live very close."

"Yes. Just over there on another street. I think that if the tower falls it will land on my street. Oh! There's Mama!" Without a backward glance, the child skipped across the walkway.

Adwan watched her grab her mother's outstretched hand and swing playfully on it as they walked off together.

"You live too close, little girl," said Adwan quietly.

Chapter 25

July 19, 5:37 A.M.
La Quinta Motel, San Antonio, Texas

"**E**veryone check your weapons."

Kamal Adwan, Ahmad Labidi, Khahid Aswar, and Iranian Hosni Haidari all followed Muhammad ben-Ali's lead and gave their hand weapons a final visual inspection, ensuring that the clips were loaded and their ammunition belts full. Adwan and Labidi would also carry small patches of plastique to blast out sections of the two stairways. Ben-Ali picked up the rewrapped broadsword and handed it to Aswar.

"Take this holy relic," he ordered. "When it is time to bring up the weapon, I want the ancient sword of the Shaheen to be with it. One of our ancestors will realize great pleasure when the blade that once fit his hand is present at the reestablishment of Palestinians as the greatest soldiers of the one true God."

Aswar took the cloth-covered symbol and placed it on the bed next to his Uzi.

"One final time. We drive to the base of the tower and wait. When the first guard arrives and unlocks the glass enclosure, I and Haidari will follow him and take control. Immediately, Adwan and Labidi will join us and we will collect the hostages as they arrive. Aswar will remain in the van until we have taken command of the tower. Then, we will bring up the weapon. Aswar, you will be prepared to detonate the weapon should there be any unforeseen resistance. I don't expect any, but it is best that we be prepared. Even in failure we will have struck a crippling blow upon the Jew-lovers. If all goes as it has on previous mornings, we should occupy the observation level by eight-thirty."

One by one, with ben-Ali first, the Shaheen left the room, their weapons carried beneath casually folded hotel towels. Each avoided the elevator and used the stairs to proceed to the lobby level, then out the back door by the pool and into the van. The drive to the tower site was a matter of only five minutes, and after removing the chain that closed off entry to the parking lots they proceeded across walkways until they reached the concrete and stone plaza surrounding the base of the tower. Ben-Ali parked the van next to the entrance of the smoked-glass enclosure. With a patience born of confidence that all aspects of their plan had been thoroughly thought out, the five Shaheen waited.

By 6:30 A.M., a few pedestrians were taking shortcuts across the tower area, but none gave the black van any particular notice. It was not unusual for maintenance crews to be at the tower base during its hours of closure, particularly during the height of the summer season, when upkeep was increased to stay ahead of the demands of visitors to the city. It was only when the first tower relief guard arrived a few minutes before 8 A.M. that the van's presence was challenged. The guard walked immediately to the vehicle and spoke to ben-Ali.

"You can't park here. You will have to move your van," he ordered.

Ben-Ali opened the door and stepped out, a draped towel over his arm. "We were told to be here at eight to assist the cleaning crew." Glancing about, he could see no special attention being paid them by the few people crossing the walk. Jabbing his Uzi hard into the guard's ribs, he let his eyes emphasize his instructions. "Unless you wish to die here, go ahead and enter the tower. I will be behind you, and I will not hesitate to kill you if you do not do *exactly* as I say."

The fiftyish-looking guard, overweight and unarmed, paled. His day had not started well and now some kook was threatening to make it much worse. His assailant was obviously quite sincere, but why would anyone want to force his way into the tower? The entry fee was only two dollars. The second jab of the gun barrel against his rib cage prompted him to immediately unlock the entrance door, and with ben-Ali pressed against his backside they entered the enclosure.

"Wait," ordered ben-Ali, holding the man aside as Haidari joined them. "Now, how many people are up in the tower? The truth. Your life depends on each word you speak."

"One," the guard replied. "I am to relieve him."

"Then, we go up."

The guard unlocked the closest elevator and they entered. The elevator rose from the base of the tower and through its glassed outer wall. As ben-Ali watched the ground fall away, he could see Adwan and Labidi leaving the van and entering the enclosure. As the elevator climbed, the visible horizon expanded. More of the city came into view and, by the time they reached the outer dome of the tower, ben-Ali could observe all of the central city and the maze of access highways. The morning rush hour was well under-way. Abruptly, his view was blocked as the elevator entered the dome and eased to a stop. The highly polished brass doors slid open. The guard going off duty was standing directly in front of them, his coffee thermos in one hand. Seeing ben-Ali and Haidari, his smile froze for a moment, then faded into an open-mouthed look of puzzlement. "What is . . ?" Haidari's outstretched gun cut off the last words, and the man backpedaled as the two Arabs and his relief strode from the elevator.

Ben-Ali herded the two guards into the security office. "The keys. I want the keys to the outside access doors."

The guard going off duty picked up a large key ring from the desk and held it out to ben-Ali.

"Which are the keys to the outside doors?"

The guard placed one of the keys between his fingers. "Unlock it," ben-Ali directed, waving the two men to the nearest stairwell. After the guard did so, there was no further need to tell him to hand over the key ring; he held it out eagerly. Ben-Ali waved the two men outside. "You will remain here. If you drop anything from the walk-way or try to signal anyone down below or in the buildings around us, you will be shot and thrown over the side when I return."

"What do you want?" asked the guard coming on duty.

Ben-Ali lowered his Uzi and squeezed the trigger. The guard screamed with pain as his left leg was shattered by the brief burst. As he fell, the other guard stepped back and raised his hands before his chest in terror. "You will not speak unless we request it," ordered ben-Ali. He locked the door before rejoining Haidari. Together, they hurriedly surveyed the glassed-in observation level before taking the elevator down to the restaurant level. As expected, it was empty, and they returned in the elevator to the ground level. Adwan and Labidi were there with two more guards and three of the cleaning crew.

"How many more will be arriving?" asked ben-Ali of the guards.

"Two more security people shortly before ten o'clock," answered one.

"And your crew?" added ben-Ali, directing his words to the other hostages.

The oldest, a graying and very nervous Mexican, responded, "There are five of us. The other two will be here anytime. Please, we are just the cleaning crew."

Ben-Ali ignored his plea. The pedestrian traffic across the walkway was increasing and, although the glass of the enclosure was heavily tinted, the activities of ben-Ali and his comrades could be detected should anyone take a studied look.

"Get Aswar and the weapon," ben-Ali directed. "Be casual."

Labidi and Adwan walked outside to the van and returned cradling the weapon. Aswar followed, carrying the wrapped Shaheen blade. Several passersby glanced over at the strange procession but walked on.

"Take it up," ordered ben-Ali. "Labidi, you stay and assist Haidari."

Adwan and Aswar, with the weapon held between them, disappeared behind the closed elevator doors.

Labidi and Haidari directed the hostages into a second elevator and nodded to ben-Ali as the doors closed.

Ben-Ali waited, observing the people on the walk until Haidari returned.

"Everyone secure?" asked ben-Ali.

"All outside and quiet—very quiet." Haidari added the last words with a broad smile. Ben-Ali's shattering of the guard's leg had made his point well.

"We must take two more at least," announced ben-Ali thoughtfully. Studying the people outside, he concentrated on a young couple who were detouring on their walk across the area, the woman leaning to peer curiously through the glass. Her escort was in a summer business suit and she wore the fashionable flared skirt and loose-fitting blouse typical of the downtown working crowd. Ben-Ali opened the door and with a friendly smile hailed them, "Would you step over here, please?"

The couple looked at each other, mildly surprised, but turned to approach the door. "Hi," said the man. "What can we do for you?"

"Could you hold the door while my friend and I bring in our load from the van?" As he spoke, ben-Ali opened the door wide. The man grabbed it and ben-Ali stepped back inside, bringing his Uzi into view. "Inside! At once!"

Reaching out, Haidari grabbed the woman's arm and pulled her forward. The man read the message of death in ben-Ali's eyes and followed wordlessly. For the final time, ben-Ali and Haidari stepped into the elevator with their catch and the doors slid shut.

Stepping out onto the observation level, ben-Ali walked briskly into the security office while Haidari escorted the man and woman to the outside platform. Adwan unlocked the door.

"Out—with the others," directed Haidari.

Obviously frightened, the woman cringed at the sight of the wounded guard lying on the deck, the left leg of his trousers a mass of glossy red paste. One of the other guards was monitoring a tourniquet while holding the man's head in his lap. The woman's escort guided her around the pair and back with the others.

"What happened?" she asked. "Who are these people?"

"They are terrorists," answered one of the relief guards.

"Oh, dear God."

"We'll be all right. They have not threatened us."

"We'll be all right? What about that man?"

"They shot him as an example. We must all do just as they say and not ask questions."

"Oh, God, dear God." The woman sank to the deck sobbing. Her escort stooped beside her and held her against him.

"We must figure a way to signal someone," said the young man.

"No, not yet. They have specifically warned us against that. We best wait and see what develops."

Ben-Ali walked around the walls of the security office and surveyed the furnishings: a worn wooden desk, several straight-backed chairs, a telephone with a tower intercom position, four walkie-talkie radios, a cabinet full of clerical and cleaning supplies. Ignoring the paper clutter on the desk, he examined the drawers. No weapons. Scissors. In the back of a room was a louvered door that led to a closet. It failed to reveal anything other than maintenance supplies and a few hand tools. Ben-Ali recalled seeing another telephone within the souvenir-counter enclosure.

Returning to the observation space he walked the perimeter. To the left of the souvenir counter was a door to one of the stairways, and adjacent to it was elevator number three. Then, the security office. Farther around was elevator number two. Beside it were ice cream and cold drink vending machines. Continuing his tour he came upon elevator number one and the other stairwell. The stairwell door had a small rectangular viewing window, and ben-Ali peered through it at the stairwells. He pushed the door open and a shrill bell began screaming, its piercing sound reverberating like a thousand banshees within the enclosed observation level. Quickly, he closed it. Adwan and Labidi came running, their weapons at the ready.

"The alarm works," sheepishly explained ben-Ali. His two companions shook their heads in amusement and joined him in his walkaround, which ended in an open area furnished only with two small tables and several matching chairs. A pair of video game machines sat against one wall.

"I counted three observation telescopes. Coin operated. Break them open so we can use them. Also, I think it's time we blew the stairs."

Adwan and Labidi unslung their weapons and entered the stairwell platform, the alarm bell once again momentarily sounding. Ben-Ali peered through the viewing window and watched them disappear down the stairs. Several minutes later, they came back up, two steps at a time, and hardly had they hurried through the door when two sharp explosions shook the platform. Identical clouds of gray-brown dust rolled up the stairwells and filled the void between the doors.

"Good, let it clear some, then check the damage. I'll get the others and we'll lock the elevators. Where did you put the charges?"

"About halfway down the shaft," replied Adwan.

"Perfect."

Ben-Ali returned to the office area. Haidari was inside and Aswar was over by the stairwell to the outer deck, observing the hostages.

"Elevators all locked in manual and the doors wedged open," reported Haidari.

Ben-Ali was pleased. His men were anticipating his commands. All access to the dome was blocked; the stairs were blown and the elevators were locked at the observation level. The area was secured.

"Haidari, get up to the roof. See if we need a lookout—and raise our standard!"

Haidari hurried off.

Ben-Ali walked over to the glass panels surrounding the observation level. He was facing north and marveled at the commanding view he had of the central city and the main roads. A freeway ran north and south to his right, and off to his left he could see Interstate 10, the highway they had used to approach the city. Also to his left were the only tall buildings. None reached the height of the tower, but the nearest high rise, a hotel with a pair of pyramid-shaped frame towers on its top, reached almost to the restaurant level. He could read the large red letters MARRIOTT on its side. Farther to the west were the slab-sided Hilton Palacio Del Rio and the U-shaped midtown curve of the San Antonio River with its tree-lined banks. He could not see any of the military installations but knew they were there on the horizon: Brooks Air Force Base; Fort Sam Houston with its Brooke Medical Center; Kelly Air Force Base; Lackland Air Force Base; and just twenty miles northeast, Randolph Air Force Base. Referring to the visitor's map he had picked from the souvenir stand, he searched for other landmarks. Using one of the observation telescopes, he could identify the international airport to the north and several of the universities. He searched the downtown area and identified the route they had used the previous morning to transit the business district. At the far end were the Military Plaza and in its center the boxlike, three-storied City Hall.

He could not be more pleased with himself. San Antonio, while not one of the well-known premier cities of America, was a perfect place to strike. When it came time to use the weapon, the destruction of such a place, with its proliferation of military bases, federal offices, universities, and cultural areas, would be a severe blow to the morale of the Americans. He regretted that the population involved so many people of Spanish extraction, for they were the exploited ones in this section of capitalistic America. But they had chosen the land as their own. So be it. At least they had their heritage of Catholicism, and for the crucifixion of the prophet Jesus they must share the Palestinian hate of the Jews. He supposed there would be American Indians within the city. They certainly should be brothers to the Palestinians, for they also had been cruelly driven from their land. He wondered how such a diverse and oppressed population could live together, much less progress materially. As a Palestinian, he and his brothers would never allow Israel to enjoy such security and prosperity.

His watch read 9:30. It was time to notify the officials of San Antonio that their city was under siege.

Mayor Tony Santos started up the steps to City Hall but paused to examine the decay of the cement facade over the arched windows of his ground-floor office. Age and the elements had eaten large chunks of cement and plaster from the projecting cornice. There must be sufficient money in the city budget to correct such an embarrassing neglect of the city's first building, he thought. Certainly, emphasis had been placed on the restoration and upkeep of the old Spanish Governor's Palace out back, across the City Hall parking lot. He was still considering the damage when one of the tall entry doors swung open and the guard called out, "Mr. Mayor, you have a phone call waiting for you in your office."

"I'm coming, Paul. We should be ashamed to let this building deteriorate like this." He entered the cathedral-like foyer and turned into the left wing toward his office. His secretary was holding open his inner office door.

"You have a call on one; he won't identify himself, just says it is urgent."

"*Madre María!* I'm not even at work yet and they're laying for me. Dolores, coffee—strong."

"It's on your desk, Mr. Mayor."

Santos whipped off his summer jacket and grabbed the phone. "This is the mayor."

The words that greeted him froze him in a half-seated posture. "Listen carefully. My name is Muhammad ben-Ali of the New Shaheen liberation brotherhood, and I and my Palestinian brothers are at this moment looking down on your city from your Tower of the Americas. It now belongs to the faithful of Islam. Can you record this conversation?"

Santos found it hard to reply. He opened his mouth to speak but the words stuck in his throat, somewhere just short of his larynx. Was this some kind of sick joke? The voice had a slight accent that he did not recognize, and it was very calm, but he had never heard a more ominous tone. Breathing deeply to compose himself, he managed one audible word, "Yes." Pushing a buzzer on his desk to signal Dolores to activate the machine, he waited. A faint beep informed him and the caller that the recorder was on-line.

"I will speak these words only one time. We have with us a nuclear weapon and will not hesitate to use it if our demands are not met. For the moment, they are the following: You and the senior federal official present in this city will proceed to the base of the tower and establish contact with the observation level on the tower intercom. Absolutely no one else is to be notified. You must realize that in addition to the nine persons we have in the tower, we are holding all of the citizens of San Antonio as hostage for our negotiations. If they are informed that we have a nuclear weapon and start to evacuate the city, we will detonate the weapon. And I remind you that we have a clear view of all arteries out of the city. If you value the lives of your fellow citizens you will do exactly as I have said or they will suffer the same fate as the infidels who manned the *Lincoln* warship. Do not reply to me. Just do as I have ordered. I will expect you to be at the base of the tower with the federal representative in fifteen minutes." A click and the irritating sound of the disconnected line followed ben-Ali's last word.

Santos held the phone to his ear, unable to put it down until he could organize his thoughts. Slowly placing it back in its cradle, he pressed his intercom button.

"Yes, Mr. Mayor?"

"Did you monitor that call, Dolores?"

"No, sir. Should I have?"

"No. Just bring me the tape, please."

His secretary entered and placed the cassette on his desk. "Are you feeling all right, sir? You look terrible."

"What? No, no, I'm all right. The call had some disturbing news. That's all."

"Let me bring you something. What on earth was it?"

"No, Dolores. Just do two things for me: call Chief Peyton and ask him to come to the office immediately. Then get me Fred Gimble at the FBI office."

"Right away, sir. Please, let me get you something."

"It's all right. Just hurry and do what I ask. And Dolores, you are not to speak of this to anyone. Do you understand? Absolutely."

"Of course." The woman turned and hurried out to her desk. She was his right hand of seven years, a woman of maturity and trust who would not disobey his order despite the gnawing curiosity that was already threatening to burn a hole in her stomach wall. Santos placed the tape in his drawer machine and played it. Halfway through, his intercom interrupted the terrible words.

"I have Mr. Gimble, sir."

Santos jerked up the handset. "Fred, don't say anything, just listen to this." Rewinding the tape, he held the phone down by the player and pushed the PLAY button. As soon as the last word sounded, he switched off the tape. "I just received that."

"Mr. Mayor, I'll meet you at the tower as soon as I can get there. This may be for real and it may not. Assume that it is. Don't speak to anyone."

"I have a call in for my chief of police. We must get people away from there."

"No. Tell him to meet us at the tower. No one else. Do you understand?"

"Yes."

Ben-Ali rejoined the others on the observation deck. "The call is made. I want you to set up an alert schedule for the weapon. As soon as I talk to the federal representative and give him our demands, we must be prepared for an assault. I want the arming switch on the weapon activated and someone is to be standing by the dead man's switch and prepared to activate it at my order. Until we determine how secure we are, we must maintain a constant readiness. I do not believe they will try anything until they analyze the situation. By that time, we shall have accomplished a major part of our mission."

Mayor Santos and FBI agent Gimble arrived at the base of the tower at the same moment. Chief Peyton was already examining the van. "What's going down?" he asked.

"Terrorists in the tower," replied Santos.

"Jesus," cursed the chief.

"Inside," directed Gimble. The enclosure was still empty.

"We are to resume contact with them now," explained Santos to the startled head of the city's law enforcement force. "Just stand by while I make the call." Before Santos could get into the ticket booth and to the intercom, the two remaining guards of the day's security shift appeared at the door. "Come in and don't let anyone else enter," ordered Santos. "We'll fill you in shortly." Confused and curious, the two men stood aside with Peyton. Santos punched the intercom button on the tower phone, tilted it by his ear in order that Gimble could also hear, and waited for the buzz to be interrupted by the observation-level station. He recognized the voice immediately and nodded to Gimble.

"Let me speak with the federal authority," directed the voice.

Gimble took the handset. "This is Fred Gimble, head of the San Antonio office of the Federal Bureau of Investigation. Who is this?"

"This is the voice of the Shaheen. The city of San Antonio is now under the control of Palestinian liberation forces. I have our demands ready for you to pass on to your president, but first I must repeat the caution I have given to the mayor of this city . . ."

"I have heard the tape," interrupted Gimble.

"I figured as much. It is well for you to take my words at their absolute value. We will not hesitate to use our weapon. Now, I give you our nonnegotiable demands. First, the United Nations will withdraw its so-called peacekeeping occupational troops from the Middle East and a new UN force of Third World countries will take its place to supervise the demilitarization of Israel. Second, the United States of America will cease all military, economic, and humanitarian aid to the illegal state of Israel and will remove all American personnel from that land. Third, the Israelis will immediately declare Jerusalem an open city and withdraw all military forces from that city, the West Bank, and the Gaza Strip. The Jewish squatters in those areas will vacate immediately. Fourth, in return for our guarantee of a land for the Jews, such land to be defined by their 1948 borders less Jerusalem, Israel will agree to occupation by the Third World UN force until such time as negotiations between Israel and the Arab states provide for a disarmament of Jewish military forces and their replacement by a joint police force of equal representation of Arabs and Jews. Finally, to ensure continued compliance with the provisions just mentioned, the Secretary General of the United Nations, the President of the United States, and the Prime Minister of Israel will provide themselves as hostages to representatives of the restored Palestinian state, such state to consist of the territory of the West Bank, the Gaza Strip, and added lands to be determined by future negotiations among the parties concerned."

Gimble finished scribbling in his notebook. "I will relay your demands to the proper authorities."

"You have twelve hours to provide us with a reply."

"That is impossible and you know it."

"No, it is merely very difficult. Our representatives and friends in the United Nations general assembly are at this moment distributing copies of these same demands and will bring the matter to a vote. As a member of that body, the United States has pledged to abide by its decisions. Twelve hours is not unreasonable for some assurance that our demands will receive favorable consideration by your government."

"I do not have the authority to represent my country in this," declared Gimble. "I must turn this matter over to Washington."

"Of course. But meanwhile, the people of San Antonio will be our guarantee of security against any attempt to dislodge us from this tower. Any action to do so and we detonate our weapon; any decision to evacuate the city will cause us to detonate our weapon."

"We will have to tell the people something. Such negotiations cannot be kept secret."

"Then tell them what you wish—but do not tell them of the weapon. Twelve hours, no more."

"They're off the line," announced Gimble. "How in the hell can we go about this and not tell the people there's a nuclear weapon up there with those crazies?"

"I don't know," agreed Santos. "Their demands cannot be met, we all know that."

"But that's not our decision. The first thing we have to do is notify Washington," decided Gimble. "All of you here," he continued, addressing the late arrivals specifically, "are going to have to work with us on this. I want you two to go outside to man this door. No one enters. Mr. Mayor, I would recommend that the police immediately cordon off this entire block and let no one in."

"What do we tell everyone?" asked Santos plaintively.

"Tell them the truth. There are terrorists in the tower and they are making demands. Only don't reveal the presence of the weapon. They have hostages, that's their leverage at the moment. It's a goddamned too familiar pattern. The people will relate to that."

"We have to tell Washington," insisted Santos.

"Of course we do. But we also relay the conditions and hope to hell we can work with this thing until we come up with a counteraction. Chief Peyton, your forces are not to know about the weapon. And my people will take those two guards outside into custody and keep them secluded until this thing is over. It is imperative that the people of San Antonio not be aware of the weapon. They will panic as sure as hell and start to haul ass over every street and road in this city, and that will trigger the terrorists. All we have to work with as far as public knowledge is concerned is the hostage situation. Is that perfectly clear?"

"But the existence of the weapon must be revealed. There is no way the U.S., Israel, and the UN will even start to discuss the demands just to save the lives of nine hostages," pleaded Santos.

"I can't argue with that. We just have to take it one step at a time. I need to get on the horn to D.C. Chief, you know what you have to do, and, Mr. Mayor, you better be thinking of something to tell the people when this thing breaks, which is going to be within minutes of now."

The Old Man ran the thick brown bar of government soap over his chest and worked up a rich lather under his arms and along his rib cage. The hot water was chasing some of the stiffness from his joints, but it would take more than that to erase the effects of the poor excuse for a mattress that his fellow spooks padded their beds with. He should have stayed in the rec room and stretched out on the couch. The breakfast made up for some of it, however. At least they knew how to recruit cooks. He'd have to skip lunch to make up for the morning caloric intake. He wished he could resign himself to the inevitable increase of flab as he grew older.

He wondered if the other members of the team were assembled yet. The vice president had scheduled a noon meeting for a quick update before lunch. It had to be close to 11:30 already. Cutting short his refreshing rinse, he stepped outside the shower and grabbed a towel. A staccato of loud knocks jarred the door to his room.

"Tom . . . Tom Padina! We're on! Everyone to the situation room. I'll see you there." The Old Man recognized the voice of fellow agent Benson.

Hurriedly, he slipped on his jockey shorts, groaned as he stooped to pull on his trousers, grabbed a shirt, stepped into his shoes, and briskly walked down the hall.

Benson, Myers, and the three military liaison officers were already in the room. The Old Man arrived a step behind Charlie Kelly. Terence Shinn was the last to enter.

"I've just been on the phone with the president," said the vice president. "The bastards are in San Antonio."

The air in the room thickened with the collective disappointment and despair of those assembled.

"I've ordered Petroviny and his team to the scene, and we will be leaving in about ten minutes. Get your things and meet me at the helicopter pad. We'll brief on the aircraft."

The Old Man was panting by the time he ran back to his room and finished dressing. He ran his electric razor across his face as he trotted out to the helicopter. I'm getting too goddamned old for this type of thing, he thought. He was the last to board. It was

eleven minutes to planeside at Langley Air Force Base and within
another five the modified DC-9 was airborne and pointed southwest toward Texas. The occupants gathered around Terence
Shinn's seat as he talked.

"Sometime this morning, a group of terrorists identifying
themselves as the New Shaheen occupied and gained control of
the Tower of the Americas in the middle of downtown San Antonio.
They claim they have a nuclear weapon and nine hostages. They
have relayed their demands to the president. Briefly, they want us
out of Israel, they want Israel to get out of the West Bank and the
Gaza Strip, and they want the UN to supervise a revision of the
Israeli state to include an open Jerusalem and a reduction of military forces. For insurance they want our president, the UN president, and the Israeli prime minister as hostages."

"They're fucking-A mad," spat the Old Man.

"That they are," agreed the vice president quietly. "Here's the
tricky part. They do not want the people of San Antonio to know
they have a nuclear weapon. They want to hold the entire city of
San Antonio as hostage and have declared that if the people start
to evacuate they'll detonate the weapon."

"They can't have it both ways," exclaimed CIA agent Benson.

"For the moment, they do," countered Shinn. "I instructed
Petroviny to set up a command post—he'll beat us there by almost
two hours—and hold his team in check until we arrive. We'll survey
the situation and decide what we have to do. For the moment, the
cover story is that the Palestinians have indeed taken over the tower
but their leverage is the nine hostages. The president has called for
an immediate meeting of the UN Security Council with the Israeli
ambassador and a PLO representative present. Charlie—" Shinn
spoke directly to his press officer, "the press will already have a cover
story. I want you to establish a central press office and control
releases from there. Everybody will be digging for that one scoop
item. I don't want it to be the presence of the nuke."

"We have a chinaman's chance to hold out for a while,"
answered Charlie Kelly. "The fact that there were two weapons in
the original Cuban transfer has never been made public, but with
the *Lincoln* disaster, everyone will be wondering in the back of
their minds—and will probably be scared shitless. I suspect some
San Antonians will start getting out based on that. And a few leaving can trigger a lot. We won't be able to get them to stay by telling
them they'll be nuked if they try to leave."

"Then we'll have to try and calm them down. A mass exodus

cannot be kept from the terrorists. Hell, they can see seventy percent of the city from the tower."

"We're between a rock and a hard place—pardon the cliché," ventured Myers.

"Look," said Benson, "the Shaheen must know that their demands cannot be met. They are outrageous to begin with."

"No, I won't buy that yet," countered Shinn. "Think about the wording of their demands for a moment. They don't call for the elimination of Israel. In fact, they are recognizing the right of Israel to exist. Arafat sowed the seed in late 1988; now, even the extremists are picking it up. There could be a very slim thread of substance for negotiation there."

"The Israelis won't hear of it," stated the Old Man flatly.

"I'm not that sure. There is a nuclear weapon involved and an American city. Probably a million or more people—including us, I should mention, once we're there. If we lose all that, there's going to be precious little support for Israel from the man in the street."

The Old Man shook his head. "That may be. But when it comes to national interests, the Israelis tend to disregard the thoughts of the American man in the street. For the moment, anyhow, we have a rather serious tactical problem. What can we really do when we get to San Antonio? If they have the weapon and it has the same devilish deadman's switch, there is no way we can assault the tower."

"That's for Petroviny to decide. Our main purpose is to stall the terrorists, act as a relay between them and the president, and try to control the situation as it affects the people of San Antonio. I'm not sure exactly what our first move must be yet."

"For me, I'm going to find a priest and go to confession," muttered the Old Man dryly, then added so all could hear, "I don't think the Shaheen have any intention of carrying on a long dialogue with us or anyone else. I admit my specialty is the Cubans—I don't know why the hell I'm included in this circus, anyhow—but I know enough about religious fanatics to feel that these terrible people are out to make their point and then take out San Antonio, period. Look how short a time the Iranian waited before he evaporated the Lincoln, a matter of hours. He presented their demands and then took six thousand souls with him to see Allah. We're in a losing situation. It's gone too far. We've waited too long to stop these people. We should have hit every goddamned Arab state that supported the PLO and their offshoot bastards from day one—from the massacre of our Marines in Beirut. That's when we should have stopped them. Barring that, we should have used the Persian Gulf fracas as an excuse to bomb Iran into a big flat plate of fused glass and eliminate at least one of the Palestinians' allies. We could have taken out Libya, Syria, and even Lebanon and nobody would have given a rat's ass except the Palestinians. Hell, we got a hint of what we could do when we slapped Khadafi on the wrists—he crawled back under a rock with his women and didn't stick his head out for months. The worthless goddamned sons of bitches have been terrorizing and murdering for *years*, for Christ's sake, all in the name of their God and claiming it has been all justifiable because of us, the great satan. And we sat over here and wrung our hands and waited for them to have a change of heart. Now we're going to lose a big chunk of southern Texas and a lot of Texans. Almighty God himself must throw up his hands at our stupidity."

No one spoke up to counter the Old Man's arguments.

Colonel Schuyler Petroviny, United States Marine Corps, was waiting at the bottom of the DC-9's boarding ladder when Shinn and his team filed off the aircraft at Kelly Air Force Base. In black special operations fatigues, and belted with an eel skin–holstered .45-caliber automatic, the short, stocky Marine stood, legs spread, with the all-business stance of a General George Patton. He was almost a physical clone of the corps' legendary Chesty Puller. Saluting with one hand, he waved them into a waiting Air Force bus with the other. As they drove toward the main gate with a police escort, he stood in the aisle and gave his briefing.

"My team is on station within the glass enclosure at the base of the tower and we've recced the stairs. Both sets are blown about halfway down the shaft. Ten feet out of one, twelve to fourteen out of the other. We can get across if we have to, but it'll take a bit of doing. The elevators appear to be locked at the observation level. I've taken the liberty, Mr. Vice President, of establishing your command post on the top of the Marriott. We can use the roof if we desire, and I've cleared out the top floor. It's thirty-eight stories and the highest building close to the tower. The phone people are installing a direct line to the White House Situation Room and secure lines to the Pentagon, Kelly, Randolph, and Fort Sam Houston. I'll give you a radioman for direct communications with me.

"The city police have the entire area cordoned off and are rerouting traffic for several additional blocks around the area."

"What word has been released?" asked Shinn.

"The TV stations have picked it all up, naturally. They were onto the situation as soon as the police arrived at the tower plaza. The mayor made a live broadcast and informed the people that a group of terrorists had control of the tower and were holding hostages. He urged them to remain calm and assured them that everything was under control for the moment. I bet he's one hell of a poker player."

"He didn't mention the weapon?"

"No, sir, he did not."

"We'll want to set up a pressroom at the Marriott," suggested Charlie Kelly.

"I've already taken care of that, sir," responded Petroviny. "A suite on the floor below the command center."

"Excellent, Colonel," complimented Shinn. "Have you had an opportunity to assess the vulnerability of the Palestinians' position? Can we get to them, providing we can figure out some way to neutralize their weapon?"

"Oh, we can get to the sons of bitches by the stairs. But how we set up an element of surprise is beyond me at the moment. As soon as we think it feasible, I'd like to send up a team and bug the observation level. It would help if we knew what they were saying to each other. We can use ceiling and wall taps from the restaurant level."

"They haven't sealed off that level?" asked the Old Man incredulously.

"In effect they have by blowing the stairs. We don't think they will keep anyone continuously at the restaurant level, but they will want to maintain access to the food. They have booby-trapped the blown section of the stairs with grenades and a maze of trip wires. We can blow it in an all-out assault, but I wouldn't try it for a clandestine penetration."

"Then how do we bug the observation level?"

"I have a pair of climbers from Alaska who can scale a mile-high greased mirror if they have to. There are access portholes spaced along the entire height of the elevator shafts. We climb the stairs as far as we can, then go out into the open shaft and on up. With the top overhang they won't be able to be seen from above. We can get to the bottom of an elevator and possibly a section of the floor of the observation level. We don't dare try and enter the restaurant level. Too risky—we could cause them to set off the weapon. But we can set the bugs."

"They'll be speaking Arabic," prompted the Old Man.

"Half of my team speaks Arabic," replied Petroviny. "My first sergeant is a native Palestinian."

"Do it ASAP," directed Shinn. "Sounds like a good idea." Being able to monitor the terrorists' conversations would give our people a critical tactical advantage, thought Shinn. Petroviny knew his business. For the first time since receiving the phone call from the president, Shinn felt as if they were well on their way to scoring the first points in the showdown with the Shaheen.

Muhammad ben-Ali swept the city with one of the observation telescopes. It was a poor-quality lens but better than the naked eye. There was a moderate volume of traffic moving on the freeways, but he judged it to be no more than a bit above normal. He could still observe considerable pedestrian and vehicle traffic within the central downtown area and the gathered crowds bunched around the limits of the police barriers. They wouldn't be there if they knew of the weapon. His twelve-hour deadline would provide for a 10:30 P.M. response. As he surveyed the surrounding area a final time, an irregular blob passed his field of vision. He swung to follow it and captured the dark form of a helicopter approaching from the southwest. It didn't appear to be military, but an air-to-air weapon could be fired from any airborne vehicle, even a TOW or Stinger missile. But if that were the case, such an assault could have been launched from the ground around the tower. No, it was not an assault, but more than likely some sort of reconnaissance. Ben-Ali picked up the intercom to the base of the tower. The FBI agent, Gimble, answered.

"Get the helicopter away from the tower," ordered ben-Ali.

"What helicopter?" asked Gimble.

"There's a helicopter approaching from the southwest. If it closes within a mile of this tower we will detonate our weapon."

"I'll take care of it! We have given specific instructions to the military and the police that nothing is to approach the tower. It is not a threat!" Who would be doing such a thing? His order had been specific. Could it be private? Or an air ambulance—*or a news team!* Jesus! That must be it! Gimble dialed the number of his agent on top of the Marriott and roared into the mouthpiece as soon as he heard it picked up, "Keep that chopper away from the tower! To the southwest! An unknown. They've threatened to detonate their weapon if it closes within a mile!" Rushing outside, he searched the skies, but the buildings of the city limited his view of the sky.

Shinn and his team, along with Colonel Petroviny, reached the command post on top of the Marriott. Mayor Santos was waiting, as were several others: Petroviny's radioman, the FBI link to Gimble at the base of the tower, Chief of Police Peyton, and several military technicians from Randolph Air Force Base who were manning portable communications consoles. Santos handed his field glasses to Shinn, who aimed them at the tower.

"What the hell is that?" asked Shinn.

"Where?" responded Petroviny.

"On the tall red-and-white-striped antenna. It looks like some kind of flag—green, white, and black stripes. Can't you see it?"

"Basically a Palestinian flag—PLO," answered Petroviny. "It has something in the center added to it."

"Yes, I see it. It looks like a sword. Arrogant bastards." Lowering his glasses, Shinn asked, "So what's the latest?"

"It has been quiet until a few minutes ago," replied the FBI agent. "But some idiot in a chopper is to the southwest. The Shaheen have threatened to blow their weapon if he closes within a mile. We have scrambled a Cobra from over at Sam Houston."

"Where on earth did Sam Houston get a Cobra?" asked Colonel Thompson, Shinn's Army liaison officer.

"It's a transient. Some captain with a wife in the medical facility there. The FAA handed him over to us. No armament—but he can make the interception. Sergeant Phillips at the first communications console has him in radio contact. The sergeant has been assigned to you, Colonel Thompson, and Master Sergeant Owens will handle your communications, Colonel Fisher."

"You people are on your toes up here," commented Colonel Fisher, Shinn's Air Force liaison officer.

"Captain Duncan," continued the FBI agent, "Sergeant Wiley is manning your position. We don't have much of a Texas Navy, but he does have lines to the Pentagon and Corpus Christi for you."

"That'll do fine for the moment. Thank you," responded Duncan.

"What are the Cobra pilot's orders?" asked Shinn.

"To divert the helicopter," answered the FBI agent.

"There he is!" called out Chief Peyton.

"Take it around upsun and approach from there," directed "Rusty" Brown, shouldering his actioncam transmitting unit. This was going to be the scoop of the year, live action of the terrorists in the tower. Could win him the Pulitzer!

"I don't know if we should get too close," advised his pilot.

"Just do as I say. A thousand yards will do it with this lens."

The pilot swung west and was about to head back toward the tower when his headset crackled with a message on the emergency frequency. "November two-niner-echo, this is Army gunship off your right side and to your rear. Reverse course and clear this area immediately or I will open fire."

"Holy shit!" exclaimed Brown's pilot, leaning his craft into a steep left turn, the abrupt maneuver throwing Brown to the floor behind him.

"Hey, I'm not strapped in back here!" yelled Brown.

"We've been ordered out of the area!" yelled back the pilot. "I don't want to tangle with no gunship. We're hauling ass. Fuck your pictures!"

Ben-Ali had watched the approach of the gunship, suspicious at first that it might be the forerunner of an attack on the tower, but when he saw the violent turnaround of the first helicopter he understood what had taken place. Excellent. But the Americans must understand the price of such acts. "Get one of the hostages," he ordered, "and have the rest back around away from the door."

Haidari unlocked the access door and he and Adwan grabbed one of the tower security people.

Ben-Ali stepped out on the open deck and struck the man full in the face with his Uzi. The guard slumped but was held partially upright by Haidari and Adwan. Ben-Ali smashed the weapon against the man's face a second time, and then a third. There were no longer any recognizable features, and blood was bubbling from the crushed opening where the mouth had been. "Bring out the ladder from the security office!" yelled ben-Ali.

Aswar joined his comrades on the open deck and they erected the ladder by the stainless steel fence rods. Ben-Ali picked up the unconscious guard as easily as he would have lifted a sack of flour, and climbed the ladder. Easing the man over the bent tips of the rails, he looped the guard's belt on one and let the man dangle over the side. Returning to the intercom, he summoned Gimble down below.

"Yes?" answered Gimble.

"Stay inside, devil, I don't want anything to fall on you."

Gimble puzzled at the order. What was going to fall on him? Oh, God, no! Horror-stricken, he stared vacantly at the black-uniformed members of Petroviny's antiterrorist team who shared the enclosure with him.

*   *   *

"Good Lord!" exclaimed Shinn. "They have hung somebody on the fence around the outside platform. He looks unconscious— or dead. Are we patched into the tower yet?"

"Yes, sir, we are," replied Petroviny. "To reach the terrorists you have only to pick up the phone in front of you."

Shinn lifted the phone. After two rings it was picked up at the other end of the circuit.

"This is the Vice President of the United States. With whom am I speaking?" demanded Shinn.

"This is Muhammad ben-Ali. I see our words have been taken seriously. Where are you?"

"I am here, in San Antonio."

"On the top of the hotel, yes? We have been watching the frantic preparations. Do you have word from your president?"

"He has your demands and is talking to the others involved. What have you done to that man on the fence?"

"You have until ten-thirty tonight. As for the Jew-lover on the fence, he is purified. You will not try the helicopter trick again."

"We had nothing to do with that. We have no idea who that was."

"Whoever, it has cost the life of one of your people."

Shinn could hear ben-Ali shout, "Cut him loose!"

"No!" yelled Shinn, but the circuit was dead. A feeling of helplessness chilling his blood, he watched the man tumble end over end six-hundred feet to the concrete. "Oh, dear God, please let him be already dead," he prayed.

The sun was low over the horizon when the Marine radioman reported that Petroviny's men were starting up the tower. "They're climbing out into the near shaft, sir, about halfway up," reported the Marine.

"Let me talk to the colonel."

The Marine handed Shinn the headset.

"Colonel, what are their chances?"

"Good. They're using lock grapples and the guide rails in the shaft, and there's plenty of stuff to grab onto on the sides of the shaft itself. A piece of cake, Mr. Vice President. You should be able to see them. It'll take awhile."

"Thank you, Colonel. We'll be praying."

The Old Man joined the others watching the climb. The fading light and distance made it difficult to pick out the two tiny figures within the shadows of the three-sided elevator shaft. "That's guts ball," he observed.

"What do you figure? A couple hours to get to the top?" mused Shinn.

"More or less. They've got about a three-hundred-foot climb. It'll be slow going."

"I'd like to have a couple of Petrovinys on my staff," observed Shinn. "He's one hell of an operator."

"Uh-huh, that's for sure. This is the first time I've ever walked into a high-level government operation that is so well organized, Mister Vice President. Petroviny had this thing set up before we ever got here."

The Old Man observed the vice president out of the corner of his eye. Shinn was calm and confident. The man showed definite signs of competency. How he got sidetracked into the number two spot had always been a mystery to the Old Man, who had long been familiar with Shinn's political career. The president could have used him much better as an attorney general or secretary of state. But he wasn't being wasted in his job at the moment. He was knowledgeable and aggressive, and the Old Man was impressed by the way he was handling the situation. Despite his gut feeling that it was a hopeless situation, he felt pretty good with Shinn running the show. "Looks like they've moved up some," he ventured.

"A couple feet, maybe," observed Shinn. "I would think those guide rails would be slippery from grease."

"Uh-huh. Too bad they don't have explosives with them instead of bugs. They could mine the whole underside of that dome by going up the three shafts. Have you approached that thought with Petroviny?"

"No, not yet. I don't think it's right to try and get into Petroviny's business, not just yet. Anyhow, there is a flaw in such a plan, but there wouldn't be if it were not for that dead man's switch. We could blow the whole top off the tower, but as soon as someone released his grip on the switch, that would be the ball game."

"They may not have someone on it all of the time," said the Old Man.

"Depends on how many are up there and how strong the spring on the switch is. Is it tiring to hold it down? I would think it has to be a little bit," said Shinn.

"I've been thinking along those same lines," said the Old Man, rubbing one hand across his stubble. His electric shaver back at Langley had done a poor job. "The only way we can approach the top is up those shafts. The stairs are mined, the elevators are locked up. We can't drop onto the top—they'd see us coming. We can't fire anything from the ground or the air. They'd see that and would have time to release the switch. Even if we caught them by surprise, it would do no good as long as they are holding the damn thing. But I keep thinking of those shafts. If there is any way to get into the dome, it has to be from underneath. If the elevators are at the observation level, the shaft is clear all the way to the restaurant level. This climb should determine that."

"Petroviny's initial inspection indicated that's exactly where they are," said Shinn.

"The bastards are clever. They seem to have thought of every-thing," concluded the Old Man.

"Not everything, Tom, not unless they have Jesus Christ him-self on their team. And I doubt that. No, there has to be a flaw somewhere in their plan. We just have to figure out what it is before they do what I know damned well they intend to do."

"The devils are up to something," said ben-Ali.

"How do you know?" questioned Haidari.

Ben-Ali stepped back from the observation glass. "Take a look. They have been watching the shaft of the tower for the past hour, all of them. Several of them have not moved an inch."

"It's too dark. I can barely see them."

"Well, I have been watching them. Something is going on at the base of the tower—or on the shaft. Of course! *On the shaft!* They're climbing the elevator shaft! That has to be what it is. That's why they've made no attempt to shut off the power. They don't want to give us any indication as to what they're doing."

"Why would they climb the shaft? All they could reach is the bottom of the elevator, and there is no opening in the bottom of the elevator."

"How about the doors at the restaurant level, or the bottom of this dome? Is there any space below the floor of the restaurant where they could enter?"

"I don't know. I'll take Adwan and check it out."

"No. That won't be necessary. If they are coming up the shaft, we'll meet them halfway." Ben-Ali's lips curled and his eyes danced with the sudden solution to the problem. "It is most probably the shaft on this side—that is why they have been looking so intensely. Come!"

Ben-Ali led Haidari to the elevator. "Run it down to just above ground level, then back up. If there is anyone in the shaft, they'll be scraped off like mud from a shoe."

Haidari removed the chair from the entrance to the elevator and stepped in. The polished brass doors slid shut.

"Still see them?" asked the Old Man.

"Yes," answered Shinn, "they're three-quarters of the way to the top. I'd say another forty minutes or so. What time is it?"

"Almost nine. Oh shit! Look at that!"

From the dark bottom of the dome emerged a rectangular shadow. It was easing slowly but steadily down the elevator shaft.

"They're onto us! Shinn! Do you see it?" cried the Old Man.

Shinn was already on the radio to Petroviny at the base of the tower. "Colonel, the elevator's coming down! Kill the tower power! Kill the tower power!"

The Old Man watched the elevator approach the climbers. Instantly aware of its movement as soon as it had started down, they were scrambling to keep ahead of it, dropping several feet at a time in their panic. But the elevator was gaining. Suddenly one of the climbers began to drop farther and faster, his arms flailing as he desperately reached out for a handhold to stop his plunge. Sickened, the Old Man watched the man fall the entire length of the open shaft. Just before he disappeared within the housing at the base of the tower, all of the lights went out and the elevator stopped. The remaining climber could not be seen in the dark shaft.

The line from the observation level rang in front of the vice president. He looked down at it. "No," he said, shaking his head. "No—I won't talk to you. *You* sweat for a while."

The Old Man couldn't keep his eyes off his watch. The sun was almost down and there had been no further activity from the tower. Shinn and the terrorists were playing a dangerous game, each waiting for the other to make the next move. For the first time, the Old Man was not pleased with Shinn's actions. He should keep a dialogue going. Keep the bastards in the tower talking; don't give them too much time to think. He walked over to the coffeepot and poured another cup. A hand touched his shoulder. He turned around, expecting it to be Benson. It was Davey Morales.

"Holy shit! You look like death warmed over," said the startled Key West substation chief.

"I'll never bad-mouth another Mexican cop as long as I live," responded Davey, reaching for a cup. The Old Man poured.

"What the hell happened? I sent word out just before we left Langley, although I didn't know if you were still in Allende."

"That saved my life."

"Sit down. Fill us in."

Shinn had joined them. "Morales?"

"Yes, sir, Mister Vice President. Excuse my appearance. I cooked in the Mexican desert all day yesterday and damn near froze to death last night. I haven't had a chance to change or clean up."

"No problem. We're just glad to have you with us. Has anyone filled you in on what's happening?"

"Yes, sir. The Air Force driver from Kelly says we have a real problem."

"Davey, what were you doing in the desert? What about Plotnikov? Did he come back with you?" asked the Old Man impatiently.

"He's dead." Davey sipped the coffee as he related the sighting of the terrorists in Allende and the resultant chase across Coahuila. "They left me to die. I figured I'd had the course. But the chief of police at Monclova was one savvy Latino. Your recall reached him and he checked Allende and found that we weren't there. Then he was told that we went hauling ass after the Palestinians. He got a police chopper from Monterrey and started a search. Had to call it off when night came, but at dawn he sighted our tracks just north of a little village by the name of Zaragoza; that's where we had left the highway. Found me about nine this morning. I was a bit dehydrated. They brought me around and we went searching for the terrorists. We found their camp, we think, but they were gone. I figure they had help and left sometime last night. Their car, an Isuzu Trooper, came back down the roadway in the early morning. I still had an AK-47 but it was jammed, and I had lost my handgun when the jeep rolled. I stayed hidden while the driver searched the jeep and made sure Plotnikov was dead. God, I wanted to jump him, but I was pretty weak and he was too damned alert and armed to the teeth. He looked for me for a while but went on, probably figuring I had started out across the sand. He knew I wouldn't get far if that were the case."

The Old Man nodded his understanding. "The others were already in-country by then, we figure, although we still don't know how they accomplished the penetration. We had wall-to-wall people on the border."

Davey continued, "We got back to Monclova in the early afternoon. I called Langley and was told that you and the team were on the way to San Antonio. The Mexicans took me across the border to the Air Force base at Del Rio. They strapped my ass in the backseat of a T-38 and zapped me to Kelly. And here I am."

"Are the Mexicans going to recover Plotnikov?" asked the Old Man.

"We picked him up on the way in and they'll turn the body over to his people in Mexico City. We weren't a bad team. And your hunch was right on. They came through Allende just like you had figured. We screwed up and missed them by a few minutes, but finally caught up with them—or rather, they let us catch up with them. We should have done better."

"We've got the top floor all to ourselves. Why don't you go clean up and take it easy for a while. We'll call you when it picks up," suggested the Old Man.

Davey tossed his drained paper cup into the trash. "I'll go hit the shower and be back up here in a few minutes. I'm cruddy, but I'm okay."

The Old Man watched Davey walk away. "Good man," he said under his breath. He repeated his evaluation to Shinn. "Damned good man—and pretty upset, I imagine. That's the second time he almost had them."

"Well," observed Shinn, "it's our turn now—for what that's worth."

Chapter 26

9:37 P.M.
Tower of the Americas

"Get the woman."

Haidari responded to ben-Ali's command by walking out onto the observation platform. The eight remaining hostages were seated against the inside wall, most with their legs drawn up to ward off the night breeze, the wounded guard prone. He had no color, his breathing was shallow, and his eyes were unmoving.

"He needs medical attention," pleaded the old Mexican on the cleaning crew.

"Silence," ordered Haidari.

"He will die," continued the old man.

"So will you," countered Haidari, swinging his Uzi around to point to the man.

"At least, some water," persisted the Mexican.

"If he is thirsty, let him drink urine," countered Haidari.

The young woman and her escort were huddled together at the far end of the group.

"You," indicated Haidari, pointing to the frightened young female.

"No! Please!" she pleaded, shrinking back against the wall as if she could force herself into it.

Two of the guards and her escort stood.

"She is just a girl," said one of the guards, taking an uneasy step forward.

Haidari raised his Uzi and pointed the barrel at the guard's chest. "You are fortunate. I do not have ben-Ali's impatience. Otherwise, you would be dead this moment. Instead, I will have the woman with no further comment, or you will wish that I had already given you the gift of a quick death."

The guard suddenly charged Haidari, arms outstretched. Haidari was caught off guard only for an instant. A short burst from the Uzi tore into the guard and the man fell forward, his momentum carrying him to within a foot of Haidari. Haidari placed his weapon a few inches from the man's head and fired another burst. The guard's skull disintegrated. The woman sucked in a great gasp of air and fainted.

"Move back," directed Haidari to the others. Too terrified to do otherwise, they stepped aside. Haidari reached down and roughly pulled the woman to her feet. His first slap did nothing, but the second and third roused her and she opened her eyes.

"Stand. You can stand. Don't tempt me to kill you here. You will come with me."

The woman, white with fear and unable to control her emotions, screamed and began to vomit. Haidari stepped quickly out of the way. When she was reduced to dry heaves he lifted her again. The woman stiffened her body and began flailing her arms, the motion twisting her in Haidari's grasp. "No! No! No!..." she repeated, her voice punctuated by continuous sobbing. Haidari grabbed her hair with his left hand and jerked her erect, covering the other hostages with his weapon. Alternately shaking her head violently from side to side and lifting it until her toes were about to leave the deck, he forced her up the short stairwell and over to ben-Ali. When he released his grip, the woman collapsed, unconscious.

Ben-Ali lifted the telephone to the command center once more. It was the fifth time in the last half hour. "This time, I will let it ring until they answer," he announced. "They will not force us to act before it is time."

A full minute passed before the ringing stopped. The Americans had undoubtedly figured that further refusal would be detrimental to their position.

"Fools! You think you can do such a thing and we will not respond? Turn on the power at once. I have the woman and in two minutes she goes over the side. Two minutes! Then you may watch the remaining hostages take the long step one at a time until they are all together at the base of the tower. After that, we detonate the weapon. It is over unless you do as I say." Ben-Ali slammed down the phone. "Take her to the fence!" he commanded. Haidari lifted the woman and carried her out to the observation platform. Kamal Adwan followed.

Turning to the Marine radioman, Shinn issued his order. "Tell Colonel Petroviny to turn on the power."

"Aye, aye, sir."

The Tower of the Americas jumped out of the darkness, its tall gray shaft illuminated by the upward-pointed floodlights at its base and the dome once more shining with its crown of white lights and the red anticollision lights on the antenna blinking steadily.

"Give me the glasses," said Shinn. Sighting the observation platform, he announced, "They have the girl outside." Quickly he picked up the tower phone and heard ben-Ali answer. "You have power," announced Shinn. "Do not harm the girl and I give you my word we will not cut it again."

"You are walking the edge of a very narrow blade—do not test the Shaheen. I will spare the woman for the moment, but she is the next to go if anyone enters any of the elevator shafts or you take any measures to deny us full access to this tower dome. Also, I remind you that you have but seven minutes to give me your president's reply to our demands."

Shinn's watch confirmed that it was almost ten o'clock. Turning to the others, he outlined their next move. "I have the president's approval to tell the Shaheen that the United States looks favorably upon their proposal and has called an emergency meeting of the UN Security Council. The name of the game, gentlemen, is time. We need time to figure out our next move—if we have any."

"Look!" called out Davey, pointing to the tower. The elevator was climbing toward the dome. "On the bottom of the elevator, it's the other climber!"

Shinn could see the man clinging to the underside of the elevator as it disappeared into the dome. "Give me the headset."

The radioman handed the vice president the transceiver.

"Petroviny, this is Shinn. Your other climber just rode the elevator up into the dome!"

"Good. We figured he was still okay. Only Matthews fell."

"Is there still a chance we'll get the bugs in place?"

"That was the original idea, Mr. Vice President. I'll have radio contact with him when he gets to where he can give me a call. I'll keep you informed."

"He's a very brave man, Colonel."

"I'll tell him you said that after we get him back."

Sergeant Henry Thompson Hoover slipped one hand down into the leather pouch clipped to his accessories belt and extracted one of the disc-shaped listening devices. Leaving himself hooked to the elevator, he peeled off the protective covering and pressed it hard against the bottom of the elevator. That's one, he thought. Looking around, he could see no way to place another one any closer to the observation level. The walls of the shaft were solid, and he was below the floor of that level. Methodically studying the situation, he let his eyes work their way down to the elevator doors that led into the restaurant level. Changing his grappling lock from the elevator to the guide rail on the side of the shaft, he worked his way down. The doors were closed, and a tentative inspection indicated that they were tightly locked in that position. The elevator itself was obviously the trigger that allowed them to open, but how? Hoover searched the outline of the doors. There had to be something, probably a cam or an electrical contact. High on the left side, he found what he was looking for—a mechanical cam that activated an electrical microswitch when the elevator reached its proper position in alignment with the doors. Now, slow down, Hoover, my boy, he said to himself. There could be someone on the other side of those doors. Reaching into his tool pouch, he slipped out his dikes and cut the wire from the microswitch. If his reasoning were correct, the electric door-opening motors were now disabled. All he had to do was move the mechanical cam and he could open the doors manually. First, he had to give a listen. Positioning himself, he placed his head against one of the brass doors and kept it there for five full minutes. There was no sound.

Grabbing the cam, he gave it a tentative tug. It was solid. Double-checking his hookup, he braced his feet against the wall and gave a stronger pull with both hands. The cam moved almost thirty degrees before the resistance became too much for him. Winded, he studied the design. There appeared to be an over-the-center position that the elevator could activate with ease, but another try indicated that it was too much for hand manipulation. He needed a lever of some kind. Unslinging his weapon, he extended the metal frame stock and wedged the barrel against the cam. Jesus, if the colonel finds out I used my weapon as a crowbar, he'll have a chunk of my ass for sure, thought Hoover. But what the hell! Tightening his stomach muscles, he forced a quiet grunt up from his gut just as he put his full weight and muscle to the stock of the weapon. The cam flipped into position! Lowering himself to the level of the floor of the restaurant, he listened for another five minutes. Still, no sound. Lord, I don't know if my credit is very good, he thought, but if it is, I'd surely appreciate a small advance.

Hoover wedged his hand against the inside of the overlapping doors and cautiously applied pressure. The door slid easily. He gave himself a one-inch opening and listened. Nothing. Opening it halfway, he pulled himself up and into the restaurant. The tower stairwell was beside the elevator. Holding his weapon at the ready, he hurried across the foyer and past the maître d's podium to the outside ring. He needed a place to study the interior. Looking back, he could see the upper-level lounge. That would be better, and the bar would provide a hiding place should he need one. No true Muslim would go near that bar. Detouring to check the kitchen — it too was empty, as expected—he noiselessly stepped up into the lounge. Before sliding behind the bar, he placed another listening device on the ceiling of the lounge. It was most probably a double layer, with an air space between the ceiling and the floor of the observation level, but it was the best he could do. Squatting down behind the bar, he whispered into his hand radio, "Colonel, this is Hoover. Over."

He had to adjust the volume from its lowest position before he caught the reply, " . . . where are you, Hoover?"

"In the lounge of the restaurant."

"Jesus! Get out of there and back down here!"

"Hey, Colonel, I'm as safe as in my mother's arms. I'm behind the bar. They won't come near me."

"There's nothing you can do there, Hoover. Place the bugs and get back down here."

"They're in position, but I don't know if they're going to pick up anything."

"We already hear the bastards. You done good, Hoover. Now come on down."

"Colonel, I can stay right here and maybe get one or two when they come down for chow supplies."

"No, you goddamned well cannot! Come down. That is an order, Sergeant."

"On my way, boss."

Before leaving the bar, Hoover retrieved a grease pencil from his pocket, hastily scrawled three words on the mirror behind the bar, and smiled with self-satisfaction. Hoover, you are one cool dude, he praised himself silently.

Bounding noiselessly down the few steps from the lounge, he started toward the elevator. The sudden movement of the doors prompted him to veer sharply to one side and brace himself against the wall. He realized that someone must have taken the elevator from the observation level and was about to enter the restaurant. Hoover let his jaw go slack, his open mouth enabling him to breathe more quietly. Reaching down, he slipped his assault knife from his boot.

The elevator doors remained open and there was no sound within. Hoover waited.

Aswar stood puzzled. Why had the doors not opened automatically? He felt a strange presence, but its meaning was unclear. Certainly no one could be in the restaurant. The drop of the elevator had earlier cleared the shaft, and there had been insufficient time for the Americans to have achieved a new climb. No, the electrical circuit to the elevator doors must be malfunctioning because of something that happened when the power had been cut off and then restored. For a moment he was tempted to close the doors and report the odd occurrence to ben-Ali. Deciding against such an action, he stepped out into the restaurant.

He never saw the figure that stepped from his left and wrapped an arm, rigid with contracted muscle, around his neck. Nor could he tell who was driving a sharp knee into the small of his back. He could only feel the sudden, unbearable pain of a blade sliding into his rib cage. A terrible bolt of lightning radiated from the sharp bend in his spine, surged upward into his head, and burst brilliantly into a million silver stars in the back of his eyes. Then, his brain died just as his throat was crushed, a desperate scream trapped inside.

Hoover heard the satisfying crack of the Arab's back as he bore down on the man with all of his strength and twisted his blade. Giving a final jerk to the body, he let it settle to the carpet. There had been little sound, and he was confident that no one above had heard the very brief struggle. But he did have a problem. He lifted his hand radio from his belt.

"Colonel, complications."

"What is it, Hoover?"

"I got me a dead Arab."

"Jesus! What happened? Are you able to get back down here?"

"Yes. One of them brought the elevator down to this level. I had to take him."

"All right, let me think for a moment—wait, never mind. Throw him in the elevator and bring him down."

"You got it." Hoover dragged Aswar inside and closed the doors.

Shinn held the mug of coffee to his face. Ben-Ali had received too calmly his message that the president was giving favorable consideration to his demands. No threats. No reiteration of the other demands. What was going on in the dome? CIA terrorist specialist Ted Benson provided part of the answer.

"We've been at this for about twelve hours. They've had the upper hand and have made their demands and have reached what we call the first plateau."

"What's that?" questioned the Old Man.

"Their first doubts. They know we sent someone up the elevator shaft. In other words, we're working on plans ourselves. They figured they had accounted for every possibility. But we surprised them with that one. Not damaging, mind you. But it has set them to thinking further. You see, up to now, we could call their bluff on a minor issue, if we were careful. We did that by cutting the power and refusing to talk to them for a while. Such a tactic will work at first, since they're still anxious to get their message out. But it only works once. Now that the first euphoria of success has passed, they've had time to reflect on the overall situation. I think the president did right by having you tell them he was favorably inclined toward their demand that we pull out of Israel. But they can't be sure we really mean it. In fact, their common sense will tell them we're stalling for time—which we are. But we have sown the seed of doubt: if we are truly considering their demand, what should their next move be? See the conflict in their minds? They may not want to use the weapon just yet."

"The elevator is going down!" suddenly called out FBI agent Myers.

"Colonel Petroviny, the elevator is coming down," relayed Shinn on the radio handset.

"Yes, Mr. Vice President, I know. One of my men is inside and we have one less terrorist to concern ourselves with."

"My God, he has one of the Palestinians with him?"

"A late Palestinian. He had to kill him."

"This could set them off!"

"Please stand by, sir. I'll get back to you in a moment."

Shinn wanted to tell Petroviny that taking out the Palestinian could be a grave mistake, but he knew that the colonel was very much aware of that. Instead, he contented himself with a remark aside to the Old Man, "He shouldn't have done that."

"I suspect he had no choice," ventured the Old Man.

Petroviny was waiting as the door opened. Two of his team picked up Aswar and carried him over to the side of the glassed-in tower enclosure.

"I've got Shinn on the horn. He's pretty pissed about this," said Petroviny.

"I had no choice, Colonel. He walked right in on me."

"What's done is done. We'll have to make the best of it. We may be able to use it to some advantage." Speaking into his walkie-talkie, Petroviny called the command post on the Marriott. "No ID. It may be awhile before they discover he's gone. When they do, sir, I suggest we say that he has defected."

"Terrorists don't defect, Colonel," responded Shinn.

"Well, tell them this one did. They obviously will discover the vacant elevator shaft. We have to tell them something. Why not claim a defection? It may work."

"It won't work, Colonel, but I'll give it a try. Except pray that this isn't the straw that breaks the camel's back."

Ben-Ali wondered why Aswar had not returned. It had been almost a half hour. "Haidari, come with me," he ordered. The two men entered the stairwell and descended to the restaurant level. Ben-Ali peered through the viewing window of the door.

"I don't see him," ben-Ali said.

"Perhaps he is in the kitchen," ventured Haidari.

They entered the restaurant, quickly closing the door as the alarm sounded.

"Aswar! Where are you?" shouted Haidari.

Ben-Ali walked to the elevator door and pushed the UP button. Nothing happened. He tried the doors, and stepped back in amazement as they slid apart. Even more surprising, there was no elevator. Leaning inside the shaft, he checked upward. The elevator was not back at the observation level. There was only one other place it could be. He peered down the open shaft, but the upward-shining lights prevented him from seeing it at ground level. Yet it had to be there. Haidari was beside him.

"What has happened?" asked Haidari very slowly.

"I don't know," answered ben-Ali. "And I am not anxious to speculate. Check this entire area first."

His Uzi at the ready, Haidari disappeared into the kitchen while ben-Ali walked the circle of the restaurant. They met back at the maître d's position and stepped up into the lounge.

"What is that?" asked ben-Ali, using his weapon to point toward the mirror behind the bar.

Haidari read the three words aloud, "Sem-per fi, Mac—what does that mean?"

"It means we have been taken for fools. Quickly let us gather some food and get back to the observation level. I want this area sealed off. We have one more task to perform before we complete this mission, but I will not let the Americans force us into finishing it before I decide."

"You think they have Aswar?"

"Where else would he be? Why is the elevator down below? We are up against very worthy adversaries, my brother. It makes this game so much more satisfying, does it not? But we can afford no more mistakes. Come, do as I say."

"What possessed you to go inside the restaurant, Hoover? They could have panicked and set off the weapon," chastised Petroviny. "You and Matthews were told exactly what to do."

"It just seemed like a good idea at the time, Colonel. I surely did want to wrap one of those Arabs around my boot knife. In the back of my mind was the hope that I'd get a chance to neutralize the weapon. It was dumb."

"And very brave, Sergeant. I may recommend you for a medal, but if I do I intend to pin it on your ass. We're just lucky you pulled it off."

"I understand, Colonel. It's just that I wish we could do something."

"So do I, Hoover, but you know how we play these games. No individual effort. Teamwork. As it is, you may have cost us all our lives."

"All right, Mr. Vice President, here is my recommendation. When they call, tell them that one of their number has defected and we have him in custody. Try and convince them of that. It may create some confusion. It's worth a try. If we can place even the tiniest trace of doubt in their minds, we gain something."

"Will do, Colonel. They're ringing us now." Shinn put down the radio handset and picked up the tower phone. "Shinn."

"What have you done with our brother?" Ben-Ali's voice would have carried to the top of the Marriott without the phone.

"He is in our custody."

"Impossible!"

"Then, he is still with you."

"No! Such arrogant lies are seriously jeopardizing our willingness to allow negotiations to continue."

"You have indicated that you are pleased with the president's response."

"That was before you violated our willingness to negotiate. Killing our brother ends our discussions."

"He is alive and well and recognizes the futility of further violence. If you and your people will join him, I will guarantee that the president is willing to continue negotiations at a less precipitous level."

"Unlike your president, you lie poorly. Aswar is dead. There is no other possibility. And so, we enter what I declare at the moment to be the final stages of our discussion. There is only one chance for continued negotiations. We wish to speak to the people of the United States. You will provide us with a television camera and a monitor."

"Then release the hostages."

"That cannot be done."

"In that case, we cannot provide you with a television crew."

"You will, or you sentence your people to death, one every hour until we receive what we demand."

"No, we will provide you with nationwide television coverage if you release the hostages. That is the only way it can be done." Shinn apprehensively looked back at Myers.

"Your answer is on the observation platform," interrupted the Old Man, continuing to hold the glasses pressed to his eyes. Shinn raised his own. Three of the terrorists were on the open platform, one holding the hostages at bay while the other two were beating one of the men. As Shinn and his people watched, the man was forced up a ladder and held at the top. Shinn picked up the tower phone. "All right, you get your television crew, but you must guarantee their safety."

"One man. He will bring a camera and a monitor. No one else."

"Take that man off the fence."

"He stays there until we speak to the people."

Shinn knew that now there was a test of wills. The penetration of the tower and the killing of the Palestinian had not resulted in the terrorists setting off the weapon. Perhaps he did have some control over the situation. "You will remove the man from the fence, first."

"Very well, we will remove him from the fence."

In an instant, Shinn realized he had pushed too far. It was the sarcasm in ben-Ali's voice. Shinn started to speak again, to accede to the request. But it was too late. The man was falling toward the plaza.

"Bastards! Cowards!" Shinn threw the phone to the floor and shouted across the space between him and the tower. CIA agent Benson grabbed his shoulders.

"Give them what they want, Mr. Vice President," advised Myers.

Already another hostage was being beaten. Benson picked up the phone, praying that it was still working.

"All right! You get the television coverage!" shouted Shinn into the receiver, then slammed it down. "Damn it all!" he continued, speaking to those around him. "I want sharpshooters up here! Get Petroviny and tell him I want snipers!"

"No, sir, we don't want that," argued Myers. "We might get one of them. Or maybe even two. But what good would it do? We can't do more than that. They won't expose themselves if we fire at them."

Shinn was shaking his head as if he could force the anger out of his skull. "Goddamn it—you're right, of course. But I'd just like to do something besides kowtow to their every whim."

"We can—now." The Old Man's words dropped like a stone on still water. "This is exactly what we need."

Every man in the command post raised his eyebrows.

"What do you mean?" asked Shinn.

"We've been conducting our response to these people based on their ultimate threat, the use of a nuclear weapon. What if these characters don't have the other weapon? Why haven't they used it? We've given them ample cause to do so. Oh, they're Shaheen, all right. I don't doubt that. But suppose they're a different bunch who are pulling off the bluff of the century? Could they really have gotten into the country with that damned thing? Think about it for a moment. Could this be a diversion? I sure hate to think that we let them walk right into Estados Unidos carrying a device the size of a hot-water heater under a blanket or something."

"We've got witnesses who said they saw some men carrying it into the tower this morning."

"Carrying what? A silver cylinder? That's easy enough to come by. Does your witness know what the device really looks like? I don't, except for what Davey has told me. Nor do any of you."

"Just what are you saying?"

"I'm saying that we have to get someone up in that tower to verify the presence of the weapon. If they are bluffing, we've got a whole new ball game and we're up at bat. We have to stall until we can verify the presence of the weapon."

"And the television cameraman can do that?"

"No, he can't. But Morales can."

"Of course!" added Davey. "I'm the only one who has seen the cylinders."

"They won't still have it packaged," cautioned Myers.

"No, but I'll know if it's the weapon. A television cameraman may not. Besides, if he does, he'll pass the word out and then where will we be?"

"Can you operate a TV camera?" asked Shinn.

"So, I get checked out. It's perfect. I'll have to be in radio contact with the television van to set up the shot and coordinate the shoot. I may even be able to talk to you without them knowing it," replied Davey.

"We need a man in the tower," continued the Old Man, "and Davey is the man we need. He has seen the terrorists, at least the original three. Two are dead, but if one of those in the tower is Kamal Adwan, we can feel pretty damned sure that the weapon is the companion of the one that took out the *Lincoln*. If there is no weapon or it's a fake, we turn Petroviny and his troops loose."

"Even if it means we lose some or all of the hostages?" asked Charlie Kelly.

"For Christ's sake, Charlie, that is not even a governing consideration at this point. This is not for publication, but those people were dead as soon as they were taken to that tower. We will make an effort to save them, but if push comes to shove, it's out of our hands. No life, or nine lives, is more valuable than the security of this country. Besides, our argument is probably academic. First, we need to confirm the presence of the weapon. One step at a time, Charlie. Just get us a camera crew."

Kelly hurried off.

"Morales," said Shinn, walking closer to Davey. "You know, of course, what you're walking into."

"If they have the weapon, being in the tower is no worse than being right here. After all, we're probably less than a thousand feet away from ground zero as it is."

Shinn smiled grimly. "I've been thinking about that."

Shinn faced the room full of press people. Until now, Charlie Kelly had been able to keep them in check. But their dissatisfaction with the sparse information given out by Shinn's press officer had called for Shinn's presence. It was almost three in the morning, but their excited conversation made the room as alive as a Vegas casino. Several started to yell out their questions simultaneously. Shinn held up one hand until everyone in the room understood his message and quieted.

"I have urgent duties, so if you wish me to answer your questions you must be brief and orderly. Yes?" said Shinn, recognizing an upraised hand.

"Sir, we are roughly twenty hours into this siege. Two hostages have died and one Marine. Do we have plans to assault the tower?"

"Not at the moment. The lives of the hostages are our first concern. We have an ongoing dialogue with the terrorists."

"Has the president responded to this crisis? Our White House correspondents know no more about the situation than we do here—which is darn little."

"You have to realize that this is a very delicate situation. Demands have been made on the United States, the United Nations, and Israel. It would not be proper for me, or the press, to anticipate the response of any of the authorities of those bodies of governments."

"Sir, the president has announced that a battle group is on station in the Mediterranean. Does that mean that we are about to strike Palestinian strongholds or sympathetic governments?"

"The president is handling the international situation. I am concerned with our domestic problem."

"Why haven't we just rushed the terrorists? There has to be a time when we consider that option."

"We have no access to the tower dome. The stairwells have been blown and mined. The elevators have been kept locked at the top except for the one you saw descend."

"Who was in that elevator, Mr. Vice President?"

"One of our people managed to reconnoiter the restaurant level of the dome. He was not able to penetrate the observation level, nor was it intended that he attempt that."

"Then, we will wait until all of the hostages are thrown off the tower before we act?"

"That is an insensitive and stupid question. We are trying to prevent the deaths of any more hostages."

"Who all are in the command center?"

"Myself, representatives of the FBI, military liaison officers, and a small staff of communications people. The mayor and chief of police of San Antonio have free access."

"No antiterrorist specialists?"

"We have two."

"How about the assault team at the foot of the tower?"

"For contingency operations as they develop."

"How long are you prepared to wait, sir?"

"As long as there is a chance at saving lives, we will continue to talk to the terrorists."

"Is there any chance they will blow up the tower and themselves with it?"

Shinn looked closely at the questioner, a reporter for the San Antonio *Express-News.* "It is always a possibility if they have the explosives to do so."

"Sir, we are not being fed enough information. The people have a right to know what is going on," persisted the man from the *Express-News.*

"The people have every right to expect the full protection of their local, state, and federal government. We will keep the public informed of all pertinent developments through my press officer, Charlie Kelly. You must understand that I have obligations that preclude frequent personal briefings. I have no more time."

Shinn walked from the room, leaving Charlie Kelly to deal with the clamor that erupted at his departure.

The camera team from KENS, San Antonio's CBS affiliate station, was waiting outside the command center when Shinn returned. The Old Man and Morales met him.

"Davey's been checked out on the minicam," briefed the Old Man. "We'll patch the TV control circuit into the command center. Davey will feed us ad-libs, in Spanish if necessary, every chance he gets. His main purpose will be to check on the weapon and the number of terrorists. In extremis, that is if they monitor every word he says, he will signal the presence of the weapon by the expression 'I say again'; if there is no weapon he will use the expression 'I repeat' instead. He can work either of those in any conversation, even if the terrorists are right beside him. Other than that, he will set up and shoot the terrorists' spiel."

"Will we go live nationwide?" asked Shinn.

"Not if they don't insist. But they will want to see themselves on the monitor and we can't reach it via closed circuit, so it will be at least local. The TV types want to go national," responded the Old Man.

"I think we should," decided Shinn. "It's early morning, but I suspect there will be an audience. Have a CBS lead-in announcement. Let's give them the full treatment—feed all three networks."

"If that's what you want."

Looking squarely at the Old Man to ensure he understood his meaning, Shinn continued, "That will prepare the people for any eventuality. I'd like to see Morales for a moment before he goes up."

Davey followed Shinn into the command center.

"Morales, feed us as much as you can. We will be asking mostly yes or no questions. Answer whenever you can do so. I will have your comm circuit piped into here."

"We've already arranged that, sir."

"Good. We'll be praying for all of you up there."

"Thank you." Davey found himself strangely anxious to get into the tower. Without a doubt, his chances of ever getting out alive were practically nonexistent. Yet, if there were no weapon, the terrorists would milk their TV coverage as long as they could, and somewhere within that time frame there could appear an opening. It was a very, very slim possibility, but it was better than no possibility at all.

His thoughts were interrupted by a touch on his elbow. The Old Man was standing beside him. "You don't *have* to do this, you know," he said quietly.

"Who else?"

"Good question. I was just fishing."

"That's not like you—with all due respect."

"Davey, you know the odds on this."

"Of course I do."

"Well, I just wanted to say that—well, when it's all over, I'll buy the bourbon."

"You're on—Thomas."

The Old Man leaned forward. "Don't push it, Morales."

Davey was ushered to the elevator by Colonel Petroviny. "They expect you to arrive on your knees, your hands clasped over your head, facing the back of the elevator. Expect to be patted down. You have any government ID?"

"Nothing but a civilian driver's license and an ID whipped up by the KENS people."

"Good enough. Good luck."

Petroviny's firm grip felt good. Davey placed his minicam and the monitor on the floor of the elevator and punched the observation-level button. Petroviny gave him a thumbs-up as the doors closed.

Ben-Ali, Labidi, and Haidari were waiting as the elevator reached the observation level.

"Stay in position," ordered Haidari as he entered and walked around Davey. "All right, outside. I will bring your camera."

Labidi ran his hands over Davey's body, thoroughly patting and feeling for any weapons. "Open your shirt and drop your pants," he ordered. He checked for wires before allowing Davey to rearrange his clothing. "ID."

Davey handed him his wallet and Haidari showed the driver's license and KENS card to ben-Ali.

"David Morales," read ben-Ali. "You are Mexican?"

"Mexican-American," responded Davey.

"Of course."

Davey shouldered his camera as he was led to an area adjacent to the wall of the security office. The monitor was set on one of two tables and plugged into a wall socket. "Let me see a picture," demanded ben-Ali.

"I have to set the transmitting antenna. The fence rods on the outside platform will provide a clear field. Is it all right?"

"Give me the lead and dish," instructed Haidari. "I will mount it for you."

Davey adjusted his headset and earphones and steadied the camera. "This is a test," he announced, "for light level."

"Let's see some flesh," came back the reply from the van.

"I need a person for correct flesh exposure," requested Davey.

"Him," directed ben-Ali, pointing to Labidi.

Davey refocused.

"That's good," came the voice from the van. "Can you answer questions?"

"Yes," replied Davey, adjusting his mike boom.

"Do you see the weapon?"

"No."

"No talking," ordered ben-Ali.

"I have to check with my control in the van for picture quality and setup."

Ben-Ali's eyes narrowed. "All right. I will be seated at this table. Is that satisfactory?"

"Yes. I should have the camera at the level of your face. May I have a chair?"

Labidi placed a chair and Davey sat. "This is good," he said.

Speaking into the mike, he checked arrangements with the van. "We're about ready up here. The monitor is showing the CBS logo."

"That is it. We'll have a fifteen-second lead-in with Dan Rather, then I'll cue you. Give me a go when you're ready."

"We are ready when you are," announced Davey to ben-Ali.

Labidi placed the wrapped sword of the Shaheen on the table in front of ben-Ali. "I am ready," said the Shaheen leader.

"It's a go," said Davey into the mike.

A voice came over the logo picture, "This is a special CBS News report."

The familiar black-haired and dark-eyed face of the CBS anchor appeared.

"This is Dan Rather reporting. We are going live to the Tower of the Americas in San Antonio, Texas, where Palestinian terrorists have held nine hostages since early yesterday morning. At their request, we are presenting a statement by their leader, Muhammad ben-Ali."

Rather faded and he was replaced by a long shot of the tower, then a zoom to place the dome full screen.

"You're on," said the voice from the van as the dome faded and the face of ben-Ali materialized, slightly off center. Davey adjusted his aim and pointed to ben-Ali, who had already watched his image appear on the monitor.

"I am Muhammad ben-Ali of the New Shaheen Palestinian liberation forces. The sacred army of Islam has been mobilized, and this is the first of a series of incursions into your homeland. The Palestinian people have joined forces with the mighty warriors of all Islam nations, and the United States of America is being brought to the court of Islamic justice. Your crime is the establishment and support of the illegal state of Israel and the displacement of the Palestinian people from their rightful homeland. We have informed your president, and the secretary general of the United Nations, and the prime minister of the bastard state of Zionists, of our demands to right this injustice. Our presence here in this tower is but the first of a continuous penetration of your land to exact retribution for the persecution and death of Palestinians and our brother Muslims. Even as I speak, our forces are preparing themselves for the jihad that will cleanse you of your sins against God and restore his chosen people to their land. We are the vanguard of Islamic justice. You have ignored the teachings of Abraham and Moses and even of the prophet Jesus, and established a land of evil. You are the great satan, America, and there is little time for you to achieve salvation. Rise up in protest to this great wrong. Force your government to comply with our demands or face the wrath of Allah!

"We will occupy this tower for twenty-four more hours. Then we will destroy it as a message of our intent. We die for our cause with the joy of martyrs. The next blow by the New Shaheen will be even more severe, and we will continue to strike until your support of the Jews is completely and forever ended. We have spoken. Allahu Akbar!"

"Stay on him, Davey. We're cutting back to Rather. Can we talk?"

"Yes."

"Find the weapon."

"Yes."

"Woodridge, what are you doing here?" asked Shinn of the presidential aide who had just appeared at his elbow.

"The president asked me to come and brief you on events taking place at the Washington level. It's all happening very fast, Terence. Let's get together with your team over at the table."

After everyone was seated and coffee was being passed, Woodridge began. "At noon, the *Post* intends to break the story that there is a nuclear weapon in the tower. They have agreed to sit on it until then, but they feel the word is out and will be all over the country by word of mouth before that."

"They can't do that! They're dooming San Antonio to certain annihilation!" exclaimed Shinn.

"We can't stop it. At first, there was just in-house press speculation. They knew what happened to the *Lincoln*, so it was just a matter of tying in the Shaheen to the tower. Somewhere there was a leak in the White House, and they've been down our throats ever since. All three networks intend to put out a special report at noon, eastern time. They claim it is a matter of civil defense, and they have a point. The San Antonio papers must have it by now."

"Even if they do, they're cooperating with us. They know the stakes," argued Shinn.

"The president is issuing a restraining order under his Emergency Powers Act, but the story is already at the city desks. Too many people are aware of it. There's no way we can kill it now. Without a doubt, the phones in San Antonio homes are starting to ring even now," continued Woodridge.

"Look, we have a man in the tower, one of our own people," countered Shinn. "He took the place of the cameraman for the terrorists' broadcast. There is the very slightest possibility that there may be no nuclear weapon up there. His job is to confirm it, if possible. And he may be able to do something, we just don't know. But whether it's there or not, when the people of this city hear or read the report that there is a nuke, even if it is worded as a possibility, they are going to evacuate. Can you imagine the chaos? And if the Shaheen have the weapon, that is exactly the situation they have stated will cause them to detonate it."

"The president says you are free to pull out your people."

Shinn sat back in ill-disguised disbelief. "Evacuate? What kind of government would do such a thing? Save our own ass and to hell with everyone else? Absolutely not. Every man here knows exactly where we stand and not one has given the slightest indication of bugging out. We'll see this through. I'm scared and I suspect we all are. What could the president have been thinking?"

"He just wanted you to have the option."

"Well, he can screw his option. As long as we're here, and we have a man in the tower and Petroviny's team at its base, we have a chance. It's past four. We need at least a couple more hours. Rather than go out quietly, I'll authorize an assault on the tower if that's all we have left."

"For what it's worth, your response is exactly what the president said it would be."

Shinn looked at the others. "If any of you wish to leave, nothing will be said."

"Mr. Vice President," spoke up the Old Man, "each of us has had his ass in the crack before. Hell, as for myself, my liver won't let me kill the aches and pains anymore with good bourbon—or even bad bourbon—and I've been laid by the most qualified whores in the Western Hemisphere, so what's left? This isn't the worst way to go, anyhow. Besides, we're in a much better position than we were twelve hours ago. Davey is one hell of a thinker. Let's give him his chance."

The silence and smiles of the remainder of Shinn's team backed up the Old Man's comment.

"Colonel Fisher, I want a pair of Air Force attack aircraft holding out of sight of the tower as soon as you can get them there. I want them relieved on station for continuous coverage, and all are to carry missiles that can be locked on the tower when the time comes. Have them check in with us on our air control circuit. Only I will issue the attack order."

"I have already ordered a squadron of A-7s to Kelly. In fact, they have arrived within the last hour and are being refueled. They have all the equipment to do the job. After dawn would be best. The terrorists will never see them until the missiles are released," replied Fisher. "I know what we're all thinking: it won't do any good if the dead man's switch is being held in the tower. But if Morales can signal otherwise—we would need only a few minutes."

"Then that's the plan," confirmed Shinn. "There is one other factor. Assuming the dead man's switch is not activated, will the destruction of the tower detonate the weapon?"

Fisher replied, "If the weapon itself is armed, there is a good chance that it will. If they have the weapon arming switch off, regardless of the status of the dead man's switch, it's possible for the weapon to withstand the shock and not detonate. We've had aircraft accidents and nothing happened."

"Then we need to get some word to Davey," suggested the Old Man.

"I assume you are returning to Washington," said Shinn to Woodridge.

"That was my instruction."

"Don't look so damned guilty. There is nothing you can do here," comforted Shinn.

Woodridge obviously was uncomfortable. "Good luck to all of you. I know there is no humor in the situation, but I guess now we all know how the men in the Alamo felt."

Shinn nodded. "Good analogy. Give the president our best. He has his own problems and they may be even more serious than ours. Now get out of here and let us get back to our work."

"This thing is pretty heavy," commented Davey. He had been sitting opposite ben-Ali since the terrorist had made his statement. "Are we going back on the air?"

Ben-Ali rose and spoke to Haidari, but as with all the conversations between the Shaheen, their words were in Arabic. Davey used the distraction to call the van, trying to move his lips as little as possible. "Still got a picture?"

"We're on tape. What's happening?"

"Stand by."

"Place your camera on the table. We will be making another statement but not for a while," ordered ben-Ali.

Davey lifted the minicam from his shoulder and made a play of casually putting it on the table, leaving it cocked in such a fashion that the red POWER ON light would be shielded. With the lens set at its widest angle, the camera would still be picking up a view of a large segment of the observation level, including the door that led out to the open platform and the security office. "I'm down— going off the phones for a moment," he announced, intentionally loud enough so that the others could hear the words and not be suspicious.

Ben-Ali and Haidari walked away. Labidi stayed with Davey, his face expressionless and his hands casually fingering his weapon, which was still slung across his shoulder. "You can get something to drink, if you like," said Labidi, pointing to the coin-operated soft drink machine. Its lock was damaged and the door slightly ajar.

Davey was surprised at such a concession. He *would* take something; his act of acceptance would form a tiny bond between him and the Palestinian, a vestige of civilized behavior. He selected a cola and took several steps toward the exterior of the observation level. Labidi did not protest, but Davey stopped. It would be better not to move beyond whatever limits the terrorist had in his mind.

Outside, the many-colored lights of San Antonio flickered from horizon to horizon, a million tiny fires distorted by the radiation of the city's heat and the passing of the mild night winds. There was steady traffic on the freeway to the east and also on the interstate, but it did not appear frantic. To the west the brightly lit Hilton Palacio Del Rio sat like a great, flat monolith, its face illuminated by a series of floodlights and a great number of room lights. Most of those inside were undoubtedly sleepless and watching the tower through their windows, certainly unaware that they were less than a half mile from a potential ground zero position.

The terrorists had occupied the tower for only twenty-one hours, but Davey was surprised to see evidence that the presence of a nuclear weapon was still not known by the general population. It was a tribute to the vice president's swift and positive measures as soon as he had arrived on the scene. Davey's thoughts also reminded him of his purpose in the tower. Where was the weapon?

Could it truly be a bluff? He sipped his drink and gently edged toward the security office, Labidi following him with his eyes.

"This is the first time I have been in the tower," said Davey casually. "You picked an ideal target."

"You do not live here?" responded Labidi suspiciously.

"Oh, I do now, since I got my job with KENS. I came here from Austin."

Labidi had no idea where Austin could be, but he was satisfied with Davey's answer to his question. "You members of the news media are a privileged class."

"I beg your pardon?"

"You have access to this tower with us and we will let you return to your people when we are through with you. You are not a hostage. It is sort of an unwritten law."

"You use us, of course."

"Certainly. That gives you a value to us above that of your life. Our message gets out to the people. That is very important, to get our message out to the people of the West. Your press is so strongly Zionist."

"We have a very free press."

Labidi grinned broadly. "Controlled by Jewish wealth."

Davey recognized a second opportunity to gain some measure of rapport with the Arab. "True enough. But the Jews do not have the influence over us you seem to grant them."

"No? I am a student of American politics and economy, or I was before I became a warrior with my brothers. Consider your national elections. The candidate with the Jewish support and Jewish money is the strongest candidate, is he not?"

Agree with him, thought Davey. You have found an opening!

"But not always the one elected."

"That is occasionally true, but the support always has an impact on the candidate's platform and performance in government. You cannot deny that," countered Labidi.

"That is part of our system. Representative government. You take care of your constituency, but not to the detriment of others, necessarily." That's it, thought Davey, don't agree on everything. Make him want to convince you, but remain sympathetic.

"You are of Latin extraction, a member of a minority group in your own country."

"Within certain limits, I guess you could say that."

"You do not feel oppressed?"

"Oppressed? The mayor of this city is Mexican-American. So

are a number of our city officials. San Antonio is a showplace of Hispanic culture. We are the fastest-growing ethnic group in the United States."

Labidi walked over and stood peering at the lights of the city, all the while keeping Davey within his view. "What you have out there in the night is what you have in every city in this land. A Jewish-controlled economy, an immoral code of conduct that sanctions the flaunting of sacred law, whether it be Christian, Jew, Muslim, or whatever. Right now, down among those buildings and houses, drugs and intoxicants are flowing freely, and fornication is a way of life. You, yourself, Morales, may be a moral person, but your fellow citizens wallow in the most corrupt society the world has ever seen. The Shaheen will erase such an abomination and its satellite Israel from the community of world nations."

Davey's heart skipped a beat, not because of Labidi's words but because of the dim reflection he could now see in the glass panels surrounding the observation level: the interior of the security office. On the table near the center of the office was a long cylindrical object. A smaller cloth-wrapped package was beside it. Seated next to the table was Kamal Adwan! Using his response to Labidi's argument as a cover, he took several steps and placed himself beside the Palestinian. "What you say is most probably what you believe, but you do not know this country. Yet you condemn it. I respect your religious belief and almost admire your zeal. But you are perverting the true meaning of the Koran—indiscriminate mass murder cannot be justified under any circumstances. Those people down there are innocent of any wrongdoing against the Palestinian people. Hell, a great number of them don't even know what a Palestinian is."

Labidi's eyes narrowed. "After this night, they will."

It was difficult for Davey to ascertain much detail in the window reflection, and he was taking pains not to concentrate on the scene within the security office, deliberately averting his gaze from time to time as if he were randomly surveying the city. But he could tell that Adwan had both hands resting in his lap; they appeared to be holding his weapon. And on the edge of the table, easily within his grasp but ignored for the moment, was a small boxlike object. That could very well be the dead man's switch remote detonator for the weapon. If so, the terrorists were not continuously keeping the switch armed! True, it was only an arm's reach away, but that lapse of vigilance could give Davey and Shinn's team the opportunity they so desperately needed. An

extremely long shot, at best, but sufficient to generate a new feeling of hope within Davey. Already, the discovery was germinating
the seed of a plan in his mind. But first, he had to get the word to
the command center.

"Will you be making another statement?" he asked.

"Ben-Ali will speak shortly after dawn."

"I need to set up the broadcast with my people down in the
van. It is already five o'clock."

Labidi nodded, noticing the first lighting of the sky to the east.
"Then let us prepare." Leading Davey over to ben-Ali, he informed
his leader of the necessity to communicate with the TV van.

"It is almost time for prayer. I will get the others. You monitor
Morales. He can use the time to make arrangements. I want to
delay until we can be sure of maximum exposure," directed
ben-Ali.

"Seven o'clock would be eight o'clock on the East Coast and
five o'clock on the West Coast," offered Davey.

"Seven-thirty, then. I wish no longer than that."

Why? thought Davey. Have you decided that will be the time
you detonate the weapon? Seven-thirty—two-and-a-half hours
until Armageddon?

Chapter 27

July 20, 6:16 A.M.
Command and Control Center, Marriott Hotel

Still wearing the headset that he had acquired from the air controlman assigned to the command center, Colonel Fisher leaned over toward Shinn and reported, "We have a pair of A-7s orbiting the tower, twenty miles out at fifteen thousand feet, Mr. Vice President. They're loaded for bear and all it'll take is your execute command and they can have their weapons on the tower in ninety seconds. That's our lead time. They'll be relieved on station every ninety minutes."

"That's excellent. What are they carrying?"

"Each one has six missiles. Daylight TV guidance with blast and fragmentation warheads. They'll take the top right off the tower."

"And everyone with it."

"Yes, sir."

Shinn sat down next to the Old Man. "What do we tell Morales?"

"Tell him the truth. He knows what the situation is."

"No. I don't want to leave him without any hope of survival. It could affect his performance. I want his judgment to reflect the fact that his actions will have a direct bearing on whether he lives or dies. No suicide stuff. In his mind, there has to be some reasonable expectation of success."

The Old Man pursed his lips, then leaned back and sighed. "Let me tell you something about Davey Morales. He is the best young operative I have ever worked with. When he first reported to my control, I had him in the thick of the most dangerous drug operations in southern Florida and the Gulf. He mixed with the *numero unos* as well as the runners and was personally responsible for breaking up a Caribbean cartel that was doing a billion dollars worth of cocaine a year. When I sent him into Cuba, he adapted overnight and damned near intercepted the weapons transfer from the Soviets to the Palestinians. Then, he actually caught up with them in that hellhole Coahuila and failed to stop them. Since the loss of the *Lincoln*, he's been carrying too much guilt, and when I suggested he go up in the tower he pulled me aside and thanked me for giving him the chance to redeem himself. Imagine that. He knew damned good and well what his chances were of ever coming back alive, but he was as tickled as a kid with a new bike. You tell him anything you want. And if there is one chance in a trillion that anyone can create the opportunity we need, Davey is that person. If we can get the message to him, when he gives us a go, we better be ready to execute before he gets all of the words out of his mouth."

Shinn nodded and placed one hand on the Old Man's knee. "When I agreed for you and Morales to be on this team, it was with the thought that just such a circumstance as this would require your expertise. It was a long shot and several people questioned your worth. I know now I made a good decision, maybe the best decision I've made during this entire crisis. You have a great deal of affection for him, don't you?"

"Like a son," said the Old Man. "I'll never forgive myself if we bust his ass because we aren't ready."

"We won't let him down—Thomas."

With the sun came the realization within the command center that down among the homes of San Antonio, thousands of telephones were ringing as friends and relatives all over the country were calling to confirm their fears. The residents of San Antonio, the ones closest to the scene, were the last to be getting the word that there might be a nuclear weapon in the Tower of the Americas. In their panic, they were still taking time to alert their neighbors, who in turn alerted theirs. A gigantic pyramid of fear was spreading at unbelievable speed, and all manner of vehicles were pouring from the residential areas onto the freeways. The traffic was thickening rapidly, and the sound of sirens and the sight of rotating red and blue lights were becoming constant as the inevitable accidents slowed traffic to a crawl or in many cases blocked the exit routes.

Downtown San Antonio was completely bare of pedestrians, and only an occasional car passed along the deserted streets. The police cordon around the area was still in place, Chief Peyton having passed the word that there was a plan underway to take the terrorists. He also issued orders that any officer who attempted to desert his post was to be shot.

Ben-Ali and his companions watched the chaos developing and realized that it actually was of little consequence to their purpose. The bumper-to-bumper traffic was barely moving and would undoubtedly be unable to move at all within minutes. Only those on the perimeter of the city would have any chance of making it to the outlying areas, and even those who reached the outskirts of San Antonio would find their suburban neighbors in the same situation. A million people were holding themselves hostage by their own inability to deal with mass panic. There was absolutely no cognizance or concern for any civil defense preplanning, as sparse as it was in the first place. Within the hour, they would be killing each other in their desperate attempt to save themselves.

The efforts of the police and the military who had been hastily mustered in an attempt to preserve some order during the evacuation were simply being overpowered. Shinn directed the radio and TV stations to issue pleas for order, but such pleas were futile.

In such an atmosphere, Davey placed his call to the TV van. Shinn held up his hand for silence as Davey came up on the TV control circuit.

"Control, this is Morales. The Palestinians are requesting a setup for a broadcast as soon as possible. *I say again*, the Palestinians are requesting an immediate broadcast."

"Got it, Morales," replied one of the KENS people manning the relay van. "We'll notify the network and be ready. Request you stay on the headset while we check."

"Will do."

Shinn shook his head. "Davey just verified the presence of the weapon. We're back to square one." To Davey he spoke into his tap to the TV circuit, "Clear?"

"Clear," responded Davey quickly, indicating they could talk.

"We're set to assault the tower on a moment's notice. From this point on, all we need is a ninety-second mark. Any chance at all?"

"It's not over until the fat lady sings," replied Davey laconically. "Stay with me."

Ben-Ali paced the floor of the observation level, periodically looking out to check the progress of the evacuation. Things were going from bad to impossible with respect to the frantic citizens of San Antonio. This pleased ben-Ali, for it signaled certain success to his plan. Even when the people knew of the weapon, they could not escape, not within a reasonable time. Certainly, other cells of the Shaheen could use the same tactics in the tower at Seattle, or the New York Pavilion, perhaps even in the Washington Monument, although such tactical penetration would no longer be as simple as it had been with the Tower of the Americas. "How soon will they be ready?" he asked Davey.

"They are setting it up now. In just a few minutes, I'm sure. I think you should change your location a few feet to take advantage of the morning sun. We'll get a much clearer picture. Normally, we use artificial lights to augment natural light. I don't even have any reflectors."

"Where do you want me?"

"Just move to your left a few feet. Here, I'll position the table." Davey slid the table to within two feet of the doorway to the security office and sighted through his minicam. By adjusting his lens he could bring the doorway into the picture while still maintaining a center focus on ben-Ali. He would have to assume that Adwan's position and stance within the security office would remain unchanged. That was the unknown that bothered him. Davey busied himself with arranging his chair opposite the one ben-Ali would use. Adwan came from the security office, carrying an oblong, cloth-wrapped object. As ben-Ali sat, Adwan placed the object on the table in front of ben-Ali and backed away to stand in the doorway. *In the doorway.* He did not return to the security office! Davey could hardly believe the stroke of luck. With Adwan there, in full view, the time for the fat lady to sing could be very close.

"We're almost ready here," reported Davey.

"Five minutes," replied the van, then Shinn came on again. "Clear?"

"Clear," replied Davey.

Shinn's voice was low and calm. "How do things look?"

Davey continued fiddling with his lens. "Possible. Be ready. Petroviny in position?"

Shinn hesitated. Davey was assuming the assault was going to be made by Petroviny and his antiterrorist team. Why not? Shinn had merely used the word "assault" and said nothing about an aerial attack. That was good, for Davey would figure that if the assault could be precisely timed, he would have a chance at survival. That was the way Shinn wanted it, and in the long run it was better for Davey not to know that the assault would undoubtedly result in his death. That was the way it had to be, just as it had to be with respect to the hostages. "Ready," responded Shinn.

"We have a go," reported the van, and Davey once more watched the CBS logo appear on the monitor. As before, it was followed by the face and words of Dan Rather, then a fade to the tower, a close-up of the dome, and a fade to the sinister face of ben-Ali. Davey pointed at the Palestinian, who began immediately to speak.

"The time of the Shaheen is at hand and I raise the sword of my ancestors in salute to the heritage they have provided us." As he talked, ben-Ali unwrapped the cloth and held up the remnant of the ancient broadsword. "This is the sword of the Shaheen, which honored itself almost twenty centuries ago when it first tasted the blood of infidels. This day, it strikes a much greater blow for Palestine. Even as I speak and hold this blade over the people of this city of the damned, there is chaos and the turning of brother against brother.

"Death to the infidels! Death to the Zionists! Death to the enemies of the one true God! To my brothers who follow us on this holy path . . ."

Davey waited until the digital timer at the bottom of his inch-and-a-half monitoring picture was coming up on the even minute. His lips, pressed against the mike boom, were hidden by the minicam. Ben-Ali's strong voice should mask the sound of his own voice. Quietly and without movement or emotion, he signaled Shinn. "Stand by. Three, two, one—mark."

Ben-Ali was continuing his tirade against the people of the great satan.

"Now!" called out Shinn.

"This is Bridesmaid. Execute! Execute! Execute!" ordered Colonel Fisher over his air control circuit.

Major "Dink" Toohey shoved his throttle forward and max-rolled his Corsair II to the left. His wingman, twenty yards off his right wing, followed with the precision of a shadow. Together, the two A-7s accelerated to Mach .95 as they dove for their five-hundred-foot attack altitude.

"Advise when locked on, Crusher. We'll take it as close as we can. Salvo on my command."

"Will do, Dink."

Toohey eased his charging Corsair II into a long, swooping flare and steadied on five hundred feet by his radar altimeter. Checking his aft quarters, he could see the nose of his wingman riding just a few feet off his right wing tip. Any moment now he should be able to identify the tower. A thin veil of morning haze still hung over San Antonio, a gray whisper of condensation that had lingered through the night. Gradually, the central city emerged from the gloom, and there in its middle, reaching up above all else, was the thin shaft and thick dome of the Tower of the Americas.

"Got it, Crusher."

"Me, too."

Davey leaned forward in his chair, raising himself slightly into a crouched position. Very slowly he eased his right leg back to give him leverage for when the time came. Twenty seconds had elapsed. Apparently concentrating on the animated face of ben-Ali but actually scanning a wider area ahead, he adjusted his position to give himself a better view of Adwan and Haidari. Although his right eye was pressed into the rubber cup of the minicam eyepiece, his open left eye could observe Adwan still standing in the doorway of the security office. Davey leaned farther forward and adjusted his lens. Ben-Ali's face filled the monitor.

Thirty seconds, Davey counted silently.

"Can anyone see them yet?" asked Shinn.

"They should be coming in from the south," stated Fisher. "They will be hard to pick up."

"I can't see a thing," observed Shinn, keeping his glasses pressed to his eyes.

"Then neither can the Shaheen," observed the Old Man.

Major Toohey's weapons-ready lights were all green. Nestled under his wings were two three-missile clusters of Maverick AGM-65Bs, and the lights indicated that the missile-guidance gyros were up to speed. He had the small blob of the tower dome in his gun sight, and as soon as he pressed his uncage switch the protective covers slid back from the noses of the missiles and their video circuitry came alive. His cockpit monitor glowed brightly with a picture of the upper portion of the Tower of the Americas. The second of the Maverick series of air-to-ground missiles, the chubby eight-foot-long dash-65B, with its enhanced scene-magnification TV camera, carried a two-hundred-and-fifty-pound blast and fragmentation warhead. Once released, it would accelerate quickly to its supersonic attack speed. Toohey and his wingman would rapid-fire all twelve missiles, starting at maximum range, then pull skyward to escape the blast forces. Toohey had been briefed that a diversion would be taking place once he received his execute signal. He wondered how it was going.

Davey continued to focus the minicam on ben-Ali, but his mind was furiously reviewing the details of his plan. Ben-Ali was a mere four feet in front of him. Adwan was perhaps five feet to one side. Haidari was a good fifteen feet away and still had his weapon casually slung over his shoulder. It would take a good three or four seconds to react and unsling his weapon. Davey intended to be through the security office doorway by then. Labidi would be out of the immediate action, since he was over by the stairwell observing the hostages. The digital timer indicated that sixty-five seconds had elapsed.

He would have to throw the heavy minicam at ben-Ali, then lunge at Adwan in the doorway and charge over him into the room. It was about eight feet from the door to the weapon. All things considered, he would allow himself five seconds' lead time. If his calculations were correct, Petroviny and his troops would be bursting through the stairwell door about the time he reached the weapon. That would distract ben-Ali, Haidari, and Labidi. If he hit Adwan hard enough, he should have time to turn off the weapon's arming switch before the Palestinian could recover and reach the deadman's switch box. Adwan then would have to depress the plunger, arm the box, and release the plunger. That would give Davey an additional second or two, which would be his cushion.

Eighty seconds. Davey cocked every muscle in his body.

The tower dome completely filled his cockpit viewer. Major Toohey depressed the missile-track switch on his control stick and watched the cross hairs on his viewer center on the dome. His missiles had lock-on.

Davey took a deep breath, hurled the minicam into ben-Ali's face, and charged head-low into Adwan. Although he outweighed the smaller Arab by about twenty pounds, it was as if he had plowed into a very determined linebacker. Nevertheless, Adwan, caught off guard, didn't have time to completely set himself, and Davey's pumping legs carried them both into the security office. Adwan toppled backward toward the table, roaring with rage and flailing his arms as he struggled to maintain his balance. Davey dove for the weapon.

The two A-7s were closing on the tower at almost a thousand feet per second. Major Toohey could already visualize their missiles pulverizing the dome of the tower. All he had to do was release the missile-track switch and the deadly Mavericks would erupt from under the wing of his speeding aircraft, their self-homing capability steering them unerringly toward the target. He pressed his thumb against the radio button on top of the throttle grip and alerted his wingman, "Okay, Crusher, stand by for my release mark: three . . . two . . . one . . . fire!"

The twelve Mavericks leapt from under the wings of the two Corsairs in four smoking streams.

Toohey hauled back on his control stick and grunted to tighten his stomach muscles as he was pressed deep into his seat by the six-g pull-up. The two Corsairs went vertical.

Ben-Ali was almost in the door of the security office when he stopped in his tracks. Just outside the wall of windows was a rain of incoming missiles. Raising his fists, he threw back his head and let the words roar into the confined air within the doomed observation level, "Satan! Satan! Satan!"

Vice President Terence Shinn stood slack-jawed as the top of the tower erupted into an orange ball of flame. Black smoke and debris hurled outward like an expanding universe. For an instant, his heart stopped and his brain ceased to function, both organs frozen in fear at the possibility that the explosion was nuclear. But the shock wave barely shook him, and the fire reached out to only a hundred feet or so. Even before he could speak he could see the tangle of metal and concrete emerging from the smoke.

"Dear Jesus," muttered Shinn. "We got 'em."

"God rest you, Davey," prayed the Old Man.

No one else in the command post spoke or moved.

Chapter 28

8:52 A.M.
Situation Room, White House

For a long moment, the President of the United States and those around him watched the devastation of the top of the Tower of the Americas. Then, as if a fresh breeze had entered the room, the bitter, sickening smell of Armageddon that had permeated the underground chamber for the past forty-eight hours began to dissipate. Across the front wall, the array of television monitors had multiplied the instant of the attack as if one were inside a fly's eye looking out. As the black smoke cleared, the president sucked in a long breath. The tower's entire dome had disappeared, leaving a stub of concrete and bent steel rods where the dome had once been connected to the shaft.

The camera holding the scene slowly panned downward and stopped at the bottom of the shaft. Irregular chunks of smoldering metal and concrete, none apparently larger than a foot or so across, lay about as if a meteorite shower had plunged to earth around the base of the tower. Off to the left side of the picture was what appeared to be a crumpled body, but as the monitoring camcorder zoomed in, closer inspection revealed that it was only half that.

"My god," murmured a quiet voice in the rear of the room.

The president picked up his direct line to San Antonio. "We saw the whole thing, Terence. Good job."

"Thank you, Mr. President. We have Petroviny's team approaching the site to recover the device. It obviously wasn't armed. Morales did his job."

"How is the overall situation there, Terence?"

"Well, as you can see, there is debris all around the base of the shaft. The column appears stable and relatively undamaged, except for the top, of course. We still have a police cordon around the area. The traffic on the freeways and all of the major arteries is unbelievable; however, most of it is stopped, and the people are out of their cars. The San Antonio police will be trying to clear the roads as a first priority. We are making announcements on all TV and radio stations telling people that the crisis is over and urging them to be patient until we get things under control. It's a municipal problem, Mr. President, and I am trying to stay out of it."

"I understand. How many hostages did we lose?"

"We believe there were eight still in the dome."

"Tragic, Terence, but a small price when you consider the alternative."

"Yes, sir, I suppose so."

The president handed the phone to one of his aides. "Stay with the vice president until we are sure there is no further danger."

"Will you be making a statement, sir?" asked the president's press secretary.

"As soon as we can get airtime. The nation needs to be informed of what has happened and why. Have me a briefing sheet ASAP."

"Yes, sir." The press secretary motioned to several others within the room, and they formed a small huddle over one of the corner desks.

"I need to speak to Malenkatov," announced the president, picking up the black and yellow–striped command-post phone. In the oval office the phone was red, but here in the command center there were seven red phones—thus, yellow and black was set aside for the Moscow line. He heard the Soviet interpreter pick up the line and then his interpreter ask for the General Secretary.

Yuri Malenkatov's basso profundo voice came on the line. "Yes, Mr. President, we are here anxiously waiting for your call."

"It's over, Yuri. We blew off the top of the tower."

"Then . . . the device? It was not detonated?"

"No."

"We are all very much relieved. You understand, Mr. President, that we have already disciplined those responsible for this tragic mistake."

"Mistake, Mr. General Secretary? Yuri, let's cut out the bull-shit. How many more devices are out there?"

"There are no others, and there will be none."

"The American people will demand satisfaction for this."

"They will have it from the Soviet Union. I will make a public announcement in five hours. By then, those responsible will have been executed and will be named."

"We would like to carry that announcement live, Yuri."

"Yes, of course. Our people will make the necessary arrange-ments. It is over, Mr. President."

The President of the United States looked up at the status board of terrorist strongholds. "No, Yuri, it is just beginning. We have come too close. You know what we must do."

"Yes, Mr. President. We will not interfere."

Rear Admiral Thomas A. Gilbert, Commander of Special Car-rier Battle Group Sierra on station in the Mediterranean, looked one final time at the decoded and verified top-secret order from Washington, then handed it to his aide. "Put it in the special file. It will have some historical importance." Turning to his assembled staff, he fixed his eyes on the tactical chart of the Middle East. Iran, Syria, and Libya were dotted with small red bomb symbols. "Exe-cute Operation Vengeance," he directed.

His order went directly to the ship's captain and the Air Boss. Immediately, the first A-6E shot off the port catapult of the USS *Theodore Roosevelt* and was followed within two seconds by a sis-ter aircraft from the starboard cat. Within ten minutes, an angry swarm of Hornets, Intruders, and bomb-laden Corsair IIs was on its way toward its Arabic and Iranian targets. Several sections of Tom-cats followed and took their combat air patrol stations.

In England, three squadrons of FB-111s lifted off for their over-France leg to a Mediterranean rendezvous with their KC-10 tankers.

Two squadrons of B-52s, their bellies full of conventional bombs, left their ready patterns over the East Coast of the United States and headed southeast across the Atlantic.

The men of the 1st Armored Battalion of the Israeli First Army looked up as flights of swift Israeli fighters passed over them on their way to Lebanon. The tanned and dusty tankers waved their arms and cheered before sinking down into their steel chariots and pulling shut their hatches. In a massive line-abreast formation, the armor surged forward.